Freshta

Freshta

by Petra Procházková

translated by Julia Sherwood

STORK
PRESS

Published by
Stork Press Ltd
170 Lymington Avenue
London
N22 6JG

www.storkpress.co.uk

English edition first published 2012 by Stork Press
1

Translated from the original *Frišta* © Petra Procházková, 2004
English translation © Julia Sherwood, 2012

 **MINISTRY OF CULTURE
CZECH REPUBLIC**

The translation of this book has been supported by
the Ministry of Culture of the Czech Republic

Paperback 978-0-9571326-4-1
eBook 978-0-9571326-5-8

Designed and typeset by Mark Stevens in 10.5 on 13 pt Athelas Regular

Printed in the UK by MPG Books Group Ltd

chapter 1

I HAVE KNOWN for a long time I would have to write all this down. I also knew I would have to write it the way it really happened. But I had to wait. Wait until those who had done so much to help me, those who had been instrumental in making me want to share this experience, were no longer alive. Yet I was absolutely sure. It felt awkward. It seemed inappropriate to have almost planned to survive someone just so I could write about them. Except this hadn't really been my plan. It existed independently of me and independently of them, but it did exist, beyond any doubt. All this flashed through my mind as soon as I decided to write about things I had been afraid to talk about my entire adult life. I realised that both of them were going to die and I would be left with plenty of time to write. No, I'd never tried my hand at anything like this before. I had just read lots of books and somehow knew I would be up to the task. I had stored everything in my memory, replaying at night the days gone by, like a film. Sometimes it made me cry, so convincing was that half-dreamt show of mine. But I never cried in the daytime, as the events were unfolding. It had occurred to me that I ought to keep a diary so that no essential events would escape me. But the diary might have been found. There wasn't a nook or cranny they couldn't get into. So I ended up jotting down vital bits of information on scraps of paper

and hiding them all around the house. Unless they found most
of them they wouldn't have understood anything. They were
really just screams, written in Cyrillic, though not in Russian
but in my bad Persian. I was the only one to whom they made
sense. They helped me recall what had happened before they
both left me. And they reminded me that there were moments
when I did wish it would happen. There were hundreds of
these scraps of paper. Some are now in front of me and if I were
an antiquarian decoding forgotten scripts, they would have
kept me busy for the rest of my life. Some are almost illegible,
others are incomprehensible even to me, even though at the
time I must have known what I was trying to say. I've forgotten
a lot, even some of the places where I had hidden some of those
memories. Never mind.

Nobody in our family liked Uncle Amin. He was short and
scrawny in spite of eating non-stop and whenever he came to
see us within five minutes he would exclaim, as if taken aback
by his own greed, 'My, I can't even remember when I last had
something to eat.' Then he would laugh that horrid laugh of
his that sounded like a hysterical little boy being circumcised.
Brave little Afghan boys don't cry during the procedure aimed
at divesting them of their foreskin. Except that on that 13th
November 2001, when Uncle Amin came to see us quite late at
night, we never got around to eating. I know it for sure because
the bit of paper relating to this day says: fork – Amin – threw
pyjamas away. Grandpa, Father and my husband were sitting in
the living room while Mother, Freshta, the children and I were
in the closet trying to figure out what to do in case Freshta went
into labour after curfew.

   'I'll just go into labour during the day,' Freshta, my sister-
in-law declared confidently, having given birth to four children
already, all of them, she claimed, around 11am, which in a war
is the best time for this kind of activity.

'You never know when it comes over you,' I said and immediately regretted it.

'You don't but I do.' Freshta couldn't resist alluding to my childlessness.

'Who knows, maybe the curfew will be lifted,' said Mother, not so much out of concern that her daughter might give birth without medical assistance as that she might be called upon to provide it.

Whenever Freshta changed her clothes Mother would either demurely look away or leave the room. I had actually never seen my sister-in-law naked either, all I knew was that she had a pair of large, firm and beautiful breasts. When breastfeeding she would proudly stick them out for all the women to see and I'm sure she did it because she was proud of them.

'I don't mind assisting,' I offered. I had always longed to be friends with Freshta. When I was a little girl I had a best friend called Nadia. We went to school together in Moscow and when we were nine we discovered in my father's desk some black and white photos of a couple having sex and pledged we'd never do that kind of thing. Nadia cried when I left for Kabul. We swore to write to each other. We hadn't kept either of these two pledges. Freshta and I, on the other hand, had never found any black and white photos of copulating couples. Maybe that's why we never truly bonded.

'Oh, I think I can manage on my own,' Freshta said with a meaningful smile that made it quite clear what she thought of my ability to bring little Afghans into this world. At that unhappy moment there was a knock on the gate. Everyone in the house immediately knew it was Uncle Amin. Everything he did he did faster than everyone else. The frequency of the rapping on the gate was about seven times greater than anyone else would have managed. It made even our dog bark at a higher pitch than usual and Grandpa shouted from the living room: 'So will someone let Amin in or do you expect me to go?' Freshta's eldest son, my

fourteen-year-old nephew Kamal, cheerfully dashed to the door.
He was followed by his brother Rustam, two years his junior,
who tripped over Freshta's youngest son Hamayun, another
nephew of mine who, still too young to curse, just hurled a fork
in the direction of his brothers with a force startling for his
twenty-eight months. Freshta gave him a slap, knocking off the
gas burner a kettle with boiling water. Getting up from the floor,
Mother stepped on the enormous scarf wrapped around her
head and the material pulled her back down to the floor. And
just as Mother was rolling about on the floor, Hamayun was
crawling in the direction of the fork and Freshta was yowling
and rubbing her scalded instep, Amin entered the hallway.
After taking his shoes off courteously he stepped resolutely
forward to share his big news. As he did so he landed on the fork
intended for Kamal, which penetrated his foot. He let out a roar I
wouldn't have expected from a man of his tiny stature and weight,
collapsing in an undignified heap on the floor and frightening
little Hamayun who responded with a slightly deeper howl of
his own, frightening Mother who was still trying to get up from
the floor and giving Freshta premature labour pains.

'*Salam alaikum*, Uncle Amin,' I said, getting up to rid him
of the fork lodged in his foot. It wasn't difficult since it hadn't
gone in too deep and so hadn't resulted in major injury, though
it was certainly in a rather inconvenient place.

'I bet it will get infected,' he squealed, making no effort to
get back on his feet. My husband came out of the living room;
behind him Grandpa stuck his head out. Father, confused as
ever, kept his calm, which spared him the sight of a scalded
pregnant Freshta, Mother struggling with her scarf and her
bulk, a howling Amin, and a screaming Hamayun.

'What's going on here?' said my husband in a tone suggesting
that an investigation in search of the culprit was about to begin.

'They've dug a poisoned fork in me,' Uncle Amin declared
in a somewhat calmer voice, as usual jumping to a premature

and wrong conclusion. He was scared of my husband. In fact, we were all scared of him.

'Who's dug a fork in you, Amin?' my husband asked.

'Well, I don't know of course but considering your family doesn't use forks it can't have been lying about by accident,' he said triumphantly, slowly getting up as he spoke. 'No, I can't,' he shouted, collapsing back on to the floor. My husband came closer, grabbed him under his arms and moved him into the living room, which was quite easy given the huge difference in weight in his favour. Mother, Freshta, me and the children hurried in as well. Fifteen-year-old Roshangol, Freshta's eldest child and a beauty like her mother, emerged from the other room. Being an adolescent she didn't think much of family gatherings.

Grandpa, who was in the same weight category as Uncle Amin, suddenly exclaimed, quite contrary to his habits: '*Ho Khodai ma*, Amin – my God, Amin, what on earth are you wearing?'

Only then did the rest of us notice that Uncle was wearing a suit. The dark brown jacket was several sizes too big, its sleeves completely hiding his hands. The shoulder pads, which reached to just above his elbows, made him look like a badly-dressed ice hockey goalie. The trousers fitted him fine, except that they were shiny at the knee and, unlike the sleeves, far too short. Once he lowered himself into the typical Afghan squat, the kind that gives foreigners cramps all over the lower body after a short while, that is, after he plonked himself down with his legs crossed and his upper body proudly erect, the trousers came up almost to his knees. His thin, hairy calves gaped in the space between his socks and trousers.

Since the Taliban had left Kabul, Amin was the first male in our extended family to put on something that Grandpa would describe later that evening as horrid. Not because the jacket didn't fit and the trousers had been worn by many men before but because Grandpa regarded European attire as something inappropriate. Grandpa certainly wasn't a religious fanatic. In fact he couldn't stand the Taliban; nevertheless he considered the classic Afghan garb with its wonderfully comfortable trousers and airy shirts reaching down to the knee a key symbol of national pride and the successful struggle against colonialism. Although he'd complained that his head would sweat under the turban the Taliban had made him wear, he was very fond of the *pakul*, the oddly fetching headgear worn by the Afghan Mujahideen fighting against all the oppressors in their history. He put it on as soon as the Taliban vanished from the city. Once unrolled, the felt hat could easily hold a sizeable quantity of maize. After moistening the hat sides, every good Mujahideen, including our Grandpa, would take much time and great care to twist it into a roll that eventually surrounded the face and the top of the hat. The smell emanating from some *pakuls*, if they happened to get unrolled, was horrendous.

Amin didn't respond to Grandpa. Gazing meaningfully above our heads to show the immense superiority conferred upon him by the information in his possession, he finally shared the news meant to bring joy to us all.

chapter 2

APPARENTLY I had been quite a good little girl. That's what my Mum used to say. My Dad was a Tajik, a sweet little fellow, and my mother was Russian, nearly a head taller than her husband, who claimed that not so long ago she'd been regarded as a great beauty. That may have been so. But I remember her only as an ageing woman with a face gone grey, the corners of her mouth permanently drooping as if she were about to cry. Later, in Kabul, when I tried to recall her, my mind kept conjuring up the wrinkled face of a woman, a stranger, urging me to return. When we first moved to Kabul my husband was rather surprised I never tried to phone or write to my family and wasn't crying myself to sleep at night. Later, when the post and telephone stopped working and the only information we had to share with the world was casualty statistics, I had a suitable excuse for not trying to keep in touch. I'm not saying I didn't miss them but I knew I would never see them again and preferred to turn my memories into a kind of fairy tale.

I don't remember anything noteworthy from my childhood. I played with dolls, went to school and got decent grades, had a few best friends and loved Soviet chocolates. My Dad never beat me, nor did he beat my Mum. My older brother – he was seven years older – ignored me, apparently claiming I was boring because I was such a quiet child.

In the holidays we used to visit Grandmother and Grandfather in Tajikistan. They lived in Dushanbe. They were a really posh couple who spoke Russian at home to show they belonged to the intelligentsia and could speak Farsi but never taught us to speak the language. In fact, my Dad wasn't really fluent in Farsi anymore even though he claimed to understand it.

After we moved to Moscow I went to secondary school and everyone expected me to go to university. My Mum would have liked me to become a doctor and Dad claimed the world was hurtling to disaster and what it needed were astronauts. I couldn't have cared less. However, with my fear of heights the idea of orbiting around the Earth seemed not just a pointless but also a highly dangerous activity. My Dad's claim, that there really wasn't anywhere to fall from space and that assorted planets would soon become holiday destinations and therefore anyone who could steer a spaceship would be at a great financial advantage, fell on deaf ears. I decided to study law. I suppose my parents thought it preferable to drugs and keeping dubious company, as my Tajik Grandmother used to refer to Moscow's youth. She knew a thing or two about drugs since rumour had it that my Dushanbe cousin had been a drug dealer who managed to make enough to be able to afford three houses and three Mercedes before being stabbed to death by his associates during a business deal that went wrong. This incident had never been mentioned in my presence and all I remember about it is that this was the context in which I first heard this word, the name of a mysterious country that was to become my fate. My cousin used to transport opium from Afghanistan and had done pretty well for himself. Many years later, when my husband's drug dealer friends sat around our Kabul house complaining how unfair and belligerent the world was, Grandpa would observe how great it was that there was something the Afghans were better at than the rest of the world. Around that time we heard on the TV that Afghanistan controlled eighty-five percent of the world's opium trade and the men in our family couldn't conceal their pride at our nation's global triumph.

But in the days I spent my holidays with my Tajik grandparents I had no idea about opium barons, and tales of people smuggling the drug across the border smacked to me of forbidden fruit and romantic adventure. That was partly why, in the stories I had told my husband about my original family before we married, I had added things that weren't quite true. I wanted him to regard my male relatives as equals of the wild men who weren't scared of anyone, not even Soviet border guards, and who transported dangerous cargo whenever they weren't fighting the occupiers. When we first met, my future husband's rhapsodies about his family made me feel inferior. I didn't really know our family tree; we had no family history, nor relatives around the world who'd made it in politics or business. I invented an actress aunt and when I was told off that actresses were often prostitutes I tried to embellish my family tree with a nuclear physicist uncle. He didn't go down too well either. Like it or not, our family wasn't a clan and not even a few made-up individuals could transform it into a close-knit community whose cohesiveness provided them with bacteria-like resistance to enable them to survive arduous periods of history.

When I first met my husband he pretended to be impressed by the stories I told him about my brother who had struck out on his own at the age of seventeen, only occasionally returning home at night for some home-made food. He was a dealer in smuggled jeans and tights, articles that in those days were in great demand but short supply. The money he earned helped him get into the international affairs department at university and after that I hardly ever saw him. It was only years later that my husband told me that a bigger bastard than my brother would have been hard to find. He himself, being a member of a respected Afghan clan, ruled over his sister with an iron hand right until his death.

I liked spending holidays at my Tajik Grandmother's. Dushanbe was a moderately exotic city with plenty of restaurants and mildly importunate young men making lewd lip-smacking noises at girls from Moscow who'd arrived in the hope that the lack of competition from other metropolitan beauties would provide a boost to their egos. This was a place where even a woman who in Moscow would pass for unusable – or usable only in case of extreme need and total drunkenness – had a chance of attracting admiring catcalls and whistles. In terms of appearance, I was quite average. I was a bit plumper than was fashionable in Moscow, with a bust that was well developed by the age of fifteen; to disguise my sizeable rear I wore only tops that went halfway down my thighs; as for my lower extremities, my Grandmother used to compare them to 'piano legs'.

'You've got quite a chassis on you, my girl,' she would say gleefully and at these moments I hated her with a vengeance. My thighs, on the other hand, were nice and shapely and in those days they weren't as flabby as they are now, although I didn't really know how to show them off while keeping my substantial calves and chunky ankles hidden. But none of that mattered in Dushanbe. Besides, fat girls were extremely successful here, to the point of attracting the envy of the thinner ones. Representing the golden mean, I was the queen of Grandma's neighbourhood. When I turned sixteen she allowed me to go out with girlfriends in the evenings, with a 9pm curfew at first, later extended to 10pm and, eventually, to midnight. By the time I met my future husband in a teahouse in the city's central park I was eighteen. Our first encounter is hardly worth mentioning. A group of dark-haired young men sat down at the next table and started stealing furtive glances at us, a group of light-haired girls.

'You're here on holidays?' my future husband asked as he walked me home later that night.

'My Grandmother lives here,' I whispered demurely.

'Your parents are Tajiks?' he asked.

'Only one of them,' I said.

'Which one?'

'My Dad.'

'Is he a Muslim?' he asked as we reached the entrance to my house. I stared at him in astonishment, as the thought had never crossed my mind.

'Oh yeah, my Dad is a Muslim, very much so,' I exclaimed and dashed inside. I caught a glimpse of his amused smile.

He was very handsome. And as his Russian was very good I took his accent to be Tajik during our first meeting. 'He's probably from the countryside and they speak Farsi at home,' I told myself. It took me a few days to learn he was an Afghan. I think I was impressed.

'Will you show me your passport?' I asked. Without saying a word he produced a little blue book containing some scribbles. His passport impressed me very much. And that's how I fell in love with him.

Grandmother must have noticed some visible hormonal changes in me and started to pump me for information. I guess she must have looked out of the window a few times to see who was walking me home. And then one day she asked if Mum had enlightened me about certain matters. I wasn't quite sure where Afghanistan was, whether my Dad was Muslim or not, I had never had a foreign passport but I was no longer a virgin. But of course Grandmother had no idea. My husband had no idea either. And I had no idea that not being a virgin could be life threatening.

chapter 3

'YES, HE'S RELATED TO US, Herra, are you listening to me?'
I was sweeping the carpet thinking that the broom had had
it, as it was shedding sprigs and making more mess than it
cleared up. Picking breadcrumbs and grains of rice off the
Persian rug Freshta had woven when she still made her living
that way, I listened with one ear to the children shouting in
the courtyard. They were running wild. Now allowed out into
the streets, no amount of warning not to rummage through
wreckage and not to touch anything suspicious could stop
their frenzied joy at their regained freedom. They kept
rooting through what was left of the formerly palatial villas in
the western suburb of Darulaman. They completely ignored
our strict orders not to stray too far from home, sometimes
venturing as far as the main mosque and the main stadium to
watch the finest Afghan riders on the most gorgeous Afghan
horses getting ready for a game of *buzkashi*, in which wild
chargers drag a headless goat across a line; a game that was
no longer banned. Freshta was strangely calm, Mother kept
saying it was too early to let the boys roam around freely, and
the men insisted that every proper Afghan boy had to touch
a mine, while I anxiously anticipated the moment a proper
Afghan boy would be brought home with a bleeding stump
where a child's little leg used to be.

'He's an important person, Herra, a member of our family. Hey, are you listening to me?' Grandpa was in one of his stationary moods again, glued to the radio and feeling the need to share his take on current affairs. Kabul was fairly peaceful now and Grandpa seemed to have started wasting away since the bombing stopped. For the past twenty-three years the excitement of war had kept him really fit. Now he was giving up.

'Who's a member of our family?' I tried to show interest because old people deserve it, whatever they're saying.

'Why, Zaman of course, the Commander of the Eastern Afghan front,' Grandpa raised his hand proudly, turning up the volume on the miniature Sony radio my husband had recently got him at the market. I tuned in to the Persian news, which I still had some trouble understanding. Although everyone said I sounded like a nomad from the eastern Afghan provinces of Paktia or Paktika, even after twelve years of living amid Afghans, radio news still posed a problem.

'Two hundred people were killed and thirty-five captured in fighting in eastern Afghanistan... the search in the woods will continue for the next few days... organised resistance is on the wane... ' the little Sony box held forth. The references to Zaman didn't sound particularly respectful.

'C'mon, grandpa, this Zaman is against our new government and against the Americans...'

Grandpa may have sometimes confused his right hand with his left, but he was on top of political events, sometimes jotting down a few bits of information on scraps of paper.

'It sounds like he's helping the Taliban, Grandpa. Perhaps he's not family after all,' I tried to offer him a way out.

'Nonsense!' he shouted passionately. 'He just doesn't want Americans in his city. He doesn't want the Taliban there either. He's a real Zaman. We're also Zamans.'

'...Osama bin Laden has not been found in the Tora Bora mountain range, dead or alive ... the search continues ... US

Secretary of Defense Donald Rumsfeld met Afghan leader Hamid Karzai at the Bagram allied airbase near Kabul...' the radio went on. I stopped sweeping and sat down next to Grandpa.

'Nothing good will come of having the Americans here...' he said. 'They'll spread out all over the place and we won't be able to get rid of them.'

'Perhaps we can profit from them.' I knew what Grandpa cared about most was the material aspect of the liberation from the Taliban.

'That's true, I just hope they won't get stuck here forever. That's what Zaman is afraid of. Muhammad is his name. He's against the Taliban but he's also against the Americans. Definitely one of our tribe.' Grandpa turned the radio down a bit and I could hardly hear the news item that thrilled me more than all the information on those who were dead, imprisoned, tortured to death and discovered in mass graves.

'Russia is sending 50 tons of humanitarian aid to Afghanistan.'

Fortunately Grandpa didn't notice my excitement. Instinctively I looked around the room to check if someone a bit more alert may have caught the news. The cargo would arrive in Kabul on board a Russian aircraft with a Russian crew, with an entourage from Russia's Ministry for Emergencies. These people would speak Russian, it occurred to me, and they'd be flying in from Moscow. They would spend a few weeks here and build a field hospital in the centre of town where they would treat the poorest of the poor. At that moment, had someone offered me a bowl of rice with raisins and slices of carrot, the dish I love more than anything else in the world, I would have been sick. Grandpa switched off the radio and placed a small pinch of snuff under his tongue. I realised it was 16th December. It had been almost exactly a month since Uncle Amin had come to tell us the news that had given some of us stomach cramps instead of joy. On 13th November, as Uncle dashed in wearing his ill-fitting suit, the radio played music, for the first time after years of it being banned on Afghan radio. It was quite an insipid tune, not exactly cheerful or lively but at least it wasn't a prayer like under the Taliban, it was proper Afghan music. And then, still bothered by the slight pain in his foot where the fork had been stuck, Uncle took the radio from his pocket and turned it on.

When children started clapping rhythmically he quietened them down and announced ceremonially: 'I have secret intelligence from the ministry. Very soon the first British soldier will enter Kabul. Not an American but a Brit. And he will be followed by peace troops that will restore order.' Nobody said a word for a while until Grandpa uttered very sadly, almost at a whisper: 'Oh well, they'll be staying here forever.' No debate on the usefulness of international peace forces for the people of Afghanistan followed. Everyone was downcast, lost in thought. And on 24th November the first British contingent duly arrived in Kabul, with further troops from countries of every stripe descending on the city in their wake. Two days later Freshta went into labour, just after 10pm. She didn't keep her promise to bring her fifth child, like her previous four, into the world at around 11.00 in the morning, thus causing the family no end of trouble. Ever since the foreigners had arrived the curfew had been enforced even more strictly than before. You could be shot without warning and the local population had been advised to phone the nearest police station and ask for an escort and a pass in the event of a night-time emergency such as a heart attack or childbirth. The only problem was that nobody in Kabul had a phone. So Qais, Freshta's husband, went to fetch a female neighbour who was said to have assisted at a childbirth before. Mother stayed in the kitchen to pray, while I held Freshta's hand; the men in the other room reflected on the news that Aria Airlines would soon resume flights to Europe. Following

a thorough examination the neighbour concluded that Freshta
would last until the morning. And so she did. It was a terrible
night that made me envious of all the illiterate village women
who give birth to fifteen children in their lifetime, without ever
requiring medical assistance. In mountain villages anyone
with good eyesight is qualified to pull teeth out with pliers,
and children come into this world assisted by experienced
women who are aware that it's a good idea to wash their hands
beforehand. In the morning my husband drove Freshta and
her husband to hospital, where, as luck would have it, another
of our relatives was in charge. Cousin Nafisa told my husband
and Qais off for dragging Freshta across town with the baby's
head almost protruding from between her legs, but she was
reassured when she saw both baby and mother were alive. Qais
stayed outside in the dust along with other future dads who
were strictly prohibited from entering the realm of women in
labour until later in the afternoon, when he received the news
he had a baby boy, Yunus, without any obvious sign of interest.
Displays of joy are rare in Afghanistan. And even though I'm
sure Qais was overjoyed, he put on a condescending air as if he
had just been told there would be lamb for lunch again. Once
back at home, though, he stared at the baby boy for four hours
solid and I think he was genuinely touched; I'm pretty sure it
wasn't just my imagination.

Baby Yunus was now three weeks old and even Freshta had
stopped thinking of the traumatic night before he was born.
After she got back from hospital she pretended she'd never
held my hand and never told me: 'If I die, take Roshangol.
They won't let you have the boys but take Roshangol and get
her out of here. So she doesn't have to die like me.' I think
Freshta didn't want this fifth child. But of course Qais never
consulted her on minor details such as the number of their
offspring. Freshta coped so bravely with everything, including
a difficult childbirth, that I was beginning to forgive her for

not having found naughty photos with me when we were little and for us not having pledged we'd never do such horrid things ourselves.

Suddenly I felt like running up to Freshta and confiding in her and her alone. Russians would be arriving in Kabul for the first time in years. They would speak the same language I used to speak to my parents. And they'd be here for the New Year. No, I'd better not tell her anything, she would only advise me coolly to give them a wide berth and to forget all temptation since everything that's tempting tends to be indecent. And I wouldn't have been able to stick to her advice. Oh dear, my poor husband, he wouldn't survive this either. Or else I might be the one who wouldn't survive.

Muhammad arrived the next afternoon. Mother and I were in the middle of cooking potatoes with tomato sauce and debating the question of whether the plump chicken sold at the bazaar came from humanitarian aid or directly from US army stores.

'They look as if they've been crossed with pigs,' said Mother and I guess she meant it as she had no sense of humour whatsoever.

'I don't think a chicken and a pig can do it,' I joked. She frowned at me. Whenever I let on that a long time ago I had happened to have acquired some academic knowledge, her face turned to stone. She was a traditional woman. Kind, faithful, resigned and awfully traditional.

'You always have to know best, don't you,' she said.

Earlier that day we had ventured to the bazaar and that was when the plump chicken problem began. I felt like some meat but blamed my craving for a chicken on my husband, as usual. The bazaars had become much bigger since November, with more rubbish, paper, plastic bags and all sorts of produce. The chickens that had recently turned up in vast quantities really looked more like turkeys.

'*Fil-morgh*,' exclaimed Mother, stunned by feeling the weight of a poorly plucked creature.

'Oh no, *khanoom*,' the trader countered. 'It's just *morgh*, a little chicken, not a turkey...' he continued, patting the bloated body as if to emphasise that turkeys couldn't be patted this way. The extraordinarily well-developed parsons' noses stuck out from their rears aggressively, at a right angle, like giant erect penises. The same idea crossed Mother's mind. I couldn't see her expression under the burka but I could picture her disgusted grimace.

'We're not buying this,' she ruled. We continued the discussion at home. 'You really wanted to buy that chicken, didn't you,' she said, surprising me with the sudden question. Mother had never been interested in what I wanted, what made my mouth water, let alone what I was thinking. Questions regarding states of mind, worries, desires or problems were taboo, except perhaps when they related to periods, pains in the womb and procreation skills, which I had been spared so far.

'The fat would have melted during roasting; the skin would have turned nice and crunchy and with some potatoes it would have made a decent meal... Plus, with a chicken that fat three pieces would have been enough to feed the whole family. A single thigh portion would have been enough to satisfy the men and as for us women, having some of the breast meat would have kept us going until evening,' I brooded.

'I know you've got used to our food, but don't you ever crave anything... anything special?' Mother said all of a sudden.

'If you mean do I miss pork, you're quite wrong...' After twelve years this was still a sore point. I wasn't missing pork at all. Nevertheless, Mother suspected that if it had been offered, I would have bolted down enough for three. In 1992, when I first moved into her house, she told me: 'Pork and sinful thoughts are not allowed here, otherwise you're completely free.' And she was right. As long as you suppressed your cravings, like the taste of a pig's tail or the desire to be attractive to men other than your own husband, you could lead an amazingly happy life in an Afghan family.

Just as the smell of the steaming potatoes started to make our mouth water we heard banging on the gate. It was a timid kind of banging, like someone bringing bad news or asking for a favour. Freshta and her children had gone to visit her sister who'd just returned from Pakistan and was in the process of reconstructing her damaged flat in the Soviet-built estate called *Mikrorayon* No. 3. My husband had been out driving his taxi since 5.00 in the morning the last few days, an occupation that provided him with plenty of foreigners and decent money. Grandpa was asleep and Father had gone knocking on the doors of foreign humanitarian missions, demanding a job in his funny English. Throwing a burka over my head I got up and went into the courtyard; Mother's words were ringing in my ears as she repeated for the umpteenth time: 'Look through the slit first to see who it is...' It wasn't necessary. As soon as I entered the courtyard I heard: 'Anybody home? Open up, women, it's me, Nafisa.'

Nafisa was the daughter of Father's sister, an attractive young woman, a smart and educated doctor, one of the few female doctors who hadn't lost their job, because the Taliban's wives needed gynaecologists too. She was the pride of the family, for she combined the qualities of a perfect wife with those of a worthy representative of Muslim progress. She still went to work in a burka even though women were now officially allowed to appear in public with their hair covered only by a headscarf. She ran Kabul's largest maternity hospital and helped deliver all the children in our tribe, most recently baby Yunus, who'd been held back a whole night. She ruled with an iron hand over her fiefdom. Generals, politicians, fundamentalists and mullahs alike flocked to her cap in hand. The minute she entered the hospital courtyard she'd take off her burka, don a tight-fitting white coat, and get on with inspecting Afghan women's vaginas. 'I would never let you to do this kind of work,' my husband said to me once. 'But I think it's a wonderful job,' I objected. 'Yes, but a dirty one. It's not a clean kind of job... you know how many women in this country have all sorts of discharges, infections, how smelly it all is...' I don't know where my husband got this information from and why he found the idea of female sexual organs so frightening but it was as if he recoiled from Nafisa in disgust. Whenever he talked to her it was as if he thought that traces of secretions or blood from the entrails of sick women might stick to her fingers. For my part, I was fond of Nafisa and hearing her voice made me forget all about the plump chicken. However, her voice sounded a bit strange. This wasn't just an ordinary visit, and in any case, she was too busy to pay people visits in the mornings. I opened the gate and the doctor slipped into our courtyard; her burka caught on a nail in the fence and as she yanked at the material impatiently a big hole appeared in the pleated garment. She ignored it. Only once she was inside did I notice she wasn't alone. She was holding something by the hand. I stared at the creature wondering if Nafisa had brought along a mannequin, the type used to display congenital defects to would-be mothers.

'Is anyone at home?' she asked me as if I were nobody. Normally she always treated me with exceptional kindness and, when we were alone she often quizzed me about life 'over there', about sex and divorce, as well as about women's illnesses and relations between mothers and daughters.

'Yes. Mother is here.' I stole a horrified glance at the creature standing next to Nafisa, who looked dumb and stared at me with enormous eyes that resembled slightly rotten plums.

'Come on,' Nafisa said and it wasn't clear if she was addressing me or whatever it was that was clinging to her hand. She entered the house resolutely and I stumbled along behind her. Only now did I begin to pay closer attention to whatever it was she was dragging behind her. Apparently it was a child. At least its height suggested something like a child. Its little legs were incredibly short and thin with absurdly tiny feet that wouldn't have supported a ballet dancer. The little body was quite compact, without any unnecessary shapes or folds, reminiscent of a giant egg. Without any transition, the egg was topped by a head, which was perfectly round and covered with a scant fuzz that, with considerable imagination, might have been taken for hair. There were three large folds on the scruff of the neck. Enormous, thick, pink ears protruded from each side of the head, lending the creature the appearance of a plump bat. The bat's little arms were as stubby and thin as its legs. It seemed the little creature couldn't lock its arms in front of its body even if it tried, that's how short they were. As it walked, one free arm swung randomly beside the body, sticking out like the chicken rump we'd seen at the bazaar earlier that day.

Nafisa noticed my horrified look and said through her teeth, as she took off her shoes: 'I hope I can at least count on you to be sensible.' I was surprised to see the creature was wearing shoes, as thimbles would have been more suited to those tiny feet. It struck me it must require a tremendous effort to keep the disproportionate body upright. The laws of physics were being totally violated here, or else everything I'd learned in Soviet schools was complete nonsense. The creature fixed its eyes on me while taking off its shoes. I had never seen eyes like that before. They were dull and enormous, twice the size of the tiny mouth and set so close to each other in the bloated little face they almost merged into a single irregular shape. Yet there was something unusual in them. A kind of tiny spark that immediately convinced me that what Nafisa had brought along was indeed a human being.

Mother came rushing out of the kitchen, the polite smile freezing on her lips. She didn't like Nafisa but never dared to question the admiration and respect the clan had for her.

'What's wrong with you, Nafisa?' she exclaimed at the sight of the creature holding the woman's hand.

'Nothing's wrong with me,' came the grumpy reply from Nafisa, usually so patient and sensitive, tolerant and understanding of everyone, including the views of women who regarded her as something akin to a prostitute, since in the liberated seventies she'd gone to university alongside young males, marrying one of their number, whom she'd chosen herself, in defiance of her parents' will.

Horrified, Mother stared at the creature and I had a premonition that a radical change in my life was about to happen.

'His name is Muhammad and he's a boy, in case you didn't notice,' said Nafisa with considerable sarcasm. Mother might have crossed herself, had she been familiar with the gesture so common where I had grown up, or she might have let out a curse. Instead she just squeaked: 'Oh dear Allah, and the holy name...' not saying out loud what went through her head '... borne by this monster.'

We sat in our living room, fitted out with a single piece of furniture, a wooden mock rococo TV table our neighbour the carpenter had built that summer. The creature stood next to the TV, drawing strange patterns in the dusty screen. So far it hadn't said a word.

'And can he talk?' I asked Nafisa.

'Can he talk? You might say he speaks poetry. He's incredibly smart, sensitive and thoughtful.'

'So ask him to say something.'

'Muhammad,' Nafisa called gently. The creature looked at her, curling its upper lip, a gesture we later came to recognise as a smile. 'How old are you?'

All three of us put on a forced smile, although in Mother's case it was rather a desperate sneer, while Nafisa had shaped her bright red lips into a theatrical grin and I had to do my best to suppress the urge to click my tongue at Muhammad the way you do at a dog. But he didn't say a word, merely baring his unusually tiny teeth at us.

'He's got this very unusual condition, I've never come across it before, at least not in this form,' Nafisa began and we didn't dare interrupt to ask why on earth she'd brought him to our house.

'It doesn't affect his brain but his physical development has been impaired.'

'Well, he's obviously got a good-sized head on him so I guess he's not stupid,' Mother said.

'No, he's just a bit peculiar,' Nafisa replied. 'Sort of disproportionate.'

'Portionate?' Mother asked in surprise.

'Disproportionate... well, you can see for yourself, can't you... he's got the arms of a one-year-old but they don't match his body at all. His legs are not great either, that's why he walks in this funny scuttle. He has to make a huge effort just to keep his balance. He keeps falling over and tumbling down to the floor the minute other children poke him. Do you see the tiny soles on those feet?'

'Oh yes, like a crow's. And how many toes does he have?' Mother inquired, getting quite animated and forgetting that what she really wanted to know was why he was in our living room right now.

'He's got the full complement of toes, like everyone else. Except that they're tiny,' Nafisa explained. 'You've got to clean his feet thoroughly, he's got very little room between the toes, they're sort of squashed together and get sore if they're not cleaned properly.'

The child watched us without moving, only his ears seemed to wiggle from time to time. The mention of dirt between his toes, for example, made those pink, almost transparent shells tremble visibly.

'Well, and then there's one more thing...' Nafisa said with a sigh that made Mother and me edge forward with curiosity. 'He's a boy but... Muhammad, come over here, please. Come and stand next to me.'

Muhammad puttered over to her obligingly and only then did I notice how carefully he planted his feet far away from one another. Besides, he walked only on his heels. He didn't seem to be making any use of his toes in his walk, which consisted of tiny quivering hops that made his fat little body and double chin shake. Only his ears protruded stiffly into space. He seemed to be in full control of those.

Nafisa gently got hold of him in the area where children's waists are usually located, although in his case it was hard to tell, as it was clearly difficult to divide his body into the usual segments. The boy wasn't dressed in an Afghan outfit, which are rarely worn by children his age. I had actually never been very fond of those baggy drawstring trousers and long shirts reaching down to the knees. 'Whatever happened to your pyjamas?' I used to tease my husband who preferred to wear military trousers with a normal, dignified fly ever since the turban brigade left town. The boy was wearing a pair of rather dirty tracksuit bottoms and a t-shirt with a picture of a duck, which was too tight and only emphasised his absurd appearance. Nafisa drew him closer and said, for some reason, in a whisper: 'He really is a boy, except that I don't know if he'll ever grow to be a man... sometimes these things do get better in adolescence.' She pulled down his pants with the skill of a doctor, revealing nothing, just as I expected. Afghan children rarely wore underwear and they didn't seem to mind or come to any harm. It just went to show that so many modern inventions are totally unnecessary. One could just as well live without them. Under the boy's clothes there was no underwear but nothing else either. Mother and I stretched our necks like two turkeys, staring into the creature's crotch from a distance of about ten centimetres. Only by getting this close could one spot the little boy's quivering manhood. Its size, and indeed its shape, was that of a rather large pea. The boy didn't move. I extended my arm obeying an unconscious urge to touch the tiny little penis and caress it gently, perhaps to make sure it really didn't conceal an even more miniature pair of testicles. Both women understood my intention at the same moment. Furious, Mother slapped the back of my hand as hard as she could and Nafisa declared: 'Oh no, they're ingrown, poor thing.'

'Allah help us, he might not even be circumcised,' wailed Mother.

'It wasn't possible.'

We were all so engrossed in studying the little boy's sexual equipment we didn't hear the gate slam nor the heavy steps in the hallway, and by the time the curtain leading to the room opened it was too late.

'Damned women!' Father roared in horror. The sight that presented itself to him was very far from desirable. He saw a baby's backside, its trousers pulled down below the knees, and facing it three women, their heads tilted so close to the imaginary sexual organ that they might have touched a regular-sized one with their chin. Although the whole scene didn't last more than a few seconds, Father, more experienced in the ways of the world, probably suspected the worst.

'Out!' he said, pointing at Mother and me. It was bad enough that his wife and daughter-in-law had witnessed what may have been a medical experiment concerning a subject as sensitive as human sexuality. 'And shut those mouths of yours,' he added a little more calmly when he realised he couldn't see much between the boy's legs either. Apparently he found us standing there mouths agape, partly from shock and partly from the immense concentration that had preceded Father's arrival. Nafisa stayed in the living room pulling up the boy's trousers apologetically.

'You go with them,' she pushed the boy and he followed us into the kitchen. Although it was dark inside the cubbyhole we used for preparing food, I noticed something changed in the creature's face. Mother threw herself into finishing lunch and I squatted in front of the boy. It was only then that I noticed something that surprised me even more than the realisation that he had a funny little ball instead of a willy. Tears poured from his eyes, those huge alien eyes. Muhammad was crying from having been humiliated and I realised he was a man. It wasn't until much, much later that I came to realise that Mad, as we called him, was the greatest man I ever knew.

chapter 4

THE HOLY MONTH OF RAMADAN was over. Having stuffed our faces, we lounged about digesting idyllically.

I watched in amazement as Sima Samar, proud and justifiably pleased to have been elevated to the rank of minister, fulminated on the TV screen. Grandpa wasn't asleep, which meant he found the speech by the new boss of all Afghan women quite fascinating. My husband was smiling as he picked his teeth. Mother grumbled that the lady went on for too long and Father was inspecting his ivories because he'd been plagued by terrible toothache for a week now. 'We have been forgotten for a long time,' Sima continued her eloquent speech, her voice dripping with honey. 'Now girls will be able to acquire an education. It clearly says in the Quran that they should. I am glad there are women in our government, albeit only two, which is not enough, but it's a good start. The country is devastated, the judiciary is in ruins, there isn't enough money in the budget but women's rights mustn't be forgotten.'

'She's right,' croaked Grandpa. 'If Grandma were alive she would applaud her.' Nobody ever dared to contradict Grandpa because, whenever he ran out of arguments, he would ostentatiously go to sleep leaving the rest of the family fighting violently over whatever was being discussed.

'Come over here, Mother, I think I've got it.' He jammed the mirror between his teeth on the left side of his mouth so that his hands were free to open his mouth as far as possible. Mother stopped dusting and knelt in front of Father.

'It's too dark in there, I'll need a torch,' she said firmly. A hoarse voice emanating from Father's throat apparently instructed her that the torch was in the car.

'Not all women who wear a chador are illiterate and the burka isn't a sign of backwardness,' the TV announced. 'Education is a priority, we mustn't lose time!' Grandpa applauded with joy.

'That's what I keep saying, off to school with the girls.'

Freshta entered the room with baby Yunus in her arms.

'The neighbour's car has been stolen, someone's got to go and do the shopping,' she announced.

'Roshangol is going to go school,' Grandpa rejoiced in Freshta's direction but she just waved her hand.

Father suddenly spat out the mirror, angrily swallowing the accumulated saliva and exclaiming: 'Roshangol will be going to school, Freshta. Surely you don't want her to stay as ignorant as you are?' My sister-in-law was taken aback. Roshangol was already fifteen but she couldn't read or write and could count only a little.

'Qais will never allow that,' she said with a bitter smile. My husband put the toothpick aside and declared in a formal tone, as if addressing a family council: 'Qais is an idiot and an embarrassment to the family. If he doesn't let the girl go to school I'll give him a thrashing he won't easily forget.' He would never have described his brother-in-law in such damning terms in the presence of strangers but in the close circle of the family there was no need to hide his hatred of the man who beat his sister.

'The Afghan population protests against the continued shelling of areas held by the Taliban. The US Air Force has resumed air strikes...' Mother turned down the TV and went to the car to fetch the torch. By the time she returned Father's mouth was propped open by the mirror again, the toothpick was rolling around my husband's mouth, Grandpa was fast asleep and Freshta was sitting in the corner with baby Yunus, a single, large, shiny and very sad teardrop running down her cheek.

In the evening our neighbour from across the street came running to our house. Under the Taliban he'd dutifully worn a turban and grown a long beard and once, when Mother had stuck her head out of the gate with her burka rolled up so that her forehead was visible, he'd waved a stick at her shouting: 'Shame on you, you naked wench!' Later that evening my husband had gone to see him and gave his hand such a squeeze the neighbour's knees gave way and he collapsed on the floor screaming: 'I just wanted to protect her, my friend!' In the bad old days he used to supply us with extra potatoes and vegetables. He was a really kind man at heart. During the wars the Russians had executed his father after they caught him delivering flour from Kabul to his relatives in Charikar with an old gun hidden under the sacks as protection against robbers. They accused him of plotting to assassinate friendly allied Soviet troops and shot him following a trial that lasted three minutes.

'Thirty dead. Dear me, thirty people dead near Puli Khumri,' he said panting as if he'd run ten kilometres, although he'd only crossed the street. He probably did it to give his words greater weight. He was the most ardent listener of *Radio Ozodi* (Freedom) in the entire Taimani neighbourhood. Only a few months earlier he'd listened to the Taliban prayers with the same fervour. After his father's death he began to serve the communist regime. Meanwhile his brother was in the mountains fighting against the very same regime and occupying army, laying mines in the roads and decapitating Russian soldiers with great gusto. 'Somebody's got to look after the family and feed the children,' had been the neighbour's excuse for going about supplying the guerrilla fighters with money and food with such dedication that he lost seventeen kilograms in spite of holding down a well-paid job.

We turned on the radio. 'The Americans have committed a tragic mistake by bombing an allied Northern Army base near Puli Khumri...' My husband frowned.

'I hope none of my pals was there.' When he talked about his friends from the trenches, which was quite often, he sounded theatrical and sometimes seemed to regret he'd left the army.

'Commander Jaffar Nadri has denied he deliberately provided the Americans with false coordinates to make them unwittingly destroy his rival in the fight to capture the regional centre of Puli Khumri...' said the neutral and bored voice on the radio but it was enough to rouse Grandpa from sleep.

'That bastard Nadri, of course he squealed on purpose.' Grandpa had an uncanny ability to join the debate with lightning speed after waking up.

Nadri was commander of a division of Ismailites, whom I'd always found appealing. They had a progressive air and weren't too numerous. They claimed to represent the most progressive branch of Islam while not seeking to harm the more traditional branches. Everything about them impressed me. However, the victorious Northern Alliance no longer needed such dubious allies. On the contrary. I never argued with my husband about this but it seemed to me that even he, being one of the victors, was beginning to show condescension to former allies from other tribes, regions and ethnic groups.

'I wonder how the people will react,' speculated the neighbour who was becoming less and less fond of the Americans ever since he'd applied for a job with the Ministry of Foreign Affairs and was told that his fervent admiration of the Taliban and subservient cooperation with the Russians wouldn't go down well with US advisors.

'What do we need advisors for?' he complained. Nobody in my family really liked him but in the name of good neighbourly relations we only showed our dislike when absolutely necessary. At that point I believe he was afraid of us. He would have given us up the minute he landed the job of a guard at the Ministry of Foreign Affairs. He was convinced that my husband had a great career ahead of him and that his reputation as an anti-Taliban fighter would assure him the job of a minefield director at the very least.

My nephew Kamal brought a *dusturkhan* tablecloth, spreading it out on the rug and giving Rustam a furious kick meant to prompt him to help serve the food. The first dinner after Ramadan was usually so lavish it took us three days to finish all the leftovers. Anything that wasn't eaten would just go to waste. We'd never managed to make use of the fridge we'd got from cousin Fared, not least because we rarely had power. Just then visitors started arriving and I obediently made my way to the women's closet. My husband regarded the neighbour as such a halfwit that he would let me remain in his presence if suitably attired – though without a burka – provided I kept my mouth shut. By contrast, the neighbour had never laid eyes on Mother or Freshta, except for the one occasion when Mother made the mistake of poking her head out of the gate. Our two aunts arrived with both uncles and an amazing array of children, Uncle Amin turned up a bit later minus wife and, around midnight my husband's friends came bustling in; nice young men with scarred, bearded faces and bullet holes in their chests. The aunts joined us in the cramped women's closet to watch TV, which that evening exceptionally continued to broadcast until late at night. A Bollywood film was on. The heroine fell in love with a young robber who requited her love but her parents wanted her to marry a slobbery rich old farmer. Eventually her beloved triumphed over the farmer and his guards and eloped with her. All this took place amidst constant singing and dancing and the couple swirling around each other. Yet they never kissed or tried to touch each other's bodies. Physical contact was limited to holding hands. She was a bit on the chubby side and rather scantily dressed.

'How can they stand there having their navels stared at all the time,' one of the aunts commented with genuine curiosity. Since her eyesight was failing she sat glued to the TV set, blocking everyone else's view. Being the eldest she was entitled to some close-up erotica. Showing off her experience, Mother uttered: 'That's quite normal in India. And in America people walk around half naked and nobody minds.'

'Half naked?' The other aunt let out a shriek.

'Well, men mainly,' Mother added with less conviction.

'Who'd want to look at them anyway,' the younger aunt declared bending forward as much as she could to see at least a section of the screen. The heroine undulated around a tree, sighing repeatedly, lifting her legs shoulder high and winding them around the tree trunk. The hero stood nearby watching her, hollering a plaintive Indian song, which suddenly switched to a wild rhythm propelling the hero and heroine into a passionate dance. The older aunt started swaying to the music.

'So Nazir works for the Americans, Herra?' The younger aunt suddenly turned to me with a gleeful smile. My husband had recently asked her and her husband for a small loan and they'd made it clear that unlike him, their sons had made it in Europe and had been sending regular contributions back home.

'Yeah, he's in charge of their car pool and also works as an interpreter,' I lied and Mother let it go without comment. In fact, my husband regularly drove out to the airport to hunt for foreigners as, fortunately, they were now arriving in Kabul in ever greater numbers and were increasingly well-heeled. Those who got on with him particularly well would hire him for several days. And just the other day he managed to wangle some work with an international humanitarian organisation. The aunt thought all foreigners were Americans and she was right in this case as it really was a US-run organisation. Except that my husband didn't do any interpreting for them and neither was he in charge of their car pool: the sole thing they had put him in charge of was an old Japanese jeep; they hired a doctor from the Wazir Akbar Khan Hospital who had studied in the US as an interpreter. The aunt nodded appreciatively. Actually, she was rather a nice woman. Every night she cried her heart out thinking of her two sons who phoned her every six months from Europe to enquire about her health. They had been sending her so much money she could afford to buy a whole ram every day, support her five daughters and hand out long-term loans to her relatives. Her youngest daughter had died recently. It was a mystery. One day she was the picture of health and optimism and the next day she was gone. People said she'd had a 'wrong pregnancy'. It was her third and the last one at the age of twenty. The aunt must have read my thoughts.

'Work, money, what good is it all when you lose a child?'

Mother nodded her approval, inadvertently glancing at Freshta. Freshta sat in the corner with her cousin and they were whispering to each other. I knew what they were talking about. They were badmouthing their husbands.

'My oh my, what a handsome man he was, but his wife ran off with a fellow who later died at Mazar-i-Sharif,' the older aunt suddenly laughed, alerting us to the fact that the film had finished and a popular Afghan singer was jigging about on the screen. It was a concert recorded in the seventies, with European clothes and arrangements and the music a cross between jazz, traditional Afghan folk music and Soviet pop. At one stage the camera wandered towards the audience and only someone with a very sharp eye would have noticed a few women seated in the first row wearing skirts that covered their legs only slightly below the knee. The vigilant censor now overlaid the graceful legs of Afghan women with some tulips. A twenty-five-year-old concert had now become restricted viewing and not only for children.

'Just look at these Americans, they don't mind going to a concert half-naked,' said the younger aunt who only had a partial view of the TV set.

'C'mon, they're our people, not so long ago I'd turned this kind of dress into a pair of trousers for our girls,' Mother said. Two weeks ago she had forced a pair of trousers on Roshangol, which the girl put on with the greatest reluctance. Later Freshta convinced Mother that the trousers were too tight and that they would suit Mad better.

'How right you are, they're our people,' the younger aunt sighed in astonishment and started daydreaming. The tulips disappeared and a scrawny little singer appeared wearing a white suit and a colourful neckerchief. Kamal stuck his head into the room and whispered: 'You're supposed to go to bed.'

He must have been sent by Qais, since no other member of the family would have thought of us at that moment. We visited the toilet in pairs skipping our evening ablutions with the somewhat unnecessary excuse that there was no power. The bathroom was so dark nobody felt like going there. As soon as we lay down next to one another on the battered old mattresses, still wearing our clothes, we could hear the oldest aunt's regular breathing. I couldn't go to sleep. I missed my husband and Mad. It was unbelievable how I'd got used to him in the short time since Nafisa had brought him into our house. On that first night, he headed for the room my husband and I slept in without saying a word, and lay down on the floor next to our mattress. Nobody dared to discuss where this weird child was going to sleep. The other children found him gross, so the room where Freshta, Qais and their progeny slept would have been out of the question for him. Plus baby Yunus screamed through the night and the place was so crowded there was only standing room left. At night they all lay there squashed like sardines and anyone who stretched out an arm would have hit their neighbour in the face. Mother, Grandpa and Father slept in the TV room, dreadful snorers all of them. And they all had to go to the toilet several times a night and although they had slept in the same place for years, they trod on one another every time, waking one another up and cursing audibly before going back to sleep. The presence of another clumsy body might have resulted in a tragedy. On that first day Mad kept trailing me without saying a word. But he kept looking around with a mixture of fear and curiosity. In the evening, after he had flopped down next to us, my husband gently pulled him close. And that's when Mad spoke. He whispered in the voice of a girl whose voice was breaking: 'I'm prone to bedwetting and should therefore sleep separately with something underneath that can be washed easily.' My husband and I sat up bolt upright in shock. Not because Muhammad finally said something but because it was a completely grown-up statement, right up to the term 'bedwetting', as you would normally find it in official medical books.

'That's alright,' my husband said firmly after a few seconds and I added:

'If it happens I'll wash it for you.'

'Oh no. I always wash that kind of thing myself,' Mad informed us, closing his eyes. He slept with us like this every night until we got him his own mattress in the opposite corner, and he never wet himself. But he used to wake up frequently and go to the toilet. Much later he confessed he had vowed to go for a pee six times every night although he usually managed an outcome only once. 'If I allowed myself to think I'd only go when I needed to, I'd fall asleep and wet myself. So I'd rather try six times and even if it only works once I can be sure it's worked.' Muhammad loved order and routine. And I loved those moments when something made him crawl over from his mattress and join us on ours. Tonight, however, both Mad and my husband were among male company, something Mad appreciated immensely. It was the first time he was sleeping in the other part of the house, surrounded by the snoring and rough breathing of bearded males with one shoulder lower than the other from the long habit of carrying machine guns.

The whole town was plastered with leaflets showing a gaunt bearded man with intelligent piercing eyes and a drooping mouth. Mad brought home a whole bunch of them.

'Osama bin Laden,' he proclaimed proudly, returning from his daily walk around the house. Mother ignored him. Freshta, on the other hand, picked up a leaflet and studied the image intently. 'People say he's disappeared,' Muhammad declared. 'They're bombing him at Tora Bora.'

'I bet he's got nothing better to do than wait for them there,' muttered Mother. Pains in her legs and spine made her grouchy. Freshta kept looking at the picture, apparently studying it with delight. Freshta had often been in a melancholy mood lately. She grew calmer once the family battle for Roshangol's right to go to school had been won, complaining less and enduring Qais' hysterical fits with greater patience. Today he wasn't at home. He had gone to gawk at the raising of the American flag on the newly repaired and fortified building of the US embassy in Kabul. He had set out early in the morning after hearing on the radio that the American flag was to fly in the centre of Kabul for the first time in thirteen years. Freshta, still brooding over their latest row, was glad he was out of the house. As usual, it ended in bruises and a bloody nose, followed by a fight between my husband and Qais, ending in my brother-in-law's leaving for his parents' house for a few days.

'I wish he'd stay there forever,' Grandpa commented although he knew that wasn't going to happen. Qais' family lived in *Mikrorayon* No. 4: sixteen people crammed into a three-room flat covered in tacky pictures ripped from calendars. The place was permeated by the stench of the toilet – even though it didn't work, women ignored the city administration's advice and made the children use it. They had had no running water for years and the sewers were blocked, but the chemical toilets between the blocks were just too far away. Qais never lasted more than three days in his ancestral home before coming back and behaving himself for a week. I still don't know how we finally managed to convince him that Roshangol's place was at a school desk. I think the main reason why Qais succumbed to our pressure was that my husband had given him 150 dollars for teaching aids and clothes for Roshangol but never asked how he had spent the money.

An all-star family cast accompanied Roshangol on her first trip to school: myself, my husband, Father, Qais and Mad. I tagged along as someone who could talk to the headmistress. Roshan and I got out in front of the school while the men stayed in the car. They looked funny as they sat there smoking nervously, surrounded by girls dressed in black and white, their heads covered in scarves but without burkas. Qais' hands were sweating. The headmistress was a very nice middle-aged woman. She had a kind smile and stroked Roshangol's head in welcome.

'C'mon, you don't have to wear a burka inside. There are no men around.' Roshangol kept mum.

'I'll have to discuss that with her father,' I said, feeling I was blushing. The headmistress was sympathetic. She had studied in Pakistan and rumour had it that her daughter had lost her virginity before marriage. She was allowed to wear jeans and a long shirt, her head only casually covered by a scarf even when accompanied by her mother and father, which presumably demonstrated the highest level of tolerance.

'But she can't sit in the classroom all covered up, surely her dad will understand that. Is he here? I could have a word with him.' The headmistress amused me. I thought it was a great idea and a little revenge on Qais could never go amiss.

'I'll go and get him,' I said cheerfully but Roshangol grabbed my hand.

'Herra, I beg you, don't bring him here.'

Grasping the gravity of the situation, the headmistress said: 'Don't worry, Roshangol, keep the burka on and just go to the classroom, my girl. I'll sort it out with your daddy in the meantime.'

Roshangol wasn't the only student sailing into the school in a blue burka. And just as in the streets men would turn their heads at the sight of uncovered women, here it was the three older girls whose faces were hidden behind a grille who were the centre of attention. We accompanied her to the classroom where girls were throwing crumpled pieces of paper at each other and a young woman teacher was writing the first letters of the alphabet on to the blackboard. The blackboard was brand new.

'It's a gift from the soldiers, the Brits,' the headmistress announced proudly acknowledging my admiring look. 'The school was opened by the Peace Corps commander, General John McColl himself,' she said with a flawless accent that left no doubt about her fluency in English. 'Do you speak English?' she asked.

'I do. And Russian too,' I don't know why I gave myself away immediately.

'You're not from here, are you?'

'My Dad was a Tajik. Is Tajik,' I corrected myself quickly.

'Wouldn't you like to teach here? We're seriously understaffed. Most of those who taught at the school in the past haven't come back and the young ones are totally uneducated. I have a woman here teaching geography who might not even know that the earth is round,' she laughed in all sincerity.

'No, thanks,' I said quickly.

As soon as we were back in the street, I automatically pulled the scarf further down my forehead. The headmistress had her hair in a bun, covered by a purely symbolic miniature scarf.

Otherwise she was dressed in a loose-fitting Afghan dress and a sleeveless cardigan that only emphasised her ample bosom. Inside the car you could hardly see for all the cigarette smoke. I knocked at the driver's window and just about managed to make out my husband's face. Spotting the headmistress he jumped out and opened the door for Father and Qais. Mad was the last one to climb out, and immediately put everyone at ease by behaving quite naturally.

'*Salam alaikum*,' he said stretching out his hand to the teacher. She took it, squeezed it and then, looking Mad in the eye, made the mistake to which all of us, Mad included, had fortunately become quite inured by now.

'How about you, don't you want to attend our school?'

'I'm male,' he smiled. The headmistress was brilliant. She returned his smile.

'Oh, I see, but never mind, the boys' school is not far from here.'

'I already know everything, I'm going to go to university, you see.'

The headmistress was silent for a while and after an intake of breath she said quietly: 'Good luck, my boy.'

Qais shifted about nervously, not knowing how to talk to this confident and uncovered woman. He was evidently sorry to have brought his daughter here. Before long she'd be parading around like this too.

'So Roshangol is your daughter?' Unerringly the headmistress guessed who the father was even though she actually hadn't seen Roshangol's face.

'Yes,' Qais whispered.

'What's the problem, don't you have a place for her?' Father weighed in.

'Oh no, that's not the problem,' the headmistress said with a serious expression. 'Our school is really for girls only, you see. She doesn't need to keep the burka on in class. It will make it difficult for her to write and she won't be able to read what's on the blackboard.'

My husband and Father exchanged horrified looks.

'You mean she's sitting in the classroom in the burka?' my husband said hoarsely.

'That's how she's been brought up, she won't take it off without my permission,' Qais averred with pride.

'So I can tell her she's got your permission, can't I? We also have clerics' daughters here, she'll be in good company, gentlemen. No man has access to the school while the girls are here. These days most of our students don't even wear the burka on the way home...'

'On no, we'll be collecting her and driving her to school,' said Qais as if he were the one who would drive his daughter to and from school every day. I knew this would be a problem since we had only one car, which was our main means of earning a living, quite apart from the fact that it didn't belong to Qais. Moreover, my husband never let Qais use his car saying he had never seen a worse driver.

'All right, suit yourself and collect her but it would really be more appropriate if she didn't have to wear the burka inside the building.' The headmistress was getting edgy. Qais was silent. Father shifted from foot to foot staring at the ground and my husband was visibly embarrassed.

'That's how she wants it herself. Her father told her to leave the burka at home but you've got to tread carefully with her, you see,' said Mad, becoming the spokesman for the entire curious assemblage and, strangely enough, nobody objected. Not even the headmistress.

'All right then. Today I'll leave her alone but please make sure that tomorrow she brings a nice big headscarf,' the headmistress grinned broadly, shaking Mad's hand, patting me on the shoulder and nodding to the men. Turning around she walked away graciously, her round hips swaying from side to side. We stood frozen for a while, watching numbly as she disappeared from sight. Mad climbed back into the car and encouraged by his achievement, particularly by not being slapped about the face for getting too involved, he gave a mighty yell: 'Let's go, gentlemen, everyone get in!' Qais, climbing into the car, was the first one to regain his senses and grabbed the fluff at the top of Mad's head.

'You miserable little imp,' Qais whispered. 'Your mother screwed donkeys and camels, you retard, you.'

'Good for her,' Mad laughed. My husband, Father and I burst out laughing. The car started and I couldn't stop myself from stroking Qais' head. He didn't move but he must have felt it. How simple life must have been for him under the Taliban. He had hated them but they had never made his wife and daughter take off the burka. Like many other men, Qais was totally unfit for this new world. So I stroked him to show I sympathised, for I really didn't envy him the life that was ahead of him, a life of constant humiliation. My husband spotted the careless movement in the rear mirror and I felt sick to the stomach. But then I leaned forward a bit and saw a sad smile appear on my wonderful husband's face and his left eye winking at me.

On the way home Qais didn't say a word. We found Freshta waiting for us impatiently, all dressed up. I saw her relief on not seeing Roshangol in the car. Qais jumped out, his self-pity morphing into rage. Freshta followed him into the house, running, the smile freezing on her face. We all pretended, as usual, that this had nothing to do with us. Only Mad was on edge, looking for an excuse to open the closed door behind which Qais and my sister-in-law disappeared. He didn't have much experience with family rows and found it harder to put up with them than the rest of us.

'Don't even think of going in there,' my husband warned him. And to me: 'Don't you get involved, Herra. Just tell them I'll collect Roshan and bring her home. They don't need to go anywhere.'

I joined Mother in the kitchen, while Father and Nazir drove away and Grandpa sat staring out of the window smoking hashish. Mad stood in the hallway peering at the door leading to the little room. We couldn't hear what Freshta and Qais were talking about, probably because they weren't talking. The only sound filtering through the door was some rustling and panting, and an occasional sob followed by a long silence. Qais emerged two hours later looking pale and tired.

'Nazir says not to worry, he will collect Roshangol.' My brother-in-law didn't respond although he must have heard me. He went out into the courtyard, looked back at the window where he had left his wife, and ran out into the street. Mad and I entered the little room. Freshta was lying on the mattress with a bleeding nose.

'It's just nerves,' she bleated. She was right. Qais never dared to beat her in her father's house, especially with Grandpa sitting next door in a haze of hashish and Mother's ears pricked up, ready to come to her daughter's rescue in an emergency.

'What did he do to you?' I inquired carefully.

'Nothing, he just said the whole experience had been terribly humiliating. Apparently some stupid cow of a teacher read him the riot act and you all laughed at him.'

Next to the mattress where Freshta lay covered by a blanket there was an ashtray overflowing with fag ends. I had cleaned it in the morning before our trip to the school. There was no way Qais could have smoked thirty cigarettes in two hours. Mad glanced at the ashtray, then at me and back at the ashtray and I knew we were both scared. But Muhammad was a really brave little chap. Crawling up to Freshta on his knees, he looked her in the eyes and lifted the blanket with a sudden but gentle movement. Freshta's chest was bared almost down to her breasts and her sleeves were rolled up, the right one slightly torn. The skin below her delicate collarbone as well as on her arms all the way to her elbows, was covered in horrific red and black burns.

From then on Roshangol went to school every day carrying a voluminous Marlboro plastic bag to stuff her burka into as soon as she crossed the school gate. After three weeks it became clear that it wasn't feasible to drive her to school and collect her every day. Mad was the only person who was suitable as an escort and had time on his hands.

'There's no way I'm going to walk down the street with him,' yelled Roshan and Mad nodded in agreement. They were very fond of each other but their affection was marked by total honesty. The things they would say to each other made my mind boggle. But neither of them ever took offence.

'No one will recognise you under the burka anyway,' Mad objected feebly.

'You're crazy Mad, I'm the only one who wears that rag to school, so on the contrary, I'm as conspicuous as a slice of water melon in the snow,' she cried. 'They'll think you're my bro.'

I started feeling sorry for Mad.

'But he is, isn't he? He really is something of a brother to you. And he's very bright... he shook hands with the headmistress.'

'The girls will laugh at me. Nobody will want to sit next to me.'

'I've got an idea,' exclaimed Mad. Nobody took any notice of him as we were all trying to comfort a desperate and furious Roshangol nestling in her mother's lap, while her grandmother wiped her forehead with a moist cloth. The hysterics had given her a fever.

'I've got an idea,' Mad said in that grating voice of his that sounded like a girl whose voice was breaking or an ageing woman, confusing everyone around him. 'I'll go and collect her wearing a burka.'

We didn't get it at first. Surprisingly, Mother was the first to react. She stopped wiping Roshangol's forehead, and said looking at Mad, 'Muhammad, you truly are the Prophet's child.'

That evening Mother and I found one of my burkas which I wore only very rarely now and which was as good as new.

My old one, from which all the pleats had come out, would do me for the odd trip to the bazaar or to the country. Mad's stature required some modifications to the classic burka style. Poor thing, the robe was hopelessly long even when he stood on his toes stretching his non-existent little neck. The nasty blue synthetic material kept gathering around his feet and one step would have been enough to make him step on the hem and bring him crashing to the ground.

'I had no idea they only come in this gigantic size,' the boy complained.

'They also come in child size but you'd never get that over your head...' Mother said. She was right. A child's burka might have fitted him in terms of length but the little hood that's meant to sit tightly on the noggin would have served him better as an aerial. Mad's head was huge compared to the rest of his body and even if we had a burka specially made for him nobody would have believed that we weren't planning to use it as a potato sack. In an adult-sized burka, on the other hand, there was some space left around his head since putting it on properly was an impossible feat, but at least there was no danger that the slightest squall would make it fly away.

'He looks like a scarecrow. He'll scare people in the street,' muttered Roshangol who was sitting on a mattress next to her mother, both of them gratefully watching our rather futile endeavour.

'Better a scarecrow than nothing,' Mad exclaimed triumphantly. He must have thought it would be an incredible adventure and couldn't wait to be able to venture far away from home on his own, without being followed by horrified looks from passers-by. Father walked into the room and his jaw dropped in astonishment. Mad stood there covered in cloth while Mother and I were measuring out how much material would have to be cut off on both sides. He looked like a fat princess. Father gave a laugh. The whole family was reconciled to the idea of Muhammad escorting Roshangol to school and back but nobody was really concerned about the girl's trauma at this embarrassingly ugly creature collecting her. Father needed no explanation to understand the purpose of our endeavour and proudly praised Mother.

'Oh no, it wasn't Grandma, it was me who came up with the idea,' Mad mumbled from under the burka, laughing in that grating warbling voice of his.

'One day you'll make it to president, Mad,' Father said with a smile.

'That's not likely, Grandpa, and besides, it's not what I really want. I want to be a commander of the UN Peace Corps in Africa.'

'Why Africa, my boy? Haven't we got enough problems in this country?' Father replied, genuinely surprised and squatting down by Mad in a friendly gesture.

'Because I understand how black people feel.'

'How can you understand black people if you've never seen one?'

'I've seen them. On TV and also the other day, at the bazaar in the centre, I saw a couple of them in uniform. They're ugly, like me. They will obey me. They'll understand and respect me.'

Mother and I started cutting off bits of the material so that it would end at his heels without revealing more than ten centimetres above the ankles at front. Even this way he cut an exceptionally deformed figure. The top presented the greatest problem. The hood attached to the robe was too small and once we managed to squeeze it at least partly over his massive skull so that it wouldn't fall off, he started moaning that it felt like being in a vice.

'You've got to lose weight, Mad,' Roshangol teased him.

'Don't be silly, if I lose weight I might fall ill. Besides, losing weight from the head is hardest. I've read about it in books.

Be glad my head is bigger than other people's, otherwise it wouldn't have occurred to me to escort you in disguise.'

The next problem was trying to make sure Mad could see at least something through the grille. The peculiar position of his eyes meant that only one of them could be near the grille.

'Never mind, I'll just use my right eye, that's my better one,' he said, beside himself at being the centre of attention.

'But what if you trip and drop the rag and we get found out,' said Roshangol, frightened.

'C'mon, we'll hold hands, surely you won't let me trip,' he implored.

'Yes, but after you've dropped me off you'll have to go home on your own and later, when you come back to collect me you'll be alone again, so you've got to see at least something.'

We grown-ups frowned, only half listening to them. All their comments basically made sense. Eventually Mad worked out that he could just pull the burka down his forehead deeper than tradition dictated and that way the grille would end up closer to his eyes. Then he'd be able to see out of at least half of each eye, and that ought to be enough for slow walking. Mother and I stitched up the hem, carefully stuck the hood with the grille on to Mad's head according to his instructions, and stepped back to take a look at him. He resembled a weedy moth, an ageing insect that's lost the ability to fly, his limp wing-cases drooping. I had never seen anything more pathetic than Mad in a burka. But under the robe he was laughing happily. He dashed out of the little room barging into the living room where Grandpa was dozing, Qais was staring into space and my husband was fixing a carburettor. Everyone froze. Mad spread his arms, waved them about and declared: 'My friends, I'm free!'

chapter 5

DECEMBER OF THAT YEAR was quite decent, bringing pleasant weather and a welter of emotions. General Fahim, the fat and balding Minister of Defence, gave his official blessing for foreign soldiers to roam freely around Kabul for the first time in history, disappointing Grandpa who had hoped to see at least some resistance from quarters other than the Taliban. My husband, on the other hand, rubbed his hands and winked at Father to show this might be an opportunity to find a job that would pay better than working for humanitarian organisations. They both believed, quite wrongly, that their knowledge of English would help them ingratiate themselves with the peacekeepers.

In pauses between fighting in Kandahar in southern Afghanistan the Americans rummaged through the wreckage, pulling out corpses and doing a tally. Apparently they had already found at least a hundred, mostly Taliban and al-Qaida fighters. I never understood how they could identify them so accurately. It was often impossible to tell a Taliban from an ordinary Afghan and since only a tiny fraction of the population possessed any identity papers – whereas nearly everyone owned a gun – it was exceedingly difficult to tell a saboteur, a guerrilla or a terrorist from a peasant, a merchant or an ordinary robber.

The shelling of the Tora Bora Mountains in the East bowled merrily along, turning the local village population into the last refugees of this war. They fled from the US bombers in a much less organised way than the Taliban troops, raining down such vehement curses on all the armies of the world that they must have been heard by everyone, including the pilots busy dropping some special type of bomb, capable of penetrating the sturdiest cave walls.

'I'll be gone for a few days,' my husband announced one evening, just as we were about to heave a sigh of relief that he had finally found a job lasting a few weeks. Instead, the Americans had put him in touch with a friend, whom they presumably wanted to get rid of forever by recommending a trip to the Tora Bora Mountains. The man, an extremely annoying German journalist armed with a camera, demanded that everyone obey his every word. It turned out that for a hundred US dollars a day my husband had agreed to act as his driver, confidant and interpreter. Grandpa, Father and I realised he was about to drive the man to the front, a place we had foolishly assumed we no longer needed to be concerned about. Snuggling up to my husband on the mattress later that night I whispered: 'Is it really worth it?'

'I'll make at least 1,000 dollars. And the longer I have to stay there the more I'll make. Don't worry, it's absolutely safe. The Americans can't afford to put a bullet through a German idiot.'

'Maybe not a German idiot, but how about you?'

'Don't worry, the German idiot will be with me at all times. He'll make a kind of shield for me, you see.'

Mad's squeaky voice pierced the darkness and I was furious he was not yet asleep, disturbing our last night together before the trip.

'An aerial bomb can't hit just one person, that's most unlikely. If there are two people standing side by side, they both get it.'

'I'd rather they sent you to Bamyan instead, where they're about to carve the Buddhas into the mountain-side again.'

'That's a load of nonsense.' Even a change of topic wouldn't silence Mad. 'They won't manage. Not just anyone can carve Buddhas into the mountain. And you can't use mechanical tools. That would lack soul.'

'Whereas your soul is rather larger than necessary, so lie down and go to sleep now,' my husband snapped. We waited ten minutes until we were sure we could hear him breathing regularly. We used to have sex quite often but had fewer opportunities since Mad moved in with us. Things were even worse for Freshta and Qais. Sharing a bedroom with six other people was more difficult than sharing a bed with Mad. Besides, with quite a bit of understanding for matters he had read about, Mad sometimes pretended he was asleep and we were only too happy to play along.

Reluctantly, I got up at 5.30am. I packed a change of underwear for my husband, a military sleeping bag with a weird upper part with sleeves and a big-eared hood, a vacuum flask full of hot tea with lots of sugar and a few slices of bread with onion. I put a towel and some soap in a plastic bag that once had grapes in it, and placed everything in a sports bag which we'd had to hide under the Taliban as it was adorned with the word Adidas even though, originating as it did from a dark sweatshop in Peshawar in Pakistan, it had no connection whatsoever with the famous brand. I turned on the radio, softly at first, to make his waking a little less harsh. Minister of Defence Fahim was finally giving his approval for 5,000 foreign troops to keep the peace in Kabul. Initially he was going to approve only a thousand but his colleagues from the trenches must have talked him into agreeing to an increase. The old King, Zahir Shah, opined from Europe that the peacekeeping force might offer the last chance of a more lasting peace. My husband crawled from under the blanket and snarled at me: 'Why the radio? Is that the best way to wake me up?'

'They're talking about Fahim, I thought you'd be interested.'

'You mustn't go out while I'm away. Don't you dare venture out. Don't as much as stick your nose out of the courtyard. Or people will say the minute I leave home you go moseying around the streets on your own.'

'I won't go anywhere. Where would I go, anyway?'

'Not even to the bazaar with Mother, you understand?'

'And what am I going to tell her if she asks me to help her with the shopping?'

'Tell her you've got a headache or a backache. She knows you're prone to such things. Or blame your stomach, you know you could easily use your bowels as an excuse every day. And if I find out you've gone out, even with Grandpa, I'll rip half of your hair out.' Perhaps as a warning he grabbed my fringe angrily and gave it a rough yank. It was painful. He was in a foul mood because he was going away and the Taliban could no longer be relied on to keep a watchful eye on disobedient wives. Lately he'd been harsher with me than in all the time we'd known each other. Since the old prohibitions had been lifted and women had gained officially sanctioned freedom, my husband had changed. He could no longer sit on the terrace at night, quietly assuring me how he would make up for all the suffering inflicted by these degrading medieval constraints. Now the time had come for him to start making up for it all. But after all these years he found the idea of me walking around town on my own, possibly without a burka, exchanging greetings with men who weren't part of our family, inquiring about their wives' health, and then catching a ride home in a cab driven by a man, more terrifying than the public execution of an adulterous couple.

Mad wasn't asleep. He was listening to us quietly and his instincts told him not to interfere. After my husband left to empty his bladder, Mad waved me over to his mattress.

'I can make you come out in a rash if you want me to. I know how to do it and you can use it as an excuse not to go out, even to the courtyard.'

'Thanks, Mad, but that won't be necessary. How do you make someone come out in a rash anyway?'

'That's a secret. But I've done it for boys loads of times when they wanted to play truant from school. They used to pay me a few afghanis. But for you I'd do it for free.'

'I don't need a rash, Mad.'

'Oh yes, you do. We're invited to Uncle Amin's tomorrow. It's his birthday. We're all going – I wonder how you're going to get out of that one.'

I had totally forgotten about the party at Uncle Amin's. And so, presumably, had my husband, otherwise he would have mentioned it specifically. It was obvious he wouldn't let me go. He just thought it was inappropriate. 'You like being at the centre of attention and do you know what our men think of that? You know very well what they think. They think you want them. You talk too much and you look them in the eye at the same time,' he used to chide me after every family gathering at which no outsiders were present and I was therefore allowed to keep the company of male relatives. Obviously, I wasn't going to Amin's.

'I'll manage without a rash, Mad. And you will tell me all about it afterwards.'

My husband returned to the room and gave me a surprised look.

'Herra, don't you have things to do? I'm leaving in a minute and here you are, having a cuddle with Mad.'

I scrambled to my feet and ran to the bathroom to look for a decent scrap of soap. As we had only one tube of toothpaste between us, I squeezed a little into a paper cone, wrapping it in a piece of carton torn from a box of washing powder. A few specks of detergent fell into the mound of toothpaste. It'll make his mouth froth nicely, I thought, smiling at the idea of a white frothy cushion of detergent bubbling out of his mouth. Suddenly Mad was standing behind me. I thought he'd come to help me pack. He took my husband's toothbrush off the shelf, placed it gently on the little pile of things, bent down and focusing hard, his eyes half shut, he spat a solid gob of saliva right on to the withered bristles. Then he smiled and left. I finished packing and went back into the room, planting a kiss on my husband's cheek and handing him the bag, with a wink at Mad.

chapter 6

EVERYONE WAS AT HOME. This didn't happen very often but when it did, it was unbearable. To be honest, I could never understand how anyone could enjoy the combination of screaming children, all the coughing, the rattling of dishes and loud Indian music. But Grandpa and Father beamed with happiness. It was *dzhuma*, the Friday day of prayer, and Grandpa was the only member of the family who had completed the full set of prayers in the morning while the rest of us honoured Allah by having an extended lie-in. My husband tinkered with the car and kept coming back into the kitchen to inform me what part was broken and would have to be replaced.

His famous expedition to the Tora Bora mountains had left his car in a rather bad shape. 'That's the last time I go anywhere with a journalist,' he had not stopped repeating since he came back. He said the obnoxious German had forced him to drive on tracks even an experienced mountain climber would have trouble scaling. Eventually they reached some kind of encampment on a vast plateau, nearly 3,000 metres above sea level, where CNN reporters sat around drinking hot coffee from coffee machines, the noise of their generators interrupting the occasional sounds of gunfire and shelling. The whole area was covered with their state-of-the-art tents, so colourful and high-tech they would have made an easy target for any sniper, even a half-blind one. The herdsmen who passed by, driving their herds away from the turmoil of war, couldn't believe their eyes and stopped to stare at these apparitions from another world, or perhaps another planet, frantically snapping with their cameras in the breaks between shelling. My husband told us he had to spend all night squatting on his haunches as his German drank whisky with his American and Polish colleagues and never thought to ask whether my husband had a place to sleep, while he got himself a nice and cosy spot in one of the tents, next to a hirsute middle-aged lady journalist. In the morning my husband pointedly said to him, 'Hello, I'm still here,' but the German just stared at him blankly and failed to get the hint. Then he went off to position his tripod in a row next to all the other journalists and wait for the smoke following the explosion of an American shell to appear on the opposite side of the mountain, sipping hot milky coffee. My husband stood by, salivating, but to no avail.

'Actually, they were quite accurate,' my husband admitted, referring to the aeroplanes that had circled around the camp where they presumed the Taliban to be based, dropping their shells right by the journalists. 'If it had been the Russians we would have had it. Their shells tended to scatter over several kilometres. But these guys can home in on a target within a few centimetres,' he said, unable to hide his admiration despite considerable irritation. 'And then this idiot asks me to go and take some pictures for him up close, saying he wanted a few dead bodies, or some wounded ones maybe, so I told him to go and do it himself,' my husband said abrasively. 'He offered to pay me 50 dollars, the lunatic. I told him I'd had enough and was willing to take him back to Kabul if he wanted to, and if he didn't he could suit himself and stay. He decided to come back but paid me only half the fee. He said I had ruined his report. For all I know he would have been happy to hang around there forever.'

'From his point of view it made sense, I guess,' I dared to counter.

'Oh yeah, it made sense, didn't it? But from my point of view, I've got a wreck of a car and the dough I got from him is not going to be enough to have it fixed. And for another thing, he never offered me so much as a crumb of bread. Although he could clearly see there was nowhere I could buy anything to eat out there.'

'Of course, darling,' I said to him in Russian, as he couldn't stand it when I showed my affection in a language everyone could understand.

'Everything is broken, the fuel pump is screwed. It'll cost loads of money. The best thing would be to buy a new car,' he announced angrily and it was clear he'd been working up to this announcement for quite a while. Although recently it had become a lot easier to find work in Kabul than it used to be under the Taliban, it still often happened that we didn't have enough rice to go round. My brother-in-law Qais still hadn't found a job and showed no intention of finding one. Nobody, including myself, would have allowed Freshta to go out to work and besides, she had no skills whatsoever. As a breadwinner, Mother was out of the question, Grandpa might have fetched some money as an exhibit in an archaeological museum, the children went to school, which in itself cost some money and, dear Muhammad, bless his kind heart, wasn't even suited to scaring naughty children. My husband had been making use of his broken English and Russian to hunt for eager foreigners who arrived to save our country from hunger and smallpox, brazenly demanding a hundred dollars a day, and sometimes striking lucky. Fortunately, more and more of the Americans who had arrived to rescue and feed us started relying on his services, as they realised they wouldn't find anyone more qualified and experienced who was willing to work for them as a driver. Twice already they had promised to give my husband a contract very soon. He was so happy to hear that he laughed like a madman and forgot to ask about the salary, which took the American humanitarian professionals completely aback. Maybe that was why the contract still hadn't materialised.

'Oh, something I forgot to tell you yesterday,' he said suddenly, poking his head into the kitchen with some greasy part extracted from the car's innards in his hands. 'We are having guests for lunch today. Foreigners. So prepare food for about five extra people.'

'Now you tell us,' Mother grumbled, genially throwing her arms open to suggest there wasn't much to be found in the kitchen. 'Go and check in the kitchen if there's any rice left soaking there,' she instructed me.

Our family had had a fridge ever since I arrived. We had kept it throughout the long years when there was no electricity. Father insisted on using it and refused to believe that in the scorching 40-degree heat a broken fridge with a closed door turned into an incubator for mould and bacteria. He used it to store all kinds of things, including once, in momentary confusion, a pair of shoes. They were all mouldy come next morning even though we'd been suffering a prolonged drought and the air was completely dry. There was a strange microclimate in that fridge. It would turn milk into inedible curd cheese, rice into a repugnantly smelly alcoholic beverage and any object people insisted on sticking in it would emerge covered in a green fuzz. Once a week Mother would patiently clean it, looking so proud while doing so that there could be no doubt she regarded the fridge as an acquisition that placed us up there with the upper middle class. Mother and I left a bucket of rice to soak and Mother summoned Freshta. As we crouched over a pile of potatoes Mother stole a glance at me: 'What sort of guests?'

'I don't know, I've no idea. He hasn't told me anything.'

'Perhaps someone has given him a permanent job,' she mused.

'It must be the Americans he's been driving around,' Freshta chipped in, as if we were expecting suitors even though it was more than certain that we women would be locked into the closet at the back of the house and asked to keep our voices to a whisper. As if reading my thoughts, Mother snapped: 'That is of absolutely no interest to you.'

'Why not?' her daughter retorted cheekily. She could always be a bit more outspoken with Mother than I, a mere daughter-in-law, ever could. 'Who knows, maybe they'll be women. It doesn't make any difference with these people. Their womenfolk are free to walk the streets and visit people without their husbands, and they don't have any problem with it... am I right, Herra?' And she gave me a prod. I had always taken pains not to say anything that might suggest I had also once lived that kind of life. After some years I learned that my family's initial curiosity gradually turned into a conviction that I had done something immoral, otherwise I wouldn't know about such things. And besides, there was the issue of my virginity, which had never been quite resolved in my family.

'They can travel around on their own, so yes, they might be women. There are many humanitarian women workers here, and even some women soldiers...' I said, getting into my stride and Mother didn't like it. But oddly enough, she smiled and said something I would never have expected from her: 'In that case, we might actually learn something new.' The smile lingered on her face for a while, perhaps the whole time we were peeling the potatoes, even though their quality certainly didn't make this a particularly joyous activity. The visitors arrived at 12.00 on the dot. Men and women both.

'Oh my Allah,' Mother whispered after looking out of the window from behind the curtain. Muhammad was standing next to her. I was the only one to notice his ears fluttering with excitement again and his tiny fingers were clenched into the delicate palms of his hands. Muhammad could predict the future, although he couldn't tell if it was going to be tragic or happy. But he knew this was going to be very, very dramatic and his sensitive ears made me realise it too.

Mother invited me to follow her to the back closet where we women congregated whenever we had unexpected guests who weren't our close relatives. The advantage of the closet was that it had a window that opened on to the adjoining room. It had been painted over with white paint but, a long time ago, Freshta and I had scratched out a tiny peephole with a hairpin and used it to observe the goings-on in male company, provided these were of any interest to us. Today we both pushed and shoved to get closer to the peephole, hissing at each other angrily. Muhammad came to the closet with us, instinctively joining the part of family that wasn't presentable to the public. The women and the strange child. We were in the same position, in a way. Sometimes I thought it was a real pity Muhammad wasn't a girl. We could have easily covered his pre-adolescent body with a burka and the problem would have been solved. But this way, on the rare occasions when he ventured out for a walk, he had to contend with curious glances, sometimes pitying, sometimes mocking, often hateful. He wore the burka only to escort Roshan, complaining that sometimes people still turned their heads in suspicion. Any cripple who had lost a limb in an encounter with a landmine could count on favourable reception here. Such people were viewed as something normal, an ordinary part of Kabul life. But a little person looking slightly retarded was regarded as something that ought to be kept at home, just like the members of our sex.

'The first high-ranking Western representative, US Minister of Defense Donald Rumsfeld, has unexpectedly arrived in Afghanistan,' the English-language service of the BBC droned through the wall. We hardly ever listened to it at home. Nobody apart from my husband and me understood English. Actually,

Father also knew about a hundred words and unlike us, had no qualms about using them at such dizzying speed that he would briefly manage to give the impression of fluency. Native British or American speakers always hesitated for a moment before they figured out what language he was speaking. Nevertheless, he never failed to dazzle them. They admired his self-assurance and the cheek required to function in a language he didn't know as confidently as if he'd sucked it in with his mother's milk.

'Al-Qaida has been defeated, all that's left is to capture Osama bin Laden,' Rumsfeld proudly informed his soldiers at the US base in Bagram, near Kabul. The announcer's voice flooded the whole house. The reason my husband had tuned into the BBC broadcast, turning the broken volume knob on the crackling old radio to maximum, was to show the visitors what kind of family they had the honour of meeting. Although they might have thought it a bit weird not to be introduced to any women. It struck me that these were the first foreigners in twelve years I could have shared a cup of tea with. And it also struck me that I wasn't interested at all.

'Oh my Allah,' Mother said, hardly remembering when women in European dress had last been seen in Kabul. Admittedly, the two women who were about to sit down on cushions next door to us were dressed appropriately. They had obviously made an effort not to cause too much of a shock on their first visit to an Afghan family. Nevertheless, the sight of them had nearly given Mother a heart attack and Freshta couldn't stop giggling like a silly little girl. The older of the two women, aged around fifty, wore loose-fitting cotton trousers and must have been freezing in the cold. Her rear was covered by a cardigan and her cropped greying hair with a silk scarf. The younger one was pretty, tall and bosomy, with light hair the colour my husband used to call 'peed-on straw'. She wore a black polo neck sweater, rather tight and showing off her breasts to full advantage. This proved too much for Grandpa who couldn't stop himself and stared at them with so much admiration that Father had to move him to a corner where he was less visible. But the breasts loomed so large they could be observed from any vantage point in the sparsely furnished room. The polo neck ended just below the woman's waist and the rest of her body was squeezed into blue jeans, tight enough to make sitting an intractable problem. The woman couldn't make herself comfortable in a cross-legged squat without risking that the trousers would rip at the crotch, which would quite certainly have been the end of Grandpa.

My husband was being the model host. He shook hands with everyone. The women's two male escorts were inconspicuous, middle-aged and not particularly attractive. Both of them wore jeans and loose jumpers.

'Several US soldiers were wounded in a landmine explosion in Kandahar. The US has promised the Afghan leadership that only a small number of troops would be deployed in military action. Fifteen European Union countries have promised to send troops to Afghanistan. Sima Samar has been appointed Deputy Prime Minister in the Afghan government, a position she will hold concurrently with her post as Minister for Women's Affairs.' The radio was blasting away so loudly we couldn't hear what our visitors and our men were talking about. Just then my brother-in-law Qais entered our closet. Freshta and I were jostling to get closer to the peephole and she had just bitten my hand, convinced it was her turn. Giving us a stern look, Qais pulled a disgusted face and whispered in my direction: 'I take it you're translating all the dirty talk for her.'

'I haven't heard any dirty talk, with the radio on full blast. But I've heard Sima has been appointed Deputy Prime Minister, that's quite something,' I said to change the subject.

'That's for their sake, too,' he pointed his head in the visitors' direction. 'To ingratiate ourselves with them. They go on and on about human rights and now they got themselves a female minister. If any one of you needs to go to the toilet, send the boy for me. I'll be keeping an eye on you.'

My poor brother-in-law was worried our bladders might get overexcited and we might run to the toilet so much we would eventually run into one of the male visitors. And that would have been a tragedy he couldn't have survived. I felt sorry for him, in a way. Admittedly, Freshta was a stunning beauty but no stranger had seen her since she reached adulthood. Mother was an old woman, her face bearing the marks of all the misfortunes that had befallen her in her lifetime and since her way of receiving all bad news – and there had been plenty of that – involved furrowing her brow, this was now lined with an almost preternatural number of deep furrows. As for me, well, I might have been of some interest to them. Not as an object of sexual desire, of course, but as an extraneous element, something unexpected, almost shocking. I had no idea then under what circumstances they would learn of my existence.

Qais, who couldn't speak any foreign language and was barely fluent in his native tongue, entered the best room and shouted with his mouth stretched into an unnatural smile: '*Salam alaikum*'. Then he turned the radio down, probably so that he wouldn't have to listen to the bad news about Afghanistan gaining a female Deputy Prime Minister. Muhammad tugged at my sleeve and, being congenitally unable to whisper, he said so loudly that everyone next door was bound to hear: 'I want to have a look, too!' I let him look and continued to listen intently. One of the women was called Heidi. A nice name.

'What are they saying?' Mother crawled up to me on her knees, clearly keen to take a look for herself.

'One of them is called Heidi. I guess it's the one with the tight trousers,' I explained.

'You think they're too tight?' Freshta had got hold of a few Western fashion magazines and now pretended to be very blasé about these things.

'Well, she can't actually sit down,' I said.

'Let Muhammad fetch her a stool from the kitchen, she'll be more comfortable,' Mother suggested.

'C'mon, it'll give them the fright of their lives and they'll run away,' Freshta protested.

'No they won't, but it will be awkward. It will be obvious we've been watching them from somewhere and noticed the trousers,' I objected.

'Hey girls, look!' Unable to conceal her extreme excitement, Mother started to wheeze, threatening to give us away. 'Oh poor thing, she really can't sit properly. She keeps shifting from side to side... oh, you poor girl... you should have worn something looser. I wouldn't mind making an outfit for her, she's so pretty...' Mother didn't seem shocked at all, which surprised me. 'Muhammad, go to the kitchen, get a chair, the little wooden one, and bring it to that lady there.' Mother no longer asked for our opinion and started to act.

The speed at which Muhammad set off made me quite concerned. Because of his tiny soles his balance wasn't great and once he started to run he couldn't stop easily as his spindly little legs weren't able to slow down such a monstrously swollen body propelled by the force of inertia. It usually went on hurtling along even after his feet had virtually lost contact with the ground. Within three seconds he appeared in our best room, his tiny mouth stretched to its full extent, which was still rather limited, and proffering the shabby stool, stained with margarine and dirt, he loudly announced in English: 'Hallo everybody!' Complete silence fell on the room. Grandpa slyly took this opportunity to move up a little to get a better angle on Heidi's breasts. Father opened his mouth, Qais rose to his feet as if that would stop what was happening and my husband spilled his tea. All four foreigners stared at the creature, horrified. Once I got accustomed to Muhammad he no longer struck me as quite as monstrous. Now I realised that he really was a monster, that instead of sympathy he elicited repulsion. But the boy persevered, for in spite of his exceptional abilities he wasn't at all self-conscious. He took a few steps towards the bosomy beauty, who at that point was sitting with her legs bent on one side, and uttered with great dignity, this time in Dari: 'Please take this chair, lady, you'll be more comfortable. And if you don't want to sit on the chair, Grandma will give you a bigger pair of trousers.' My husband was the first to come to his senses. He offered quite a fluent translation of Muhammad's speech, leaving out the reference to Grandma and looser clothing. Then he stood up, took the chair out of Muhammad's hands and asked him, stroking his enormous head: 'Could you please bring us some bread, tea and rice? Give me a hand, be a good boy.' Muhammad glanced towards the peephole the three of us were crowded around, but I was the only one to notice his conspiratorial wink.

chapter 7

'WHAT ARE THEY SAYING?' Freshta clung to me as if there was a flicker of a theoretical possibility that she might look through the hole at the same time as me. 'C'mon, you understand what they're saying, so you just need to listen. You don't have to be at the peephole to hear them.'

'Ever heard of lip-reading?' I asked triumphantly, suspecting she hadn't. As I expected, she shook her head. 'When I can't hear them properly, and what with you whispering so loudly and fidgeting about and them talking one over the other I certainly can't – well, when I can't hear them properly, plus my English isn't perfect, it helps to see how their lips move. It helps me understand them better.'

'You're just saying that. You want to look at those guys.' I was shocked, no longer thinking this was funny.

'You cow,' I hissed.

Even before I called her a cow, Freshta realised she had gone too far. That's why she took the insult in her stride, but also partly because she still wasn't used to the fact that this was quite a nasty insult in my book. Although the word didn't have the same force in Dari, I had instructed Freshta a long time ago, that should any Russian man ever call her a cow she should slap him in the face and kick him between the legs, as it was the same as an Afghan calling her a *faisha*.

'So cow means slut?' she had asked.

'Not quite. Cow is *gau* in Dari...'

'So why do you call each other that? Is it the same sort of thing as calling a man a camel?'

'Not really. In our country the camel isn't regarded as a stupid animal, we only know camels from the zoo, so we don't use the word that way.'

'But camels are really nasty. Their spittle is poisonous, they're horribly stubborn and their souls are as black as the night sky,' Freshta said sagely.

'All right, I will suggest it to our men.' My joke didn't make Freshta laugh. She clearly had something else on her mind.

'So why do you call each other a cow?'

'We don't. But if someone makes you really angry and if she's a woman you might call her a cow. Don't you call each other names?'

'We do. But not animal names. *Kosmodar* is not an animal...'

The word *kosmodar* was something along the lines of 'son-of-a-cunt'. Or rather, 'daughter-of-a-cunt'. It was a really filthy word, one Freshta and I had heard quite often from Qais.

'OK, you look and I'll listen. But you'll have to tell us if something happens that I can't hear.'

'Like if that beauty goes to sit in Grandpa's lap,' Freshta brayed in a guttural voice, and Mother pulled a horrified face.

We positioned ourselves near the peephole. Freshta glued her beautiful eyes, adorned with those incredible eyelashes of hers, to the glass and I was petrified that our precious foreign visitors might hear the eyelashes rubbing against the glass and discover that their nice and handsome young Afghan locks his womenfolk in the closet to make sure no strangers ever set eyes on them. I found the mere thought extremely embarrassing. It wasn't because they might have felt sorry for me or thought the nice young handsome Afghan an idiot, nor because it might have given them the idea that things were not going all that smoothly in this country. Nor because they might have been given the idea that it was us women who didn't want to talk to foreigners. No, I was afraid of one thing and one thing alone: that they would laugh at the warped concern shown by my husband, by Qais, or even by our Father. For even Father, in his heart of hearts, was afraid that someone might look at his ageing, care-worn and somewhat grubby wife, the sight of whom wouldn't arouse a sex-starved bull, let alone a foreigner accustomed to seeing hordes of half-naked beauties on TV screens and beyond. In other words, I blushed at the thought they might think our men were concerned that seeing us would make the foreigners think of *gunna*. That sinful ideas would flash through their mind and vivid sex scenes with me, Freshta or Mother in the main role might inspire them to take the short step that separates fantasy from reality.

'Everyone thinks about it.' When we first moved to Afghanistan, my husband explained to me the importance of modesty and covering up, in very moderate terms at first. 'It's not that someone forces you to do it,' he would say amiably and quietly, usually holding my hand. 'It's just that the local men really are more sex-starved and sex-crazed than men in your country. They're not used to seeing women and the sight of an ankle is enough to give them a hard-on.'

'I see,' I listened in amazement, and gradually started to believe this talk. 'You've got fair hair, a beautiful figure – do you really want every second man to have an orgasm when he sees you? The Quran is very sensible in this respect, Muhammad knew what he was doing when he ordered women not to be provocative.'

My husband had never read the Quran. I don't think he had read anything apart from his textbooks and required school reading. Nevertheless, he had obtained a copy of the Quran in Farsi and didn't allow it to be placed on the floor, using it instead to jam a window that flew open at every blast of wind.

He regarded my Russian edition as less valuable even though he knew that the genuine Quran had been written in Arabic and that therefore a Farsi translation really wasn't much more than a second-rate teaching aid. He still knew by heart a few passages that had been hammered into his head in primary school and could even translate them. The rest of the text had reached him piecemeal, mostly thanks to Grandpa who liked to quote certain *suras* on every suitable or unsuitable occasion, usually incorrectly and with his own additions, but with an ardent desire to convince the dumb people around him that Muhammad had wished mankind well and that a number of prohibitions had merely been invented by overzealous followers. 'Women should lower veils over their bosoms. And they should display their adornments only to their husbands...' Grandpa often used to say, both when it was necessary to defend the covering of the face as well as when fighting with our men for our feeble rights. Freshta, secure in the knowledge that her family would defend her from Qais' fury used to shout: 'You see, so where does it say anything about the burka? All it says is that breasts have to be covered.' Grandpa nodded in agreement, Qais stared blankly, first at Freshta then and at me, as I'm sure he thought I was corrupting his wife, filling her head with nonsense and telling her dirty stories from my childhood. It wasn't true. I think Freshta actually liked wearing the burka and she only let herself be drawn into this discussion with her husband because from time to time she quite enjoyed a row with him that didn't result in bruises and clumps of torn-out hair.

Sometime later I found the *sura* on wearing the veil in my Russian edition. It was there exactly the way Grandpa had recited it. And I've never found any other *sura* in the Quran referring to clothing or locking women up in darkened closets when visitors came. That's simply because no such *suras* existed. Although I had always quite relished attracting the glances of male admirers, I realised that the idea of every second or third man having an orgasm at the sight of me didn't strike me as in the least appealing. I suspected my husband exaggerated, maligning his fellow clansmen just to hide me from the world in a shapeless bag. Gradually I began to understand he just wanted to spare me constant exposure to catcalls such as: 'Hey babe, you've got nice, plump tits, how about your cunt, is it nice and plump too? Let's have a lick, babe...', although I still thought he was exaggerating. But then one day, as I walked down the road comprehensively covered by a burka, quite fluent in Dari by then, I heard young men, their mouths all twisted, shout at girls: 'Hey babe, you've got nice and plump tits, how about your cunt, is it nice and plump too? Let's have a lick, babe...', and I knew that had my baby daughter lived longer than fourteen days, I would have made her wear a burka from around the age of three right until a decent fellow took her home to safeguard her virtue as her lawful wedded husband and that I would have protected her from the eyes of these uncouth boys even more fastidiously than my husband was protecting me.

The four foreign visitors, however, had no idea about any of this. And before I would have had a chance to explain it to them, they would have taken us for a really backward family and been embarrassed that we could have suspected them of having sinful thoughts, something that I'm sure couldn't have been further from their minds. Although, actually, a glance at Freshta reminded me that even I couldn't help having sinful thoughts at the sight of such beauty.

The left half of her body pressed against me, while one of her arms rested on her thigh and her eyelashes fluttered against the glass. Radar-like, I aimed an ear at the crack from which the voices emanated. Freshta smelled lovely, something I had always envied her for, especially as I had always had problems in that department. I tended to have discharges, dirt under the fingernails, and sometimes I would forget to brush my teeth. It used to annoy my husband and he would say to me: 'Darling, you really are quite minging, you've got to do something about it, what will people say...' So I did my best, smearing camphor ointment under my armpits and shaving my pubes as thoroughly as everyone else.

'So what are they saying, damn it, Herra?' Mother inquired this time, as Freshta was apparently happy just to watch the group of cheerful, nice-looking white people.

'That we've got a nice little house, how many rooms we have and how many people live here.'

'And what are our men saying?' Mother wouldn't let up, making me miss a lot of information while I was interpreting.

'Our men are saying we've got nine rooms and there are many of us living here.'

'What made them say nine?' Mother asked in surprise.

'I guess they're including the outhouse, the closet, the hallway, the bathroom, the little room, Freshta's room and the living room... that makes nine. Ten, actually, if you count the garden. Eleven, if you count the garage.'

Mother seemed proud: 'Well, well. Eleven rooms, that's not bad at all.'

I started listening to the conversation again and this time I found it really interesting. By now it was clear that Dominic and Heidi were in charge, while the other two were apparently just short-term visitors. It turned out that the greying woman had come only for a few weeks as a member of what they called the launch team. The well-built man with almond eyes and a gentle, girl-like face, whom I didn't find attractive at all, wasn't American. He was just saying that he was from Belgium to which our men nodded, exclaiming without much conviction: 'Ah Belgium, I see, well, well, well, Belgium, hmm, the gentleman is from Belgium, who would have thought that, how interesting, Belgium...' Obviously, none of them had much of an idea as to where that country was located.

'One of the men is from Belgium,' I informed the women.

'Where is Belgium?' Freshta turned to me, her eyes reflecting a level of interest Qais would surely have branded as sinful and punished with a few slaps. At that point, I didn't pay much attention. However, later on, after it all happened, I remembered Freshta's eyes. I still don't know what could have given me the idea.

'In Europe.'

'Is that a country next door to yours? Have you been there?'

'It's not next door and I've never been there. I've only been to Poland once, with my Mum, we bought some suntan lotion and later my Dad told us off, saying it was all shoddy stuff. Otherwise my parents and I have only ever travelled around the Soviet Union.'

Freshta was evidently not interested in my childhood memories. The one thing that caught her attention was the suntan lotion. She couldn't understand that there could be a place in the world where women aspired to get a tan. In Afghanistan, by contrast, they were prepared to scrub their skin with gravel, just to make it a little bit paler.

'What's that chap's name?' she wouldn't stop asking.

'I don't know, I missed it as you keep rabbiting on. He's just some Belgian guy.'

'The woman has stood up. She probably needs to go to the loo,' Freshta squealed and Mother threw up her hands to warn her we might be heard, which might have resulted in an unimaginable tragedy.

The woman who had introduced herself as Heidi did stand up but not to go to the loo. She stretched her legs and tugged down her jeans, which must have been cutting her in the crotch in a position she wasn't accustomed to. Then the boys started serving food. We had been cooking all morning. At my husband's command we added more raisins to the rice than usual, cut the carrots very finely and cooked the chicken so thoroughly it fell apart under the fork like a piece of cake. The big salad bowls looked ravishing. I couldn't wait for the leftovers.

'Are your women not at home?' Heidi asked out of the blue.

'She's asking about us,' I said excitedly. Freshta quivered like a horse at the starting gate, Mother rubbed the corners of her mouth, and I was all ears. But all that followed was silence. My husband didn't translate Heidi's question. He pretended not to have heard it.

'They could send the two girls over here for a while, couldn't they?' Freshta suggested. She had a point. But I was sure my husband didn't want the foreigners to realise that our men had forced us to hide from the sight of their male escorts.

'Do your women have a job?' the indomitable Heidi asked again and this time her question could no longer be ignored. 'I mean, have they started going to work again maybe? I've heard the government has appealed to all women who had worked before the Taliban to return to their jobs.'

My husband translated and Grandpa nodded. Father decided to set the record straight.

'Well, there's Qais' wife,' he said, pointing to my brother-in-law, who was grinning stupidly. 'She has five children. One's very small, so she's always been at home with them, looking after all of us, together with her mother. Her mother has never worked either, it wasn't customary before, and then she was too old and the household kept her busy. And then...' I grew stiff since it was my turn now and I expected the men would deny my origin, as it might have aroused the foreigners' interest.

'There's Nazir's wife.' On hearing these words my husband blushed. As if he knew that what was about to follow would embarrass him more than anything ever had before. 'Herra.' Father pronounced my name with a certain hesitation, as if trying to decide if it was appropriate or not. Strangers, or rather anyone who wasn't part of the family, were never told the names of wives, sisters or mothers. Once, while we were still in Moscow, my husband told me about the huge row he had caused when the university registrar asked him to fill out a form which required giving his parents' names. He carefully entered his father's name in block capitals but left the box for his mother's name empty. After an almighty row involving some of the strongest terms of abuse imaginable, the Soviet bureaucrat summoned a higher-ranking official. 'My mother is no prostitute for you to call her by her name,' my still-unsullied future husband howled. The official was inclined to be lenient, nodding to show he was sympathetic, in line with the spirit of internationalism in which he had been raised. 'You know what, my lad,' he said, blurring his words somewhat as it was already 6.00 in the evening, 'let's put deceased.'

'How can you ask me to bury her alive,' my unhappy husband exclaimed on the brink of tears.

'OK then, how about just crossing it out,' the official suggested.

'That will look as if I'd never had a mother, as if I'd been found somewhere in a ditch like in your country, as if I'd come from an orphanage. But we don't have orphanages in my country.' My husband just wouldn't give up his right to uphold the age-old tradition dictating that the names of one's female loved ones may not be uttered in public under any circumstances. The official understood none of this but must have realised it was a serious matter. 'So how about putting an invented name,' he said. In spite of the large quantities of vodka ruling his brain he was still able to come up with ingenious ideas. My husband, getting ready to emit another desperate cry, was taken aback by this suggestion. He thought about it and declared: 'Fine. Let's put Natasha.'

From the moment he brought me to Kabul the only males to whom he had introduced me by name were blood relatives. And not even to all of them. With everyone else he referred to me as 'his wife'. He also instructed all the children, when talking to their friends, under all circumstances to only ever mention 'their mother, grandmother and aunt'.

'Forget their names the minute you go out into the street. Or do you want your school friends to mock your mother calling her by the worst kind of names?' The boys shook their heads to show their disapproval and observed the ban religiously.

'Herra?' repeated Heidi, not realising that no one else had been mentioned by name. She looked at my husband and then said, with a smile that would have disarmed any man: 'What a beautiful name. And where is she?'

My husband sat with his fingers buried in his knees, a vein on his neck throbbing. His face was flushed and he was completely paralysed by momentary hatred of his father. I don't think that something as intimate as my name being mentioned in the presence of foreigners bothered him as much as the fact that Qais had witnessed this terrible humiliation. Qais was agape, a smile frozen on his face. He reminded me of a clown I once saw in a circus as a child. Grandpa realised what was going on and cut in, even though my husband forgot to interpret. 'Our Herra. She was born in Moscow.'

I thought my husband would jump up, rush out of the room and shoot someone to get rid of the bile rising from his stomach to his head, threatening to erupt from his ears any minute.

'Translate, Nazir,' Grandpa prompted him and I knew exactly what was going on in the heads of everyone present. The foreigners were aquiver with curiosity, Father with mild embarrassment and unease, my husband with desperation, anger and hatred, and Qais with a passionate and gleeful joy at the humiliation of his hated brother-in-law. However, nobody ever opposed Grandpa. His years and status trumped Nazir's fury and to defy him would have been tantamount to high treason.

The foreigners were visibly surprised and fascinated. Mother and Freshta realised something unspeakably dramatic was happening.

'They've stopped chewing,' Freshta announced mysteriously, adding: 'I heard them say your name, Herra. What's going on?'

'Nothing. Wait,' I snapped at her.

'She's an educated woman,' Father followed up on Grandpa. 'She has a university degree. She speaks several languages.' My husband was translating Father's words on autopilot and Qais burst into mindless and rather loud laughter.

'But that's wonderful,' Heidi squeaked theatrically and Dominic nodded.

'Yes, that's great, does she speak English?'

'Yes, she used to translate the BBC news for us under the Taliban,' Father said proudly. 'We were the first in our neighbourhood to hear about the planes hitting those tall buildings in your country.'

'So where is she?' Heidi crowed exultantly, evidently regarding this as a ground-breaking discovery. We would soon learn why.

'She's hasn't been too well so she's gone to our relatives to recover, one of our cousins who's a doctor offered to look after her.' This time my husband made sure he did the talking in order to limit the damage. 'Qais' wife has gone with her,' he nodded in the direction of my brother-in-law who was choking with laughter like a kettle bubbling over with boiling water. 'And just today my mother has gone over as well to check how my wife is doing.' Suddenly my husband calmed down, relaxing after the long speech, as if a huge stone had been lifted from his chest now that he'd averted disaster. Just at that moment, however, Mad, who had been half-asleep since he found the previous conversation boring, woke up and got up sleepily to join the queue for the peephole. As he stood up his foot brushed against the cradle that held baby Yunus and woke him up. Baby Yunus began to whimper, arousing Freshta's maternal instincts, reinforced by fear of discovery. She leapt to her feet forgetting she was pincered from one side by me and from the other by the bulk of Mother pushing to get closer to the peephole. Meanwhile Mad had waddled up to us, stopping right above Freshta. As she straightened up nimbly, her rear knocked Mad off his wobbly stick insect-like extremities which couldn't quite cope with the weight of his globular body. Against all expectations Mad didn't fly back but, in an attempt to keep his balance, fell on Mother. Desperately trying to hold on to something as he plummeted to the floor, the only thing his little hands could find was Mother's braids loosely covered by a headscarf. Mother stifled a scream but as she tried to rid herself of the clinch of this giant tick, she hit the glass panel of the window to the living room with her elbow. At the same moment Freshta collapsed back on to the floor, her body dropping on to mine, and her legs flew up in the air, kicking mother in the face. The glass shattered most fortuitously, falling into the other room without injuring any of us. We tried to keep quiet even though a view of the visitors and our husbands had now opened up to us as we silently writhed in extremely undignified positions, eventually settling into a tableau I will remember for the rest of my life. There was Mother, her headscarf pulled down and her hair all messed up; a semi-recumbent Freshta, her head in my lap and her legs resting in Mother's generously proportioned lap; Mad kneeling behind Mother and Freshta, holding on to my breast with one hand, the other still buried in Mother's hair and finally me... with one shoulder bared, as my shirt had been pulled down by Mad's fierce grip, but otherwise presenting a fairly dignified picture, my knees demurely covered by Freshta. An oppressive silence fell. We gawped at the group of visitors and husbands, they gawped back at us and nobody made a sound. In those long seconds I couldn't think of anything one might possibly say in a situation like this. I think this was the first time in his life Grandpa was glad Grandma was no longer with us.

'And these are our sick women,' he said quietly and my husband obliged with a translation.

chapter 8

MOTHER AMAZED ME. Altogether, over the twelve years I had spent mostly under the same roof with her, she had surprised me about six times. This time she nearly gave me a shock.

'It was me who asked them to watch and Herra to translate,' she suddenly announced into the melee of shouting, Qais' yelling, Freshta's sobbing, the children's screaming and doors slamming. The house was in utter chaos. Except for me, almost nobody heard what mother had said. But she spoke again. This time the sound she coaxed from her throat was one I would never have expected from her.

'It was me who told them to watch, Freshta didn't want to and neither did Herra, I was the one who made them watch,' Mother yelled so loudly that her face went all red, the veins on her neck started showing as on a constipated baby, and her eyes almost popped out of her head. She stood in the middle of the living room looking like a goddess of justice, the headscarf that had slipped on to her shoulders revealing the plump knot of hair to which, at the critical moment, Mad had clung like a tick. Everyone froze in disbelief, as if under a spell. Qais, who was standing by the door, began to shout at Freshta, who was lying in a heap on the cushion, to start packing her things right away, but stayed there, paralysed with his mouth half open, the remaining words stuck in his throat. The children were exiled into the other room to prevent them from witnessing the adults' insanity lest they be tempted to follow their awful example. My husband, who had been running up and down the room – chased by Father, who in his turn, was trying to calm him down – and was ready to leap forward again, stopped in his stride and stared at Mother, his eyes wide with astonishment. Since advancing age had slowed down Father's reflexes, he didn't respond fast enough, bumped into my husband and froze, glued to him with his head resting on his son's shoulder. From his favourite corner Grandpa made vociferous contributions to the row until Mother's screaming interrupted his torrent of words about the importance of forgiveness, tolerance and prospects for the future.

Before this happened Mother had never ever stood up for me. In the early days, before I could speak Dari fluently but already understood at least every fifth word, I had often caught her exhorting Freshta not to get too close to me. Or comforting her son, my husband, that everything would be all right and I would calm down eventually. Sometimes she would set Father against me claiming I was a slob for not being able to wash dishes in semi-darkness and in the three drops of water we had to contend with during the five-year drought. With no consideration for me she tailored my clothes to make them even more shapeless, pulled the headscarf over my forehead even when we were in entirely female company and on a few occasions she went so far as to wash my husband's laundry after me insisting that grease stains had to be rubbed between the knuckles for at least twenty minutes. I suggested that it might make more sense to buy better quality, if more expensive detergent which, with a bit of luck, one could procure at the bazaar even under the Taliban. She chastised me with the disapproving look of a frugal housewife who had gone through life washing clothes in this way, sometimes managing to make do with plain sand.

Mother must have been plucking up courage for that fateful scream for a long time, for the mayhem had now lasted for more than three hours. The visitors accepted the explanation that we had returned unexpectedly and quietly slipped into the room next door, freshly recovered from our illnesses. They invited us for a return visit at the US humanitarian base and after they departed discreetly, my husband assembled all the children in the little room behind a door blocked with a chair, and prepared to preside over a kind of family tribunal.

But before he could catch his breath, we heard Qais shouting in the hallway.

'You slutty bitch,' he screamed, dragging Freshta into the courtyard by her hair. Normally he didn't dare attack her physically in her parents' presence but now he had completely lost control, forgetting where he was. My husband leapt up like a predatory feline and grabbed Qais by the throat. But since Qais wouldn't let go of Freshta, she ended up being worse off. She squealed like a mouse caught in a clumsy trap.

'If you want to leave, pack your things and get out of here in a calm and dignified manner,' Grandpa called in a trembling voice but nobody was paying any attention to him. Father started pulling the two young men apart but he wasn't strong enough to make any difference. I was actually quite relieved to see attention focused on someone else and hoped my husband's anger would subside before it turned on me. He managed to drag Qais back into the room along with Freshta who hung from his arms by her hair like a rag doll. Then his fist landed on his brother-in-law with real force and we all heard a dull, cracking sound. Qais' lower jaw was dislocated to the right – had he tried to clench his teeth, they would have been out by at least five centimetres. That didn't stop him from shouting although the sounds he made were rather inarticulate. Only after a second blow did he let go of Freshta but not before sending her with a kick under the window, where she cowered on a cushion. At this moment Father, puffed up like a cockerel, approached Qais from the back, and acting with great deliberation and concentration, gave him a huge slap across the face. This was more symbolic than painful but it marked a significant breakthrough in our family relations. For this was the first time Father had ever hit his son-in-law. Until now he would just listen to Freshta's sobbing, gritting his teeth and grumbling that she got what she had wanted, and when it was over he would give Qais a good talking to. But he had never hit him. Qais shuddered, unable to speak. He just mumbled something and we could tell by the tears in his eyes that he was in great pain.

'Give him another one from the other side, that'll make his jaw lock back in,' Grandpa shouted sensibly and it was obvious he would have been happy to take care of it himself had his strength permitted. My husband gently pushed Father away from the most advantageous position in front of Qais and after sizing up his brother-in-law he stretched out his arm and clenched his fist, slowly rehearsing the blow. Qais stood there gawping at Nazir without moving.

'Just don't overdo it, or you'll put it out in the other direction,' Grandpa offered his advice although it seemed he wouldn't have minded had this unconventional medical procedure not worked at the first attempt. Then the blow came, probably even more violent than the one that had dislocated the jaw from its original position. There was another crack and Qais spoke.

'Leave me alone,' he rasped. I thought it sounded funny and chuckled. My husband turned to face me and said in a quietly admonitory voice: 'Just you wait, your turn will come too.'

Before we realised that Qais really was in need of medical attention and came to terms with the fact that it was up to us to ensure he received it, my brother-in-law managed to unleash a torrent of abuse at my sister-in-law, while my husband kept pummelling his back, Father tugged at their sleeves, and Grandpa kept throwing his arms up in despair. Mother repeated: 'I was the one who told them to watch and Herra to translate!'

Perhaps it was because she had never stood up for me before that my husband believed her. I could see it in his eyes. But it was also because he wanted very much to believe her. He had been despondent ever since they first announced on the radio that the Russians were about to deliver humanitarian aid to our country after many years, this time without tanks. And ever since the first foreigners arrived he had been on edge. To this day I don't understand what made him invite those people to our house in the first place. After all, he should have known they were bound to notice me eventually. That someone would tell them about the woman from Russia who spoke English. I never stopped wondering about it and only now that it's all over have I figured it out. He wanted it. He wanted to show me off. For years I had been more of a liability and he had never impressed anyone with me. His friends mocked him, Mother felt sorry for him, and Father and Grandpa were the only ones who seemed to have any respect for me, appreciating that a lowly being such as a woman had learned how to read and write. Yet the whole family agreed it would have done him no harm to take another wife, a normal one, who would have borne him viable children, wouldn't talk too much, would wash out grease stains by rubbing the material between her knuckles, and have sex with real or feigned enthusiasm whenever her husband felt like it.

'I'd never do such a thing to you,' he would whisper to me at night when I complained about Mother and her endless lectures on the advantages of polygamy, which she herself had never experienced.

'We'll take an abandoned child, the place is teeming with them,' he would comfort me. And then we were given Mad. Our fourteen-year-old little monster, the precocious imp, someone even less suitable for showing off than I was. But he was quite fond of both of us really, in spite of everything.

And sure enough, later that night my turn did come. By the time we had cleared up the mess, driven Qais to hospital and, alas, brought him back home, since it was said that everything would heal by itself – that is, if anything had been broken at all – my husband had calmed down a little. Mother hadn't said a word since confessing to the heinous act of inciting us to commit something as unspeakable as watching foreigners through a peephole. She joined me in the kitchen while my husband, swearing profusely, packed Freshta, Qais and their progeny into the car to be rid of them for a couple of days, and said: 'Herra, you should thank Allah for having such a forgiving husband.'

'Thanks,' I hissed. I wasn't keen on all the praise she was inclined to heap on her beloved son. His older brothers had died before I moved to Kabul. One of them was said to have bravely fought the Soviets, while the other one was given to driving too fast and didn't survive a head-on collision with an armoured personnel carrier belonging to his own army. I knew his brothers only from black and white photographs with polished spots where their faces had been. Only later did I see Mother covering them in passionate kisses and muttering to herself. That was probably the reason Mother had lavished all her maternal love and devotion on my husband, who was the only one of her three sons left to assure her of a happy old age.

'Make sure you apologise properly at night, they tend to be peaceable in bed...'

'Did you also have to apologise to Father?'

Mother smiled. 'No, he's never raised his hand to me. But there was the uncle in Jalalabad who split his wife's head in two with a scythe because she spoke in the presence of visitors.'

I raised my hand to show that, first of all, I was familiar with the gruesome family legend and second, even if I hadn't been, this really wasn't the right time for her to recount it in all its gory detail. Apparently it really had happened but in spite of all the horrendous stories of violence in Afghan families I couldn't quite believe that an uncle could really have driven the blade of his scythe into his wife's skull just because she had uttered a few words. According to the story, some of the uncle's school friends had come for a visit. His wife with her small children, the youngest only four months old, had retreated to another room. Since tradition dictates that not only must a woman's face not be displayed but her voice must not be heard either, she kept quiet, as befitted a good and obedient wife. However, having looked after her naughty children for four hours, her nerves had frayed and she was on the verge of fainting with rage. The baby was screaming and it became increasingly difficult to find something to stuff its mouth with, while the other kids ran around like maniacs, climbing on their mother's neck and pulling her hair until one of them pushed a stick up her nostril. Holding the youngest offspring in her arms she felt defenceless and couldn't stop herself from saying: 'Leave me alone, you brats!'

Perhaps she hadn't even shouted, just raised her voice. When the visitors were gone, the family story goes, the uncle dragged her into the courtyard and asked how she dared bring shame on him in front of his school friends. She said something cheeky, presumably to the effect that nobody had invited his school friends to stay the night. The uncle grabbed a scythe, the family legend continues, and drove it into his wife's head. They say she died relatively fast. The legend ends here and I still can't believe it happened quite that way. Our men must have come up with this story to demonstrate how nice they were compared to the common-or-garden variety of uncle, as it provided them with an instructive bedtime story that would put us off committing similar improprieties. It was one of the first stories my husband told me after I moved to Kabul.

'And is it really true?' I asked him, my eyes filled with horror.

'It really is,' he replied enigmatically.

'And why didn't he end up in prison?'

'Because the woman he killed was his own wife, not somebody else's.'

'I see. And what about you and the family?'

'He was the one we're related to, she had just married into our family. Besides, I was only small, I might not even have been born then.'

'I see.'

'But it did happen,' he insisted stubbornly.

'Well, maybe a few hundred years ago and in quite a different place, right?'

'I don't know exactly when it happened but he was definitely our uncle.'

I comforted myself that this tale was more likely to have been invented to scare disobedient wives. That it had never happened, certainly not in our family. Something else had struck me back then, when I was still a newcomer to Kabul. I was perplexed that my educated husband, who had roamed Moscow discos selling blue jeans to female students, taking their hip measurements with the palm of his hand, that my beloved husband should have wanted all this to be true. That he wanted me to believe it and was proud of his uncle who had driven a scythe into his wife's head.

Mother released me from my evening duty of scrubbing the kitchen and the bathroom and sent me to bed.

'Get everything ready and be nice. Tell Mad to go to sleep straight away,' she advised. I really resented her at that moment. She was prone to dispensing this kind of crude advice but I felt she was the least suitable person to offer marital counselling. She had enjoyed a wonderful life with Father, who was just like Grandpa and the older he got the more like Grandpa he was, eventually becoming nearly perfect. When they were young Father used to take Mother to concerts; twice she'd been to the cinema in Kabul, frequented almost exclusively by men, but she had been so keen... He used to buy her western clothes and when the Russians came to Afghanistan and introduced the basics of socialist emancipation, she and her Muslim women friends decided to take driving lessons. Mother had failed only because she couldn't tell right from left and failed to switch into reverse when so instructed. Father was quite relieved, as he had dreaded the day he would have to let her behind the wheel of his car.

I went to our room and resentfully chased Mad to his small mattress in the corner.

'Don't even think of trying to join us tonight,' I snarled and he pulled a face.

'You bet.'

'Do you want a slap in the face?'

'No I don't, just like you, but unlike me you won't escape,' he retorted and I felt like kicking him. Sprawled out on the mattress, with his round little body, round head and thin extremities, he resembled a spider. A spider begging for someone to pierce his belly and make him take off like a deflated balloon. But I didn't kick him. I made up our mattresses and reached for the Prophet Muhammad's biography, starting from page one for the umpteenth time. After re-reading it so many times I had almost become fond of the Prophet. And I reckoned I could hardly pick a more appropriate work to send an immediate signal of profound remorse.

'I can't understand how they could have let the Brits do this,' I heard Grandpa from the room next door. 'People will be cheesed off,' he said commenting on the news that the command of the peacekeeping forces had been entrusted to the Brits, who had gone down in history for their failed attempts to subjugate Afghanistan.

'We shouldn't have let them leave,' Mother brooded. Father kept quiet.

'The Germans, the Germans would have done a better job of it, things have always been better under their rule,'

Grandpa continued. He had managed to catch the news in spite of the commotion.

'Nobody seems to care that we had waged a war against the Brits for years...' Grandpa was working himself into a state of frenzy.

'We should go and get Freshta tomorrow, we can't leave her there,' Mother started pestering Father who remained stubbornly silent, if he was in the room at all. But then again, it was unlikely that Mother would have started to discuss Freshta's departure with Grandpa.

'They say they'll install running water and fix the sewers. That'll be the day. These Brits. They've never done any good around here and now they'll be digging our toilets.' Grandpa was in a rage. 'If they start parading around here in short trousers with their girls half naked, our people will dump their sewers on them and smash water pipes on their heads.'

'I'll go and get her tomorrow,' Father said. 'Don't worry Father, nobody will be running around here half naked, that would be too much for our womenfolk, and it might give them ideas.' Oddly enough, Father was still trying to crack a joke.

'That's really nice of you but you'd better not take Nazir along, he's too quick-tempered,' Mother declared as she crawled under the blanket, judging by the rustling.

'I think it's their New Year today!' Grandpa suddenly exclaimed enthusiastically.

'What year would that be?' Mother said, fascinated by this piece of information.

'2002, but it's not for another month, they're just getting ready now,' Father said sleepily.

'Getting ready in what way?' Mother was surprised.

'OK, you're right, it's not happening yet,' Grandpa admitted and I heard the door slam. My husband was returning home. I had heard the car pull in and the smooth sound of the engine reassured me he had calmed down completely. He entered our room and took off his cardigan, trousers and shirt. He didn't even wash. He joined me under the blanket and took my hand. I felt relieved, so relieved. And then, all of a sudden, he squeezed my hand making it into a fist, crushing it with a grip he had learned in the special forces. He had shown me this trick many times before. He used to laugh when he heard me squeal with pain and always let go immediately. This time, however, I didn't squeal. Clenching my teeth and forcing my ankles together I writhed in a desperate attempt not to scream while he kept pressing and pressing, staring at the ceiling, possibly without even blinking. It went on for an eternity, until I began to feel sick. This is what the Red Army soldiers must have felt when the Nazis tore out their fingernails to make them reveal the partisans' hiding places. I would have confessed to anything. Tears welled up in my eyes and the pain that was turning my stomach now started choking me. And that's when he said: 'It hurts me even more.' He let go and turned his back to me. Over his shoulder I peered into the darkness where Mad was sleeping and it seemed as if the light of two strange yellow torches shone at me. It was Mad shining his eyes at us.

chapter 9

WE SAT on our mattress facing each other, savouring the few hours when we had the house to ourselves. Everyone else had gone to visit relatives in Panshir. Nazir claimed he had to buy some beds for the Americans, who had complained of stiff necks from sleeping on mattresses and had insisted on doing their shopping on a Friday. They had now given him a steady job, apparently not put off by the memorable visit to our house.

'But Friday is a holiday, everyone has a day off,' Mother grumbled. 'Can't you tell them it's a holiday?'

'They don't work Saturdays and Sundays and besides, they need their car and interpreter every day. Do you want them to fire me?' my husband replied amiably. None of us wanted him to get fired as his was the only regular income in the family and sustained an astonishing number of people.

'I told them they could meet you next week...' my husband said in a quiet voice once everyone else had piled out into the street and into the car and, following a series of jerky stops and starts, Father, no longer used to regular driving, managed to get the car moving north east. 'You'll be paid 400 dollars. For now.'

If it hadn't been for Grandpa, Father and eventually also Mother, my husband would never have allowed me to work for the Americans. When they first asked him to keep an eye out for a suitable local woman, someone fluent in English, bright and perceptive, he had blurted out cheerfully without thinking: 'That's my wife!' He regretted it the minute he finished the sentence.

'There's no need to chat to them and definitely no need to go trekking around town with them or to attend their damned meetings,' he lectured me, grabbing my hand tightly. 'Promise you won't?'

'My love, I don't even know what sort of work it's going to be and if I will be able to set any conditions. Did they tell you what they've got in mind?'

'You'll be in charge of a women's centre. Some kind of social support and advisory centre for women in need. War widows, refugees without a breadwinner... that sort of thing.'

I stroked his cheek. 'Well then, there'll be no problem, you'll see. The only people I'll ever talk to will be wretched Afghan women. I'm not interested in foreigners anyway...'

'Oh yeah, that was quite obvious the other day when you broke through the glass just to take a look at them.'

'Nobody broke through anything, the glass broke because Mother was too heavy and Mad was clumsy. They made me...'

'Don't even mention it, just thinking about it makes me sick.'

'Father said you used to black out from fury when you were little. You were born that way,' I said trying to tease him. He wasn't amused.

'I'll take you on Monday. And you know what, I'll just pop down to the bazaar and get you something nice to wear to make you the prettiest woman there.'

'Nazir, my love, I've got more clothes than I need, I don't need any more.'

'Oh no, it's all awful stuff...'

'Can I come with you, my love?' I knew he wouldn't like that. He hated it so much when I went out with him that I'd given up asking. Whenever we did go out, I was more on edge than he was, anxious that I might do something wrong and make him angry.

'You've got to wear a frown. In this country, if you smile it means you want all the men.' In spite of my twelve years of experience with Afghan men he still felt the need to enlighten me in these matters. And so, although I had already said good-bye to the burka several times, I preferred to slip it on just to make sure the garment would hide my smiling face, as I had never been very good at frowning.

'Herra, please. It'll be much faster if I'm on my own...'

'But how will you know what to get me?'

'C'mon, I know best what suits you and what's suitable for the job.'

'OK, I'll bake a cake while you're gone.'

'There's a good girl. Bake us a cake. It will make Mother happy.'

'What about you?'

'Yes, me too, but don't let anyone in, OK?'

The door slammed shut after my husband and five minutes later Nafisa arrived. There was a knock on the door and I went to the terrace to enquire who was there, in a guarded and quiet voice... I knew I was meant to pretend nobody was at home but I was curious to see who was so eager to come and see us on a Friday. I squealed with delight when I saw the well-built shape of the maternity hospital director undulating under the burka in her own inimitable way.

I welcomed the rare opportunity to spend some time with Nafisa on my own.

'Two women died on me in labour last night,' she sighed before complimenting me on my hair. Freshly hennaed, it did look rather lovely.

Although Nafisa was rather pretty, in our family she was regarded as a dissolute woman, too outgoing for her own good. At the same time, she was the pride of the family, being better educated than anyone else and enjoying the reputation of being a devoted doctor. She may have been a bit too sinewy, the colour of her neck slightly reminiscent of poultry, but all in all she was a very attractive lady. Some considered her a model of a loving wife, others claimed she beat her husband at home, wondering what she was up to at the hospital at night. 'It's not healthy for a woman to spend so much time outside of her house and never lift a finger at home,' Mother would say, denouncing Nafisa whenever her name came up. 'Just leave her alone, she has a job and a family to cope with, and could knock spots off any man,' Grandpa would snarl at her. But everyone, including Mother, welcomed her with open arms since she treated us free of charge and was better acquainted with our vaginas and ovaries than our own husbands were.

'How's Muhammad?' Nafisa asked after a little chitchat. I thought I detected a residue of guilt in her voice. Perhaps she felt she should have kept him herself.

'We can't find a school for him. He gets bullied in the boys' schools and the girls' schools won't have him. I tried home-schooling him but he knows more than I do.' I wasn't going to complain to Nafisa about Mad. After all, we were all happy to have him and she knew it.

'How about you?' she asked, slightly inappropriately, I thought.

'What about me?'

'I hear you're starting a job.'

'Oh yeah, this coming Monday. I'll be advising women on how to improve their lot. I'll send the most hopeless cases your way, so that at least they die in clean sheets in your hospital.' Nafisa laughed.

'They'd have to buy those sheets first. I haven't got a single one left. But seriously, it sounds like a great job, Herra, and it'll be a nice break from the crowds at home.'

She was quite right. After so many years of being confined in the same space with the same people, there were times when I was willing to die just to be on my own for a while, even though my husband used to frighten me by saying our entire family was going to end up in paradise so we would all meet up there anyway. Sometimes the sinful idea sneaked into my mind that I should get up to some mischief to make sure I ended up in hell where I might make some new friends. Besides, in my husband's view I had long been going to hell in a handcart.

'And how's Freshta?' Nafisa was ticking off members of the family one by one as if she were expected to compile a report on us.

'Freshta's not going to get a job.'

'That's not what I asked, that's pretty obvious. First, she's got no skills and second, that moron of hers would never let her. Are they living here at the moment?'

'It varies. Qais is penniless so while they're here at least their children have enough to eat. Sometimes he drags her to the *Mikrorayon*, then they're back here again. It's madness. The same thing over and over again.'

'Does he still thrash her?'

'No change there; sometimes he does, sometimes he doesn't.'

'She ought to divorce him.' Whenever Nafisa suggested this in the past, I had voiced my disapproval as if I were the one defending the peculiar custom of depriving divorced women of the custody of their children while she was a progressive champion of the right to permanent marriage.

'OK, but what about little Hamayun and baby Yunus.' I breathed a sigh of experience.

'Well, she could keep them for a few more years...'

'Qais is a lunatic, he's capable of ripping the baby off her breast.'

Suddenly Nafisa laughed and produced a cigarette from a pocket hidden under her shirt.

'Want one?' All at once I felt a real craving for a cigarette. My husband smoked, so did Qais, while Grandpa indulged in ever more substantial quantities of hashish and Father wasn't one to say no to a cigarette or hashish either. The whole house reeked of tobacco so there was no danger of being given away by the smoke. I stretched out my hand and Nafisa placed a Hi-Lite cigarette between my fingers. The box said 'Made in Japan' but we all knew the cigarettes had been rolled by nimble-fingered Afghan refugees in Pakistani sweatshops. Nafisa put one into her mouth too and struck a match but managed to light it only after several attempts. 'We can't even produce matches,' she muttered with the cigarette in her mouth, looking like the president of a women's organisation fighting for the right of women to carry arms, smoke, drink vodka and mete out physical punishment to their husbands.

'I'm sending my daughter to Europe,' Nafisa announced, blowing smoke towards the ceiling in a theatrical gesture. She pulled a face when the smoke went right up her nose.

'What about your husband?' I said in surprise.

'He's against it. But I'll make her go anyway. Not the boys, I'll keep them at home for the time being. They're not at risk here. But I want the girl to learn something abroad. I want her to study to become a doctor. Doctors are always needed here.'

'And what if your husband simply doesn't allow it?' I persisted, as I couldn't imagine getting myself into this kind of fight with my own husband.

'He won't. He's not as stupid as your menfolk. I can't understand how Uncle can put up with it. He used to carry your Mother in his arms and now he doesn't mind seeing his own daughter being battered by an uneducated moron and his own son walking you around town on a leash.'

That hurt. My husband had never taken me anywhere on a leash. Nafisa was alluding to a long-forgotten family visit at her place, still under the Taliban, when I had suddenly felt sick after eating mutton. Nafisa had persuaded my husband to let me stay the night and collect me the next day. Since it was late Nafisa dropped me off on her way to work in a taxi. My husband screamed at her so much even Mother shook her head. 'I can walk my own wife around on a leash if I feel like it,' he had shouted, red with rage. 'Oh yeah, and you might as well muzzle her and thrash her with a stick,' Nafisa had shouted back. It was an ugly scene, quite rare in those days, when we spent most of the time sitting at home. I thought my husband was just worried about me. It certainly wouldn't have been much fun to have been caught by the morality police and quizzed about the kind of men we had at home to allow us out on our own, let alone let us resort to something as immoral as a taxi. But Nafisa had a special permit as she had helped to give birth to thousands of little Taliban, sometimes visiting their homes, and therefore wasn't deprived of her freedom of movement.

'Actually, he wants our daughter to go abroad too, he's just scared to admit it to himself,' she suddenly said softly, taking my hand. Her gesture surprised me, for Nafisa had never been given to excessive displays of affection. 'He's a good guy, really, but sometimes I have to gently explain to him that what I want is better than what everyone else wants.'

Nafisa's husband was also a doctor. We all felt a little sorry for him. When other people were around he seemed very timid and Nafisa kept shouting him down. She had asserted her right to accompany him to some of the newly reopened restaurants and when they had visitors she would gracefully cover her hair with a headscarf and join them for a convivial chat about politics and some tea. Occasionally she would allow her professional vocabulary to slip into the conversation, describing her female patients' innards in such vivid detail it made her husband blush and their male visitors' jaws drop. Once, in Father's presence, she held forth on how much she hated having to sew up hymens

and how she wanted to kill all the parents who dragged their
thirteen-year-old daughters to her surgery demanding that she
check their vaginal passages. 'A girl happens to jump up and tear
her hymen, and they bring her to me and want me to make it
good again,' she boomed. For a long time after this, my husband
claimed she was totally depraved. 'And then there're all these
poor girls who come to see me because they slipped up and
are now scared they'll be found out when their parents pick a
husband for them. And the worst thing,' she bellowed, 'is this
girl who's slept with her future husband and now they both
want me to sew her up so they can wave a bloodied bed sheet
for their family after the wedding night. So I told them to take
a cockerel to bed with them and cut its throat in the morning,
they'll have plenty of blood.' When she said that, Nazir and I
exchanged a long knowing look. In our case a cockerel would
have been no use.

Nafisa was deafened by the clamour of her own sonorous
voice so I was the first to notice the sound of an engine. She
had just finished telling me that her husband would in fact be
more than happy to send their daughter to Europe because he
was really a kind and wise man who only sometimes pretended
to be a harsh tyrant to satisfy their friends and family. Not with
much success, I thought. My husband, on the other hand,
had recently started getting better at it. I leapt up, pulling the
cigarette out of Nafisa's mouth. She opened her eyes wide and
croaked: 'What the hell... is he here? So what...' I buried the
cigarettes, still burning, in flowerpots beneath the window and
started waving my arms around wildly to disperse the smoke.
It seemed so thick you could cut it.

'Calm down,' Nafisa yelled and got up, annoyed. She had
managed a couple of clumsy arm movements in solidarity when
my husband appeared in the doorway, laden with packages and
smiling the smile of a slightly overgrown child, which made
me forgive him instantly for doing anything hurtful. He didn't

seem to mind that Nafisa was in the house and didn't even ask how she had got there when I wasn't supposed to let anyone in.

'I've got something wonderful for you,' he shouted, beaming happily. Now it was my turn to wish Nafisa weren't there. I wanted to have his happy mood all to myself. Whenever he brought me little gifts he would purr blissfully like a little tomcat. He loved dressing me up just for himself sometimes squeezing me into clothes so tight I would have been embarrassed to wear them even to bed. 'You'll wear it one day, when we go to Moscow,' he promised but we both knew there would be no trips to Moscow. Now my husband dropped the packages on the floor and started gently to unwrap the most monstrous one, covered in scraps of dirty paper, eventually extracting an object of indeterminate colour and shape. As he raised his arms above his head an enormous pair of trousers concealed his entire body. Nafisa rose in silence, taking a few steps towards the weird garment, her shoulders hunched like a vulture that has just landed. I froze in astonishment, unable to move. It was a pair of military trousers. Or rather, if it had been only that. It was a pair of trousers someone must have ripped off a dead or wounded US airman, albeit one not conforming to army regulations. He must have been over six feet tall, weighing well over 300 pounds. The trousers were adorned with countless pockets, which Afghans adore, a faded US flag on the right leg and a permanent-looking stain on the left knee.

'Isn't that something?' my husband exclaimed from behind the fabric. '50 dollars! But I haggled it down to 46. I said to him – c'mon, you call yourself a patriot? How can you ask so much for a piece of American trash? Of an Afghan Mujahideen? And he said, OK, give me 46 and it's all yours,' my husband laughed happily and his arms, which he had raised above his head started to shake, lending the trousers the appearance of a theatre curtain closing for the seventh time after thunderous applause.

'That's... incredible,' I said in Russian, adding after a few seconds: 'My darling.'

Nafisa was still speechless. She carefully reached out towards the material as if needing to pluck up courage before stroking a wild animal. After touching the trousers carefully she whispered: 'It's waterproof.'

'Yes, it's rubberised. You can roll about in puddles and not a single drop will get through,' my husband roared in a voice suggesting he was close to ecstasy. 'Try it on, Herra, I know it'll really suit you,' he added in Russian. He let the thing drop to the floor where the material collapsed into a shapeless heap with a thud worthy of a parachute. I looked at my husband, tears welling up in my eyes. His own eyes were radiant with happiness, the joy of a child given a toy electric train mixed with a hint of disappointment at living in a city that has had no electricity for years.

'Yes, my love,' I uttered in the language Nafisa did not understand since Afghan society has a low tolerance of affectionate exchanges between husbands and wives. 'I'll try it on, I'm sure it'll be a good fit.'

'I know your size, don't I?' my husband replied with a roguish smile, honouring Nafisa with a wink in his inordinate joy. She slowly sank back into the cushions, a smile frozen on her lips.

I bent down towards the heap comprising the trousers. I was going to fling them over my arm casually and walk gracefully to the other room but they weighed more than I did and almost pulled me down to the floor, so the best I could manage was to get hold of one leg and drag it along with a loving expression on my face. It must have weighed several dozen pounds and would have made a jet crash, had a pilot worn it. It was a garment suitable only for the pilot of a heavy bomber.

My husband went back to Nafisa and left me alone with his present. I wasn't sure how to fasten it to my body. Although my hips were quite generously proportioned and I was certainly not thin, the belt alone, roughly stitched to the top of the trousers, would have been enough to cover the whole of my body. The only way I could stop the trousers from falling was to gather the thing tightly around my waist and fasten it somewhere above my breasts. In fact, the trousers could have made decent sleeveless overalls. I soon discovered they reached almost to the top of my head but I didn't give up. I used some string to tighten the trousers above my breasts, turned the bottoms up nine times, which was not easy as the numerous pockets that for some strange reason were located on the lower sections of the legs also got in the way. I pulled on my loosest shirt so that the bumps on my body formed by the tough impregnated fabric would be at least partially covered. I made a move to show off the result but, impeded by the stiff garment, instead of walking graciously I staggered about like someone who had stepped on a landmine and had to walk on prosthetic limbs hand-made by a carpenter uncle. Nafisa lost the power of speech for the second time, my husband for the first. To my horror, after ten seconds he exclaimed: 'Beautiful, Herra. I knew it. They'll have something to stare at tomorrow.' And they sure did.

We set out first thing in the morning. I was extremely nervous, mentally rehearsing English idioms I had completely forgotten over the years, trying to imagine what I ought to know and praying in a mixture of Arabic and Russian to our common God for my husband to be sent away on an assignment as soon as possible. My airman's attire took up the entire front seat, spilling over into the driver's area and hindering my husband in changing gears. As he enthusiastically threaded his way through the morning traffic he kept glancing at me in delight, infecting me with his joy. In line with his instructions I covered the upper half of my body with a top that had always been too big but lately, given my increased bulk, only just fitted around my hips. The top won my husband's approval and I couldn't tell if his vociferously expressed admiration for my appearance was genuine or whether it was just a shrewd way of disguising his joy at having achieved his goal – I was about to meet foreigners for the first time in years, looking like an overgrown potato. That was one of the reasons he decided a burka wasn't essential today. He spent half an hour picking it up and hanging it back on its nail, until Mother felt the need to intervene: 'Nazir, I don't think she'll need it. She'll be in the car and once you get there, she'll just have to nip over to the office or whatever it is they have there...' Even Mother realised that a burka might be a bit out of place in a work environment and it might be rather off-putting for the foreigners to have to conduct a first interview through a grille. We brought the burka in a plastic bag, just in case. 'You never know...' said my husband.

Armed guards stood outside a building with barbed wire on the walls and freshly painted gates. My husband knew some of the men. They hugged, exchanged kisses and chatted, holding hands. I stayed in the car, knowing that the first difficult moment was about to come. Just as I decided to grab the burka my husband came back to the car and said: 'Lower your head and walk inside, quick.' I staggered out of the car clumsily, the trousers rustling like a rattlesnake. I felt the gaze of the men with sub-machine guns and blushed. Waddling like the first astronauts on the Moon I made for the door. '*Salam alaikum,*' the men said. '*Va alaikum salam,*' I said, sailing into a nice garden where a few Afghans with spades, shovels and pickaxes were dashing about. Wherever I looked something was being built or repaired. A giant satellite dish lay outside the large two-storey building and a small group of Afghans in European clothes stood above it waving their arms. My husband pushed me with a furious whisper: 'In you go, quick...'

Everything smelled of new paint, the floors were carpeted and the doors were fitted out with imported handles. My husband knocked on the second door on the left and I realised I hadn't seen him knock in twelve years. It made me laugh. 'Come in,' a voice said and my husband opened the door. Wiping the smile off my face, I entered an office full of computers, notice boards covered with bits of writing and maps, and filled with what, in Afghan terms, seemed like vast amounts of furniture.

'This is my wife,' my husband sang out, pointing at me with pride. The head of Dominic, the man I remembered from the visit to our house, peered out from behind a computer. Heidi was standing by one of the notice boards and her hand froze mid-air as she spotted me. I bet she forgot what she was about to write. The ensuing silence lasted longer than the rules of etiquette dictate. Dominic was the first to come to his senses.

'Pleased to see you, madam. I believe we've met before.' I took a deep breath but my husband cut in first: 'She's a lawyer and she speaks Russian, English and Dari. I've already told you...'

'Yes, Nazir,' said Heidi interrupting him. 'We're glad you were able to come. I think it won't take long for us to come to an agreement. I suppose we can start today...'

'She just needs to know what exactly she's expected to do, I mean, that is, if you're interested in her...' My husband interrupted the American.

Heidi raised her eyebrows, which, as I later discovered, was a sign of considerable displeasure.

'Of course we'll explain everything to her, Nazir.'

'But she doesn't know how to use a computer, she hasn't had an opportunity, you see...' Nazir grinned in demonstration of his positive attitude. I kept smiling for the simple reason that I forgot to stop.

'Shut your mouth,' my husband said in Persian, without altering the enthusiastic expression on his face. But I could tell he was really angry with me. I lowered the corners of my mouth and clenched my fists. At that point Dominic got up, took a few steps towards us and shook my hand. Heidi did the same. I squeezed their hands as much as I could to show I wasn't a puppet.

'Take a seat,' Heidi invited us and I rustled as I sank into an armchair, probably an import from Dubai. My husband sat down gracefully on a sofa with an appreciative nod to me. If I ever found myself in public, he had always instructed me to find a seat where no male would be able to sit next to me. No Afghan would have dreamt of trying to do that. On the rare occasions when male and female members of a family gathered in the same place, all the women would crowd on one side of the room and the men on the other to avoid any chance of physical contact. Now I intuitively remembered his oft-repeated lesson, selecting a chair meant only for one person. Heidi sat down next to my husband who didn't seem to mind. Dominic made himself comfortable facing me.

'I can drive her in first thing in the morning every day so there'll be no problems with her arrival,' my husband's voice rang out and Heidi gave him a surprised look: 'But why should there be any problems? I'm sure we'll work everything out with... what's your name?' she said, turning to me unexpectedly. Before I managed to open my mouth, my husband uttered, stressing both r's: 'Herra, Herra is her name.'

Heidi frowned. 'Right, Herra... Do you think you could give us your CV? In English, and you can do it by hand, for the time being.' I nodded quickly, to give some sign of activity.

'Yes, she'll definitely write it but surely she can do that at home?' My husband started getting up cheerfully, evidently assuming the interview was over and I could do my homework in the safety of our house, without witnesses.

'Nazir,' Heidi suddenly said quite sharply. 'Can your wife speak at all?' The same embarrassed silence descended as when I rustled into the room in my US army trousers and Dominic and Heidi weren't quite sure if the idea was to provide entertainment or whether in their few weeks here they hadn't quite grasped all the mysteries of Afghan national dress. After a slight delay, my husband's face turned red as he recognised subtle mockery in the American's question. 'Yes she can,' he said sternly.

'Nazir,' Heidi continued in the same tone. 'We need you to drive to the Ministry of Public Works and the Ministry of Foreign Affairs. I think you should go now.'

'I think it would be a good idea if Dominic came along, things get done faster with a foreigner around,' my husband declared confidently with a triumphant wink in my direction. Poor man, he still thought he was in charge of the situation.

'Nazir, if we thought it would be a good idea for Dominic to go with you we would send him. But right now we're the ones deciding who goes where. Perhaps it would be better if I came...'

Nazir was frightened to death. He leapt from the sofa in a flash, his face completely frozen. The thought of leaving me alone with Dominic plunged him into a state of total despair.

'Let me go on my own first and then we'll see. The key officials might not even be there today and you might be wasting your time... I'll be back soon...' Fortunately, the two Americans agreed. My husband gave me a fiendish look, indicating I wasn't to move from the spot. Taking a few steps towards the door he turned around and said in Persian: 'Don't talk to him.' The look he bestowed on me was a mixture of anxiety, boundless devotion and hatred. I knew that look well. It was exactly the same look he had given me during our first night together. Except that on that occasion he had a compelling reason. Not this time. After all, he was bound to remember our time in Moscow, when it had never occurred to him there might be anything wrong with me talking to strange men, sometimes even giving them a friendly smile. He scowled and left with a gentle, courteous bow. Everyone heaved a sigh of relief. For a while nobody said anything until we heard the engine start in the street.

'Really, he won't let you say a word,' said Heidi, leaning over to me adding: 'It must be hard to have a husband like this, right?' With a meaningful look she glanced at the hideously shapeless lower half of my body.

'I'm happy to work for you. Can you explain what will be expected of me?' I said in a studiedly correct English, the way I had rehearsed it the night before, doggedly staring at Heidi and her alone. That day I managed not to look at Dominic once. But I had to make a huge effort.

chapter 10

'THEY ARE ALL BUNGLERS, just like the Russkies. Exactly the same,' said Grandpa, traversing the area between the living room and the kitchen with unusual agility, waving his arms and shaking his head. The drawstring in his trousers stuck out from under his shirt, which indicated he was highly agitated as letting one's drawstring be seen is regarded as very embarrassing and anyone who lets a stranger's eye rest on it risks social disgrace. 'A hundred people, a hundred, that's an awful lot even for Afghanistan... isn't it? A hundred people! One minute they're here and the next they're gone. It didn't surprise me when the Russkies did this sort of thing, but these guys...' In Grandpa's usage, the term 'Russkies' sometimes denoted not just the 'Soviets' but anyone who did anything to annoy him. 'And how about you? I hope at least they're treating you well?'

His remark puzzled me. Until then Grandpa had been among those family members fighting on my side of the barricade and putting pressure on my husband to accept the Americans' job offer, albeit for mercenary reasons. Once I accepted, he had given me an appreciative pat on the back and said: 'Please make sure you are a dignified representative of our people. We shall all be judged by you.'

'They just want to be helpful,' I objected now.

'Well, so did these guys, except they've hit our villages instead of the Taliban,' Grandpa had been glued to the radio all morning, jotting down bits of news on a piece of paper. Occasionally he would attend a meeting of our neighbourhood council of elders, he had even joined a preparatory committee for the *Loya Jirga*, the Afghan people's assembly, and was now clearly planning to thrash this out with his colleagues. This kind of blunder was rare for the US Air Force but when it did happen it usually resulted in many casualties. However, since Kabul had been peaceful for some weeks now, we looked upon the grieving villagers in the East with sympathy but without offering to do anything much to help them. Only Qais came up with the half-witted idea of sending the children to throw rocks at the US Embassy but my husband cut him down to size with a rather convincing argument. 'They'll throw one rock and they'll be shot dead. Why don't you go throwing stones yourself, because if anything happens to you quite a few people will be relieved.'

'So what exactly is it that you do there?' Grandpa asked all of a sudden and I didn't know what to say. So far, as Heidi would say, I was being inducted into the basics of humanitarian and development aid issues. I was learning how to live with charts, regulations and the wishes of rich sponsors who lived so far away they couldn't possibly have any idea who was using their money and for what purpose.

'Well, I'll be looking after women who have problems. But I still have a lot to learn, they're waiting for me to finish my training. Basically, the programme is aimed at women who've lost their husbands during the war and also at women whose husbands are good-for-nothings, disabled, violent or stupid...'

'Aha, and who's going to determine which husband is stupid and which one isn't? I bet it'll be the females themselves, right?' The information seemed to have suddenly aroused a residue of male solidarity in Grandpa, even though he usually tended to champion the rights of the weakest, often lecturing my husband on how to treat his wife and women in general. In his own way, Grandpa was a solitary Afghan feminist at heart. Recently, after my husband had chucked a pile of my Russian books down the toilet (in one of his many acts of punishment for what he deemed to be my inappropriate behaviour at work) Grandpa found a long rod, and after tinkering with it in the garage for a while he went out to the outhouse carrying a weird contraption. He used a rag to attach the handle of a pair of pliers to one end of the rod; another, much thinner parallel rod was affixed to the tool's other grip in such a way that the pliers could be operated with a bit of dexterity. He lay down on the ground in front of the foul-smelling hole and since he didn't bother placing anything underneath he lay there amid the droppings our children had left behind after emptying their bowels in the morning. He spent over three hours with his head down the hole, panting and occasionally emitting a triumphant cry. Eventually he managed to retrieve most of the books covered in excrement, their pages sodden with sewage. He himself looked as if he'd taken a bath in the sludge at the bottom of the hole. The problem was that whenever he caught a book he had to extract the rod very carefully, moving it hand over hand, forgetting that the hut ceiling was lower than the length of the rod. The end of the rod hit the ceiling each time, sending the book fluttering and splattering faeces all over Grandpa's face. Then it fell back into the bog and the operation had to be repeated. The most terrible incident occurred as the old man fought to rescue the *History of Russia*, a thick volume by Zaichkin and Pochkayev, which for some mysterious reason got stuck to the pliers and wouldn't drop out even after the rod had collided with the hut's wooden roof. Instead it started swaying wildly, smashing its sludge-soaked pages right into Grandpa's face. But even that didn't deter him.

The whole family pretended nothing was happening and everyone avoided going anywhere near Grandpa. My furious husband was out in the courtyard playing with his nephews but didn't dare to stop Grandpa from rescuing works of literature. Grandpa, in his turn, hadn't dared to interfere when my livid husband was chucking my library down the toilet. Only one person apart from Grandpa eventually plucked up the courage to protest at Nazir's mean deed. It was Mad. After watching Grandpa for about an hour he approached him quietly, grabbing his feet without a word of warning with all the strength his tiny hands could muster. Unfortunately Grandpa, frightened that someone was trying to throw him down the hole head down, waved his legs pointlessly with a wild yell of: 'You criminal!' That, in turn, frightened Mad who let go of Grandpa's legs and the only thing that saved him from falling into the depths were his shoulders whose width exceeded that of the hole. Eventually Mad took on the commendable task of extricating the rescued books from the pliers and wiping the faeces off Grandpa's face when he could no longer see. Finally, Mad washed all the books, spread them out in the courtyard to dry and asked me to teach him Russian.

'I'd like to read something. How long will it take me to learn?'

'That depends on you, Mad. I think in about a year you should be able to use a dictionary, at the very least.' Six months after our Russian lessons began he started studying a rather difficult volume entitled *Animal Husbandry*.

When the people from the US humanitarian organisation first suggested I work for them, Grandpa was the first to react. He said to my husband: 'Nazir, my boy, I wished all my life that Grandma could have gone to school and learned at least how to sign her name. Your wife does know how to sign her name. So we might as well all benefit.'

Although my husband never argued with Grandpa or his Father, he invariably ended up having his own way. The family elders had the right to raise objections but lacked the strength to do anything about the practical consequences of any acts of disobedience. They had never allowed me to complain about my husband and, to be honest, it only occurred to me to do so once, some three years after I came to Kabul. 'Why do I have to wear the burka at home when our cousins come to visit?' I resentfully turned to Father whom, along with Grandpa, I regarded as an ally. 'Because that's how Nazir wants it and it's his right. Do you want people to think you're a slut? And that my son is a weakling and a henpecked husband?' Never again did I say a word against my husband, which ensured I could always count on Father and Grandpa for support. Not on Mother though. She never supported me. On the contrary. She and Nazir would sometimes whisper in the corner and I knew she was comforting him: 'Don't worry, she'll get used to our ways. Just be patient and don't let up.'

Father had never beaten Mother. It wasn't the done thing in our family. Qais was the first one to introduce such customs to our house, earning himself the label of a pathetic, backward thug in the eyes of the whole clan. Freshta had never really been an ally either. Sometimes I thought I detected some glee in the way she observed the fights and scuffles between me and my husband, almost as if she were relieved that someone else had made the same mistake and picked the wrong husband. Unlike her, however, I was convinced – except for the odd brief moment of doubt – that I couldn't have picked a better husband.

'Grandpa, my Americans are totally opposed to what their army is up to in this country. Or at least, slightly opposed, you know.' Grandpa was looking out of the window but he was listening. He didn't reply but gave me a puzzled look. I had said 'my Americans.'

Mad was just as eager to pick up 'Western manners' as my husband had once been. He quizzed me about details of Moscow life, just like Nazir had many years ago. Except that in Mad's case it wasn't the kind of empty admiration whetted by videos we used to watch in the evenings, which made Mother feel faint since they showed 'huge numbers of naked people

running around,' as she used to say. Incidentally, she did have
a point. The recently reopened video shops that had sprung
up on every corner offered films of the trashiest kind. Most
of the female characters were promiscuous bitches, who had
barely finished having dinner with a new acquaintance before
jumping into bed or on to the back seat of a darkened Mercedes
with them and emitting guttural noises of pleasure. For the first
time in years my family suddenly remembered that I had come
from 'over there' and started grilling me about things I had no
clue about. Even Nazir, who had spent several years in Moscow,
seemed to forget that Moscow was hardly the West – in fact,
for many people it was the quintessential East – and that I was
far from being the most suitable person to represent, let alone
defend, Western civilisation. But for some inexplicable reason
I enjoyed playing along.

'Is it normal for two women to live together like this in your
country?' Father asked one evening after watching *Basic Instinct*
in English, having viewed it three times in a single night, I
hasten to add. The copy was quite worn out, as the film was
apparently quite popular with newly-liberated Afghans, which
meant, luckily, that the most titillating scenes were almost
invisible.

'I'm not sure but lesbian couples do exist in our country.
I don't know about living together but they do walk around
holding hands.'

'You really don't know where to draw the line! Now girls are
making out with girls...'

'And it's not just girls going out with girls, Father, it's also
boys with boys. They walk around the streets with their little
fingers hooked together like you and Uncle Amin,' I said,
cracking up.

When I first arrived twelve years ago I was stunned to see
bearded men with sub-machine guns on their backs walking
around with their little fingers hooked together, sharing

frequent hugs and exchanging passionate kisses on the cheek every time they met or said goodbye. This sight elicited my first wrong-footed question and I was told it was just a custom, which had absolutely nothing to do with sex.

'It's just a custom, girl,' Father retorted now, insulted. 'And it's not just Uncle Amin, this is what all men do when they're friends and it doesn't mean anything. Here in Afghanistan we don't have any of your sickos, or at least there are fewer of them in this country than anywhere else in the world. I'm quite sure of that.'

'Four percent, Father. Just like in my country...'

'I can assure you, Herra, there are many more of them in your country than in ours.' Father wouldn't give in. Considering he was my father-in-law this was an exceedingly open discussion, perhaps too intimate. He was growing irritated, and I wondered if embarrassment and virtuousness wouldn't get the better of his curiosity. But eventually he went on: 'In that film, you know...'

'Yes, Father, I know, I watched it when you were out, with Freshta,' I declared triumphantly, proud not only to have seen it but also to have the nerve to admit to such a deed.

'Good for you but you ought to have spared Freshta, it must have been quite upsetting for the poor girl. But what I wanted to ask you,' Father kept beating about the bush. 'You know these two girls who are together, the writer and the other lady... well, the pretty one, she also has a fiancé...' Father was strangely inarticulate and it took me a while to figure out what he was aiming at.

'Father, they swing both ways, you see, they like both men and women.'

Father just shook his head, showing he'd had enough.

'You know, Herra, if you'd been through a war like we had, you wouldn't have time for things like that. I'm just worried that now we have peace these things will start happening here, too. I don't know what's worse.'

Hearing this freaked me out. It freaked me out so much a lump appeared in my throat, the one that appeared there whenever I was scared. Because Father wasn't the only one who thought this way. My husband started to pee in a sitting position about ten days after we returned to Afghanistan. It was one of the things that puzzled me most and had me secretly in tears for months. A Russian man wouldn't be seen dead peeing in the same humiliating posture as these proud Mujahideen. It took me a week to find the courage and ask my husband what had got into him. I first spotted him one morning behind the well squatting on his haunches, with his head lowered and both hands clasped around his crotch. He had his back turned to me and I thought he had found something precious. Only when I came closer did I see he concentrated on directing his stream on to the ground. For some reason it brought tears to my eyes. I turned around, ran back to the house in desperation and started sobbing in the little room. Freshta was breastfeeding one of her children and gave me a perplexed look. My Persian wasn't yet fluent enough for me to explain a woe of this intimate nature. Freshta put the screaming child aside, came up to me and stroked my head.

Later, when Nazir took me for a drive around the city to show me the museum next to the Darulaman Palace, I noticed three men sitting by a fence in the same position he had assumed near the well. Yes, I'd been right. On the other hand, there was something reassuring about the horrific discovery that all Afghan males wee sitting down. My husband wasn't a deviant, it was what everyone did around here.

'It's very practical,' he explained. 'It's always windy here, there are no public toilets and if I were standing upright I'd splatter my trousers.' He was right. The wide Afghan trousers provide welcome relief from sores in the scorching hot summer but they don't have a fly and have to be tied by a drawstring which makes it rather difficult to answer the call of nature without suffering any damage. And there had hardly been a single day without wind in Kabul in the twelve years I had spent here. I never got used to the strange spectacle of men all around the city, sitting on their haunches and sprinkling pavements, rubbish heaps, roadsides or wilting lawns. Sometimes they would all go for a collective wee. They would perch in a row like chickens and relieve themselves in a synchronised display. Women in burkas would pass by without even crossing to the other side of the road, their side vision obstructed by the grille while the urinating men thought the women under the garb were invisible and possibly blind. I can see how during the war, when shooting went on in the city for twenty-four hours a day this might have been a highly useful habit. A Mujahideen engaging in this activity was much less vulnerable in a sitting position than if he'd been standing upright the way we're used to. Nevertheless, we often argued about ways of urinating.

'It's embarrassing, undignified and disgusting,' I would cry in fits of fury, claiming Russians used urinals for peeing, cutlery for eating and chairs for sitting.

'But you murder unborn children, so who are you to reproach us for adjusting to nature,' he would mock me sometimes, or he would fly into a rage and bang his fists on the wall, condemning me, my Mum, brother and Dad for failing to subject my Russian aunt to a public whipping in Red Square because she let herself be knocked up while unmarried.

'You're happy to pee in public but you don't allow women to go out.' Sometimes he wound me up so much I didn't care what I was saying.

'Well, in Moscow I saw lots of drunken boys piss in the underpass near your block and they didn't even bother to put it away when a woman passed by.'

'They do that when they're pissed, but you're sober and you don't put it away either when a woman passes by,' I countered.

'Because unlike you, we never get pissed,' he exclaimed triumphantly, and that usually put a stop to the argument.

As a matter of fact, something quite different was going through our minds. I was thinking that the drunks in the Moscow underpasses really were rather more disgusting than an Afghan man in a dignified squat taking care not to splatter his trousers. My husband, meanwhile, thought that people shouldn't be allowed to turn the streets of Kabul into public toilets and that the odd shot of vodka wasn't such a big sin after all.

Hardly a day went by without Mad approaching me with some outlandish question. His curiosity and eagerness to learn absolutely everything about the strange world I had once inhabited knew no bounds. This time, however, he seemed exceptionally preoccupied. All the skin on his face was folded into worried wrinkles and this was the first time I noticed he'd been blessed with another skill the rest of mankind had been deprived of. He was able to form wrinkles not just on his forehead and the area around the mouth but also on his nose, chin and right in front of his earlobes. He had an expression to suit every situation. He could put on a look that was sombre and curious, or sombre and angry, sombre and inquisitive; his expression could indicate that he was thinking of something jolly, sad, tragic or dangerous. Most of all, I was fascinated by the expression he managed to achieve by forming several wrinkles along both sides of his face, right in front of his ears. It made him look like a very aged Dunno. This was exactly how I had imagined the famous character in Nikolai Nosov's stories when I was little. Even as an old man, Dunno would still be cute and funny but the wisdom he eventually would have to acquire would be stamped on his face. But Mad had never heard of Dunno.

'What's wrong, Mad?' I asked, slightly concerned, since he looked as if his face had lost weight overnight but was still covered with the same amount of skin only now all creased and crumpled. Actually, Mad resembled an alien. The idea flashed through my head merely as a comparison. Only later did I seriously begin to wonder if Mad wasn't really an alien.

'I don't know if it's appropriate to ask a woman about this sort of thing,' he said, the wrinkles washing over his face like waves of an ocean.

'C'mon, Mad, the two of us aren't like a man and a woman,' I said, immediately regretting it. 'What I mean is, you're a man,' I tried to limit the damage, 'and I'm a woman, but what really matters is that we're friends.'

Mad looked me in the eye and for the first time since he had come to live with us, he said quietly: 'Best friends in the world, right, Herra?'

'I think you're right, Mad, we're the best friends in the world.'

'In that case, can you teach me how to pee standing up, the way your men do?'

My jaw dropped and I stared into his lumpy little face thinking that if he now started to cry, his tears would pour down the hollows like little brooks, joining into rivulets and forming tiny ponds here and there, that with a bit of luck a small sea might appear below his lower lip where his crumpled chin formed something of a mountain plateau. Mad's sea of tears.

'I'm afraid I'm not really an expert in this area, Mad.'

'Herra, please. Of course I know you're not an expert, I just need some theoretical grounding. Not practice. That I'll manage on my own.'

'I see. But surely you've seen it in movies, they do sometimes show men going to the toilet...'

'What I don't understand...' Mad began and although he was blushing, the skin in the hollows retained its original colour making him look like a zebra. 'I'm not quite clear how to...' He sighed again and blinked hard. 'Well, how to prevent the drops from dispersing excessively when the water falls from such a great height.'

'Mad, where did you read that?'

'What?'

'The thing about the drops dispersing.'

'Nowhere, it's obvious. When water hits the ground from a great height it scatters to all sides. Urine is bound to behave in the same way.'

'I see,' I said with understanding. I had to think of Dominic who had asked me a few days earlier why Afghan men sit when urinating. His question embarrassed me, and his disdainful tone made me angry. 'Do they all do it?' he kept pestering me although he must have known how terribly awkward this kind of discussion was for me. Fortunately, nobody else was present. 'Yes, they all do,' I mumbled. 'Your husband, too?' Now Dominic had gone too far. Next thing he was going to ask me to describe my husband's genitalia. Blood rushed to my cheeks, I looked around to check there really was nobody in earshot and chirped cheerfully: 'My husband also poops while standing.' Dominic swallowed hard and looked at me, shaking his head in disbelief: 'Our presence in this country will be necessary for a very, very long time,' he said theatrically and I just shrugged.

'Right. They must have a special trick. Because in films I haven't noticed stains on your men's trousers after they have relieved themselves.' This problem had apparently preoccupied Mad for some time now and he only turned to me after reaching a dead end.

'Perhaps it's got something to do with the fact that we have urinals.'

'Urinals?' to show his surprise he immediately smoothed out his forehead, which made him look like a UFO that's been in an accident.

'Yes, urinals, it's what we call the contraptions in toilets men urinate into.'

'I see,' he said restoring his forehead to its original preoccupied appearance.

'Well, and when you pee into the urinals, which by the way have raised sides, you don't splatter yourself at all.'

'Right, I understand that, of course,' he said edgily. 'But I wasn't talking about civilised ways of peeing in a toilet. I meant in the open, in the street...'

'Well,' I said, realising I had never looked into the technical side of this issue and therefore wasn't sure what to tell Mad. 'You probably have to aim it at a precise angle.'

'I knew it,' he exclaimed in triumph. 'That's exactly it. What angle?'

'I'm afraid you'll have to test it yourself.'

'Right,' he said, resignedly. 'I hope those twits won't laugh at me and get in the way of my experiment.' Mad meant Kamal and Rustam and their naughty friends who tended to pee collectively sitting down, and had probably never thought there was another way.

'By the way, Mad, why do you want to learn this?'

'Because the only way you can really get to know someone is by understanding how they do the most basic things and why they do them the way they do. And I want to get to know your people. When I visit your country I don't want to feel like an illiterate moron.'

'I see you're planning to visit the West,' I smiled.

'So are you. We'll go together. You and I. Just you and I.'

I forgot to pull down the corners of my mouth and kept smiling like a half-wit even though I didn't think it was funny at all. Mad lowered his eyes and pulled his face into an expression that seemed to suggest delight. Mad was up to something.

chapter 11

EVER SINCE I had first heard of Mullah Omar I always thought there was something twisted and romantic about him. He wasn't a good-looking man, that's for sure. While he was in charge of the Taliban we had known even less about him than we did now that he was hiding from the Americans in Helmand Province. I have to confess I hadn't really known much about him before. But now the thought that he had only one arm and one eye, was smelly, sweaty and stubborn in asserting his ideas, gave me a kind of titillating sensation. I was aware of how inappropriate that was, for I agreed with everyone else that his ideas were depraved. Freshta, on the other hand, rather fancied Osama bin Laden. The first time she saw him was on one of the leaflets the Americans had dropped from their helicopters alerting us to the person we should report if we happened to run into him.

'Look at his sensuous lips,' she said, pointing to the blurred picture.

'Yes, and the piercing eyes,' I had to agree.

'What a proud man he is,' Freshta declared.

'But he's a real bastard, too,' I added, frightened by my own feelings. How could I feel attracted, even in purely physical terms, to a guy who murders other people just because they don't pray five times a day? My husband didn't pray five times a day and Father even less. Nevertheless, I suspected that in spite of their fierce hatred of the Taliban, they, too, had some respect for a man who stood by his principles so fiercely and consistently, however misconceived they might be. In Afghanistan people respect everyone who stands up for their beliefs, with a grenade launcher if need be, regardless of how stupid they are.

'He's got a face like a bird,' said Freshta, revelling in Osama's picture.

'But he's the reason the Americans are here now.' I poked her in the ribs, even though personally I was quite happy about the soldiers' presence.

'Oh well, having the Americans here isn't all bad,' she replied. 'If it's all his fault, I won't hold it against him.'

'You'll blub when they catch him and execute him, won't you?' I frowned.

'C'mon, don't be silly,' Freshta countered, pouting in that inimitable way of hers that would have driven bin Laden to the heights of ecstasy.

'You know he's quite a ladies' man, don't you?' I giggled as Freshta seemed to be buying it.

'Yes, and he's into boys as well, at least that's what people say.'

'Oh well, who wouldn't fancy boys,' I burst out laughing and Freshta finally had a good laugh with me.

A few days later, when Mullah Omar and bin Laden were no longer on our minds, my husband brought home a videocassette. With an important air he announced we'd be watching a film tonight. Since he included us women in the invitation, we knew it was going to be a fairy tale, a Bollywood movie from which all the naughty scenes had been excised, or a documentary featuring dolphins.

'I got it on loan for one night only,' he emphasised and invited Uncle Amin to the show as well. The crafty Uncle turned up just before dinner and was rather disappointed to find neither meat nor rice on the menu, only bread, salad and aubergine with sheep's cheese and tomato sauce.

While Mad and the boys were putting the dishes away we waited impatiently for the boring Afghan TV news to end. A scrawny young announcer with meticulously coiffed hair abundantly covered in grease informed us that: 'the US ground forces jointly with the Afghan armed forces and with the support of coalition air forces have searched three areas – near Kandahar in the south, in Helmand Province and near the border with Pakistan in the east – for Mullah Omar and Osama bin Laden, all in vain.'

'Surprise, surprise...' Uncle Amin offered his commentary on the news, as he liked to do, to the infinite irritation of everyone present.

'If the local population in these areas can't be persuaded to cooperate, the two men will remain in hiding in Afghanistan forever,' the young man announced dramatically, making Uncle Amin squeal in triumph: 'That's just what I was going to say. The silly Pashtuns cook chicken and roll hashish joints for them every night. And then they complain that the Americans drop bombs on them. Well, if they're playing host to Osama they just have to expect the odd shell.'

Mad had taken up a position right in front of the TV set, crossing his tiny legs and folding his little arms in his lap. Kamal and Rustam were sprawled next to him, while Mother, Freshta and I leaned against the wall between the windows. The men had lined up on a mattress next to the longest wall.

'Uncle,' my husband said, 'when I start the film, there'll be no talking until it's finished.'

'Why pick on me?' Amin snapped, taking offence and sinking his rear in the mattress. 'All I was going to say is that I went to see the Russians yesterday. They've built a kind of field hospital in Wazir Akbar Khan. Everything is free of charge.'

I had a weird feeling in the pit of my stomach. I didn't even know why. Right at that moment my husband looked at me, as if he could see right through me. There was a mixture of concern and anger in his eyes.

'We don't need anything for free, least of all from the Russians,' he snapped back.

'And we now have four-and-a-half-thousand peacekeepers from seventeen countries,' Amin hollered, proud to have caught our attention. 'Today a couple of delegations came to the ministry and we told them to be kind enough not to parade around half naked, not to booze and ogle our women.'

'Have you been interpreting?' Father asked.

'I serve there in the capacity of an advisor,' Amin said, miffed. He failed to point out there wouldn't have been anyone for him to interpret for, since there were no Russians among the peacekeepers. The only thing he could say in English was 'Hello' and 'How are you?' and he had also taught his children to say '*baksheesh* please'.

'What is it you're advising on?' Father kept prying.

'On how to keep their distance because Afghans are allergic to foreign uniforms, which might get slightly crumpled if they're not careful,' Uncle chuckled. He himself had never tried to cause anything to crumple on anyone, and quite sensibly, given his flyweight stature. As a precaution, after the Taliban came to power, he had taken refuge in his native Panshir Valley where he dispensed wisdom to Russian journalists who turned up there from time to time. As his back might have broken under the weight of a sub-machine gun he never even tried to get involved in the war.

'Can we start the film now?' Grandpa shouted from his corner. He couldn't stand Amin and thought him a disgrace to the family. He had never forgiven him for being the one who had talked my husband into going to university in the Soviet Union. Grandpa had dreamt of sending his grandchildren to Great Britain or Germany and had made them study English from an early age. But Amin, who never wanted to be the lonely black sheep of the family, had acquired a great many contacts during his own studies in Moscow, which he later put to good use by sending his relatives back to Russia and setting them up for shady deals in mink and *astrakhan* hats and denim. My husband used to bring the stuff back from the Soviet Union by the truckload and I only learned later that Uncle used to take a cut of the profits.

'If you don't start the film right now Amin won't be able to get home,' Grandpa said, hoping to finally scare us into starting the screening to prevent Uncle from overstaying his welcome.

'I've got a pass,' Amin retorted dismissively, although he could never be quite certain that a strict patrol would not shoot him before he managed to show it. The curfew was supposed to be lifted next month but nobody quite believed it since there was still shooting every night.

Approaching the TV ceremonially my husband pressed play. Complete silence ensued, interrupted only by Mother's cracking of sunflower seeds. A city with tall houses appeared on the screen. A male English voice commentated on an event that had shaken the world, the voice claimed. We had heard a lot about it on the radio but this was the first time we got to see it on TV.

'That's New York!' Mad exclaimed happily. Nobody responded. We watched with absolute concentration, just as my husband had demanded. We saw aeroplanes hitting something the voice referred to as the 'twin towers' several times and from several angles, then crowds of people running up and down the streets, some weeping. The voice sounded agitated and insistent and the buildings that had taken a direct hit from the aeroplanes were on fire. Suddenly the voice groaned and the camera focused on tiny figures jumping from the windows of the burning buildings. Eventually both buildings fell, collapsing on to the street in an orderly way.

The people started sprinting away from the area where the skyscrapers had landed holding white handkerchiefs to their mouths and chased by mountains of dust nearly as tall as the buildings around them. People huddled in shops with glass windows, leaving deserted cars in the streets. The scene teemed with policemen and firefighters. When the dust settled, in the place where the two tall buildings had stood there was now an unsightly heap of wreckage and lots of paper flying around. Then a man, whom the announcer introduced as the mayor of the city, started talking in a sad voice. A woman was crying because one of the people who had jumped from the windows after the jacket of his expensive suit caught fire was her brother. A suit like that might cost several thousand dollars. The voice didn't say that but I knew it. Lots of people on screen were in tears, some cursed the terrorists, and men with muscular arms swore that America would win this war. But the city had clearly lacked decent anti-aircraft defences since not a single shot had been fired at the planes, whereas during air raids in Kabul machine guns started barking the minute the first dot appeared in the sky. The recording finished with a panorama of skyscrapers in the setting sun and a sad male voice stating that several thousand innocent people had lost their lives there.

'That was September 11th, the day Osama attacked America,' Mad announced before my husband had a chance to open the discussion. Mother leaned over to me, whispering: 'Was that it?' She sounded rather disappointed.

'How about some tea?' Amin said and Rustam leapt up obediently, as serving tea was his duty.

'It was a great tragedy for them and they haven't stopped talking about it to this day,' said my husband, sounding like a schoolmaster. Lately he'd been given to bouts of pontificating and I was sure he just parroted at home what he had picked up during long drives with his white bosses, who practically never stopped discussing the situation on the front and in the world. They hardly ever talked to me about politics. The only thing Heidi talked to me about was 'women's issues' and she was growing increasingly disappointed with my inability to provide her with the sort of information she longed to hear.

'Just over three thousand dead, big deal,' Grandpa uttered with disdain, disappointed like everyone else that my husband hadn't brought an action movie or at least a juicy record of a bloody battle where we could root for one of the parties. This event, on the other hand, didn't seem to have much bearing on us. Amin unwrapped a sweet, stuffed it into its mouth and after washing it down with unsweetened tea he lisped: 'Oh well, those Americans, they've never had a war at home and now they're making so much fuss about two collapsing buildings.'

Women were normally not expected to join this kind of discussion but as today we had been explicitly invited to watch the film together with our male relatives, we felt obliged to make a contribution.

'Those two high-rises were quite ugly anyway,' said Mother, slapping Rustam who had dripped some tea down the back of her neck as he weaved his way through those of us who were sitting.

'If they hadn't made those buildings so tall nobody could have hit them,' Freshta commented, injecting the first sign of practical and logical thinking into the proceedings. 'Is New York the capital?' she asked.

'Freshta!' Mad shouted, offended. 'Surely you know that Washington is the capital! But this city is really important because it's got loads of rich and important people as well as the UN and also loads of foreigners, but mostly Jews.'

'And what else was destroyed?' Freshta enquired.

'Nothing,' my husband replied, as if he had been expecting more from us.

'Can you drive all the way to America?' Kamal dared to ask a question.

'Not unless you have an amphibious vehicle, you twit,' Mad jumped at him, appalled to discover such dramatic gaps in his cousin's knowledge of geography. 'There's a sea in between. A really big sea, an ocean.'

'So how did Osama get there?' Mother tapped her finger on her forehead to show her real grandson wasn't as dim as Muhammad's patronisingly intellectual answers suggested.

'He must have flown there, Mother,' Freshta explained.

'Why should he fly there, you silly woman. There you go, talking nonsense again.' Amin finished sucking on the sweet and was beginning to display a dangerous level of activity. 'He never went there! If he'd been on one of those planes the Americans wouldn't have to hunt for him in the mountains, isn't that obvious? The guys who flew the aeroplanes must have died too, didn't you see the explosion?'

'Were they Afghans?' asked Mother, horrified. 'Poor dears, someone must have done something really bad to them.'

'Those guys were no poor dears,' my husband said. 'They were idiots.'

Father got up and gave us all a tired look. 'The women and children ought to go to bed. Grandpa is tired and Amin is in a hurry to get home.'

'I'm not in a hurry,' Amin started stuffing another sweet into his mouth, waving his empty glass at Rustam to signal he wanted more tea. 'I'm just thinking, if someone flew a plane into our ministry of foreign affairs it would never be shown on TV and nobody would declare a war just because of us.'

Freshta, Mother and I started to get up. The boys were taking the dishes away and Mad was the only one still sitting, frowning with his chin the way only he could, which indicated extreme concern.

'If a plane flew into the ministry of foreign affairs nothing would happen because the building would probably be empty,' he suddenly announced sagely, making my husband laugh. Since the fall of the Taliban ministry officials had been receiving no salary and consequently showed less and less enthusiasm for their work, leaving the buildings empty. Most of them had been appointed only a few weeks ago. The guys with turbans and long beards had emptied their offices so fast they didn't manage to take all their folders with them. So there was an abundance of folders but a distinct shortage of paper and a number of decrees and orders had to be typed on ancient typewriters on the back of old Taliban leaflets exhorting people not to listen to foreign radio stations as that would block their way to paradise. The new ministry officials were instructed to supply their own chairs, which the Taliban regarded as the devil's invention and a depraved whim of Western civilisation, they had to sweep up the grim corridors, repair broken windows, and change into European clothes as far as possible. In spite of this, many ministry officials insisted on wearing traditional Afghan clothes to work, which was regarded as undesirable. Afghans in baggy pyjamas supposedly didn't cut a dignified figure next to Americans or Europeans dressed according to the latest fashion.

'All that fuss over three thousand dead, yet they were never bothered by the odd million dead Afghans,' Amin added with disgust.

'If, for example, they wanted to fly their plane into the Darulaman Palace, they'd have to change their mind at the last minute because they would realise that someone has already done the job for them,' Mad went on speculating. 'Another thing that would make it more difficult to hit a building in Kabul is that nothing particularly stands out here.'

'But those boys were right on target. I wonder how long had they been in training. Maybe they were trained here. By the way, were they actually Afghans?' Amin couldn't hide his excitement at the thought that an Afghan could have committed an act so significant as to keep the whole world talking for months and years. 'The Americans must have been really impressed with our pilots!'

'But it's good they're here anyway,' Grandpa muttered under his breath.

'Well, Grandpa, it's too early to tell. Because they haven't really come to help us. They've come because they're really, really scared of us.' My husband picked up the cassette, drummed his fingers on it a few times and unexpectedly helped me to get up. 'What if they flew their plane into the Kremlin?' he smiled at me. I opened my eyes wide.

'Then the Russians would come back, so it's much better they flew to New York because now we have the Americans.' Everyone had a good laugh and I could see they agreed with me. My husband was proud of me. It always made him happy to hear me refer to Afghans as 'us'. Grandpa curled up on his mattress getting ready to mumble his evening prayer under the blanket as always when he was very tired. His parting words to us were: 'Pray to Allah tonight that no such thing may ever happen again. Because then they'll come looking for Osama in every Afghan house and believe me, they're just as good at hitting their target as those poor boys of ours.'

My husband cuddled up to me in bed and said: 'Heidi asked me to show the film to my friends and family. They want to know what we think about it.'

'What will you tell them?'

'That we were all really upset and are terribly sorry.'

'Are we sorry?'

'We're not but Heidi promised to give me a rise next month and I'll be getting a mobile phone tomorrow.'

'What phone?'

'A mobile phone. It's like a normal phone except it has no cord. You carry it in your pocket and it lets you make calls to the whole world. And anyone in the whole world can call you. I can talk to the guys every day. And Heidi will pay for everything. I mean, her bosses will pay.'

'But it's dishonest,' I objected, 'to say we're sorry when we're not.' I was angry Heidi didn't offer me one of those magic phones as well. But then I realised it was just as well. If my husband knew I could phone anywhere in the world I'm sure he'd say I had contracted an incurable illness and would never let me go back to work.

'Oh, c'mon, what does honest really mean? Heidi gets 12,000 dollars a month plus a risk supplement. I get 300 and not a penny for the risk.'

'That's true, but then again you don't have to worry about going back to a place like New York where people tremble in terror every time a plane flies overhead, while we hardly even notice when our house gets hit by a bomb. The Americans are worse off at home than we are here in Kabul.'

'There's no place in the world that's worse than Kabul, Herra.'

chapter 12

'I DON'T UNDERSTAND why you've got to go to the zoo, of all places. It's the worst zoo in the world and yet you insist on going there. It'll be terribly crowded, full of annoying brats and there's no guarantee you'll see any animals,' my husband said, but his tone seemed to indicate he had already given the green light to our zoo outing.

'If you're too busy we could go with Grandpa instead,' I suggested.

'Grandpa is about as useful an escort as a premature baby. If you're not careful, he'll fall into the lion's den.'

'He won't. And the lion they've got there is blind, it would never find Grandpa anyway.'

'That's nonsense, Herra. I'll drive you there and I'll come back to collect you. But as far as I'm concerned, these outings of yours are just a waste of time. And they're driving me mad. You know I'm not keen on this kind of thing.'

'Oh please, it will be our first outing in seven years,' I pleaded although by now it was clear that I had won. Everyone wanted to go to the zoo, including Mother, who hardly ever left the house and basically regarded every venture into the outside world as something akin to sin. For the sake of familial harmony I put on my burka, and caught myself noticing I didn't really mind. In fact, I almost enjoyed wearing it thinking of scruffy brats shouting at me: 'How about a shag, you cunt,' which happened quite often whenever a male escort was out of sight. Grandpa would be no deterrent for these cheeky youths, and the poor chap would feel less useless as a bodyguard if I kept my face covered.

The next day we all piled into the car, with some difficulty. Freshta stayed at home with baby Yunus nursing a headache and claiming she couldn't stand the smell of monkey urine but the real reason was that Qais had told her the night before she should just try and see what would happen if she tagged along with us. Mother, Roshangol and I climbed into the car boot, Mad, Rustam and Kamal with Hamayun in his lap squeezed into the back seat and the neighbour's son Mahmud, Kamal's and Rustam's best friend, sat in the front seat, next to my husband.

The zoo is surrounded by ruins of what had once been magnificent buildings on one side and by a filthy dried-up sewer on the other. Most of the animals that had survived the front passing through the city several times were mentally quite unstable. The animal houses were riddled with bullets and all the monkeys had been crammed into a microscopic cage right by the entrance. My husband handed us over to a friend who had fought under the command of the illustrious Lion of Panshir, Ahmed Shah Masoud, but whose love of animals had trumped his love of sub-machine guns, making him join the Taliban to keep his job as zoo director. He had had a limp in both legs since 1993, when for some unknown reason all the opposing forces fighting for this part of Kabul decided to shell the frightened animals but he refused to desert his wolves and bears. Although Afghan commanders Dostum, Rabbani and others had targeted the surrounding neighbourhoods rather than the zoological gardens, eventually everything was reduced to ashes. The wolf cage collapsed on to the director, the wolves ran away and he spent sixteen hours trapped under the wreckage with an open fracture of the right thighbone and a broken ankle on his other leg. He didn't dare call for help for fear that someone might put him out of his misery instead. Fortunately, the wolves must have been just as terrified, otherwise, given the limited supplies of food, they would certainly have feasted on his freshly carved up legs. The director survived. He was found and rescued. Three of the six wolves were caught. The rest were casualties of war. An elephant and two giraffes, whose only sin was to offend the Mujahideen's aesthetic sense, suffered the same fate, as did ninety-three further specimens of exotic fauna. All that was left were twenty exhibits and a director with a wounded soul.

The first place the children dragged us to was the lions' enclosure. I for my part wanted to see the monkeys that were kept next to the entrance in a cage so tiny they had to enter into negotiations if they wanted to turn around. Their newly-developed collective decision-making skills will soon transform them into rational beings, I thought to myself. A few boys, aged around ten, had sharpened the ends of some sticks and were now poking them through the cage bars, prodding the monkeys in every body part they could reach. A crazed baboon was the one and only monkey I've ever seen visibly sweating. Grandpa, leading our group, tried to reprimand the boisterous youths. They laughed at him but none of them said anything rude. Some kind of deep-rooted, centuries-old respect for the old, however foolish their behaviour might be, had survived in these children of war. They, too, had survived and their best hope for the future was that they might die during a respite in the fighting.

Mad seemed uncharacteristically quiet and bewildered that day. He didn't lecture everyone within earshot as usual, quoting whole paragraphs from encyclopaedias and annoying everybody except Grandpa and me. I took him by the hand and whispered: 'What's your favourite animal?'

'An earwig.'

'Why an earwig? They're disgusting, aren't they?'

'Because nobody else loves them. If we loved them they might not be as disgusting.'

I gave him a puzzled look and instantly regretted my question. 'So you think if I love you enough you'll be the most handsome boy in the world?'

'It's too late for that. I'll never turn into a real boy, that's for sure. Allah has created earwigs so people would find them repellent and he's created me to make them realise that if they act like swine they will end up looking like swine too.'

'Mad, for heaven's sake, what are you talking about, you're not a swine!'

'I'm not but the people who produced me were real swine. And lots of people who have to look at me are real swine, too. I'm sort of God's revenge, you see,' he said with a hate-filled laugh.

I was cross with myself for letting him draw me into this conversation, at the zoo of all places. This really wasn't the right moment, especially as I'd decided long ago I would never ask Mad any questions. When he first came to live with us, Grandpa assembled the whole family and said: 'We're a family and none of us is perfect. Now we've been given this peculiar child. He may not be perfect either but Allah forbade any of you to ever say anything of the sort to him. He must have ended up here for a reason, and we must be grateful to Allah for giving us this sign.'

We all followed his counsel, including the two scamps Kamal and Rustam. At worst, as on this occasion, they ignored him. They were running around the zoo frantically, throwing stones at other bands of boys and Mad's laughably tiny feet couldn't possibly keep up with them. In spite of that he suddenly broke loose from me, trying to catch up with his cousins. However, hopping as he was on his scrawny legs, he resembled a wounded duck, his disproportionately large body making him sway like a badly steered yacht in a strong wind. The zoo director interrupted his conversation with Grandpa and asked: 'Is this your child?'

'Oh yes, this is our boy. And a very nice and smart boy he is. He just has some health problems.'

'I'm only asking because I'm worried he might fall into the lion's enclosure,' the director said apologetically. He must have felt the child's way of running wasn't unlike the way he himself might look if he tried to run on his mangled limbs.

The director was a decent, civilised gentleman who realised that Mother, Roshangol and I were keen to learn as much as we could about the animals but didn't dare to ask. He also knew it wasn't appropriate for him to address his explanations directly to us, so he directed them to Grandpa instead, making sure we could hear everything, trailing behind as was expected of well-behaved females.

The lions' enclosure was enormous and, unlike everywhere else, it was extremely well kept and modern. Only the lions were in short supply. Actually, there was only one. The old, mangy and extraordinarily sad animal was lying in the middle of the enclosure and didn't respond even when a boy hit it with a rock the size of a brick.

'He used to have a lioness,' said the director, positioning himself with his back to the enclosure and leaning on the wall so that as many people as possible could hear him. 'The lion's name is Marjon. Once a group of Mujahideen came in and they made a bet that one of them would climb in and stroke Marjon. The man had almost made it when the lioness got enraged and attacked him. She bit his head off.'

The boys suddenly stopped fighting and flinging rocks at the animals and started paying attention. They gathered around the director in a semicircle and listened.

'Two days later the brother of the Mujahideen whose head had been bitten off arrived and threw a grenade into the enclosure. He'd declared a blood feud and kept his word. The lioness lost her front paws and bled to death. The lion survived but got shrapnel in his eyes and he's now blind. But he's got every right to it, really, he's twenty-seven years old.'

Mad's eyes stared incredulously from the director to the wretched lion and back. Kamal and Rustam listened with their mouths open. After a few seconds, one of the boys shouted: 'Bet I can climb in and kick him in the snout!' We all pretended not to hear. The lion, having survived well beyond the age befitting the circumstances, his place of residence and his animal species, seemed resigned to an encounter with an Afghan brat, from which the brat was likely to emerge victorious. The director turned around and headed towards the next cage.

'He won't harm them, he's got no teeth. We have to mince his meat into pap for him. But the wolves, they're quite another story. The mesh on their fence isn't strong enough so we try to make sure there's always an attendant at hand. A few people have had their fingers bitten off. Those beasts are wild and they're always hungry. They're treacherous and inscrutable.'

'And this is Chucha, our little darling. For some reason the Taliban didn't like him and slashed his snout with wires.' The bear that may once have cut a dignified figure was now huddling in the corner of a tiny cage. A swarm of flies sat on the gigantic festering hole that used to be his snout. 'A Canadian organisation promised they would look after him.'

The director spoke without emotion and I wondered if he had any left. My husband used to relate fascinating stories about him and I could never tell fact from legend, since Afghans like to spin tales around the most ordinary endeavour. In any case, before he was wounded he allegedly used to carry animal feed into the zoo in the dead of night, crawling through trenches with a bag full of foul-smelling leftovers on his back, dividing its contents fairly among his charges. Under the Taliban he had won a religious–academic dispute regarding the zoo's raison d'être. He had allegedly dared to mount a defence of the animals' right to life in front of Nuruddin Turabi, the notorious and extremely dim minister of justice, who claimed that the Quran had banned the keeping of animals under inhumane conditions. The director convinced him it was within his power to make the conditions humane and stop the animals howling with hunger and horror, frightening the whole neighbourhood even more than the air raids did.

Suddenly we heard an explosion. This was nothing out of the ordinary; at home something like that wouldn't have made us look out of the window. But here it was out of place. We all rushed to the source of the noise and I forgot that Mad couldn't keep up with us.

'It's all right, it's just some boys. They threw a harmless firecracker into the monkey cage,' one of the eleven attendants shouted, running towards the primates' cage to meet us. At that moment I realised we had lost Mad. Tugging at Grandpa's sleeve I whispered: 'Grandpa, we've lost Mad, we've got to find him quickly, the kids around here are throwing grenades at monkeys and for them Mad is just an animal of a marginally higher order...'

Grandpa looked around and waved at Mother: 'Herra will go to the right and I'll go and check around the lion enclosure. Mother, you stay here and don't move.' Although he was a good organiser and loved dramatic situations he had rarely had an opportunity to participate in them in the past thirty years even if he had often been their cause. The director was trying to disperse the unruly boys, lashing at them with a twig he found on the ground but they just laughed at him, dodging him with a sense of complete impunity. Due to his broken legs the director didn't stand a chance of inspiring respect, let alone threatening anyone.

The grille of the burka hampered my ability to see Mad, should he have appeared to my left or right. Grandpa, on the

other hand, was long-sighted and short-sighted at the same
time, and with a bit of luck was just about likely to find his way
back to the place where we parted and where he had parked
Mother. I headed past a cage that was far too large for the bunch
of rabbits running around in it. Later on the director explained
that the cage had been inhabited by porcupines but they had
died of starvation during the 1994 war, and now he used it to
keep rabbits as food for predators. Right behind the rabbit farm
there was a path laid out with an unusual aesthetic sense and
dotted with patches of sand. It ran past completely wrecked
dwellings that once housed large predators, or at least so I
assumed, looking at the ruined fortifications. I was about to
turn around and walk back when I spotted another cage behind
the ruins and something inside it running to and fro, again
and again. It was a wolf. Another one was sitting in the corner.
The mesh in the fence was more than flimsy and there, at the
end of the enclosure, sat Mad, facing the third, largest animal
with enormous yellow eyes. They were staring at one another.
My stomach constricted so much I was nearly sick. Mad had
squeezed his short, tiny hand through a hole and was stroking
the wolf's head.

chapter 13

HEIDI WAS SITTING at her desk staring at the computer. Dominic stood next to her bent low, his elbow leaning on her shoulder. He was staring at the computer, too. I waited a few seconds, then knocked and walked in. I hadn't yet got used to knocking and always felt I was doing something indecent. I wondered why at home nobody ever knocked even though it might have been quite beneficial. And useful. We often do things we don't want to be seen doing. Like putting on make-up or combing our hair.

I also found it strange to walk into a room and find a man and a woman touching even though they weren't married or siblings. Another thing that struck me as weird was that they didn't feel the need to jump away from each other. Once I had walked in on Uncle Amin holding his ugly wife's hand in the kitchen. They parted company frantically and Uncle later complained to my husband about my bad manners. But I couldn't have knocked as they had only a piece of cloth instead of a door. That might explain why we didn't bother knocking here. We had curtains instead of doors.

'Hi,' they greeted me cheerfully. Their broad smiles made them look like cartoon characters.

'Hi,' I said, proud of my progress in English.

'We'll have to sack these locals. It'd be better to have people working in the villages who also live there,' Heidi contended.

She was talking to Dominic. Not to me. They never talked to me about locals. I was a local too.

'So, Herra, are you happy?'

'Yes, but I have some questions,' I took care with my grammar as I hadn't yet mastered the tenses and preferred to keep to the present. My deficient English wasn't the only reason.

'Herra, what do you do to stop men groping you between the legs when you're in town?'

In my preoccupation with the finer points of grammar I didn't catch the meaning of Heidi's question. It took me a couple of seconds to realise what she was asking. The only thing that saved me from fainting was the fact that I don't have a propensity for it. Otherwise I would have immediately hit the floor and felt much better for it.

'They keep reaching between my legs and pinching me, and they go for my boobs, too...'

Heidi shook her head in disbelief and continued to stare at the computer.

'Oh well, it will take them a while to get used to us...' Dominic said. Neither of them noticed I was in a state of shock, standing with my mouth wide open, fists clenched and eyes popping out. If they had cared to take a proper look at me, they would have realised they had done something unspeakable. But I had no such luck. And Heidi seemed intent on dwelling on the issue of groping.

'I never go to the market without covering my hair, I take care not to do anything provocative, I try to engage them in a normal conversation... and those little bastards, they just keep smiling and then suddenly they're all around me and before I know it they're between my legs.'

I sat down in the white garden chair we bought the day before at Chicken Street for a considerable amount of money.

'So what do you do when they start groping you?' Heidi said. She was beginning to sound impatient and I realised I would have to come up with a sensible answer.

'I never get groped,' I said. I felt like crying. If only Dominic would go to the toilet I could have explained everything to Heidi... Or if he just wouldn't prick up his ears quite so much.

'Are you all right?' he asked instead, showing some concern.

'No, I'm fine. Just hot, I feel a bit hot. We went to the zoo the other day, I must have got sun stroke.'

'How come you don't get groped, you must be kidding me...' Heidi seemed rather put out to learn I was spared the groping but it made her even keener to find out why she was being singled out.

'I never go to the market without Mother.'

'So why doesn't Mother get touched up as well?' Dominic burst out laughing and I was sure this would be the end of me. Mother. That twit. As if someone would dare grope our Mother. He'd be dead by the morning.

'He'd be dead by the morning,' I said emphatically, wiping the grin off their faces.

'Nobody ever touches Afghan women. It's not allowed.'

Dominic raised his eyebrows and asked, sounding slightly offended: 'You mean it's all right to touch foreign women?'

I thought about it but couldn't think of a diplomatic answer.

'You see, our men know it's not allowed,' I smiled, satisfied with my response. 'If Heidi wore a burka nobody would come anywhere near her.'

'You think I'm crazy?' Heidi shrieked in an unnaturally high voice. 'We come here to fund a women's education programme and fight for their emancipation, we try to get them to work and make sure they have equal rights and you expect me to walk around Kabul wearing that piece of rag!'

'I'm not saying you have to, just that nobody would touch you if you did.' Heidi irritated me. From the first minute I saw her. I guess I found her too energetic, too provocative, too affected. And too strident. She rarely asked me any questions and when she did, they were usually pretty stupid.

'You mean I'm supposed to drive a car in a burka? I could only drive in a straight line, you can't see what's to the side with that thing on. And it must be so hot, why can't you make them out of cotton at least…'

'That's impossible, Heidi, cotton can't be pleated and a proper, elegant burka has to be pleated at the back. What would it look like otherwise…?' I said, still wearing an idiotic smile, hoping to ease the tension.

'You're right, that wouldn't look good at all,' Dominic uttered stupidly, probably getting bored with this conversation.

'Oh my God,' yelled Heidi, by now furious that none of those present seemed to show any appreciation for her struggle for the liberation of Islamic women. I knew she had written a study on the subject, having caught a glimpse of it on her computer. 'Oh my God, I can't believe this. What are you going on about? Dominic, have you lost it or what? Who cares if it's pleated or not when these idiot males foist a rag on their wives so that nobody can see them? What kind of a place is this where a woman can't go out into the street on her own, gets beaten up at home and locked in a sty whenever strangers come for a visit? And you prattle on about some stupid pleating.'

'Well, I don't know, but perhaps we have to be more patient…' Dominic replied with what looked like a conspiratorial wink to me. 'Herra here also wears a burka in the street, don't you, Herra?'

'Of course. Do you think I want to hear wolf whistles?'

'You wear a burka on your way to the office?' Neither me nor Dominic thought Heidi would regard this discovery as a major impediment that might threaten my entire future.

'I hardly ever wear it, only sometimes, when I feel like it and when I'm not accompanied by my husband,' I said truthfully. But she wasn't listening at all.

'Herra, you're meant to be in charge of a women's centre, to help women become liberated and hold their heads high and you're telling me you crawl down the street in a burka?'

'I don't crawl. I walk completely normally.' I didn't feel the slightest inclination to convince her that in fact I hardly ever took my burka off the nail. I enjoyed egging her on.

'But that's terribly embarrassing for all of us. After all, our local staff are meant to serve as an example and not be more backward than everyone else.'

'She didn't mean it like that, Heidi,' Dominic tried to put her at ease. 'After all, it's not that long since the Taliban left.'

Seeing Dominic so helpless and Heidi beside herself with rage filled me with glee. Edgily, Heidi lit up a cigarette and all of a sudden, I felt like lighting up. She could tell.

'Want one?' she asked in an annoyingly rasping voice.

'No thanks, I don't smoke.'

'It's kind of hard in a burka, isn't it?' She wouldn't let it go.

'It might burst into flames, like a walking flaming torch. And I might choke on the cigarette smoke wearing it. But I don't smoke when I'm not wearing a burka either. It's bad for you. Only prostitutes smoke in this country,' I said, relishing the terror in her face. 'Your men invented the parachute, ours invented the burka,' I added with pride. I used to drive my husband crazy with this comparison. He would scream at me that if it hadn't been for Ibn Sina Abu Ali al-Husayn we Europeans still wouldn't know how to remove a burst appendix. I used to think he was just kidding me but I never contradicted him.

'C'mon, Herra, a parachute is a useful thing, it's progressive and doesn't restrict anyone – on the contrary, it helps widen people's horizons.'

Heidi suddenly calmed down and assumed one of her familiar postures – the lecturing one.

'If it hadn't been for Ibn Sina Abu Ali al-Husayn you'd never have learned how to remove a burst appendix,' I blurted out before I knew what I was doing.

'Appendix? Hussain and the appendix? What Hussain, you mean the one in Iraq? He removes people's guts, not just appendixes, and he does it without an anaesthetic, doesn't he?' Dominic was now taking Heidi's side, perhaps also in an attempt to be witty.

'I mean Avicenna. He wrote the *Al-Qanoon fi al-Tib* and invented the theory of illumination. He said the act of creation was the result of God contemplating himself.' I was relishing the opportunity to score a point. I wasn't quite sure if my memory served, I was quoting from the Soviet encyclopaedia my husband and I sometimes read before going to sleep. Recently, however, I preferred to read to him from the Quran in Russian although this had a detrimental effect on the poor fellow. It made him realise how many of the things he had believed in weren't in the holy book at all. We would then look for an explanation in a lexicon of Islamic terms published in Moscow many years ago. Heidi was quite disconcerted. She forgot to close her mouth and the cigarette stayed glued to the right corner of her mouth, the ash about to drop on to the keyboard.

'You'll drop ash on to the keyboard,' Dominic said quietly. Heidi glanced at him with malice in her eyes and flicked her ash on to the keyboard. She got up and headed for the door. At that very moment the door opened and our driver Hamid burst in without knocking.

'Can't you see we're typing here and stuffing our faces with pork?' she screamed at him and stormed out. Hamid's English was almost non-existent.

'Are we having pork today?' he asked me in Persian. I started laughing but very soon stopped. 'Your husband is here, the bodyguards won't let him in,' Hamid informed me and ran away. In line with new guidelines issued by our American humanitarian bosses, local non-office staff were not allowed access to the offices. They had unrestricted access only to the courtyard and had to make an appointment to be received inside. My husband, a mere driver, was thus confined to the area outside the building, with the other mere drivers. I failed to persuade him I wasn't to blame for this new rule. I tried in vain to convince him that the rule was introduced because Afghan staff used to sit around the building making noise and distracting the Americans from their intellectual endeavours. He labelled me 'one of them', and once went as far as to accuse me of being the one who had put this idea into Heidi's and Dominic's heads in the first place just so that I could chat to them, smoke and drink alcohol unhindered, in short, lead a dissolute life. I looked at Dominic in horror. He was glad to see Heidi gone and he wouldn't have understood anyway. But I knew I had to get out of the room, having suddenly and unexpectedly found myself alone with a man who wasn't my husband. Blushing, I rushed to the door and collided with my husband who entered with a forced grin on his face.

chapter 14

MY HUSBAND drove at breakneck speed. He was fuming. I knew I was in trouble the minute he entered the room and caught me in flagrante with Dominic, or rather, the minute I stormed out of the door as if in flight, while Dominic stood there wondering what was going on.

'Hi,' he said to my husband.

'Hi,' my husband replied, dazzling him with a smile I immediately recognised as one of his forced and rather hate-filled ones. Slipping past him I shouted in Russian: 'Hello, darling, I'll get my stuff and we can go, I've finished for today...' I don't know how he managed to carry on a conversation with Dominic about the latest fighting in the North between 'that twit Dostum' and 'General Atta' while at the same time discreetly saying to me through gritted teeth: 'You're finished here!'

It was hot in the car. Our little Toyota pushed through horse carts, boys on bikes and shiny jeeps that had recently been appearing in the city in ever greater numbers. My husband's upper lip was twitching, which indicated extreme agitation.

'Why are you cross? Has something happened?' I had never learned to hold my tongue at critical moments.

'You're nothing but a whore. A Russian prostitute, that's what you are. You're a slut and you're making me sick.' His swearing was always much earthier in Russian than in his native tongue, probably because he'd had much more practice in Russian. People in Afghanistan watched their language much more, as a single wrong word could have major consequences. I ignored his insults. Ever since I started working for the Americans, becoming a local, that is, a local staff member, I'd been called all sorts of names. A slut wasn't even the worst. I don't know why but I didn't find it too offensive. Instead, I started to feel sorry for him after our first fights. The poor man was obviously rather desperate. Just then he gave me a mighty whack on the thigh. He had never given me a real thrashing, only sometimes, when he was unable to control a fit of fury, he would throw something at me or hit me, but he always did it in such a way as if he were inflicting pain on himself. Muhammad once gave me a long and serious lecture to explain that 'Uncle doesn't know the real meaning of the word prostitute, otherwise he wouldn't call you such horrible names.'

'So what does the word mean?' I asked him, amused. He closed his fish-like eyes to think and then announced slowly: 'A prostitute is a woman who sells rotten meat to men. She smells really bad and can give them an infection.' He said it so tenderly and lovingly, it was almost scary.

'Who told you this?'

'I found out myself, gradually. Actually, I figured it out from various allusions, from things older boys have said.' Muhammad still used a kind of learned language whose origins remained a mystery to us. Although he wasn't quite sure what a prostitute was, his knowledge of many other fields was impressive. He could list the capital cities of nearly all the countries including those I didn't even know existed, and his knowledge of developments in medicine and philosophy were at a university student's level. I resolved to find the right moment to fill this gap in his knowledge and enlighten him on the real meaning of the word prostitute.

I knew there was no point trying to explain anything to my husband. He really hated Dominic and Heidi with a vengeance, regarding them not simply as 'horrid American invaders' but also as depraved individuals, bastards and awful sissies, as he used to say. After being banned from entering the office his original tentative fondness turned into a fierce hatred and contempt. We had known each other for years but there had never been so much distance between us as we sometimes felt now.

All of a sudden he hit me again, with much greater force.

'Why are you laughing, you whore, you,' he exclaimed in despair. And I realised we really must have quite a supernatural bond, otherwise how would he know I was grinning broadly under the burka. It must have been love.

Muhammad let us in. In spite of the rather unusual shape of his ears his hearing was excellent. Certainly better than that of many ordinary mortals. His eyesight was probably better, too. Whatever physical beauty, agility and grace nature had taken away, it had compensated for it with highly developed senses, including some mysterious ones other people lacked. The poor soul tried to direct my husband into the narrow garage but from his frantically waving little arms it was impossible to tell whether he was telling us to go forward or back. But it wasn't his fault that my husband crashed into a little column on the left, smashing his back light.

'What a moron!' he yelled switching to Russian, showing some sense of decorum and affection for our ward even in his state of frenzy.

Muhammad laughed. This time his intuition failed him. He got slapped three times, albeit so gently it made me envious. Everyone was at home. I was relieved. The row would be postponed until later and the settling of scores at night, with the parents sleeping on the other side of the clay wall, would have to be rather restrained, at least in terms of sound effects.

Thanks to one of his senses Muhammad realised things were not exactly hunky-dory.

'Is he angry with you?' he whispered, tugging at my skirt.

'He is a bit angry,' I smiled, so as not to traumatise the boy.

'What have you done?'

'He found me talking to Dominic in the office and there was nobody else around.' I got used to telling things to Muhammad the way they happened. He usually surprised me with a mixture of ingeniousness, childish naivety and exceptional sensitivity and his response often provided me with useful clues on how to get out of trouble.

'Was he touching you?' Muhammad asked.

'Certainly not, why should he have been? We were talking about work. Heidi was there too but she left just before Nazir walked in.'

'She's a right cow to leave you alone with Dominic. How can she be so stupid, she doesn't understand anything.'

Once again, I had to admit Muhammad was right.

'But they don't see anything wrong with being alone with one's boss. For them it's OK to talk to women...'

'I know that, of course,' said Muhammad interrupting me and sounding agitated. 'I've seen loads of films. But sometimes they also touch them and have intercourse with them without God's permission.'

My eyes popped. I had never heard Muhammad utter the word intercourse before. But from the natural way he said it, without blushing, this was clearly not the first time he had used the word. His relationship with God was also rather unusual, unlike that of most other Afghans. For him Allah was a kind of older friend whose job was to keep an eye on us but not to rule us. That's why it was possible to have intercourse without God's permission, that is, out of wedlock, although every instance of intercourse outside marriage was being recorded somewhere and unless we made up for it by a sufficient number of good deeds, the final score would not be in our favour. By that logic prostitutes ought to do more good deeds than anyone else, Muhammad once explained after I had corrected his original concept of what these women did for a living, since this was their only chance of getting to paradise even if they had slept with thousands of men who were not their husbands and had no intention of marrying them. He seemed quite preoccupied with prostitutes. The idea of a fallen woman seemed to titillate him. However, as I later discovered, it was just a sign of enormous empathy and a kind of scholarly interest. Muhammad claimed he didn't regard prostitutes as evil and immoral but rather as women who were in search of something. It was male depravity that forced them to adopt this disgusting behaviour but as far as they were concerned they were only doing a good deed.

'But you know that prostitutes charge money for their services...' I pointed out gently, to spare him future disappointments.

'C'mon Herra, I know that, of course. But there are exceptions. Some show mercy and offer sex for free to those who are poor.'

'Where did you get that, Mad? I've never come across a prostitute like that.'

'I just know,' he said uncompromisingly. 'Besides, Uncle also calls you a prostitute although you don't charge him money...'

'That's quite different, Mad, he doesn't mean it that way....'

I recalled that in the middle of this conversation we heard tomcats screeching in the street. Muhammad's ears fluttered and he announced: 'They're fighting because there's a shortage of prostitutes among the cats and some tomcats can't find any. Muslims also fight because we don't have enough prostitutes. If there were more prostitutes there would be fewer wars.'

'Go to the back room and stay there for tonight,' my husband said, peering out of the living room where the whole family had assembled, chatting and drinking tea. I was glad I didn't have to participate in the idyllic family reunion. 'Muhammad will go with you and keep an eye on you,' he added.

Muhammad smiled. 'Of course, Uncle, I'll keep an eye on her.'

Muhammad took care not to address me as Herra when my husband was around. Nazir didn't like that. Only he, Grandpa, Father, Freshta and Mother were allowed to call me Herra. For everyone else uttering my name was too intimate. It took me a long time to convince him that people at work couldn't refer to me as she and that I couldn't demand it either. Consequently, Heidi, Dominic and the other foreigners freely called me Herra. Whenever this happened in my husband's presence he would blush. 'But when we first met, all your student friends called me Herra. And you didn't mind,' I raised a futile objection. That was a different time and different place.

I went to bed with a heavy heart. I knew he would come down on me once everyone had gone to sleep. Nazir climbed under the blanket next to me without a word and looked at the place where Muhammad was turning and tossing. Once Mad seemed to have gone to sleep he pinched my thigh. I knew this wasn't foreplay. Then he pinched me again, a little higher up where the skin is especially delicate and sensitive. I squeaked.

'Be quiet or I'll strangle you,' he whispered into my ear. 'This is for today.'

By the morning the insides of my thighs were blue and purple from his pinching and I was really glad that women in Kabul didn't wear shorts and miniskirts. My eyes were glued together with dried sleep, the remnants of my tears of fury and pain. We got up and I told Muhammad to wake up. He opened his eyes, smiled at me and when Nazir went out to wash his face he whispered to me: 'He's a piece of shit, a real and genuine piece of shit.'

chapter 15

I RECOGNISED FRESHTA in the crowd even though she was wearing the same burka as most women in the long queue. Over the couple of weeks since our advice centre had opened word had got around the city and its environs that 'there were handouts', drawing several hundred women every day, like moths to the light, to come and try their luck. I would offer them literacy classes, tried to convince them that one-off humanitarian aid wasn't ideal, that they ought to sign up for sewing or embroidery courses and that our lectures on hygiene were also worth attending. This was what Heidi had taught me in lessons listed in her computer under the abbreviation CW, community work.

I recognised my sister-in-law as soon as I saw her hastily approaching the crowd of blue burkas. My heart sank. Something terrible must have happened for Freshta to have left the house on her own. Qais never allowed her to go shopping or visit her girlfriends without a reliable escort, meaning Father or Mother, or sometimes Nazir, but preferably himself. I looked around but didn't see anyone from our family.

'My husband died six years ago, he had fought like a lion. But he left us nothing...' An elderly woman whose turn it was went on talking to me, not noticing that I stopped listening.

'Excuse me, would you mind waiting for a moment?' I asked her distractedly, closing my file, pushing the woman out of the office and running towards Freshta. She had already started elbowing her way through the crowd to reach me. We met halfway.

'What are you doing here?' I blurted out, hoping nothing had happened to Nazir.

'Stop the silly questions,' she howled, forcing me back into the building. We entered the office, leaving the grumbling crowd outside. Women who pushed ahead were usually nudged hard and sent to the back of the queue. Freshta got away with mere curses since most of the women thought I was a foreigner in Afghan clothes, which stopped them from attacking me physically.

I closed the door. Freshta took off her burka, revealing a face as pale as a sheet. Her beautiful full lips quivered in agitation, her eyes were full of tears. Her chin trembled and green snot hung from her nose. It was immediately obvious that nothing had happened to Qais. The idea had often crossed my mind that if he were to step on a landmine and were torn to shreds, Freshta wouldn't shed a tear. Sometimes she may have even wished for it to happen. Later I was told it was quite safe for a slim Afghan to step on a landmine and that it took something much heavier, such as a camel, to make it explode. That left anti-personnel mines. But these normally just rip out a piece of one's leg and with a bit of luck the victim ends up in some kind of development programme where he gets kitted out with a decent flexible prosthetic and perhaps even a job manufacturing artificial knees.

'Did Qais allow you to go out on your own?' I asked stupidly.

'Are you mad?' she sobbed. 'He's gone to Jalalabad. He'll be back in two or three days. If we don't find her by then... I'll shoot myself.'

'If we don't find who? Would you like some tea?'

'I don't want any tea. Why don't you just listen to me and do something? Tell your Americans to help me. What are they here for if they can let such a thing happen...'

'What kind of thing, Freshta? Calm down, I don't know what you're talking about.'

'Roshangol's gone. When I woke up this morning she wasn't there. She took a few things... Including my little mirror, you know the painted one you gave me and the new lipstick. He'll kill me. He'll most certainly kill me and if he finds her, he'll kill her too.' Freshta clutched her hair with both hands and clenched her fists. She pulled out a clump of hair. She really was desperate. The door opened and little Muhammad's puffy eyes peered inside.

'What are you doing here?' I snapped.

'I followed Freshta. She's very upset. Roshangol has run away from home.' Actually, it was probably useful to have Mad here. I drew him inside and closed the door.

'Why has she run away?' I asked, addressing both of them as at that moment Mad clearly had more common sense than Freshta.

'The moron wouldn't let her wear the new dress,' Muhammad exclaimed. 'It was so pretty, green with silver embroidery up here,' he said stroking his chest gently. 'Before he went away he told her she wasn't allowed to wear it and yesterday afternoon Freshta said she couldn't let her wear it without his approval...'

'You bet I couldn't. If he found out we'd both be in trouble. Do you have any idea what he might do to us?'

The green dress had been on the agenda for several weeks now. Nazir bought it for me at the bazaar. It was meant for our planned trip to Moscow that was never to materialise but it turned out to be too tight for me around the hips. We gave it to Roshangol. It suited her fabulously. Neither Nazir nor I thought this demure dress would send Qais into such a rage. 'I wouldn't let her wear this to bed, let alone among people,' he screamed, so loudly Grandpa had to scold him: 'My boy,' he said, 'my boy, the only people allowed to scream in this house are myself, my son and his son. You can go and vent your rage in your father's house. And if you don't stop yelling at my granddaughter and her daughter, my great-granddaughter, I'll have to thrash you like a dog.' These were very strong words for Grandpa and they exhausted him so much that before he managed to put a full stop after the last word he tilted his head back, opened his mouth, closed his eyes and started snoring like a foghorn. He fell asleep. Our Grandpa was quite wonderful. Qais frowned, giving the sleeping old man a hate-filled look. Then he said through his teeth: 'Allah will punish you for having brought her up this way.' He stormed out of the house and into the courtyard and disappeared, slamming the gate. Freshta grinned maliciously. Roshan hastily put on the new dress and indeed looked so gorgeous and provocative I couldn't help thinking Qais knew what he was talking about. 'Well, it's definitely not something you should wear to the bazaar but I think it'll do fine for when we have visitors,' I advised her, knowing full well the visitors would have to arrive when Qais was not at home. 'Herra,' Roshangol replied, offended, 'do you think I'd show myself to a stranger dressed like this? My father would kill me. He gave me a thrashing the other day just because I dabbed a little lipstick on my lower lip at home. I was planning on wearing it on special occasions but dad's making so much fuss now...' Freshta took her daughter to task, then asked her to check that her father wasn't lurking behind the gate waiting for us to start putting on make-up and doing our hair so he could deliver stupid lectures on female morality, chastity and fidelity, then give his wife a good kicking, wake up Grandpa, be told off and eventually go to his parents in a huff and stay there for a few days. They would bring him back eventually, and although they'd be upset they'd calm down after having a quiet word with Grandpa and Father, and would leave with an apology, leaving Qais with us. My husband would spit on seeing him to stop himself from slapping him in the face, and Grandpa would say: 'My boy, your parents are very nice people, but why, oh why have they brought you up such a moron.' Grandpa never used this kind of language with anyone else. Father wouldn't say a word to Qais and the rest of us would pretend everything was absolutely fine.

Muhammad didn't participate in the conversation about the green dress. But he didn't take his fish-like eyes off us. Then he went back to our room and started rummaging through my Russian books, which he perused so often some of the pages had been virtually rubbed out. He didn't say a word until the evening, informing me just before he went to bed: 'I've figured it out but I'll tell you tomorrow, not now.' I had no idea what it was he'd figured out and what he wanted to tell me tomorrow, and the next day I forgot all about his promise. My husband drove me to work and when we arrived home in the evening we found the family in the middle of another fight. This one, too, was about the dress. When he realised what the row was about my husband shouted: 'I'll never buy you so much as a sock again!' Then he turned on his heels, jumped into the car and drove off. The family was in ferment, Mother was crying, Freshta's teeth were clenched and Roshangol's face was so pale and puffed up I expected her to faint any minute. Grandpa was about to deliver one of his wise speeches and Father was sipping his tea furiously. Muhammad stood facing Qais, looking him in the eye, which wasn't easy given the difference in height.

'You brat, you useless bastard, you shitty cretin!' Qais was screeching like a baboon and the more Mad smiled – and smile he undoubtedly did – the more Qais strained his vocal cords. What had happened was that while I was gone Mad went to my trunk, which I had forgotten to lock, and took out a camera. The digital camera had already caused a few rows at home. Heidi had given it to me to document the workings of our advisory centre but very few women were prepared to have their picture taken.

The green dress clung to Roshangol's breasts and hips like a liana and Mad snapped a few pictures. He made her adopt alluring positions, including some rather suggestive ones. He

enjoyed pretending to be a photographer and Roshan felt like
a model. She pouted and rolled her eyes while Mad whispered:
'Raise your chin a little bit, yes, there we go, nice and graceful,
now show us your teeth, your lovely teeth...' He even approached
her a few times to adjust a fold on her dress or tuck a strand
of her thick black hair behind her delicate little ear. For Qais,
who had been watching them in secret, four minutes was as
much as he could bear before he had a fit. He hit his daughter
twice on the head, so hard she stayed frozen in a sitting position,
staring at the wall glass-eyed. Only Grandpa's entering the room
saved her from further punishment. And while Grandpa was
protecting his granddaughter, Qais set upon Mad. He kicked
him in the belly and since Muhammad's scrawny legs were quite
shaky and unable to resist a moderate gust of wind, he collapsed
immediately. Qais kept kicking him furiously until Grandpa,
stooping and frail as he was, grabbed the TV aerial that was
sticking out of our window and slapped his granddaughter's
husband across the back. Mad got up and straightened up in
front of Qais, while Grandpa, who had had enough, lay down
and Roshangol continued to stare at the wall vacantly and
nobody else dared to enter the room. That was the point at which
my husband and I arrived. As I took my camera Qais warned that
some day he would kick all these devil's inventions to pieces...
Then he focused on Mad. But there was no more beating. Even
though Grandpa had dozed off, Qais was actually a bit scared of
Mad. 'You revolting little dwarf,' he said with so much hatred in
his voice it made me nauseous. Mad kept on smiling. This was
the last and biggest row about the green dress my husband had
bought me at the bazaar.

'Was she planning to go somewhere wearing the dress?' I
asked gently.

Freshta gave me a tired look and replied: 'Herra, you really
are from another planet. She never wanted to look at it again.
I have no idea what happened. I promised her she could wear

it for her husband once she got married. We talked about it last night.'

'Is she getting married?' I exclaimed, horrified. Grandpa had been trying to persuade Qais to let Roshangol complete at least five years of education before marrying her off. In the short time she had been going to school she had already learned to read and write. Kabul now offered plenty of courses for girls who had missed out on their schooling under the Taliban and she had a chance to learn English or computer skills. Qais gave it some thought, his sudden prudence inspiring a little respect in me. My husband had offered to buy her English textbooks and notepads so Qais wouldn't have to pay for anything. There had never been any explicit talk of marriage.

'Not now. In a few years' time, of course,' said Freshta breaking in on my thoughts. 'Qais has already picked his uncle's son. A very nice boy, apparently. And he's going to be quite well off...'

'I bet he's a moron like Qais,' Mad said calmly, and I gave him a slap.

'What else did you talk about yesterday?' It occurred to me that Roshangol's escape might have something to do with her conversation with Freshta.

'I was telling her how I met Qais. How handsome and nice he was. I promised her she could choose her bridegroom herself. But she started crying and said: "Mum, do you really believe that? We'd have to kill dad first." That made me cry too. And then she asked me if I thought she would ever wear the green dress again. And that's when I explained that she should save it for her husband, as the only thing she could expect from other men would be lecherous looks and dirty talk. She asked me how come the women in Indian films could walk around with their breasts semi-naked and her dad was happy to look at them. Do you know what she told me, Herra, do you know what my little girl said to me? She said looking at them gave her dad a hard-on... That's how she put it. My sweet little kitten. I thought she didn't even know what boys have between their legs...'

'Freshta!' I snapped at her, adding softly: 'There's Mad, don't forget Mad's here...'

There was no point whispering as Mad was all ears and didn't find it the least bit strange that we should freely discuss such matters in his presence.

'That's true. I've noticed it too. It always made Roshan laugh,' he said sagely.

'And then we went to bed. We were looking forward to altering my old brown trousers... you know, the ones made of the fine fabric. Father had brought them back from Mazar and they're too tight for me. I wanted to alter them for her, they'd go nicely with the top she got from you. You know, the yellow one with ruffles... Well, and by next morning she was gone.'

'Has she taken the green dress with her?' I addressed my question to both of them. Mad didn't say a word, Freshta sobbed and looked at the boy. He nodded with an expert air and pulled a piece of green fabric from his pocket. It was frayed at the side as if it had been torn out forcibly.

'I found it in front of the toilet. It can't be sewn together anymore but it still might do as a smallish scarf.' Mad has always been very down to earth. I picked up the piece of cloth and as I felt it between my fingers I realised Roshangol was never coming back. And even if she did, she would no longer be our Roshangol.

Dominic stormed into the office just as Freshta was getting up and saying she was going to jump into the river.

'You've got a huge queue out there, Herra! This is not good enough! You've got to be better organised.' Then he spotted Freshta. He didn't recognise her. He didn't know she was my sister-in-law, the one who had made a spectacle of herself falling through the glass door, because when that happened he must have been even more shocked than us. He did, however, realise straight away that she was in utter despair. 'Oh, I see, this is some kind of an emergency?' Freshta didn't understand a word of English but Mad's ears wiggled.

'Hello, mister,' he said. Dominic was taken aback. He must have thought the lady had given birth to a monster and come to us hoping we'd help sort it out. Perhaps she needed surgery for the child and I had told her it was too late for that, or something of the sort. But then he realised he had seen Mad before although he couldn't remember where.

'Her daughter has disappeared. She's fourteen. She's run away. For the family it's a major...' I wanted to say a tragedy but then thought it might not be quite such a disaster after all. 'A major disgrace...'

'Is there something we can do for her?' Dominic asked in a kind and sympathetic tone, as required by his job description.

'To begin with, we can give her something to calm her down,' I said to get rid of him for a moment. Like a good boy he ran off to get the tranquillisers that he had come to rely on himself and which Heidi apparently couldn't go to sleep without.

'Freshta, you've got to find Nazir. Right away. Nazir is the only one who can help you. He's probably at the Germans' office. He was sent there on an errand. Do you know where it is?'

'And what can he do to help me?'

'He'll find her. The Germans' office is in Shar-e Naw, next to the park. Mad will go with you and can ask around. Go and find Nazir, then come and get me. We might come up with something.'

The door opened again and Heidi came in. Just what we need, I thought, my cheeks flushed with anger.

'Is this serious?' she asked in an official tone.

'It's a matter of life and death,' I said, truthfully.

'Why life and death?'

'Her daughter has run away. If her husband finds out he might kill her.'

'Kill who?' Heidi could be really thick sometimes. But she made me stop and think for a while.

'Both of them, actually,' I said quietly. It was true. Heidi stared at Freshta, then at Mad and unlike Dominic she remembered immediately having seen the creature somewhere before. After a few seconds she said sternly: 'This boy is yours, isn't he?'

'Hallo, how are you,' Mad sang out. 'That woman want jumping into river,' he said making only four mistakes in the English sentence.

'Is that true?' Heidi looked at me, clearly not sure if the three of us weren't making fun of her.

'She's desperate, you don't know what it means for a fourteen-year-old girl to run away from home.'

Freshta got up. She was now standing next to Heidi and the American was looking at her, enraptured. She must have realised she had never seen such a beautiful woman before.

'Ask her what I can do to help her.'

'She wants to do something for you but to be honest, I don't know what she could do to help us now. She's a bit of a cow,' I said to Freshta in Dari. Mad giggled hearing my last words and a perplexed Heidi kept glancing from one to the other, finally resting her eyes on me.

'Do you need a car? Is there anything you can do for her at all? Perhaps Dominic and I could go to her house and have a word with her husband...'

'No, Heidi, that's not a good idea. Let her go. We can't help her. Please believe me. There's nothing we can do for this woman at the moment. The river is dry anyway so even if she does jump she'll get stuck in the mud and won't come to any harm. And besides, I don't think she'll kill herself, she's got other children at home. So it's best if you just forget about her.'

Mad burst out laughing and I was surprised he had enough English to understand the bit about the mud.

'Is this the kind of advice you generally offer people?' Heidi said sarcastically.

'If they ask for sleeping pills or for flour to bake bread, I send them to the Germans. But as for those who are about to get killed by their own husband, I don't know how to stop it... We shouldn't get involved.'

Freshta started getting ready and pulling the burka over her face. Heidi took her hand.

'Wait, lady, you can stay with us for a few days if you like. We shall protect you...' Heidi was prone to bursts of emotion at the most inappropriate moments. Right now she was trying to persuade my husband's sister to renounce her family and abandon her children, husband, mother, brother and father. Only Heidi was capable of coming up with this kind of nonsense. If she'd had her way, I might have been at risk, too.

'In that case you'd have to take her to America with you, Heidi. That would be the end of her in this country. Not even a single night, do you understand? Let her go, she'll figure something out.' Heidi finally let go of Freshta's hand and watched in fascination as the tall and beautifully proportioned blue figure disappeared in the crowd of other blue women. Mad scuttled out behind her.

'Next,' I shouted and Heidi gave me a disdainful look: 'Your job is to help them break free of these idiotic antediluvian traditions of yours. And the best you can do is give them an address where they can get a sack of flour?'

'I'm sorry, Heidi, but I'm not going to help you change these idiotic antediluvian traditions. Because they won't stand for it.'

As soon as Heidi left, slamming the door with a disdainful smile, a woman entered. She was the one I had pushed out to listen to Freshta's woes.

'My husband has died, you know...' she wept like a real pro, tears welling in her eyes at her command.

'Here you are, take this piece of paper, it says you're a war widow. Take it to the warehouse around the corner. You'll get flour and sugar, if they have any left.' The woman halted the flood of tears and smiled.

'What about oil, my girl, do you think there might be any oil left?'

We didn't find Roshangol the next day or the following day. After the meeting in my cubicle, Freshta, Nazir and Mad collected me and the three of us circled the city aimlessly, taking turns shouting: 'Look over there, isn't that her...' even though none of us believed Roshangol was wandering around town and none of us knew how to look under a burka to check if it really was her. On this occasion even my husband, who had always claimed he could tell a beautiful woman from an ugly one under a burka, and that he could spot me, Mother or Freshta right away, was just as clueless as the rest of us. Freshta was in tears, which blurred her vision. That's probably why she shouted less frequently than the rest of us.

Eventually we realised it was pointless and went back home. The first row occurred before we even got out of the car since none of us wanted to be the harbinger of bad news and tell the rest of the family that we had lost Roshangol and been disgraced not just in the eyes of the whole family but, as Nazir put it, 'the whole country'.

'C'mon Nazir, my love, who cares if someone's daughter has run away? Why should we be disgraced in the whole country?' I said this in Russian to reassure him but I only managed to incense him.

'You're so stupid, you've been in this country for twelve years and you're just as stupid as you were before you came. People will care, even if they don't know us. They've got nothing to do and spend their evenings gossiping about things like this, who did what, where, and why... Other people's tragedies are a great opportunity to forget one's own. As if you didn't know that. Isn't that what you, Freshta and Mother do?'

He was right. We women usually mulled over everything that happened to anyone, discussing who had been raped by whom, who had got married, who had run away from whom and who was beating whom and where... And this was how people would talk about our family now.

The best news of the day was that Qais was still in Jalalabad. Grandpa, Father and Mother were beside themselves as Freshta and Roshangol had never left the house for a whole day before without a word of explanation.

'So how are things at home?' Father asked by way of welcome, thinking Freshta had gone to visit her father-in-law, even though he found it strange, as his daughter had never visited her in-laws unless forced by her husband. So it was strange that she would have gone to see those annoying people of her own accord when he was away.

Freshta started crying like a newborn baby. It was impossible to get a sensible word out of her. And so it was left to Mad, since I kept quiet and Nazir felt a sudden urge to start tinkering with the car. The family received the news in silence. Father was silent, Mother was silent too and so was Grandpa, and Muhammad also fell silent after finishing his long and admittedly, rather articulate and sensitive speech. Then, all of a sudden, Grandpa got up with difficulty, looked at all of us in turn and pronounced with a sad, sad smile: 'We're beyond help if our own children run away from us.' Then he sat down slowly, propped his head on a cushion and fell fast asleep.

That evening we all joined in a collective prayer asking for Roshangol to be found before Qais returned. However, Grandpa's prayer seemed rather perfunctory. As if he didn't really wish for it to happen. I suspected he was rooting for Roshan, hoping she would end up some place where nobody would rip a green dress off her delicate body and beat her about the head. I prayed, too, even though I had never quite mastered all the accompanying gestures. Nobody seemed to mind. Mad came up to me later that night and whispered: 'I can teach you if you want. It doesn't matter that you're not a Muslim, it won't do any harm for you to learn how to do it properly.'

'You're right, it won't do any harm. Thanks, Mad. Let's start next week, shall we?' He squeezed my hand and fell asleep next to me under the blanket. Nazir went to bed much later, after he, Grandpa and Father had discussed the next steps.

'What was it you had figured out?' I asked Mad, half asleep. Nazir climbed under the blanket and when he bumped into Mad, who'd rolled himself into a ball, he swore in fright that some small animal had got into our bed. 'That imp is here again...' he cursed but then lay down next to Mad with a kind smile. I slept really soundly that night, surrounded by the two people I loved more than anything else in the world.

'We have to find out from her girlfriends if she had a suitor. That's usually the reason – a girl normally elopes with a boy the family is opposed to. Freshta herself had threatened to elope if we didn't let her marry Qais. We should have broken every bone in her body, it would have been better than this...' Nazir was six years younger than his sister but when, aged seventeen, she got it into her head to marry a Pashtun, and one from a totally unknown family, and not even the best family at that, he responded like an adult. He later confessed he had wanted to go as far as killing him but Grandpa had talked him out of this ill-advised course of action.

'But who will talk to her girlfriends... Mother, I suppose?'

'No, you will. You'll talk to them.'

I was more than happy to hear that. It must have been the first time the family acknowledged I could do something really useful.

Nazir drove me to work an hour earlier than usual to give

me time to negotiate. It went quite smoothly. Heidi was in a good mood and listened to my slightly embellished story with an open mouth. Occasionally she even smiled at Mad, and when she pulled a lollipop out of a drawer it was obvious she was in a perfectly charitable mood. Taken aback, Mad accepted the treat and commented in Persian: 'Does she think I'm a monkey or what?' Heidi, who must have thought he was thanking her, caressed the delicate fluff on his head that passed for hair.

'You were right, Heidi,' I started tactically. 'I've been thinking about that woman, you know the one who wanted to jump into the river…'

'Well, and did she?' came Heidi's rather silly response.

'No, she didn't. But if she doesn't, her husband will rip her to pieces,' I said, exaggerating slightly. Qais might not have ripped Freshta to pieces but he was quite capable of splitting her head with an axe.

'What are you going to do?' Heidi whispered, as the story was starting to sound as thrilling as an Ed McBain mystery.

'That's why I brought our Mad along, I think he can help. There are things I can't ask about but people tend to open up to children and they might reveal something they're not supposed to.'

'Oh, I see,' said Heidi, and added: 'So where are we going?'

'You see, Heidi, the presence of foreigners may be a bit disruptive in situations like these.' I tried to impress her by sounding worldly. I knew she would want to be part of our investigation. 'With you around people won't say anything that might be embarrassing.'

Heidi thought about this. She had totally forgotten how angry I had made her the other day.

'But can you tell me at least what you're planning to do?'

'We're going to try to find her.'

'And then what?'

'I don't know. We'll try to save her.'

'So that means you won't force her to go back home, right?' said Heidi showing an unusual degree of sensitivity.

'I won't.'

I failed to convince Dominic and Heidi to give us a car without a driver even though, in the hope of increasing our chances of success, I had managed to persuade my husband to let me drive, something he was normally dead set against. The first time I sat behind the wheel in Kabul, I remember it was on the 3rd December 2001, it felt as if a new revolution had broken out. Cars were stopping and hooting, skinny, sad policemen beamed with happiness and even if the world's CEO in person happened to drive in the opposite direction, with a suite of bodyguards in tow, they would have made him stop and let me pass unhindered. This was the one occasion when Afghan men didn't shout indignantly or jeer and insult me and responded with a mixture of admiration and amusement instead. My husband, who was sitting next to me in the car, tormented himself by counting the number of men who stared at me, lewdly caressing my face as he put it, but he was very proud of me nevertheless. Admittedly, he had originally tried to wedge me into the driver's seat in a burka but it didn't take him long to realise that this was likely to cause a major car accident. I couldn't see to my left or right. Peripheral vision, or rather its total absence, is one of the major disadvantages of a burka. Its inventor evidently didn't expect anyone to drive a car while wearing it. But then again, at the time when men began to force women into burkas there weren't any cars around. Pulling out of the garage I promptly bumped against a neighbour who was pushing a cart loaded with cabbages to the bazaar. And since you can't stop a fully loaded cart that easily, the unavoidable encounter inflicted rather more damage on our car than on the neighbour and his cart. My husband gave a moan, cupped his head in his hands and was about to give up on his brilliant idea of a drive around the city with me behind the wheel. I convinced him it was just a minor deficiency brought on by a combination of nerves and the dense grille blocking my view. That was the first time in many years I was able to go out without a burka. My husband even helped me pull the garb over my head, throwing it on the back seat with a hint of disdain, though I might have been only imagining that.

As we drove around town I felt like the queen of Afghanistan. People were waving at me and the joy felt by the few women we came across radiated through their burkas. Everyone understood this meant more than just the departure of the Taliban from Afghanistan. For about a month Nazir enjoyed being the pioneer of female driving. Then he learned that Uncle Amin overheard someone saying at a Mujahideen meeting: 'People say Nazir's Russian whore wants to launch driving courses for women. She would've got a public thrashing under the Taliban. Nazir seems to have lost control over her.'

I don't know whether Uncle Amin invented this story or if it was true, but the fact was that after that my husband no longer enjoyed being the object of admiration and put a stop to my driving. It was a miracle that he now agreed to let me drive into town on my own, accompanied only by Mad. However, his niece's scandalous disappearance and his sister's despair meant so much to him he was prepared to live with potential gossip and coarse innuendo.

'Drive carefully, everyone will take you for a foreigner if you're behind the wheel of an American car. But the minute you see anyone you know, look away so they don't recognise you,' he said. His advice was utterly useless as it would have been too dangerous to keep looking away while driving. And in any case, Dominic didn't let me use their car on my own. Not because he thought there was anything wrong with a woman driving but because he didn't trust my skills, and besides the use of office vehicles was subject to a battery of regulations.

He kept the paperwork in a smart grey folder and produced it despite my protestations, to prove he wasn't a free agent.

'Look, here it says something about material responsibility… all drivers have to sign that in case of an accident, and if they are found to be responsible, they will be liable for any repairs. Surely you don't want to take that risk.'

'I'm as good a driver as any Afghan, plus I know the rules of the road and I'm more careful,' I protested.

'But your name is not on our official drivers' list. What if we get an inspection, how will we explain that?'

Hmm, I thought to myself, we were always notified at least two months before any visitors from the US headquarters arrived. Bodyguards and cars to collect them at the airport had to be organised, hundreds of letters written, the whole team was put through psychological training, everything in the vicinity was inspected and the barbed wire on top of the walls was repaired. The likelihood of an unexpected visit was therefore about as great as my husband letting me wear a miniskirt. But there was no point protesting, Dominic was basically worried about the car. Fortunately he allowed us to pick our own driver. Zulgay was a great guy. He was a brilliant driver, always laughing and brimming with optimism, even though he had buried two wives, had a mother who had been bedridden for six years and was dribbling and incontinent, and a third wife who was barren and malicious. In my excitement at being sent on this mission I threw all caution to the wind and forgot every principle which, after twelve years of indoctrination, should have been in my bloodstream and so I was ready, accompanied only by Mad, to get into a car with a man who wasn't part of our family, who was an Afghan and a family acquaintance at that. Honestly, none of this dawned on me until it was too late.

The huge Toyota, its aerial proudly erect, was an imposing vehicle but hardly suited to an inconspicuous search of the slums. We first headed for Roshangol's school. We were all in good spirits and Zulgay fortunately didn't ask why we were going there and what we would do once we reached our destination. He cracked one joke after another and I found some of them genuinely funny. We arrived at the school on time, just as the girls were leaving the gates, chattering happily to one another. I spotted Anahita in the crowd. She was our niece's best friend, a beautiful girl with huge eyes and eyelashes so long she could have used them to fan herself in a heat wave.

'Ana,' I shouted, using the nickname only her closest friends knew. She stopped in her tracks, unsure whether she should leave her little group. I got out of the car and took a few steps in her direction. Suddenly I realised she was about to flee, that she didn't want to talk to me and was terribly scared. Then she changed her mind. She came up to me, putting on a neutral expression.

'I don't know where she is,' she said without hesitation and with a hint of contempt.

'I have no intention of hurting her or of making her come home by force. I just want to help her. If she doesn't want to come back, I won't make her,' I rattled off my points. At that moment Mad appeared by my side.

'Trust her. She's not lying. It's true, Qais, her dad, isn't home, you know. She won't get punished...' Although Mad did his best to look trustworthy, Anahita couldn't help laughing.

'Oh yeah, her dad used to beat her just for staring out of the window for too long, so I'm sure he'll praise her now, you silly thing.'

Mad was offended. I wasn't.

'Anahita, at least please tell us that she's safe. That she's going to be OK? Do you know how her mother must be feeling? And do you know what her father will do to her mother? Are you aware of that?'

'Sure I am. And so is she. But she just couldn't take it any more. I don't know if she's safe. I don't know anything except that she didn't want to live with you any more. She's been saying so for a long time. And she didn't elope with a boy, if that's what you're hinting at. I really don't know where she is.' Turning abruptly, Anahita walked away. It would have been pointless to follow her. Dispirited, we got back in the car. Zulgay started the engine and was about to leave when a burka pushed itself into our window.

'I'm her teacher.' I recognised Fatima, a nice but rather dim teacher who did her best to impart the knowledge of English to her pupils although her own command of the language left quite a lot to be desired. The bright headmistress, the one who had made Qais come out in a rash when we first met, tolerated the teacher at her school only because she couldn't find anyone more literate. Fatima spent her evenings swotting up on vocabulary and dictating it to her students the next day. Roshangol once declared she could introduce herself and enunciated with full concentration: 'Me nahmay iz Roshangol and me tone is Kabul.' Nobody seemed to have informed the teacher that in English some words are pronounced rather differently from the way they're spelled. As a result she crammed her students' heads with expressions she alone could understand, creating an Esperanto of a kind that, I later discovered, was used in a number of Kabul schools. However, it was one of the male teachers who taught Kamal, our eldest nephew, who took the biscuit. The man had recently been found to be illiterate. Funnily enough, instead of being sacked, he was just told to study at a faster pace than his students so that he could gradually share his freshly acquired knowledge with them. The headmaster of the school that all my nephews attended was a university professor who had spent his whole life reading books, spoke five languages and wrote beautiful poetry. He belonged to the Afghan elite and championed the teaching of Greek since he felt the students' minds weren't sufficiently occupied. In his boundless indulgence he ended up tutoring his illiterate subordinate in the evenings.

Fatima looked around to make sure nobody was watching her. I was reluctant to suggest that she climb into the car with us. Afghans believe only prostitutes get into a car driven by a stranger and the mere fact of inviting her in might have put her off talking to us. To my immense surprise she suddenly started to climb into the back seat.

Taken aback, Mad shifted in his seat to make sure he didn't as much as hint at touching her. Although still a child, he knew that the most fleeting contact was something so unforgiveable he might as well have shot himself afterwards. For sooner or later the husband would have come to kill him.

'She's with the Hazaras, possibly in Charikar,' the teacher blurted out after smoothing down her burka and casting a couple of quick glances at Mad. He maintained a neutral expression since, unlike the rest of our family, he didn't find the idea of Hazaras potentially being part of our family particularly shocking, claiming that as descendants of Genghis Khan's raiders and raped Afghan women they were of good genetic stock; nor, in his view, did the fact that they belonged to the Shiite branch of Islam matter in any way, since the decision as to which religion was best wasn't going to be taken in the near future anyway. In addition, he thought there was something quite charming about their slanty eyes.

'At least that's what I've heard, you know what girls are like, they can't keep a secret.'

'Holy shit,' I let slip. 'And who is she with, at the Hazaras? We don't have any relatives there.'

'We do,' Mad interrupted. Nobody had ever explained to us how exactly Mad was related to us. Grandpa was probably the only one who had an inkling of the state of affairs and knew why Mad's appearance was so far from that of a proud Persian, resembling rather something born out of an involuntary union between a slant-eyed Kazakh and a Russian village girl. His origin was never discussed, on principle.

'I have relatives there,' Mad said unusually softly. He grinned as everyone looked at him in amazement. 'But I haven't seen them for a long time.'

Charikar was about an hour's drive away. A road that had once been covered in tarmac led through the Shamal plain, smashed up by all the wars that had rolled across it, past withered and neglected vineyards dying for lack of water and past wrecked, ancient irrigation systems. The road was lined with the hulks of Russian tanks, which over the years since the Soviets had left Afghanistan, had been stripped of everything remotely usable, including gun barrels that had been fashioned into primitive water pipes. When Charikar had been a major Soviet base the Russians were quite happy there and engaged in lively trade with the local population. These days all that was left of the occupying forces were vast cemeteries and barracks, used by the Taliban after their departure, followed by the Mujahideen, then by the Americans and now by the new Afghan police, comprising former Taliban, Mujahideen and famished locals. The road was thronging with traffic, drivers madly overtaking one another to prove to themselves they were the best drivers in the world. It was forbidden to drive on the soft shoulder in places marked with red stones, to indicate mines, but the signs were heeded so rarely it was quite astonishing that so few people actually stepped on a mine. Or drove over one.

'Zulgay, please, don't drive on the soft shoulder,' I pleaded in vain with our driver who completely ignored the warning signs marking the boundaries of minefields. He had fought with the Taliban under Masoud together with my husband, and believed one would die whenever one was destined to and there was no way one could influence what had been preordained. We survived the trip to Charikar.

I liked Charikar. Under the Taliban my husband and I had gone there a few times for a kebab because the local police had seemed more tolerant and the local people less fanatical.

'Mad, do you know where we're going?' asked Zulgay who had been silent until then.

'No, but I think I know where to ask,' Mad said, sounding so grown-up I suddenly felt my presence was unnecessary.

We stopped outside a clay hovel surrounded by a half-demolished wall and I immediately made out the contours of a woman's face behind the torn sheets of polythene hanging from the windows. Mad got out of the car and gestured to me to stay inside. He returned some twenty minutes later, unusually red-faced and deadly serious. He gave a nod, signalling that we should go. I couldn't stop myself from turning around. A young woman in extremely ragged clothes stood by the wall. She could still have been a child. But she didn't resemble Roshangol at all. We didn't say a word almost all the way to Kabul. Then Mad said quietly:

'Everything is all right. We don't have to worry about Roshangol any longer.'

'Did you see her?' I asked, dying of suspense.

'No, I didn't and I don't think I ever will. Neither me nor you.'

'Come off it, stop being so secretive. Out with it,' I kept pestering him, my nerves on edge.

'But you have to promise never to tell the details to anyone. Not even to Nazir. It might put her at risk.'

'I promise,' I said licking two fingers of my right hand and raising them in a symbolic oath to show I meant it.

'She's in Bamyan. She's happily married. She doesn't have to wear a burka because Hazara women don't wear them. She gets lots of fresh air because she's high up in the mountains, surrounded by beautiful countryside and has plenty of water. And there's no Qais.'

I've never learned anything more about my niece. We told everyone at home we had lost track of her somewhere in Charikar but were certain she was in good hands, most likely married to a decent young man. As for the fact that he was a

Hazara and that she went to live with him in Bamyan, we kept that to ourselves. Forever.

Freshta broke down when she heard the news. It wasn't just for show. Only now did she realise she would never see her daughter again. I spent the whole evening sitting with her on the patio and if there had been a bowl in front of my sister-in-law she would have filled it with tears. She cried silently, without sobbing, taking my hand every now and then and whispering: 'I know she had to do it. She saw Qais forcing himself on me every night and must have known how dreadful it was for me. She told me she was so scared… And silly me, I tried to make her believe it could be quite nice sometimes. She got her first period recently. And she knew that was it. Qais had been asking me about it for a year now and I kept lying to him, saying it hadn't happened yet. He would have married her off straight away. But he found out. Do you know what that brute did? He looked at her panties the other day. He must have felt it, he's got an instinct…'

My husband came out on to the patio. He sat down with us, stroking Freshta's head.

'Maybe she'll be better off where she is than here with us. But if I knew where she was I'd go there and strangle her. Disgracing our family like this.' Then he turned to me, saying: 'You must have lost your mind. To go around in a car with a strange man.' But he sounded surprisingly gentle, sad rather than cross.

'C'mon, it was only Zulgay, and Mad came with us,' I objected.

'Shut up please, just shut up. Mad is invisible in the car and Zulgay is not a relative of ours. As if one disgrace in the family weren't enough.'

'I'll never do it again,' I promised sincerely.

'Oh yes, you will, Herra. And you'll do worse things too,' he said with resignation, putting an arm around his sister's shoulders. He never touched me that evening. I slept on our mattress with Mad and my husband slept in Mad's place. He had never done that before. He had sometimes spent the night in the car in protest but he had never gone to sleep on Mad's mattress.

'Mad,' I whispered once I could hear regular breathing from the far corner. 'Who was it you went to see today?'

'It doesn't matter,' he replied sleepily.

'Is it a secret?'

'Sort of. Actually, not really, more of a disgrace.'

That was one disgrace too many for me in a single day. After all those years I still didn't understand all the things that counted as a disgrace in Afghanistan.

'Your disgrace?'

'Mine too. I was actually born out of that disgrace.'

'And that was your mum?' I dared to pose the key question.

'No, it was my sister,' said Mad, turning his back to me.

chapter 16

IT WAS A GOOD IDEA, and Heidi deserved credit for it. 'If any of the women have health problems, you'll refer them to our clinic so that a doctor can determine what's wrong with them. We have an agreement with the American and German military hospitals, they'll deal with the more complicated and rare cases. And the Russians, they'll take anyone.' Heidi was suitably proud of having squeezed out enough money from her spreadsheets and budgets to cover medical aid. She was obsessed with helping women and insisted that the two American doctors on our team focus on my women. Heidi was right. Every day I listened to women telling stories involving a difficult labour, prolapsed uterus, fetid discharge, back pain, swollen eyes, fingernails and hair falling out and, invariably, all I could advise them to do was to take ibuprofen. My advice was always received gratefully. Ibuprofen was the only medication we handed out to the poor wretches in large quantities. It must have been a gift from a company that had overstocked, and this was an easy way to do a tax-deductible good deed.

Heidi and I were drinking tea and I found myself in complete harmony with her, which was strange but, lately, not all that uncommon. She was nuts. A complete crackpot. One day she'd drive me crazy, the next day she'd make me feel something bordering on affection. But gradually I came to realise that Heidi was genuine about everything she did. And, unlike Dominic, she didn't care how much risk allowance was added to her monthly salary. She was genuinely happy whenever we succeeded in anything. That this didn't happen as often as I would have liked was another matter. Heidi knew nothing about us but was obsessed with a desire to help, to become a Mother Teresa and leave behind thousands of rescued bodies and souls. I think as a child she had dreamt of becoming a singer but it soon transpired she didn't have a voice. But determined to commit great and good deeds, she turned to saving the poor. Her previous assignment had been to south Sudan and she told me how dreadful it had been.

'Was it much worse than here?' I asked her. She gave it a long thought.

'Not much worse. Actually, not at all. The people there didn't know things could be any better. They'd always had a difficult life. But you used to enjoy quite a decent life, right?'

Now I had to stop and think. 'When I came to this country, it wasn't much fun anymore. But our Mother used to go to the cinema,' I said proudly, omitting the fact that she had only been to the cinema twice altogether. Nevertheless, these outings were still the stuff of legend in our family. Admittedly, women used to walk around Kabul wearing skirts above their knees in the seventies, I saw it on video. Men used to take them to Soviet-style pop music concerts and even though they made them sit in special 'female' rows they didn't force them to wear trousers under the skirts. Now we were in the era of tights. The only time poor Heidi ventured out to a UN meeting wearing a skirt down to her ankles with tights underneath, young brats waiting outside our international saviours' impregnable blue gate greeted her with lewd shouts of: 'Hey, you've left your trousers at home, you'll get a breeze up your...'

This didn't impress her at all. Heidi was kind but rather dim. I don't mean to say she was stupid. She was good with computers, she could drive as well as I could, churned out beautiful charts and her accounting was impeccable. And she would happily answer all my questions about new American movies which, in her view, were considerably less idiotic than the ones that were available on worn-out cassettes in Kabul. I suspected she didn't like me very much but she tried not to show it. What bothered her was that, having voluntarily left a country marginally more free than this one, I hadn't valiantly opposed the wearing of the burka and the discrimination of women and I always spoke of my husband with reverence and devout loyalty. I knew she had hoped to meet someone in Afghanistan who had been persecuted by the Taliban, gone into hiding and afterwards emerged as a knight in shining armour, embarking on a tireless struggle against the despotic fundamentalist regime. She kept asking whether, by any chance, any of my Kabul friends had been in charge of an underground women's movement fighting against the men who ruled us with an iron fist, and wondered if I had ever done anything that might pass for a protest. Nothing came to my mind. Neither a courageous friend nor my own heroic deeds. Eventually Heidi had to make do with me, an ordinary and slightly diffident, not very talkative and certainly not too courageous, half-Russian, half-Tajik woman. She gritted her teeth and tried to befriend me. She wanted everyone around her to be happy. Once she offered me some tinned pineapple. It had a nasty smell and I spat it out at once. She took half an hour to explain how good it was, although it was an acquired taste.

'You've got to get used to it,' she intoned, 'it's like with men. They also smell bad at first, then you stop being bothered by that musky smell and eventually you come to enjoy their scent,' went one of her lectures on sexual enlightenment.

'I don't find my husband smelly and never have. Except when he slathers himself in cologne, which makes my nose twitch, but not otherwise.'

'Have you never been with another man?' she asked and didn't even realise how rude that question was. Or perhaps it wasn't, since nobody else was around. I was taken aback. And terrified. How could she have any doubts? Didn't she know that Afghan women never sleep with more than one man in their life? Well, two at most but then the second one is usually the last because once he discovers he wasn't the first, he's quite capable of stabbing his wife. And if he doesn't, his own dad or brother will do it for him. Either way, to make sure the poor girl doesn't have to live in disgrace, someone will take her life. Perhaps widows can afford not to be virgins. And the odd divorcee. I kept quiet for too long, and Heidi was intrigued.

'So have you or haven't you?' she asked with a roguish smile. 'You're scared to tell me? I've been with just over ten. They've all left me, otherwise I would have got married a long time ago. It's not such a big deal in our country for someone to have slept with twelve or twenty men. It's not considered too much.'

'I know that, of course,' I snapped. I was disgusted. I found the idea of twelve men unspeakably offensive and obscene. My husband always used to say that changing partners was the root of all diseases. He claimed to have heard it on the radio back in the Soviet Union.

'I know it's normal,' I told Heidi, having calmed down a bit and suddenly feeling like confiding in her. Luckily she stopped me by recapping her conquests. 'I've never had any other man except for my husband,' I shouted loudly over her statistics and to suppress my own bad conscience.

'You know what, you haven't missed much. They all have the same equipment. Some are thinner, others shorter but basically I think it's all about something else,' she said distractedly.

'What is it, then?' Now I was beginning to get interested.

'The relationship, of course. Love is the thing. When you love someone you will forgive him even if he's not very good in bed.'

'Yeah, that's for sure,' I agreed. After that we had a few more conversations about men, Heidi knew lots of lewd jokes mocking men which I didn't find funny at all but always laughed at heartily out of politeness.

Today Heidi was extremely excited and on edge. The women's clinic was almost ready, the doctors were looking forward to it, and our sponsors were over the moon.

'Our military experts will be here soon, to help you build your army,' she said out of the blue.

'But we do have an army...' I objected.

'What you have is not an army but a group of enthusiasts who can shoot,' she asserted as if she were a military expert. 'Did your husband fight in the war as well?' she asked.

'He did. In Panshir. He served under General Masoud. You know, the one who's been blown up...'

'I know,' she snapped, proud of having read up on Afghanistan's history and present-day situation before arriving here. 'He was very handsome,' she added.

'But short,' I said.

'And did your husband kill anyone?'

'I think he did kill some Taliban. And his dad shot six Russians dead,' I boasted and then froze. I realised I was speaking of Russians as if my best friend Nadia hadn't been Russian, my mother hadn't been Russian and I myself hadn't been half-Russian.

'And what's it like living with someone who's killed another person?' Heidi kept pestering me.

'He doesn't do that at home,' I replied angrily, getting fed up with her prying questions and changed the subject quickly. 'Do you know that Afghans have been protesting outside your Embassy? They're demanding compensation for their relatives killed in your bombing raids.'

'Yes, I heard it on CNN. They're out there protesting now. The fact that we're here should be enough for them, shouldn't it, and the fact that we're giving them everything for free. And besides, we haven't really killed that many people.' I said nothing because Heidi was right, up to a point. We all admired the Americans for their accurate shelling. They only got it wrong a few times, for example when they destroyed the dog kennels of a humanitarian organisation that used dogs in mine detection, as well as a few civilian homes, but mostly their shells fell where they were supposed to. But one learns from one's mistakes and I was sure they would get it right next time.

'One of your planes crashed yesterday. You've got eight casualties,' I said, suddenly unable to disguise my glee. Fortunately, Heidi didn't notice.

'It must be terrible for the parents of our boys back home.'

'Actually, there were only eight wounded,' I corrected myself and Heidi didn't realise I had got it wrong on purpose.

'Thank God for that. But if your son comes home without a leg that's not much fun either.'

'We have many relatives without a leg,' I lied. In fact, we had only two: an elderly uncle who had gone out to graze sheep and stepped on a mine, and a nephew who had been rummaging for something to salvage in the ruins and this had cost him a limb. Heidi fixed me with her eyes, saying solemnly: 'And we're here to make sure you'll have no more relatives without legs.' There was nothing to add. It really was easier to talk to Heidi about women than about the war.

'Heidi, I don't think our women will be willing to see these doctors.'

Heidi raised her eyebrows. 'I've discussed it with Dominic, he said it might be difficult at first but everyone would be happy later...'

Heidi regarded Dominic as an expert on local conditions and on Islam. He had read the Quran in English and sometimes even quoted from it. He had lived in a number of Islamic countries and was the more experienced of the two of them.

'Female doctors would be preferable,' I insisted.

'But we don't have any, all we have is two male doctors, including one gynaecologist.'

'All right, but I'd like to see an Afghan woman who will let your doctor examine her ovaries.'

'Do you really think this will be a problem?' she asked, genuinely surprised, making me feel sorry for her. She longed for people to feel grateful to her and tell her what a great woman she was, but had yet to find someone who would oblige her.

'I've got an idea,' she suddenly piped up happily. 'We'll hire Afghan nurses. If your women don't want our male doctor to touch them, the nurses will examine them following his instructions. Better something than nothing.'

I had to smile. It might not have been a completely useless idea after all. And she was certainly right about one thing. Better something than nothing. I went back to listening to the woes of Afghan women who had waited for me in the dusty queue, hoping, while I was inside drinking tea, that I would save their child dehydrated by cholera or bring back their husband who had been killed in the war or had lost his mind and wanted to bring home a third hungry wife.

The clinic was Heidi's pride and joy and I had to admit that a mere visit to the little air-conditioned building with running water would be quite an experience for any Afghan woman. Self-importantly, Heidi demonstrated her idea of how the examinations would be conducted. A white screen divided the room into two parts, with a bed and a gynaecological table on one side. 'Don't worry, they've seen these things before,' I reassured her when she expressed concern that Afghan women might be frightened by the equipment. I knew that only a few of them would have seen this kind of thing and those who had would never climb on to this kind of humiliating contraption in the presence of a man.

'That's been taken care of,' she assured me. 'Stand over here,' she pushed me to the end of the gynaecological table. 'Look into that mirror over there.' Then she went over to the other side of the screen and stood in a place marked with white chalk. At that moment her reflection appeared right in the middle of the mirror, behind the imaginary patient who wasn't able to see her, while Heidi couldn't see the examined woman's crotch. Stooping down, she whispered as if someone might hear us. 'Now you're the nurse. And you don't know what to do. OK, look here now.'

I stared at her in the mirror and had no idea what she was up to. She lifted her right hand to her chin, stuck out her index finger and bent it three times in the joint.

'You want me to go over to your side?' I asked, confused.

'Jesus, no. This is a gynaecological warm-up. It's only as-if, we're testing. It will be different with a real doctor and a real nurse. Now we're just checking the clinic's technical set-up,' she continued in a whisper, although there was no need for it.

'Why are you whispering?'

'So that I don't scare the patient. C'mon, get on with it.'

'Get on with what?' I stared into the mirror in disbelief thinking that perhaps I ought to invite the wife of the annoying neighbour from across the street as a neat little revenge.

'Get on with the warm-up,' Heidi raised her voice. I saw Heidi's face contort into a grimace in the mirror as if she were about to do something very important. The stooped posture made her look like a trainee witch. Her hand was still in the same position, the index finger erect and warming up. Then, after slowly opening her bent elbow she swiftly swung her arm forward.

'Thaaat's it,' she gasped.

I repeated her gesture.

'Jesus Christ,' she screamed.

'What is it?'

'You're totally in the wrong place. Near her eye.'

'What eye?'

'You've just gouged out the patient's eye, the vaginal entrance is a lot further down.' I quickly moved my arm downwards to the area where I suspected the patient's crotch might be. 'Now you've really messed up,' Heidi yelled again, having apparently identified with the doctor's role so much she forgot we were just pretending. 'Where on earth have you put the patient's eye now?'

'C'mon, it's only as-if.' Now it was my turn to squeal.

'There's no as-if. We're testing if it's possible to estimate distance and direction by means of the mirror. It's crucial for the examination. You see everything in reverse so we need to check if that's going to be a problem.'

'Heidi, surely they'll be trained nurses, they'll have an idea of what to do, at least a little bit... I'm sure they won't need anyone to show them where to stick their fingers. Our women are the same as yours, I mean they've got those things in the same place.'

'Don't give me that. You've told me yourself that everything is done differently here. They'll have to do as our doctor tells them. C'mon, try again.'

I focused and waved my finger, repeating loudly: 'OK, finger warm-up, here we go. Now slowly forward...' I watched Heidi repeat her gestures in the mirror. Suddenly her face contorted and she started performing bizarre somersaults with her finger. 'Now snoop around the vagina,' she ordered.

'I am snooping, but she's got something in there...'

'Take it out then.'

'Wait, Heidi, a nurse can't do that. Seriously, all a nurse can do is examine a woman but if she can't tell what's wrong, what's the point anyway?'

Logic was beside the point at this moment. Heidi was so excited by the gynaecological clinic it was impossible to talk her out of anything. She bent her knees, bringing her head to the level of the somersaulting finger, opening one eye and staring with the other. I tried to imitate her.

'Excellent,' she praised me. 'Can you see anything?'

'Yes, there's a baby in there,' I declared, gasping to indicate considerable effort.

'OK, now remove your finger,' she commanded.

In a synchronised gesture we both withdrew our fingers from the imaginary woman and sighed with relief. Actually, I could see it wasn't totally pointless. The mirror worked perfectly well and it really was the only way American doctors would be able to examine Afghan women. We were both happy and Heidi gave me a contented pat on the back. Suddenly I felt quite fond of her. That's why I didn't tell her that in my opinion a gynaecologist relied mostly on his sense of touch and the mirror would be useless. He wouldn't be able to see inside anyway and just by observing the nurse... As if reading my thoughts, Heidi suddenly said: 'I know this isn't perfect, a doctor really needs to feel with his hands. But even if the nurses don't understand him fully because they won't have much English, at least they can communicate in gestures.' I had to concede there was something to it.

The waiting room was next door. Heidi had decorated it with pictures of assorted human entrails, but luckily it wouldn't have meant much to an untrained eye. Only one picture was problematic. It must have been originally a school aid. It was a life-sized picture in full colour. It showed a man's body, apparently devoid of skin and interspersed with veins and muscles. Lifting a red flap on his belly revealed his stomach and intestines, with a medium-sized male organ prominent underneath.

'We couldn't find a woman,' Heidi looked at me apologetically. 'But the main thing is that they familiarise themselves with the human anatomy while they sit here waiting.'

'Heidi, this won't do. We'll have to cut this off.'

'C'mon, kids in our schools get to see this in the fourth form,' Heidi clutched her damp, straw-coloured hair and rolled her eyes.

'I know but if we don't, firstly no man will let his wife come here and secondly, the Sharia court will come down on us and we'll all end up in prison.'

'Don't be silly, that's what things were like under the Taliban but surely not now?'

'This is what it was like before the Taliban as well, Heidi. But this,' I said, squeamishly touching the penis reproduced in graphic detail, 'this can't stay here as it is.'

This made Heidi very unhappy indeed. She had tears in her eyes. 'But we have to educate the women a little. Bit by bit. Do you really want to live like this forever?' she exclaimed, throwing her arms up in despair. 'In this... stupid way?'

She couldn't think of a better word.

I went back to the surgery and found some cotton wool and bandages on the shelf, and returned to Heidi, who was still staring at the loins, weeping openly. I scrunched up a bit of cotton wool and wrapped some bandage around it.

'Do we have any glue here?'

'No,' she hiccuped. 'Just plasters.'

I found the plasters in the drawer below the bandages. I formed a shape roughly corresponding to the size of the penis, stuck it on and cheerfully said to Heidi: 'Look, this will be perfect. We can take it off once they've got used to it. I'm sure you'll live to see the day.'

Heidi wiped her tears away and helped me cover the penis with the plasters. We stepped back to inspect our work. It was much more appropriate for a surgery than it had been before.

'It looks as if he's been bitten by a camel,' she said earnestly.

'You see,' I said, trying to sound reassuring. 'It's got educational value as well.'

Leaving the picture with the bandaged sexual organ behind, we went for a cup of tea. As I was about to go home that night I heard Dominic asking with undisguised curiosity: 'What's that supposed to be, a warning for people not to sit on landmines?'

'You're an idiot,' she said with an experienced air. 'Don't you know that Afghan women couldn't stand the sight of something like that? And quite right they are.'

chapter 17

HEIDI LOVED THE DOG. She had found it in the dusty street about a hundred metres from the entrance to our women's centre. The dog was revolting and extremely dirty. Heidi brought it into the office and set it down next to the printer. Dominic peeled his eyes off the screen and beamed: 'Oh, the little darling, a little puppy, what a sweetie-pie...' he said in a voice grandmothers adopt when they're intent on spoiling their first grandchild. Lisping and narrowing his eyes in bliss he stroked the head of the animal that must have carried all sorts of diseases and been infested with fleas and other parasites; he scratched the dog's belly thrusting his face right into the animal's snout, making the poor creature tremble with fear. Heidi bounced around the room looking for something.

'We'll make a kennel out of a carton. Nazir, can you get dog granules and artificial sand for dog excrement in Kabul?'

My husband, who was standing right behind me, completely forgot that we had actually come in to ask whether I could leave early tonight. Since Roshangol's disappearance the problems in our family had got to the stage where we could never be sure what we would find when we came home from work.

'What granules?' my husband asked, observing Dominic's frolicking with the dog in disgust.

'It's a special kind of food supplement for dogs, it contains vitamins and all the nutrients necessary for a dog's healthy development,' Heidi now joined Dominic and they were trying to outdo each other petting the animal.

'I don't think you can get this kind of thing here. Dogs are not kept as pets in this country. Only some people keep them for dog fighting.'

My husband was right. In my early days in Kabul, when I felt lonely and alienated, I had wanted to get myself a dog. Carefully choosing his words to be sure I would understand, Grandpa gently explained to me that dogs had no place in the home, except perhaps in their capacity as bloodthirsty guard dogs or as a source of income, provided they were good at dog fights, which were very popular in Afghanistan. 'The Prophet Muhammad divided all animals into two categories, those that are clean and those that are dirty,' Grandpa held forth in a tone I was very fond of as it sounded less like a lecture or a fanatical sermon and more like a fairy tale. 'That's why we cherish the camel, the horse, the goat, the sheep and especially the cat. Muhammad adored cats,' Grandpa said, looking around as if the story he was about to tell me might have been slightly inappropriate for a man of the Prophet's stature. 'Once, as he meditated, a cat fell asleep in his lap. It made itself comfortable on his coat but he had to get up. It may have been a call of nature, who knows, the records don't say why he had to get up at that very moment. So rather than waking up his beloved animal he got a knife and cut out a piece of the material from his coat. He simply cut off the part on which the cat was lying, leaving it to rest there. That's how fond the Prophet was of cats.' Grandpa paused again, this time for a long time and then he leaned towards me, so close he was almost touching me, and whispered: 'Except that I can't stand cats, I prefer dogs, big, sturdy ones. Unfortunately, Muhammad has classified them as unclean animals along with snakes, rats, fleas and pigs. I'm not keen on the rest either, but I do love dogs.'

I told him that when I had lived in a block of flats in Russia we had a cocker spaniel and as time went by my Mum preferred the dog's company under her blanket to my Dad's. Grandpa laughed so much he had tears in his eyes and his chin shook, making me worry that he might injure himself. So I made sure to keep the rest of the story to myself and never told him how Misha the cocker spaniel got so cheeky Mum could no longer watch TV after 10.00 at night because he wanted to go to sleep and hated being in bed without her. My friends' parents liked to tell jokes about my Mum's relationship with the dog while I had never thought there was anything wrong with this close bond, which would have been regarded as depraved here in Afghanistan.

This is why my new family wouldn't let me have a dog. However, my husband really cared about my happiness and one day he got me two rabbits. I called them Gargosh and Margosh, a garbled version of the word for 'rabbit' in Dari and fell in love with them just like my Mum had with her cocker spaniel. Except that I wasn't allowed to bring my pets into the house, especially after they had found their way into the hall and chewed up Father's brand new pair of shoes. I argued that they had picked the shoddiest pair, made entirely of plastic and lined with spaghetti insulation, so it wasn't such a big deal. To no avail. My rabbits got locked in a windowless crate and I was allowed to let them out to graze for only a few minutes each day. I knew it would drive the animals crazy. I talked my husband into constructing a cage I could place on the half-dried out clumps of grass that were getting increasingly rare as the drought was taking hold, so that we could enjoy the sight of the rabbits and they would enjoy being in the fresh air. The problem was that they would demolish a square of grass within a few minutes, leaving only clay and dust. They nibbled up the roots as well, thus increasing the number of barren spots in our garden and threatening to turn it into a desert. Everyone was too busy to move the cage around the garden at regular intervals to ensure uniform grazing. Admittedly, I also tended to forget about them, sometimes leaving them in the same spot for several days. Qais suggested we eat them and I knew the only person who could save them was Grandpa. He had a fantastic knack for inventing totally unnecessary things, and this time he came up with something quite brilliant. He spent a whole night redesigning the cage and refusing to see anyone. He even missed his afternoon nap, which suggested he was completely absorbed in this activity. He demonstrated his innovation to the whole family just before sunset and his response to the Mullah's call to prayer was: 'It'll have to wait a bit tonight...'

We all congregated in the courtyard – Mother and Father, my husband, Freshta, Qais and all the children that had been born by then. The cage had been solemnly covered by a piece of cloth, formerly Mother's skirt, now used for wiping down the patio. The object under the cloth seemed strangely aquiver as if it weren't a piece of inanimate metal but a bag of fleas.

'Abusing animals is a godless act,' Grandpa proclaimed grandly. 'Torturing dumb critters is *haraam*.' Then he gave me a pointed look as he had recently enlightened me on the meaning of *haraam* and expected me to show off my knowledge in public.

'Acts not allowed by Islamic law, in other words, prohibited and therefore punishable,' I intentionally recited in a child-like voice, like a schoolgirl who had crammed her lessons.

'Correct,' Grandpa said. 'That is why I've devoted so much time to the welfare of rabbits who happened to end up in our house. I've chosen the more merciful alternative. We could have swiftly cut their throats with a sharp knife to spare them the suffering and could have turned their flesh into a tasty meal. Since, however, we have acquired them for the pleasure of our children and our daughter-in-law, I've decided to make their life easier by means of this extraordinary invention, which is bound to meet with wide acclaim in the neighbourhood.'

Most of those assembled listened with a deadly serious look and only I, having not yet fully penetrated the mysteries of our family's customs, alternated between smiling and enthusiastic nodding to make sure I didn't put a foot wrong. Grandpa paused. The children kept mute too, thrilled like everyone else. Eventually Grandpa pulled off the cloth with a stick he had specially prepared for the occasion, revealing a sight that stayed etched in my memory for a long time as a symbol of the exceptional Afghan ability to invent things beyond belief. The cage contained our two rabbits, Margosh and Gargosh. I was quite certain their popping eyes were staring at Grandpa. Both wore some kind of leather collar around their necks, with two little sticks protruding on the sides that reached all the way to their bottoms. One end of each stick was attached to the collar and the other to a kind of thimble that had been pulled on to their tiny tails, giving the tails an unnaturally erect and apparently swollen look. The contraption continued from the tails to their hind legs. Here Grandpa used a different kind of material – medium-thick wires, which led out of the tails, tightly enclosing the rabbits' thighs to ensure the thimbles wouldn't come off the tails, or the wires off the legs. However, the key part of the harness was connected to the narrower part of the cage. It was a leather strap, reinforced with thin wire so that it would allow movement but only in one direction – forward – in order to prevent the animals from becoming totally entangled in the jumble of wires and strangling themselves. The harness was attached to the cage, turning the animals and their barred dwelling into a seamless, solidly connected mechanism. Naturally, the cage itself had also undergone significant modifications. A wheel had been affixed to each of its corners. Since Grandpa couldn't find four wheels of the same size, three had come from an old cart Father used to transport large loads from the market, while Grandpa must have found the fourth one somewhere else, as it was all bent and broken.

Proud as a peacock, Grandpa took a deep breath and began to demonstrate the functioning of the apparatus with the help of the stick he had used to pull off the cloth.

'See the rabbits grazing peacefully, here?'

'Yes!' the children exclaimed, amazed and surprised that Grandpa, who usually spent most of his time sleeping, was up to such an achievement.

'Once a rabbit has grazed down the whole area where it was located, it won't feel like rooting in the dried ground and looking for roots. On the contrary, it will spot another clump of grass a few metres away. Without this invention it would have to resign itself to watching its food longingly and waiting until one of you deems to move it. This way the animals can move towards fresh food independently, without human assistance. Let me demonstrate.'

Grandpa got hold of the cage with both hands and rolled it on to a concrete section of the patio. The desperately writhing rabbits were dragged on to the red hot path along with the cage. Strangely enough, they didn't get strangled or entangled in the leather straps.

'You think I hadn't tested it properly? Do you know how many times they slipped out, how many times they ended up hanging by their tails, and how many times they got out of the collar?' Grandpa gasped proudly, completely exhausted by moving the cage.

'Right, and now watch how the rabbits will react,' he exclaimed. He produced a creased and slightly wilted cabbage leaf from his trouser pocket and held it close to the front of the cage, to which the rabbits' heads pointed willy-nilly. They must have been very hungry; perhaps Grandpa had forgotten to feed them regularly while he worked on his creation or maybe he had specially starved them to show them off. He pushed the cabbage right up to the cage but in such a way that the animals couldn't munch it up from the inside. The leather straps were too short anyway, not allowing them to touch the cage walls. Seeing the tasty morsel they wiggled their little snouts and set out. The harnesses tightened, the cage shook and even though the whole thing looked quite horrific and nobody believed it could possibly work, after some effort on the rabbits' part the whole monstrosity started to move. The rabbits basically pulled their little house in the direction where they sensed food.

'Unfortunately, I couldn't figure out how to make them turn independently. I'll have to give it some more thought. But if we make them face in the direction where there is a sufficiently long strip of green, we won't have to worry about them for a few days. The great advantage is that we can leave them outside the house as well. They won't be able to run far on their own, unless somebody steals them.'

None of us said a word. I think our men had been ready to tell Grandpa off for wasting his time on this nonsense but seeing that the rabbits actually managed to pull their cage and were trying to get to a sufficiently green area, they were left dumbstruck.

From that day the wandering cage with Gargosh and Margosh became a fixture in our garden. Unfortunately, with time they learned to trudge across the green strip of grass all the way to the garden beds where Mother grew lettuces and tomatoes, making it their favourite spot. For quite a while the mobile cage was the centre of attention of all the children in our street, who regarded it as the best toy, frenziedly fighting for it and carrying it outside the limits of our house to subject it to various experiments. The rabbits even got used to the boys lifting the cage and leaving them suspended in their harnesses like skydivers in a parachute, their extremities spread out, with the little wisps of their tails sticking out of the ring looking like a gear stick. The children would run around with the rabbits swaying in the wind, frozen rigid, as if they had realised that jerking around would just entangle them in the straps, constricting them even further. The boys would leave the rabbits in the middle of a dusty road and bet on how long it would take them to reach a grass patch. The animals usually needed a few minutes to rest and recover, leaving plenty of time for betting.

If it hadn't been for Uncle Amin the rabbits would be providing entertainment for successive generations of children to this day. One day Amin stormed in, excited and impetuous as usual, to inform us of something important most of us had known for a long time. He rushed into the courtyard, stopping in front of the patio. He didn't notice the rabbit cage until the rabbits approached him from behind, as he waited for Father to come out to welcome him, lost in thought. By then the rabbits had mastered their peregrinations with their little house to a degree that allowed them to move with considerable speed, and they bumped right into poor Amin's leg. Glancing in their direction and spotting two hairy balls entangled in a harness in their mobile cage he screamed an obscenity and, horrified at being assailed by an unknown form of life, kicked the entire assemblage toward the house with all his force. And although the rabbits survived his assault without too much harm, complete with their cage and harnesses, the events that followed spelled their demise. Uncle Amin, fascinated by Father's demonstration of the contraption, took Gargosh and Margosh with their cage outside the gate to test how far they would get, leaving them in the road when Mother invited him to come in for tea and almonds, something he was particularly partial to. He was interrupted from his munching reverie by the screeching of brakes and loud swearing. Instead of running out to see the damage he had caused he just drew his head between his shoulders pretending he hadn't heard anything. Kamal rushed out into the street, soon returning with tears in his eyes, carrying two little bodies, one squashed and its entrails spilling out, the other slightly better preserved, its hind legs gently twitching inside the harness. This was the first time we heard either rabbit make a sound. Until now both of them had maintained a stubborn silence. But now, to everyone's astonishment, short, delicate and rather high-pitched noises of desperation emanated from the little snout of the shattered creature with a broken spine and crushed pelvis. I realised we had to find a quick way of putting the animal out of its misery. Calmly approaching my nephew, I took the dying creature out of his hands, grabbed it by the legs and with a mighty swing of my arms smashed it against the floor. There was a crunch, then the strange voice sounded again, this time more powerful and piercing. Blood and mucus spurted from its snout and it was all over. 'Kamaz has run them over,' Kamal sobbed without commenting on my heroic deed.

'They've covered quite a distance!' Amin exclaimed, his mouth full of almonds. That's when I decided he was really a rude idiot. In the evening when, drowning in tears, I told my husband what had happened, he said: 'Do you know the Russians killed Amin's son? He was only four months old. Amin's wife had taken him to Charikar to visit relatives. A bomb dropped on their house. She survived but the child didn't. And Amin's brother died in prison under the Taliban. He was tortured to death. We heard they had cut off a finger each day to make him confess the location of secret arms caches in the Shamal plain, to tell them which member of the family was in Masoud's army. If he had squealed it would have been the end of our whole family. After his seventh finger was cut off he chose to die instead. But I am really sorry about the rabbits.'

Heidi and Dominic named the dog Reagan. When they chose the name they laughed like mad and refused to tell us if it was meant as an act of revenge or a tribute to American statehood.

'Dogs shouldn't be given human names, even if they're names of stupid politicians,' my husband said to me. 'And animals shouldn't eat out of the same dishes as people, even if they've been cleaned.'

Nevertheless, Heidi insisted on letting the dog eat at the table with everyone else, giggling aloud whenever it went after our plates with all its four legs. She bought it vitamin-enriched cat granules (since dog granules were not available in Kabul), at fifty dollars a packet, and couldn't understand why the beggars lining the street outside the only supermarket in town gave her nasty looks.

'You don't like dogs because you believe they barked when Muhammad fled from Mecca to Medina,' she once declared seeing my husband's disgust as he ostentatiously reached out for a new spoon after Reagan greedily sniffed at the one he'd been using. 'And that gave him away,' she added, putting the dog on the floor to show she respected foreign customs.

'Nonsense,' my husband replied. 'While he lived in Medina, Muhammad had decreed that all street mutts should be put to death because they scattered rubbish about and spread diseases. But he really loved cats, he even cut his shirt for one.'

'That's at least something,' Heidi retorted, mortally offending my husband.

Although she meant no offence and tried to be friendly and helpful, she was oblivious of the fact that behind her back the locals were spreading lewd stories about her.

'Did you know that Muhammad drank wine?' she asked me during one of our private conversations on subjects not suited for Afghan ears.

'Who?' I said, missing the context. We were sitting outside the office sorting index cards with information on women who had visited the centre that day. I was putting those for whom we would try to find a job or a place on a programme to one side, while the other, smaller pile consisted of those we had referred to our clinic for an examination.

'Muhammad, of course.' Heidi recently boasted that she had bought the *Short Encyclopaedia of Islam*, and worked hard at studying it before going to sleep.

'When the men of Medina started turning up drunk for prayers, he got angry and cracked down on you...'

'Not on us,' I objected defiantly. I couldn't believe Heidi still had me pigeonholed as a Muslim, forgetting my background, although I had explained it to her a hundred times. 'And it wasn't a total crackdown either. You should forget your encyclopaedia and read the Quran. It's actually rather nice poetry,' I advised her. It was just as well my husband didn't hear me. He couldn't stand it when I referred to the holy book in such degrading terms.

'I find it boring. It's incredibly long-winded, you have to slog through dozens of pages to extract one bit of information. What I need is a summary.'

'You'll never understand anything from a summary,' I sighed but I knew what she meant. I could never relate to this marvellous book quite the same way our Grandpa and my husband, or his Father and Mother did. Sometimes I infuriated them by unwittingly leaving the Quran in some unsuitable place. Once it got mixed up with a pile of books that I had brought from Russia and used to prop up a trunk that was falling over. It led to a major row and I was forgiven only because I was regarded as dim-witted but nice.

'Want one?' Heidi produced her favourite clove cigarettes and offered me one. She smiled at my hesitation: 'The door's locked, Nazir has to knock, you'll have plenty of time to throw it away.'

'I don't like those.' I said.

'All right, what about a Marlboro?' She pulled out another box. I took one expecting to feel guilty. But I didn't feel the slightest pang of conscience, let alone guilt.

'Yesterday I was groped again in Shahr-e Now Park. Just imagine, a boy leapt on me from behind and grabbed me between the legs. Even though Zulgay was walking right behind me. Before he had time to react the boy was gone. Then a whole wild bunch of kids laughed at us from further away, shouting something.'

'I see,' I said absently, enjoying my cigarette.

'I wonder what it is they say when they see a white woman?'

'Instead of reading instruction manuals on Islam you ought to learn a few key words. Like *kos*... if that's what you heard, they probably shouted: "Show us your cunt".'

'*Kos* means cunt?' Heidi asked in surprise, raising her eyebrows. 'I think they did shout something like that. And Zulgay couldn't stop chuckling.'

'If you really must go for a walk in the park, you should go to the Gardens of Babur. They have guards there and Afghans are not allowed in when foreigners are strolling around,' I suggested, remembering how angry I was when I first heard about these weird customs being introduced in Kabul. This country that has always been so wary of foreigners, where even under a king who modernised left, right and centre and pursued European women, where foreigners have never been allowed to hold major positions or set up their own businesses, now boasted places where guards segregated the locals from white people. White people, of course, had unlimited access to almost anywhere, unlike the darkies.

'And not far from the centre there's a park only for women. They take their children there for walks. Nobody will call you a cunt there. But then again, you can't bring a male escort...'

'Oh, it's all far too complicated. I just refuse to go to a park and be abused by little brats. And I refuse to buy ice cream that might give me the runs or cholera,' Heidi said resolutely, apparently closing this chapter of her stay in Afghanistan. She had initially refused to obey the instructions that forbade her from leaving the organisation's headquarters on her own. Later she realised they had a point. Eventually she stopped going out altogether. She would only ride in a car with darkened windows and whenever she spotted a bunch of ragged children she would toss them a handful of sweets. I found it irritating but I knew she used to get out of the car, stroke the cute little olive-skinned boys on their heads and press a piece of chocolate into their little hands with a sweet smile. Until one of them shoved his hand between her buttocks, another one shouted '*baksheesh* please' and a third one screamed, to the delight of people far and wide: 'I'll eat your cunt for ten dollars.' After that she stayed in the car. Heidi and my husband seemed to have undergone a strange transformation around the same time. Both had withdrawn into their cocoons as if they had both been through an experience that had touched their innermost selves, forever altering their original propensity for openness and kindness.

I spent hours arguing with Dominic against the new rule banning my husband from entering the office without explicit permission. Afghan visitors had always had to undergo a body search at the gates, there was even a special booth for women, where our colleague Rahima would thoroughly pat down every female visitor. But the ban on entering the building was quite new.

I reproached Dominic for not treating foreigners from other organisations in the same way, for example international peacekeepers, some of whom would drop by for a cup of tea, or diplomats from various embassies who would come for a visit or just drop by. The Indian consul, who had come to discuss a prosthetics factory project, had been stripped almost naked because of his darker colour and instead of talking about the project Dominic had to spend an hour explaining this awkward misunderstanding. I have no doubt that our bodyguards could easily tell an Indian from an Afghan and suspect they had stripped him down to his underwear on purpose.

Then one day my husband and I were sent to the Bagram base where US soldiers were ensconced behind several walls and barbed wire. Surrounded by new minefields meant to deter would-be saboteurs from getting anywhere near them, the soldiers – at least the bomber pilots among them – knew Afghanistan only from the air. The weather was nice and my husband and I were having a great time. For once we were on our own again, albeit in a car, but alone nevertheless, and could chat about all sorts of things without constant interruptions from various people, mostly Mother. Every now and then my husband gently touched my knee and laughed like a child, pretending he had confused it with the gear stick.

'Fits my hand perfectly,' he said kneading my knee and licking his lips sensuously. I laughed too, happy that all we had to do in Bagram was pick up a package a friend of Heidi's had brought back from the US, and could then drive back slowly and at leisure, dragging out the trip to fill the rest of the working day.

The last time my husband had been to Bagram was when his unit was stationed there. The former Soviet air base had passed from hand to hand during the war with the Taliban and major battles for the airfield runways had transformed it into something resembling gardens dug up by giant moles. Because of its strategic position, considerable size and isolated position, as soon as the area to the northwest of Kabul was cleared of the Taliban, the Americans chose it as their main military base immediately after arriving in the country. Looking around we both noticed how much everything had changed. The access roads were covered with fresh tarmac and the closer we got to the base the more frequent the checkpoints became. The first one was manned by grinning members of the new Afghan army, recruited mainly from the less successful soldiers of motley units commanded by local Afghan warlords. The officer corps was comprised of men who had been trained as part of an education programme in the Soviet Union. Few of them spoke English although Russian commands were quite commonly heard in the exercise grounds. My husband had nothing but contempt for the new 'American lackeys' as he called them. 'Afghans who served in foreign armies have always come to a sticky end,' he declared. He was irate when he learned that our leader Karzai had surrounded himself with American bodyguards. 'What sort of a head of state is he to be guarded by members of an occupying army,' he shouted at Father, who would just shrug off 'insignificant' matters such as this. Afghan soldiers in brand-new uniforms greeted my husband with great respect. He got out of the car as required, hugged the checkpoint commander, smiled and enquired about his health and his children. They had fought together against the Taliban at Kunduz.

'He was a bit of a coward,' my husband remarked when he got back to the car. The next checkpoint was mixed. Afghans were standing outside on the road but the freshly whitewashed booth was manned by two hefty Americans with huge quantities of grenades around their waists and long knives behind their belts, as if they had just leapt out of a TV screen. They didn't greet us, and without even lifting their rears from their chairs they shouted instructions to their Afghan subordinates in English. They were obviously convinced we couldn't understand them.

'Make him get out of the car,' a blond man in dark sunglasses said. My husband gritted his teeth and I was petrified at the thought of what he might do if they continued in this vein. I pushed back my headscarf, revealing my blond fringe and turning to face them so they couldn't fail to spot my white Slavic face.

'Hello, Ma'am,' they called out, clocking me straight away. 'Where are you from?' The other, ginger-haired soldier actually stood up and took a few steps towards our car. I gave them the name of our organisation in my best English. My husband left the car, approaching the soldier from the side.

'Don't move,' the soldier shouted. 'Stay right where you are, by your car.' Afghan soldiers leapt towards my husband, explaining something very respectfully in a whisper. He cursed in his native tongue, calling the Americans sons-of-bitches and bastards. They didn't understand a word and I was tempted to suggest they learn some of the key words in Dari, as I had suggested to Heidi.

'You can go on, Madam. Is someone expecting you?' the ginger-haired one asked.

'Yes, we're expected, of course,' I replied, mentioning the name of Heidi's friend. The two men smiled and waved at me. My husband climbed back into the car, paler than I was.

'You do that again and you may as well move in with them,' he said through gritted teeth. He was livid.

'They don't know you're my husband. They think you're the driver and I'm a foreigner...'

'So what? Who's at home here, you people or me?' This was the first time my husband counted me among 'you people'. Many years ago he and his family had thought of me as someone who belonged to an alien camp whose members were basically 'others or worse'. But gradually, partly due to my complete isolation, I managed to blend in with the Afghans, making the distinction between us and them redundant. This was the first time in years the dividing line had surfaced again, and it frightened me.

'They're scared of terrorists, you know that... but who cares about them, just forget them,' I tried to bring back a semblance of the happy mood that had reigned in the car only minutes earlier.

'You're behaving like a slut,' he screamed all of a sudden and if the windows hadn't been rolled down his voice would surely have shattered them. 'You smile at them and use your body and your mug, just to gain an advantage...'

'C'mon, darling, what are you talking about?' I pleaded, horrified. 'I just wanted to make sure they let us pass...'

'I see. So if they told you to show them your naked bum to let you pass, you'd do that? Like all the women in your country?

The ones who sleep with their teachers to pass an exam? You're prepared to take off your headscarf and flash them a seductive smile just to make sure we can pass?' His screaming was quite horrendous by now.

'No, of course not, you know you're talking nonsense now. I'm not like that... I didn't smile seductively.'

'I don't know what you're like anymore,' he said, suddenly calmer. 'You've changed since they've arrived.' He stepped on the accelerator making the car jump up and down on the smooth road and deliberately veering on to the bumpy shoulder. I was quite sure that he smiled with satisfaction every time I bumped my head on the ceiling. He had also changed since they arrived.

The main checkpoint was manned only by Americans. A few Afghans stood around but they were assigned lowly tasks such as carrying water. One was painting the barrier while another held the bucket, looking around listlessly. When we stopped, a well-built black man stepped to my side of the car. He saluted and asked: 'Who have you come to see, Madam?'

I knew this was the end and my husband would do something rash. I told him the name of the female officer and when the man left to make a phone call I turned to my husband with a plaintive look.

'Let's just get this over with and get out of here as soon as we can. What am I supposed do? Heidi will go mental if we don't bring her package. It's not my fault they're like this.'

My husband sat staring at the gate without a word. I had never seen him so desperate and furious at once. The black soldier returned and, without deeming the man behind the wheel worthy of a glance, politely explained to me that the car and the driver had to stay behind, while I would be driven to my destination in one of their nice cars. After inspecting my humanitarian organisation pass he returned it with an apologetic shrug. 'Nothing doing, those are the regulations.'

'You're not going anywhere without me,' my husband hissed and he meant it. 'Tell him you can't go in without me.'

'Mister, please, I've got my own regulations to follow and I'm not allowed to go anywhere without my escort. He's got the same papers as me...'

The black soldier didn't let me finish and shook his head resolutely.

'That's out of the question, Madam. Your escort would need a special permit to enter a military installation.'

I was waiting for my husband to blurt out something in English, to give them hell, call them occupying swine, then back the car out in fury, spraying everyone with dust and speeding away before we could complete our assignment. But he just sat there paralysed, squeezing the steering wheel so tight his knuckles went white.

'So will you let me go? Nazir, please, we mustn't cause a scandal here, I know it's terrible but what else can I do?' I said, perhaps even more desperate than my husband. The black soldier was waiting.

'You move and I'll kill you,' my husband said. I was on the verge of tears. He'd never done this before.

'I'll tell him you're my husband...'

'Shut up,' he snapped. 'Get out, you slutty bitch and make sure you come back quickly so I can break every bone in your body,' he said, speaking so loudly that the man painting the barrier turned around this time. He gave us a surprised look, smiling inanely. I felt sick with helplessness. Lately I'd been feeling this way more and more frequently. The sense of despair and helplessness made me nauseous. Perhaps it might help if I were actually sick, I thought. If I could only be sick all over the black officer and collapse, it would be obvious I had no other way out of the tricky situation. But however nauseous I felt I couldn't actually will myself to be sick. We could see muscular American soldiers running in circles around an area with freshly planted trees, stripped down to their boxer shorts in the heat. A dark-haired woman in uniform with short trousers was talking to a colleague, laughing so much she bent double. Suddenly my husband leaned over, reaching across me to my door, jerked the handle open and gave me a rough prod in the side that sent me stumbling out of the car like a bag of rice and badly scraping my knee. The American gaped at me and then did something that made my situation even worse. Bounding over to me, he offered me his hand and helped me get up.

'Are you all right?'

'I'm OK,' I smiled because I couldn't think of any other expression at that moment. I was too scared to turn around but heard my husband start the engine. He turned the car around sharply, kicking up dust.

'Your driver seems to be on edge,' the soldier remarked politely. 'Shouldn't we arrest him?' he asked professionally.

'No!' I screamed. My response must have surprised him. He shrugged with a shy smile. I imagined him regaling his friends later that night with this story. I wanted to explain to the black soldier that it was my edgy driver who was at home in this country, that he had been stationed at this base before any American ever set foot here, and that he wasn't really my driver at all but my beloved husband. But I didn't manage to say a word and just stared doggedly ahead so that I wouldn't have to blush meeting the glances of people who had witnessed a white woman being kicked out of a car by her driver like a stray dog. But nobody at the base paid me any attention. Once I was certain I was out of the sight of my husband, who had parked the car with its back to the gate and stood ostentatiously as far away from the entrance as possible, I took off my headscarf. Nobody leered at me. Nobody shouted 'Let me eat your fat cunt', nobody threw stones at me. It didn't take long to find Heidi's friend. The place teemed with air-conditioned army tents, Afghans sweeping the paths and soldiers smoking and playing football. It was a different world, which somehow reminded me of my old life in Moscow, perhaps because everyone seemed so relaxed and behaved so naturally. The package was large and heavy. Heidi's girlfriend showered me with kisses but didn't offer me any tea or water. I suppose they kept count of everything and their spreadsheets didn't include a column for visitors. With an ulterior motive I asked her to walk back with me. I hoped that seeing a woman by my side would calm my husband down a bit. But I couldn't tell her that, I knew she just wouldn't understand. She couldn't accompany me to the gate. She didn't have permission, so instead she assigned me a very young soldier and a car to drop me off outside the main entrance, as they weren't authorised to leave the gate. In spite of the size and weight of the package I almost ran all the way back. I could see my husband in the distance and was grateful that he had waited for me. Indescribable terror constricted my stomach. The black soldier offered me his hand again and I couldn't refuse. If my husband had seen the gesture, I knew I would be lost. You coward, I said to myself, you've shaken hands with the man, you have to pull yourself together now. Glancing at the package the soldier said, 'I'll get one of the locals to cycle over to your car and tell that moron of yours to come and get you... so you don't have to haul it yourself.'

'Don't worry,' I said in an unnaturally high-pitched voice, because in addition to my clenched stomach my throat had gone really tight. 'I'll dash over... I need to stretch my legs anyway after the long drive.' The cord around the package was cutting into the palm of my hand and I was leaning to one side under the weight of the box. I could hardly walk and running was completely out of the question. I started nevertheless, gathering all my strength to take off, pretending I was full of energy. I moved in leaps and hops that must have looked like anything but a graceful gallop as I gasped and swayed from side to side like a wounded duck. The black soldier must have followed me with fascination, but I never looked back. The engine started before I reached the car. My husband was watching my advance in the rear mirror. He must have seen me shake hands with the black soldier. I climbed into the front seat, put the package in my lap and attempted a smile. I was covered in sweat and gasping for air, and my heart was pounding so violently I expected to have a heart attack any minute. My husband didn't even look at me. Suddenly he made a strange gesture and I felt a burning pain in my left cheek. My mouth filled with the sweetish taste of blood. Then everything went black and I was finally sick. My husband started driving and said, suddenly sounding quite cheerful: 'You slut, you took your headscarf off in front of them, as if you were one of them. You whore, you.' He didn't say another word all the way back to Kabul.

Heidi bathed Reagan in the most expensive shampoos and allowed the dog to share her bed, whenever Dominic wasn't sharing it with her. Once I plucked up the courage to ask if she was planning to marry Dominic. She tilted her head back and laughed as heartily as I'd never seen her laugh before. 'C'mon, he's got a wife and two kids. This isn't serious. It's just a kind of holiday romance.' I was outraged. Not because Dominic and Heidi were having fun from time to time but because she talked about it with such a disdainful detachment. Had she cried her heart out to me about her beloved Dominic being married and threatened to hang herself I would have understood and wished her many hot and passionate Afghan nights. It would have been very romantic but this way it was just a rather crass story. I thought back on my university days, when all my girlfriends gradually worked their way through every decent male student on our course, and even though I myself had succumbed to the school beau after two days of wooing, looking back now it all seemed extremely immoral to me. And the week I had spent in bed with Andrei (the young man who, as I later discovered, had simultaneously enjoyed two other girls from the year below) now struck me as equally indecent. I had come to regret it later although I knew my friend Nadia would have laughed at me. After all, she didn't need to be a virgin in order to get married.

Reagan was sniffing piles of paper covered with names and case and family histories of the women who came to us seeking charity. For some reason the dog loved the smell of paper. I relished inhaling cigarette smoke, feeling free and superior to all the wretched Afghan women who could only light up a hashish cigarette at thoroughly conspiratorial all-female get-togethers once they reached an age so advanced they were beyond criticism.

'Tomorrow I'll be spending the day between the centre and the clinic. If the doctor needs anything more complicated to be translated you'll have to assist him.' Heidi was enjoying her work more and more by the day and I, too, had to admit we were beginning to offer a tiny bit of relief and assistance to the women who flocked to us. It certainly made a difference to those who had no money for medication and medical treatment in hospitals where nobody would even say '*salam alaikum*' to them for free.

A car stopped in front of the gate. I recognised the sound of our engine and shoved the cigarette into Heidi's hand. She ended up holding both her own horrible aromatic one and my half-finished Marlboro. Infected by my panic, she stubbed out both of them and stuck some peppermint chewing gum into my hand. I started to rummage through papers, rolling the gum around my mouth frantically. My husband entered the courtyard. In front of the door to the office he was stopped by a scrawny guard who blushed in embarrassment and apologised a thousand times for having to ask us women for permission to let him in, something that had already brought about several sharp exchanges between Dominic and my husband. Heidi cheerfully waved to the bodyguard, suggesting everything was all right.

'Hi, Nazir,' she called theatrically. 'How are you?'

'Not bad,' he said, eyeing me with suspicion. I have no idea how, but he always knew if I'd been up to something. However, since he suspected me of being up to mischief even when I behaved impeccably, I decided eventually I might as well stop being so docile. A row was inevitable either way.

'And how are you?' he asked Heidi, since he didn't want her and Dominic to know that some of their exploits were driving him insane.

'I'm good. Herra is brilliant, everything's working really well. We've got hundreds of clients, some will soon start on an education programme and the clinic is beginning to work, too.'

'You're really smart,' my husband said. 'Can Herra go now? We're having a family celebration tonight,' he lied.

'No problem, I can finish off here by myself and if there's anything I can't cope with it can wait until tomorrow. We'll need at least a week to do the filing.' Heidi got up, only now offering my husband her hand. Then she gave him a friendly pat on the shoulder. 'You've been putting on weight, my friend, you have to watch it. European women like skinny men.' My husband laughed. The way he horsed around with Heidi I sometimes thought that if I hadn't been around their innocent exchanges might easily have developed into sexual flirtation. Once, when I tried to deflect his unfounded accusations of flirting with my foreign colleagues by pointing out how he comported himself with Heidi, he just said: 'You're crazy. Do you think I could ever be interested in that disgusting woman? I'm only doing it for your sake, to make your life easier at work.'

I covered myself in a scarf and stroked the dog.

'See you tomorrow,' I waved to Heidi, already halfway to the gate. She was standing on the patio with arms akimbo and I'm pretty sure she was looking at my husband with lust, flames of true female jealousy flickering in her eyes.

Once we were inside the car, my husband suddenly took my hand and brought it close to his face. It flashed through my mind that he was about to kiss my hand and I stiffened in surprise. That had never happened before, not even in Moscow when he had wooed me in a totally un-Afghan way, bringing my mother flowers. But he grabbed my fingers instead, bringing them close to his nose so that they nearly blocked his nostrils, and inhaled.

'Were you smoking?' he said in his scariest voice.

'No, of course not, I can't stand it...'

'You're lying. You've become pretty good at lying! How can I be sure you don't spend all day in there having sex, if you won't even admit that you were smoking...'

'I just passed the cigarette to Heidi a couple of times, she's been smoking like a chimney lately... she asked me to stub it out for her, the ashtray was too far away.'

'What do you think you are doing, Herra,' he howled like someone possessed. 'I don't even want to look at you, you dirty lying bitch.'

chapter 18

I HAVEN'T BEEN BLESSED with an ear for music or any technical aptitude whatsoever. When my Mum first made me sit at a piano, aged seven, my head began to throb and I found the alternating black and white keys boring, too rational and aesthetically unappealing. At university I mastered the art of typing but never got beyond using three fingers. And although we did have a little typewriter at home in Kabul, nobody apart from Grandpa and Father could use it, not least because the machine, made in Iran, looked as if it had been manufactured by the same company that produced the constantly exploding pressure cookers.

'You'll have to start doing your filing on the computer,' Heidi said one day. Until then I had always watched in awe as Heidi's and Dominic's fingers struck the keyboard at an astonishing speed and then as a piece of paper would emerge from a gently humming printer, everything neatly sorted and typed up with the key bits of information highlighted in bold. I was enraptured by the neat tables and regarded the astounding regularity and orderliness as the machine's greatest asset.

'You can have lots more drawers and pigeon-holes and an endless number of files on a computer... many more than you can keep on your desk,' said Heidi who soon discovered that I enjoyed recording all kinds of information and sorting it into various categories. Over the past few weeks I had developed a perfect colour-coding system for our visitors. The ones totally dependent on aid and incapable of managing on their own were assigned the colour red, while those marked in yellow, though not capable of managing on their own as they had lost the family breadwinner, may have had a fifteen-year-old son or lived with relatives. The white ones were widows, sometimes with small children, but possessing some useful skills. For example, they were good at sewing or embroidering. The black ones were notorious frauds, who would join the line in front of our office as well as other humanitarian organisations, just for fun. Some of the women in the black category managed to get help simply because of their persistence. Sometimes adding them to a list was enough to placate them. 'I'll put you into this file,' I explained, 'it's the black category, the one for women who need special assistance. If we get a consignment of nice shoes or wooden furniture, you'll be the first to get it,' I would say to reassure the frauds who responded with a conspiratorial wink showing they understood and that we were on the same wavelength. Some would slip me a bunch of grapes under the desk and one even tried to force a few hundred afghanis on me, but I managed to return the money before she disappeared through the door, delighted by the prospect of a set of sofas from Dubai. And since we never received any consignments of shoes or furniture, except perhaps some intended for foreign humanitarian workers, the fraudsters would eventually stop showing up.

I would note all the crucial information on each woman on a separate piece of paper: when and under what circumstances her husband had died or, as the case may be, which limb he had lost; how many children and how many years of education she had had, where she lived, what kind of food she ate, whether she could read and write or had any skills such as sewing and embroidering. Women with health problems were identified by a green mark on the margin, which helped us keep track of those who visited our health centre. I was proud of my filing system and the idea that the piles of paper and notes might be useless disconcerted me.

'You can store all this information in little boxes on your desktop. Everything will be much neater; you can easily open them and add any information you need at a click of the mouse...' Heidi was convinced she could win me over and I would come to see the advantages of the computer. She had much less trouble convincing me to use a digital camera. My husband didn't object as I couldn't use the camera to get in touch with anyone; on the contrary, it was almost exclusively at the disposal of our family whose members, like most Afghans, loved having their pictures taken, even though nobody was allowed to see the photos of women, which was regarded as indecent. We didn't manage to take many pictures at our centre and Heidi blamed me until I let her see for herself that local women responded to the camera by covering their faces, shrieking with horror and sometimes taking to their heels.

'This will be a long process,' Heidi acknowledged.

She did, however, resolve to teach me to use a computer and was determined to see it through. She tried all sorts of tricks.

'If you can't use the computer and communicate with the world on the internet you may soon lose the position of responsibility that you have today...' I felt like telling her she was the one who ought to be looking for another job, unless she learned the barbaric local language and managed to survive in this country for more than twelve years like I had. But she meant well. Eventually she started by teaching me computer games. And that's how she finally won me over.

'The internet has opened up vast new possibilities for mankind,' she announced once I had mastered the basics of switching the machine on and off and restarting it by myself. 'By going online you can communicate with the whole world almost in real time,' she said spreading her arms to indicate the vastness of the world.

'Including Russia?' I couldn't resist.

'Including Russia,' she shouted triumphantly.

'Online?'

'Well, almost online'.

'And how much does it cost?' I asked, ever practical.

'Almost nothing, that's the beauty of it!' Heidi beamed in her new role of a salesman. 'Well, actually, in this country it does cost something,' she said, cooling off. 'You don't have phone lines here so the connection has to go via satellite. It's kind of like a sputnik, you know, that's what makes it a bit more expensive. Do you know what a sputnik is?'

I was quite offended. When I was little my Dad had drilled the foundations of astronautics into me and later on, my husband and I had lived in the mountains, which must have been much closer to outer space than anywhere in America.

'The Soviet Union was the first country to send a man-made satellite into space,' I declared proudly. 'And Kabul is 1,800 metres above sea level,' I added, determined to dredge up every bit of my encyclopaedic knowledge attesting to the rapid technological and scientific advances of my new homeland.

'I can't argue with that,' she said with a condescending smile. 'The altitude, I mean. But the internet has yet to make inroads here. After all, loads of people can't even read and write.'

I didn't detect any signs of contempt or mockery in her voice, only complete conviction that she would rescue Afghanistan, that she was the Western Messiah everyone here had been waiting for to provide them with primary and secondary literacy skills and to turn them into free and enlightened individuals. Just then my husband entered the room. He was in a good mood, and cheered up even more seeing that Heidi and I were on our own, without male company.

'And we had an astronaut, too, Abdul Ahad Mohmand was his name,' I added, jumping up from the computer. I suspected my husband might not be too happy to see me broadening my horizons and ready to communicate with the whole world. 'We did have an astronaut, didn't we?' My husband had no idea what I was talking about and Heidi couldn't wipe an inane smile off her face.

'Oh yeah, he flew to the stars on a mortar, didn't he?' she said but my husband wasn't unnerved by her lame joke. The story of the first Afghan astronaut was one of Grandpa's favourites and, as I had verified in period sources, it was one of the few he hadn't embellished at all.

'Definitely not on a mortar, not even on a monkey,' my husband said with a crooked smile. 'He flew in a spaceship.'

'And did he get far?' Heidi began to show genuine interest. She gestured to my husband to take a seat, shaking her head incredulously. 'That's news to me. Are you serious?'

'Of course. It was a slightly political affair but it's definitely true, he did go into space and showed extraordinary courage as well as the customary Afghan iron will. Even the Russians conceded that much,' said my husband, who was normally not given to theatrical scenes but this was an episode of Afghan history he was really proud of. And probably with some justification. In 1988, when it was clear that the Soviet army would soon withdraw from Afghanistan in disgrace and with huge casualties, Moscow dreamt up a mad scheme to enhance the status of Soviet–Afghan friendship by putting it on a footing other than military. The Russians offered Kabul a place on a spaceship. Everything was arranged in great haste, including the selection of eight candidates who met the criteria of excellent physical and mental fitness and tribal links with local communist leaders. Everyone assumed that Muhammad Jahi, a relative of the Afghan deputy defence minister and member of the communist party leadership, would be the one to be sent to space.

'Except that the fool had swallowed a key as a child,' at this point of the narrative my husband, just like Grandpa, put on a mysterious face and lowered his voice dramatically. I would normally interject that it was extremely difficult for a child in Afghanistan to swallow a key as there was quite a shortage of keys as well as locks. Grandpa would wave his arms in irritation and shout angrily: 'OK, so maybe it was a screw or a stone or a cartridge he swallowed, who knows, but he did swallow something and had to undergo surgery.'

Heidi, who was not as nitpicking as I and less familiar with the country she was hoping to bring back to its feet, didn't react to the issue of the key. After a meaningful pause my husband continued.

'During a medical examination Soviet doctors discovered that as a result of swallowing a key the politically most suitable candidate had become permanently impaired, which disqualified him from the space expedition. Gradually all the others were found unsuitable and Abdul was the only one left. The Soviets didn't give him much training, in case he changed his mind and also to make sure they pulled off the stunt before the ultimate military defeat, as that would have looked rather bad. Allegedly they reckoned that, given his country of origin, he didn't need any special training to prepare him for extended sojourns in a wasteland. All that mattered was that he should survive the flight and take a few photos of Afghanistan from up there. Which is what he did, and thanks to him we got our first decent map,' said my husband, lighting a cigarette and courteously offering a light to Heidi as well. She was flabbergasted.

'So what was it he did to demonstrate the extraordinary Afghan willpower?' she asked impatiently.

'Wait, that comes later,' I rebuked her. And it surely did. The final part of the story, the account of his return to Earth, was one of my favourites and my husband might have been even better at telling it than Grandpa, who had lately often succumbed to tiredness and tended to forget names, times and places.

'He spent nine days up there, together with Vladimir Liakhov. He was a typical Russian, with no sense of shame or decorum,' said my husband, grimacing to indicate how disgusted he was. 'You see, to return to Earth they had to get into one of those little apparatuses for transporting them down here, Soyuz TM-6 it was called. And the apparatuses didn't feel like it.'

'The apparatus didn't feel like it,' Heidi corrected him. She was so fascinated she forgot to smoke.

'So they managed to squeeze inside and tried to start it but it failed twice and they had to stay up there for a day longer. But you have to imagine, they had no water, no food and no...' here my husband came to a halt and I knew why. Next he was supposed to mention they had no access to a toilet since nobody had expected them to be cooped up there for that long.

'And there was no WC,' I helped him out.

'That's right, there was no WC. Well, and because we Afghans always think of everything and believe that everything might come in handy, our man had brought along his sleeping bag and a couple of things in plastic bags. And that's what saved the Russian guy.'

'How did a sleeping bag and plastic bags save the Russian guy?' Heidi didn't understand and I knew it would be up to me to explain this awkward episode.

'They spent 24 hours in the capsule without food and water and couldn't pee, you see. So the Russian guy peed into a plastic bag and didn't care that he was on camera.'

My husband put on a triumphant expression. 'Not just on camera but with our astronaut watching, too...'

'Hmm, so what's the big deal?' Heidi frowned to signal that we were beginning to get on her nerves.

'Why, of course, the Russian peed into a plastic bag like a moron and disgraced himself in the eyes of the whole world,' said my husband emphatically.

'And where did your Afghan guy pee?' Heidi asked the logical question.

'He managed without peeing,' said my husband, getting up and pointedly looking out of the window to underline the seriousness of the moment.

I was worried that Heidi would blurt out something extremely inappropriate. Fortunately, she kept quiet. But after a while she said: 'C'mon, you're kidding me...' At that moment Dominic stormed into the room and before he managed to say hello, Heidi rattled off: 'Did you know there was an Afghan astronaut?'

'No, I had no idea,' Dominic stopped in his tracks, then rushed to the computer.

'Wait, this is really interesting,' Heidi wouldn't let it go. 'Really, they claim they also had a man in space.'

'Heidi,' I whispered unhappily. 'C'mon, you really don't believe us? I read about it in a book, it's general knowledge...'

'Well, if it's general knowledge I should be able to check it on the internet right away,' Heidi said with a triumphant air and I knew that this time victory would be ours. Dominic smiled and my husband gave me an inquisitive look. I shrugged. After some jostling around the keyboard, some typing and head shaking, Heidi and Dominic eventually nodded in appreciation as they read in unison: 'Oh yeah... it did happen more or less that way. He was awarded the Order of the USSR, the Order of Lenin and the Afghan Sun of Freedom award. It says so here.'

'Looks like they've crammed an entire library into that piece of junk,' my husband said angrily on our way home, disappointed that our US employers weren't suitably impressed with the Afghan astronaut.

'They haven't but they can connect to a library. Anywhere in the world. They can even get access to the Moscow university library... that's what the internet can do, you see.'

'I know what the internet does, damn it,' he snapped at me

furiously. 'People use it to write to each other without having to go to the post office.'

'That's it. And today Heidi explained to me how it works because she wants to teach me.' My husband stepped on the brakes so suddenly that the car behind nearly rammed into us.

'Why on earth would you need to... get in touch with someone out there in the world?' he hissed furiously.

'It's got nothing to do with getting in touch with anyone... I'm just supposed to enter information into some boxes on the computer and...'

'If you so much as touch that machine, I'll break both your arms. And legs. Who is it you want to write to? And what about?'

'I don't want to write to anyone. The whole thing was Heidi's idea, I don't care either way...' I was about to burst into tears, upset by the unjust accusation.

'Tomorrow you're going to tell them you're allergic to the computer. Invent something, a rash on your eyelids, whatever. I've heard it happens quite often. Tell them that as soon as you touch the computer you come out in a rash.'

'I can't quite see how I can claim I come out in a rash if I've never seen a computer before the one in their office.'

'We've had an astronaut so we could have had computers too,' my husband shouted and started driving again. After a while he announced much more calmly: 'I've got an idea. Tell them doctors have warned you the computer is a potential risk to pregnancy. And since you've already lost two babies you're obviously concerned. That will work, won't it?'

'That will work fine, my love, I'm sure it will.'

Over dinner, which was unusually lavish that night, what with chicken swimming in grease and salad drowning in goat's milk yogurt, my husband said out of the blue: 'Mad, I think you ought to attend a computer course. It's the thing of the future and you've got a head for this sort of thing. Do any of you have any idea what the internet is?'

They all shook their heads unanimously.

'It lets you get in touch with the whole world, it enables you to communicate freely with people all over the place, go to a library and read every book that's there,' said my husband gazing out of the window with the same expression he had put on to indicate his pride in the Afghan astronaut who had managed to hold back his urine for 24 hours just to make sure he didn't have to expose his sexual organ to his fellow astronaut and the eyes of the world. The same world to which we could now connect by means of the internet. 'And you should all learn to speak English properly,' my husband shouted sternly, resolutely shoving a whole chicken leg into his mouth.

I had managed to dodge Heidi's offers of computer lessons for about two weeks when my husband came to fetch me and ran into her in the doorway.

'How about teaching both of us?' he asked directly, without further ado. At first Heidi didn't know what he was talking about but figured it out when she noticed my husband was staring at the computer.

'Of course, but only in the evenings, it mustn't eat into our work, Nazir. Around three times a week should be enough. In about three weeks you will be able to correspond with anyone you like, even President Bush.'

She was right. My husband mastered the basic operations immediately. I took a little longer, sometimes deliberately lagging behind him to make him happy. We had additional tutoring at home from Mad, who signed up for a course run by the Japanese close to our neighbourhood. When his course teacher, a young Afghan woman from Pakistan, complained, blushing, that he had illicitly visited porn websites, my husband burst out laughing. He made Mad write down all the relevant addresses on a piece of paper. Apart from that, Mad was the best student bar none, and when the teacher asked us where the young man had been educated we just sidestepped her questions. We didn't know the answer. We had never asked him about it, mindful of Nafisa's advice not to torment the traumatised boy with questions about his past. Only Grandpa knew where Mad had come from and why he was now part of our family.

When the time came to set up email addresses, my husband casually remarked to Heidi: 'Herra and I can share the same address, to save you trouble.'

'It's no trouble, Nazir.'

'Well then, the expense.'

'It's free, Nazir, no worries, you can have an address each and you can write to each other if you ever travel anywhere separately.' The idea incensed my husband so much he gave me a proper talking to back at home on the mattress.

'Why can't you tell her you don't want to have your own address? Why do I have to tell her that? I'm sure you want your own address so I can't see how many people you write to, all your old Russian friends, including the man who was the first to have you.'

'You know what, Nazir, I'll tell Heidi tomorrow that I don't want an address or anything to do with the internet or the computer,' I sobbed, knowing what would follow.

'You want me to look like an idiot, like a dim-witted, jealous, backward Muslim who won't let his wife go out shopping on her own.'

'But you don't let me go out shopping on my own.'

'Well, that's for your own good, you wouldn't be able to find your way home from the city centre on your own.'

'That's because I'm constantly led on a leash like a dog.' I was furious, not because I couldn't have my own address but because I was being told off for something that wasn't my fault.

'OK, go out then, I've kept you on a leash like a dog... no, like a bitch because that's what you are, a bitch. So off you go, you bitch,' my husband stormed out of the room and didn't return that night. He slept in the car. All alone, demonstratively hurt, humiliated and desperate.

'Don't go after him,' whispered Mad, jumping on the opportunity to move to the still warm, freshly vacated place on my mattress. 'Minister Rahman was killed at the airport today. He'd been trampled to death, just imagine. And the stupid English soldiers just watched it happen even though they were only five metres away.'

'Why was he trampled to death?'

'People wanted to go to Mecca and there wasn't enough room on the plane. And Rahman was the air force minister, surely you must know that?'

'I did, it just slipped my mind.'

'I'm actually quite glad it happened.'

'Stop it, Mad, you can't be glad about someone getting killed.'

'Well, in that case I'd have to live in a permanent state of shock. It's good because now, at least, the Americans know what sort of people they're dealing with. In this country, if a plane is delayed the minister gets trampled to death. It's a kind of local tradition. The next guy will be more careful. In America people calmly wait for the next connection and the main thing is, their ministers aren't stupid enough to go and explain to a crowd of furious people desperate to go on a holy pilgrimage that they're going nowhere because the only decrepit aircraft we have left can't lift its bum off the ground.'

For some reason, Mad was outraged at the news of the minister's death. And through the wall I could hear Grandpa muttering something about it as well, almost in his sleep. It occurred to me that the minister's widow might well show up in our office the next day and I might include her in the category of war widows, perhaps giving her an extra few pounds of flour as someone who's well connected.

'He'll be cold out there.' I changed the subject.

'He feels sorry for himself, but for no reason.' Mad took my hand. 'I already know how to set up an email address and I'll do it for you. Tomorrow. You'll have a password that only you and I will know.'

'And what will it be, Mad?'

The chubby imp turned to his side to get a better view of me but since his extremities were too short relative to his body, he lost his balance at the critical moment, and tumbled on to his back. I helped him turn around, laughing. I realised Mad was awfully jealous of my husband.

'Death. I'll make it death2002,' he gasped.

'Mad, don't be silly, what's the point of this silly password?'

'Because you'll never forget it. You'll see.'

chapter 19

THE DOOR OPENED, revealing Dominic. His lips had spread
into the widest smile he was capable of. For the past three days
our humanitarian headquarters had been gripped by euphoria.
The owners of a fat bank account, a rotund gentleman and a
rather stout lady with flaming red hair, had come to visit us.
Right after their arrival Heidi introduced them to me as 'our
bemefactors'. Everyone piled into the room where I received
clients just as Mad was helping me persuade an elderly sick
woman who kept bringing children into the world regardless
of her advanced age and general state of decrepitude that
she shouldn't let them drink water from puddles, at least
not without boiling it first. Mad had lately been coming with
me to the office and Dominic was so impressed with his
performance he started paying him a small salary. Nobody
minded Mad, who had a great gift for ingratiating himself
with women. Totally disarmed by his indeterminate age and
gender, they treated him as a confidant, telling him things
they would never have shared with me. They told him about
being widowed and forced to marry their deceased husband's
brother. Some complained about their husband demanding
that they perform every single marital duty while others
grumbled theirs would never join them on the mattress.
Mad sat on a chair with a thick pillow underneath his bottom

so his chin wouldn't lean against the edge of the table, fully in control of the situation.

'Men are simple creatures, they require long-term nurturing, understanding and support,' he explained to a fifty-year-old woman who was trying to stop her husband from bringing a twenty-year-old girl as his second wife to their half-ruined house, which sported a UN banner for a roof.

'Let him bring her,' was Mad's advice. 'Make her learn all the household chores, make sure she serves you, looks after your children and is the last one to sit down to meals... She'll provide relief in your old age.' He concluded the therapy session by giving the women food stamps and advising them on what kind of dress would suit their figure. Since most Afghan women dressed in the only style permissible in the country – loose-fitting trousers with an even looser-fitting dress on top – this kind of advice didn't require any special qualifications. Mad was fully absorbed in the conversation with one of the women when the visitors entered the room.

'Hello, how are you!' yelled the red-haired lady, rushing to my desk. I curled up into a ball, frightened by this sudden aggressive outpouring of affection from a complete stranger. I was nailed to my seat and couldn't even lift my arm in greeting, so the gigantic person was forced to lift me up to peck me first on my left, then the right and then the left cheek again. As she shrieked 'My girl, you're so lovely!' at the top of her voice for some reason, my client sought refuge in a corner from where she stared at us in horror. When she realised the other hefty creature was male, she hastily pulled the burka over her head but in her distress she couldn't fit the grille over her eyes. Mad stayed put behind the table, instinctively drawing his oversized head between his shoulders, which made it look not only as if he had no neck at all but also as if the lower part of his face were an integral part of his chest.

The red-haired woman let go of me, dropping me back into my seat, and ill-advisedly pounced on the poor woman in the burka. She grabbed her where she presumed the woman's shoulders to be. However, due to the misplaced burka, it was her sunken chest she grabbed with one hand and her back with the other. She planted three smackers on her through the dirty cloth, hurting her nose since where she expected to find the woman's cheeks she encountered quite a different part of her face.

'Oh, isn't she cute, and look at this lovely child,' she said, noticing Mad. The man, who was a head shorter than she but still solid enough to appear quite stately, stood by the door smiling happily and smoking a foul-smelling cigar. Heidi smiled as well and gave me a mischievous wink to indicate everything was going to plan. Mad, who had never been called a 'lovely child' before, was petrified. He stretched out his short arms as buffers to prevent a display of love and affection. However, Madam misunderstood his gesture. She must have thought Mad was reaching out to her in the hope of physical contact. As she spread her arms, the folds of flabby flesh that started swaying on her arms made her look a little like a butterfly.

'Oh, my little...' she stopped to think what description would fit Mad. 'My little rosebud,' she said, finding the right word and enveloping Mad in her enormous bosom. For a while I lost sight of his head, as it merged with the body of the lady, who shed a tear of joy.

'Everything you do is fabulous, really fabulous!' She swayed from side to side as if wanting to bury Mad who tried to push her away with his little arms but found himself in a precarious position. His head was submerged between the woman's breasts, his body enveloped in the arms of a giant who kept tugging at him as if she wanted to pull his head off and throw it away. Fortunately, she let go of him before he suffocated. His hair, electrified by friction, stood on end, he was breathing heavily and his ears were all crumpled from the tight clench. But he recovered before I did.

'How are you,' he shrieked in his hoarse old-womanish voice, surprising the lady. Suddenly she wasn't quite sure if she hadn't just snogged an elderly hobgoblin.

'This is Mad,' Heidi said from the door. 'A very clever boy, he's helping Herra with the project I've been telling you about.'

'Wow, that's incredible. Fantastic, isn't it, Paul?' the woman shouted.

'He's helping her with the gynaecological clinic. Isn't that progressive! And look how nicely equipped this place is, so clean and cosy,' she surveyed the room that was rather cramped and cold, consisting of bare walls and a simple table with three chairs.

'Very impressive,' the man agreed, adding: 'We've got to go, darling, we're expected at the UN. And don't pounce on them with such ardour. They don't seem to like it very much.' I felt a sudden surge of sympathy for the gentleman.

'Sure, Paul. Oh my goodness, look at those charming women queuing outside,' she looked out of the window at the street below, clapping her hands like a child that has just received a present. 'You're doing such great work here, you're such wonderful people, so selfless and kind... Paul, would you take a picture of us, please?'

The woman stood behind Mad and taking me by the hand, pulled me forcefully towards her. Then she realised the woman in the burka was frozen in the same place. She was so horrified she didn't manage to fix the grille on her burka and couldn't see anything at all. 'Tell her to come over here, we'll have a nice picture taken. Could she take that thing off?' the woman shrieked.

'That might not be a good idea,' Heidi said gently, 'local women don't like having their picture taken, especially if there are men around... and they won't take their burka off.' I was grateful to Heidi for finding a sensitive way of explaining the problem.

'Never mind, why doesn't she stand next to us in her charming blue outfit,' the lady ordered in a rather overbearing tone and Heidi cautiously approached the Afghan woman and gently pushed her towards our little group dragging her by the burka. The poor woman didn't put up any resistance and stood there looking like a shrouded statue on wheels.

'Smile nicely, say cheese, everyone,' the red-haired woman shouted and Mad translated her request into Dari. I expect the poor thing in the burka did her best to obey the order and smile but it didn't really improve the photo. The fact that her grille was turned to the side didn't help matters either, making it look as if she were facing away from the photographer. Luckily, it was all over in a jiffy.

When everyone was gone, Mad gave a loud snort and said: 'What a shame Grandpa wasn't here, I bet this woman would have taken him for my first-born son.'

My husband and I stood in front of a beaming Dominic. We were dressed up to the nines, our hair all coiffed and smelling of perfume. Even the bodyguards had peered out of their hut at us as we passed by to admire my husband. The actual object of their admiration was his European suit, which we had purchased at the local bazaar and whose only flaw was its rather outmoded style and weirdly short, almost three-quarter length sleeves. Earlier that day Heidi ceremonially informed me that since it was our sponsors' last night in Kabul we would all go out to a restaurant and I was expected to come along as the lady had fallen in love with me and wanted to chat to me about the future of Afghan women. On our way there it occurred to me that Heidi had never mentioned my husband but I wasn't prepared to accept that after all our intimate conversations it could have crossed her mind to invite me to a restaurant on my own. That's why I happily informed my husband that Heidi, Dominic and the two of us were taking our two weird benefactors to the Herat Restaurant where Afghan food specially adapted for foreigners was served. But we were standing in front of Dominic who stared at us with a smile frozen on his lips.

'We'll drop her off at home after dinner, Nazir,' he blurted out. He must have realised my husband hadn't donned a smart suit just to escort me to the office and be sent back home without being wined and dined as well. I didn't say a word and felt like the greatest coward on earth. And anyway, the huge lump in my throat would have stopped me from saying anything. My husband turned around abruptly and before I could do anything, he jumped into the car, started the engine and shot out of the gate skidding sharply. I stayed with Dominic, clutching a tacky handbag that was nearly empty. We were both embarrassed.

'It's just for a small group of people, you see, not that we've got anything against Nazir but they want to throw a little party here in the courtyard tomorrow to say goodbye to the Afghan staff. I guess we didn't make that quite clear...'

'I think I should go home,' I said timidly, as Heidi appeared behind Dominic, wearing a short-sleeved dress, her head uncovered and her lips painted crimson.

'We've got to go,' she squealed, dragging Dominic inside. As for me, she just waved at me to follow. She didn't give me a chance.

'I don't...' I said, raising my voice, 'I don't feel too well, I have to go home.'

'Are you crazy?' Heidi was baffled. 'You know how important this dinner is for all of us and for your own future! They might even offer you a grant. We need their funding for the next year but it's not yet certain we're going to get it. It's entirely in their hands... We won't be long, Herra, please don't hold us up.'

I felt dreadful. Throughout the evening I didn't manage more than a few dozen words and both Heidi and the red-haired lady were quite unhappy with me.

'What's wrong with you, child?' the woman kept asking me. 'Aren't you hot in that scarf?'

My head was covered with a hand-embroidered black shawl and I wouldn't have taken it off at any price, not even on a European beach. I found it comforting. I wouldn't have been seen dead looking like Heidi or the lady with her rolls of fat protruding from every opening in her clothes and her wrinkled cleavage so deep the waiter could see all the way to her lap as he bent over to pour some water for her.

Heidi and the lady kept bursting into peals of laughter. The men spoke in softer voices, occasionally interrupting their conversation on subjects I didn't understand with exclamations of appreciation for the beautifully presented and tasty food.

'We'll go home first and then the driver will drop you off,' Dominic told me discreetly as we were getting into the car. Zulgay, who had been the visitors' chauffeur for the past few days, smiled at me with compassion.

'Aren't you hungry?' I asked him in Dari.

'I haven't eaten all day. They took two and a half hours over lunch but wouldn't tell me when I should collect them so I waited outside the Italian restaurant and couldn't even pop out to buy some bread,' he told me angrily, but the thought of his 500 dollar salary stopped him from venting his fury.

At this moment, as if they had understood, Heidi shouted: 'We forgot about Zulgay, and there was so much left over! Herra, could you pop back in, perhaps they haven't put it all away yet, they could put it in a box for him.'

I blushed in embarrassment and anger.

'He said he wasn't hungry,' I retorted.

The lady took the front seat and the four of us were supposed to cram into the back. The driver of the second car that had driven us to the restaurant had been unwisely sent home.

'I'll sit in the boot,' I said and was about to squeeze into the place I was used to. On family outings Freshta, Mother and I would always crawl into the boot from where we would watch the road disappear in the rear window, like three happy little chicks.

'That's out of the question,' Heidi said, rejecting my suggestion. 'We'll all fit in.' And without further ado, she squeezed in next to Dominic. Then the fat grey-haired man climbed in and with a friendly smile pointed to a space next to him, about ten centimetres wide.

'I want to sit in the boot,' I declared loud and clear.

'Forget about the boot,' the lady laughed histrionically and remarked in a playful tone: 'Paul will be happy to let you sit in his lap, won't you, darling, the girl's as light as a feather...'

'Can you open the boot for me?' I asked Zulgay in Dari, adding in English: 'I'm not sitting in anyone's lap. In this country we're not allowed to touch men who are not relatives. If I did that I'd be publicly executed tomorrow in the main stadium.'

Everyone stopped talking. The lady turned visibly pale in spite of the dark and her husband blushed. Heidi stared at the floor and Dominic started massaging his knuckles in embarrassment.

'So cruel, so cruel...' the red-haired lady sighed. 'I thought those terrible days were over. This is another thing we should do something about, Paul.' If decapitation really had been on the agenda the next day, I bet this lady wouldn't have missed it for the world. I climbed into the boot and felt good for the first time that night. The familiar Toyota was parked outside our office gate but my husband wasn't inside. Then I spotted him. He had changed back into his shabby Afghan 'pyjamas' and wore an Arab scarf wrapped around his head, like he used to when running around the mountains with a machine gun. He looked gorgeous, like a Persian prince. He waited for everyone to get out of the car and enter the building. Dominic and Heidi pretended not to see him but they couldn't have missed him. Then he approached Zulgay.

'You have a great wife,' Zulgay said and opened the boot for me. Against all expectations my husband gave me his hand to help me get out. We got into our car and before starting the engine he asked: 'Would you like to drive?'

'I would,' I said and, even though I didn't really feel like it, I knew it would make him happy if I accepted this rare offer. Demonstratively, to make sure the bodyguards could see what was happening, he let me move into the driver's seat, then lit a cigarette and said, waving to his friends: 'Now, step on it!' I immediately went into a skid and we both laughed. Then he pulled the shawl off my head and tugged at my earlobe. 'Thanks, Herra,' he said, cupping his head in his hands.

chapter 20

THAT DAY was significant for two reasons. Qais found three items relating to intimate feminine hygiene in Freshta's handbag and Grandpa wet himself. Everything happened so fast I can't even remember which tragedy occurred first.

Mad had been fidgety since the morning and by midday he was visibly out of sorts. He was always like that when he was about to ask me a delicate question. It was Friday. The men had left for the mosque, Mother and Grandpa were praying at home and Freshta and I were tackling the laundry. Fortunately, the children were running around in the street, playing a new game they had recently invented, a very silly one, according to Mad, and certainly not one he would participate in. The real problem was that the game involved running very fast, which for Mad was sheer torment. Not only was he always last, a fact he tried to disguise by claiming he had to help look after the toddlers, but the physical effort usually made him nauseous and it was considered a real disgrace to be sick in public. That's why he preferred to stay at home most of the time or spend time with me at the centre, prying into women's souls. Sometimes I suspected him of enjoying women's chores and chit-chat. On this occasion, too, he was helping us with the laundry, fetching water and scrubbing with stones and sand at stubborn spots that the Pakistan-made detergent couldn't cope with.

Mother was in the kitchen making lunch while Grandpa watched Friday's festive religious broadcast on television, loudly correcting the speakers. 'Certainly not!' he roared with laughter that was clearly audible in the courtyard. 'People are only secondary, an ephemeral episode from a historical point of view,' he shouted.

'Grandpa,' said Mad, leaning into the open window. 'Grandpa, don't be mad at them, they can't hear you on the other side of the TV screen anyway!'

Grandpa, welcoming a live audience, declared sternly: 'The Forgiving *sura* says the earth and nature are much more important than human beings: "Surely the creation of the heavens and the earth is greater than the creation of man: but most men know it not",' Grandpa's croaky voice sang out a verse from the Quran, giving Mad some food for thought.

'Oh yeah, Grandpa, a dog is much better looking than our Qais, for example...'

'How can you say things like that?' Freshta laughed. Mad's throat emitted something we had by now recognised as genuine laughter, although most visitors were under the impression that this harsh sound expressed despair and horror rather than joy and amusement.

'Grandpa, what do you think, who's a better creation of Allah's, woman or man?' Mad winked at me, suggesting he knew the answer and was just testing the old man.

'Woman, my boy. He managed to make woman much more accomplished and better-looking than man. After all, He created Adam first. And whenever you do something for the first time, my boy, you're bound to make mistakes. You end up with some bits that hang out, some that are protruding, superfluous or missing... You're bound to do a better job the second time around, especially if you're God. So it's obvious that Eve, as His second attempt at creating a human being, has turned out a much better specimen. Is man capable of giving birth? Can man breastfeed?

And do you realise that women are much cleverer than men, which is precisely why they conceal this fact in order not to provoke men?' Grandpa was quite serious now and Mad stopped laughing. 'Except, my boy, man has other advantages, and he's here to protect the woman and their offspring. And because man protects the woman and is prepared to sacrifice his life for you and for your mothers, you just have to treat him with a little more respect, obey him and try to make his time in this world nicer for him. Just look around and see how many war widows we have, many more than war widowers. A woman, even after she dies, continues to live through her children more than a man does. So as long as she brings children into this world she never really dies.' As he said these words Grandpa looked at me with unease. He realised I had never managed to bring into this world a creature that would make me live forever. It wasn't meant to be. And Grandpa must have realised it wasn't very sensitive to talk to me in this way.

My non-motherhood was never discussed in my presence even though it must have been the greatest grudge the family held against me, as well as the most incomprehensible part of my relationship with Nazir. 'OK, he may love you more than anything in the world but that's not a reason not to go to bed with anyone else.' This was Freshta's way of trying to convince me of the advantages of polygamy. She actually longed for her husband to bring a second wife home but poor Qais must have found other, secret ways of gratifying his lust on his trips to Pakistan where plenty of desperate, lonely women who had lost their breadwinner had turned to prostitution, but officially he had never taken another wife. He returned from his latest trip elated and in excellent spirits. I suspected Freshta could smell other women on him and that's why she considered Roshangol's disappearance a kind of private revenge.

Seven days had passed since it happened. It took Qais eight hours to start looking for Roshangol. I am still convinced it was no coincidence that Mad was hanging around at the critical moment so it would fall to him to be the harbinger of bad news and deflect Qais' wrath from everyone else.

'Tell Roshangol I've brought her a present,' he announced before dinner, absent-mindedly cutting his fingernails with a new pair of scissors he had brought back from his trip. 'Has she been studying all day, or what?' he wondered without interrupting his manicure.

'No she hasn't,' replied Mad who was now alone with Qais after Freshta and I quietly sneaked out into the kitchen pretending nothing was happening.

'So what is she up to? Ever since she started going to school she's been hiding somewhere and has seemed rather gloomy.' It was rare for Qais to explore his children's feelings but after being away from them for a few days he was all care and affection.

Mad rose to take up a better escaping position, knowing it wasn't a good idea to give bad news to Qais when there were scissors in his hands, no matter how tiny.

'Roshangol has run away,' Mad announced calmly just as Qais thrust the scissors into the root of a hangnail. He hissed with pain and didn't seem to have heard what Mad said.

'I told her she wasn't allowed to visit neighbours and that I certainly don't want her to hang around there all day. These people don't mind if their own daughter loiters around the streets letting strange men ogle her.'

'She's not at the neighbours. She's run away from home. We've been looking for her all week.' Having finished the sentence Mad turned around and waddled towards the hallway as fast as he could. Qais leapt up and went after Mad, and collided with Grandpa who was just entering the room. In the confusion Qais stabbed himself in the hand with the scissors he was still holding. It must have hurt like hell, as Qais screamed and froze with his hand outstretched, the scissors, made in China, sticking out of it. Grandpa, whose eyesight was very poor and who had no idea what had just happened, thought Qais wanted something and mistook the outstretched arm for a challenge or a greeting. He squeezed Qais' hand rather unfortunately and managed to push the scissors even deeper into his flesh, making him collapse in pain. Mad kept his presence of mind, grabbing Qais' wrist and pulling the scissors out with a single jerk.

Admittedly, he also pulled out a bit of his palm, although this fact was at first obscured by gushing blood. The rest of us watched the scene from a distance and thinking that Qais had been rendered harmless for the time being we now gathered around him and started comforting him like a small child. I really don't know why but suddenly we all felt really sorry for him, certainly not because of his injury, which wasn't all that serious. Qais sat on the floor like a drenched chicken, blood dripping from his hand into his lap and his shoulders shaking as he sobbed without shedding a single tear. Qais was one very unhappy man.

I didn't go to work the next day because Heidi and Dominic were in meetings at the UN all day and the surgery was closed that day as well. Qais sidled up to me as I was dusting the living room.

'You did it on purpose,' he said without beating about the bush.

'Did what, Qais?'

'You've sent her away, I know it. Because you all think I'm a bad father and a bad husband.'

'You must have gone round the bend, Qais. She's left of her own accord, really, we all nearly went out of our minds looking for her.'

'Herra.' It was rare for Qais to address me by name. He sounded so gentle and friendly I stopped dusting the TV screen and looked him in the face. It looked sallow and crumpled after a sleepless night. His hand was bandaged with a white handkerchief through which blood still kept soaking. 'Why did she do it, please tell me, Herra? I didn't touch Freshta, I promise, I spent the whole night asking her why...'

'And what did she say?'

'She said I would figure it out myself one day.'

'That's probably true.'

'But I want to know right away.'

'Well, Qais, you see... I guess she didn't want to marry someone like you.'

Qais' momentary insight didn't last long. Later that night he dragged his wife and children to his parents' home and we were quite relieved not to have to witness further embarrassing scenes.

To me it was obvious that in moments like these Freshta wouldn't have minded if Qais had brought another wife home. This idea used to make her roll her eyes furiously, to blush and spit with uncontrollable disgust. But she gradually came to believe it might actually be a relief to be able to share looking after Qais and his fits of rage with someone else. And based on her own experience she insisted polygamy would be a brilliant solution also for Nazir and me.

'You know, Herra, you could almost have your own children thanks to the other wife,' she would tell me. I think it was Mother who put her up to talking me into this. She believed that my husband, her son, wanted to have his own children even if it meant having to look after another wife. 'Herra, we could find someone who is not too pretty, quite dim, perhaps even mute. Only for, you know what I mean... procreation purposes. He wouldn't ever need to talk to her. That's what he's got you for. You wouldn't have to talk to her either. Nafisa could help us pick someone well-built, with a nice healthy uterus, she knows about these things...' I never contradicted Freshta. She had become very pragmatic in these matters. Long forgotten were the hysterics she had allegedly been in when she took it into her head to marry Qais in spite of the whole family gritting their teeth in fury. Now she expected everyone else to be just as pragmatic, including myself and, until recently, also Roshangol, claiming it was a woman's lot to endure everything and to look forward to a better afterlife. She didn't really believe it herself. And I have never found out what my husband really thought about this. He has never told me. But he has never suggested bringing another wife into our marriage either. Once I overheard him respond to a hint from Mother: 'Mother, God has decided not to bless us with children and he must have had his reasons. He will give us something else instead.' And then Mad turned up. We had never talked about it but we knew he was the gift God had sent us to compensate for my inability to continue living forever through my children.

Now Grandpa's eyes rested on me longer than was decent and Mad was also aware of the delicate situation. He knew he was the substitute God had sent us and tried to make up for the fact that he was just a substitute and hardly qualified as a perfect descendant. 'He won't give us any grandchildren,' my husband would say to me when Mad was out of earshot. He always said it with a smile, to assure me he didn't really mind at all. Because of his illness Mad couldn't have children and Nafisa explained that when he grew up he wouldn't be able to have intercourse and moreover, that he didn't stand much chance of living to a ripe old age. 'I just hope he will outlive us,' I worried. 'That shouldn't be a big problem here in Afghanistan,' Nafisa laughed. In moments like these I wished I wouldn't survive my husband and Mad. I guess my wish wasn't strong enough.

'And a woman who dies in childbirth goes straight to heaven, she is a *shaheed*, a fighter who's died in a war,' Mad shouted, to distract the others from my infertility. Then he paused. He remembered that he had been meaning to ask me an important question since we got up in the morning. But before he could pluck up the courage our men arrived. They were merry; high on tea they had been drinking with friends, and cheerfully hungry.

We sat down to eat, Grandpa still muttering under his breath but the worst of his outrage at the incompetence of the present-day spiritual leaders had passed. Besides, his favourite dish, kufta, delicious meatballs in tomato sauce, was being served for lunch. Qais was the only one not sharing the meal with us on the rug. He had brought his family back from his parents' house a week after their dramatic departure. They were on the verge of starvation and our food supplies hadn't yet managed to fill their stomachs. I was about to swallow my first mouthful when we heard a scream from the other room: 'Mad, come here immediately!'

This was highly unusual. Qais rarely spoke to Mad, they didn't have much to talk about. Mad was constantly making fun of him and his only handicap was his clumsiness, which slowed him down when trying to dodge slaps in the face. In our family, as in most Afghan families, it was forbidden to hit children before they reached adolescence and Qais was always criticised for his behaviour and regularly lost the argument as to whether Mad had entered puberty or not. 'I don't have wet dreams,' Mad would mock him from a safe hiding place to prove that he had either been through adolescence already without anyone noticing or that he hadn't got that far yet. Now he obeyed, got up and waddled off slowly, casting a worried glance in my direction. We could always hear every sound from next door, let alone Qais talking, as he was incapable of whispering and often woke up everyone and their dog in the entire neighbourhood when he believed he was speaking softly.

'What is this?' he hissed at Mad. The rest of us started eating, pretending we weren't listening. But the delicious meatballs stuck in my throat. Something was telling me that the subject Qais discussed with Mad was related to the matter the boy had been meaning to consult me on since that morning.

'I don't know,' Mad replied indifferently. 'Just a bit of something or other.'

'What do you use it for?'

'I don't use it, I just have it.'

'And what do you have it for?'

'I don't know yet, I haven't looked into it.'

'And where did you get it from?'

'I found it in the street.'

'In the street, I see, you spawn of the devil...' Qais finally burst into his usual shouting and my husband wearily got up from his meal. Soon he returned with both of them. Qais' face was flushed and Mad's was as pale as a sheet. Qais was clutching something that must have been very tiny as it fitted into his clenched fist. My husband was holding Mad's hand and it was obvious he didn't know what to think. Mad was sniffling, crumpling his chin in his inimitable way.

'Let's see what you've got there,' my husband ordered Qais. Qais hesitated and then stretched out his arm slowly and reluctantly, seeming almost embarrassed, and then opened his palm, even more slowly. I couldn't tell at first what had prompted a row dramatic enough to interrupt a festive meal. But when I got a closer look I burst out laughing, spitting out a partly chewed and rather unsightly shower of meatballs and rice. Only then did I notice that Freshta had gone stiff. She looked as if she had been carved out of granite. Her eyes were popping and she had ground a handful of rice into pulp. I stood up to take my husband aside discreetly to explain everything. But Qais, standing with his legs apart, blocked our exit and shouted: 'I want this to be sorted out right here and now. I want to know why Herra is laughing, and why you, her husband, are not interested in finding out what this thing is that we've got in our house? And what it's for!'

Obeying a strict glance from Father and Mother my husband gestured for me to return to my seat.

'Can anyone tell me what this disgusting thing is for?' Qais shrieked and I knew it was my cue.

'It's not anything disgusting,' I replied.

'It's some female disgusting thing.' Qais would not let it go.

'I don't think this is an appropriate conversation to have over a meal. I'll explain everything later, Nazir,' I said trying to maintain the decorum that is normally a must in Afghan families. Curiously enough, when it came to intimate feminine matters our males could be uncomfortably direct. Menstruation was frequently discussed without any inhibitions. For instance, a cleric who lived in our street once asked if I was menstruating, as that would bar me from entering a holy place.

'Absolutely not!' Qais yelled, 'You tell us now.'

Nazir motioned to me to speak and it occurred to me that this was a chance to exact a nice little bit of revenge for male intransigence.

'It's a tampon, it's very efficient in absorbing the menstrual fluid,' Mad suddenly jumped in, shocking everyone, including myself. Qais looked from Freshta to me and very, very slowly and silently lowered his eyes towards the little white roll in the palm of his hand. Nobody said a word. Qais put the little object in his pocket, sat down next to his wife and started eating.

'I got it for Freshta, from our doctor, she has a chronic infection and has to observe strict cleanliness,' I explained to my husband after lunch under my breath.

'I will kill that little imp,' he said gritting his teeth, without listening to me. 'Who allowed him to go through women's stuff?'

'He's inquisitive.'

'I thought it was protection against children, you see,' my husband said suddenly and it took me a while to understand what he meant. 'And I'm sure that's what Qais thought too. That Freshta uses it to avoid getting pregnant. But I still don't understand how this can possibly work...'

I stood up, took an identical tampon from my bag and asked my husband to fetch some water. He came back with a bucket.

'Just a drop will do,' I smiled. I dipped the tampon in the water for a few seconds and when he saw it stretching and swelling, my husband started to laugh. 'But even if Freshta had used it against children, so what? She and Qais have plenty of them already and he can't earn enough to keep himself, let alone the whole family,' I objected.

'Except that twit thought she used it as protection against having children with someone else. He's been unhinged ever since Roshangol ran away. If he could find her he would kill her. I do understand him to an extent, and nobody would condemn him if he did,' my husband went on laughing and I thought this might be the right moment to raise something with him.

'Let's get away from here, my love, let's go to Europe for a while. To Russia, for example. Just for a few... a few months.'

He stopped laughing.

'With Mad. It can be arranged now, we'll apply for passports and get out of here for a while.'

My husband looked as if he were still laughing, the smile not yet replaced by a stony face. Just as he breathed in to answer my question Mad stormed into our room. 'Grandpa has weed himself,' he announced with tears in his eyes.

None of us knew exactly how old Grandpa was. Nazir wasn't even sure of his own age, let alone Grandpa's; Freshta and Mother didn't care about details like that and Qais thought that trying to determine someone's exact age was positively harmful. 'We deserve as many years as we've been dealt,' he used to say, rather sensibly. All we knew was that Grandpa was very old. In the years I had lived in Kabul he hadn't changed at all. He had always been the same withered, sleepy, sometimes garrulous and incredibly bright and sensible old man. But this was a stark reminder of his age as well as a warning that our Grandpa's dignity would soon be a thing of the past.

After lunch, a relatively quiet and swift affair given how much food had been piled on to the rug, Grandpa got up and went out into the courtyard. He watched Mad hopping around the sun-scorched lawn. I don't know if he was aware that Mad was trying to learn some kind of European dance he had seen in a video in preparation for a journey that would never take place. He stretched his little arms to embrace an imaginary partner, albeit one who – given Mad's unusually formed body and overly short limbs – would either have had to be endowed with arms at least two metres long or have a sunken chest to reach her partner. Although Mad couldn't sing at all, he was trying to hum something rhythmical as he pressed the virtual girl to his chest, closer than local custom would have deemed decent. In fact, dancing itself was deemed indecent. Grandpa was smiling when Mad suddenly froze with his right foot thrust forward and his left foot suspended in the air, a highly unstable position, particularly for someone like him. He stared at a wet patch slowly forming on Grandpa's wide trousers. Grandpa felt something cold and noticed the material began to stick to his skin. He looked down, and was horrified at the mess he had got himself into. Mad was the only person who witnessed the scene. Calmly raising his eyes from his trousers, Grandpa stared at Mad, who understood him without a word. Finishing his dance move and humming the last bit of his tune, slowly as if nothing had happened, he went back into the house, to bring us the bad news. Now we had definite proof that our Grandpa was an old man.

In the evening the whole family congregated, unusually, in our little room. Grandpa was asleep, changed into clean clothes, angry at the whole world, tired and discomfited. My husband helped him go to bed without a word, impressing upon him to shout 'Nazir' if he needed him. The little room wasn't big enough for everyone to be seated comfortably. The children had been invited as well. The floor was taken by Father, who had become the official tribal elder as of today, as the clan leader mustn't wee himself...

'He's always dreamed of carrying out the holy hajj,' Father said without enlarging on the wetting of the trousers. 'We have to figure out how to get him to Mecca.'

Nobody said anything although everyone thought it would be extremely hard to complete the long, arduous and important journey now that Grandpa had lost control over his bodily functions.

'I'll find the money,' my husband declared with determination. He'd been thinking about Grandpa's wish to visit the great place of pilgrimage for a long time but until now had apparently not realised that Grandpa's time was limited. Sometimes he even teased him: 'You've got to keep fit, Grandpa, so you can run around the Kaaba. And are you aware that you have to cover the distance from Mina Valley to the base of Mount Ararat by yourself? Do you know you're not allowed to ride a donkey, let alone a Mercedes?' Grandpa used to laugh but he knew that the time when the holy pilgrimage would be beyond him was getting ever closer and even though he wasn't a fanatically devout Muslim, he did wish to make the journey to Mecca.

'I'll help you out with the money,' Qais whispered as if worried that his offer might be deemed undesirable after the unpleasant tampon row.

'Thanks,' my husband said. In a way he was relieved that he no longer had to explain why we couldn't go to Europe or anywhere else for that matter. It had never occurred to him that my parents might be as important as his. 'You've got a brother, he can look after them,' he would object whenever I expressed concern about their old age. 'Plus, where you come from, it's not compulsory to look after old people until the day they die. You stick them in an old people's home and they get a state pension. So there's no reason for you to worry about them. But I can't leave my parents here.' And he was right. He couldn't.

'We'll have to scrimp and save, and perhaps Herra could ask her employers for a loan. Do you think they might agree to advance you a few months' salary, my girl?' Father continued and I nodded eagerly. Seeing Father's contented smile I felt for the first time that I was really part of our clan, the big family Mafia, whose uncles and cousins, no matter how much they gossiped about one another, when push came to shove, would grit their teeth and share their earnings with relatives they might have never met.

'Next year is his last chance. And someone's got to accompany him.'

'It's got to be you, Dad, of course,' my husband said and everyone nodded their consent. Father didn't say anything at first. He rubbed his chin and then came out with a surprising idea: 'I think it's our Mother and Mad who should go.'

chapter 21

'TO BE HONEST, I don't understand why you don't send Grandpa to a hospital somewhere in Europe instead,' Heidi grumbled when I asked if I could receive my wages six months in advance so that Mother and Mad could accompany Grandpa on his last holy pilgrimage. 'If he's sick he should be in hospital, not in Mecca,' she fussed.

'He's not sick. He's just old.'

'How old is he?'

'I don't know. But he must be very old,' I said to Heidi, leaving out the fact that Grandpa was incontinent and explaining only that he didn't have much longer to live and that we needed quite a lot of money to make his last wish come true.

'It's a crazy idea, Herra. You should use the money you're earning here to get fertility treatment for yourself. Perhaps you could have artificial insemination in Europe. Don't tell me it wouldn't make Nazir happy to become a father...'

'But I can get the advance, can't I?' I said to put a stop to the useless conversation.

'I guess so,' she mumbled.

We were standing a few metres from the latest asset sent by our headquarters. Tall and well-built, John was Polish-born but had lived in America for years. Nevertheless, to me he seemed a kindred spirit and I felt a little tug at my heartstrings every time we met. I didn't fancy him at all, I just found him attractive as a person. Strangely enough, Nazir didn't object to him at all. Perhaps because he knew I wasn't partial to blond men, and also because John was a gynaecologist.

'He's seen so many women in his lifetime he must have lost all interest,' my husband assessed him soon after John turned up in Kabul, and then urged me to turn down any offers of medical examination. Heidi and John started discussing my fertility problems, my past failed pregnancies and still-born babies but they soon realised I wouldn't let a man examine me even if he stood behind five screens, discreetly instructing a nurse through a mirror. Absolutely not. John had now been working in our clinic for several weeks and still hadn't had a chance to examine a single Afghan woman. I watched him standing behind the screen, using his few words in Dari and eloquent hand gestures to show the nurse in the mirror how to examine the poor wretches on the gynaecological table. He would always wait for the patient to cover herself in her burka before discreetly emerging from his hiding place to dispense medication, ointments or, on rare occasions, administer an injection. Some women allowed him to move a corner of the burka aside, roll up a sleeve and prick their arm with the needle. Others didn't mind him placing his stethoscope on their burka to check their heartbeat or listen for any wheezing. He would laugh and say: 'It's like licking ice cream through a plastic bag.'

John shared my and my husband's sense of humour. 'He's a great guy,' Nazir once commented, and my jaw dropped in surprise. It had been a long time since I heard him give such an accolade to a foreigner. In the evenings he would sit with John on the patio without rushing me home, which was also unheard of. In addition, John spoke some Russian and that meant we could talk without being understood. I think Heidi resented it a bit but she didn't show it.

John didn't play tennis either, or go swimming at the UN compound that was out of bounds to the Afghans who might have contaminated it with diseases or bombs. He took us out for dinner a few times, while Dominic and Heidi always found an excuse to turn down his invitation, scared of catching an intestinal parasite from badly cooked meat in a restaurant frequented by the local middle classes.

John also came to visit us at home a few times. He shared a few hashish cigarettes and smoked the hookah with Father and Grandpa, brought Mother a box of chocolates but he hadn't yet seen Freshta. He even seemed to have broken Qais' resistance to all things foreign, conceivably because, after being beaten at cards twice, he duly paid Qais 300 afghanis.

The women who came to my advice centre soon started demanding to be examined by 'the nice white doctor'. I'm pretty sure they didn't mention at home that they had allowed the nice doctor to touch them but since John soon learned a few words and basic phrases in Dari, he was also able to chat to them. Sometimes an accompanying husband would force himself into the surgery. Whenever that happened I was brought in to interpret and explain the rights and wrongs and to enlighten both partners on marital issues of the most sensitive and intimate nature. Although I always chose words Afghans were able to accept and understand I knew my husband wouldn't have exactly approved of my involvement in these conversations. Nafisa, on the other hand, was overjoyed to see me do something useful at last, and kept begging me to let her come for a visit. When I mentioned it to John he boomed that it would be fantastic, wonderful and brilliant. It certainly was.

I had never expected Nafisa to arrive with not just one, but three patients in tow, as well as our Mad. Lately he had been complaining of stomach pains and spent most days on the mattress reading books, browsing through Russian dictionaries and constantly making notes. 'What I write down I never forget,' he claimed. But I really missed him at the centre. I was worried about him, too. Since Nafisa warned me several times that 'people like him' don't have a very long life expectancy, I was seriously concerned every time he coughed.

'I need a consultation,' Nafisa said with a suggestive laugh, and I felt a bit embarrassed for her. As soon as she saw John she started swaying her hips and it occurred to me that our husbands might have a point when they try to protect us from foreigners' prying eyes.

'Control yourself,' I hissed in Dari and Heidi must have realised something was making me very unhappy.

'Can you please focus on interpreting only, Herra?' she asked like a boss who habitually humiliates her underlings in order to get over her own inferiority complexes. Although in Heidi's case it was more of an attempt to be welcoming to new visitors, whereas I was regarded as a team member or relative who doesn't always have to be treated with kid gloves. She was beside herself with happiness as cooperation with local organisations and establishing contact with female members of the Afghan intelligentsia had been one of her key goals. Moreover, as I gained deeper insight into Heidi's soul I detected a little bit of envy. It was almost as if she were missing a little bit of domestic violence. I mean, the idea must have appealed to her that someone might be so much in love with her he would beat her from time to time. Once we talked about this at great length but our long, futile discussion about why in Afghanistan it is considered more or less acceptable for a husband to give his wife a deserved thrashing led to nothing.

'Really, I can't understand how you can defend such barbarity.'

'Well, nobody forces you to understand it.'

'Does your Quran say it's OK to beat women?'

'Their Quran says women should be treated kindly and justly. Harsh punishments such as whipping are allowed only for strikingly immoral deeds such as adultery,' I said, deliberately goading Heidi.

'Holy shit,' she yelled as if she had just been caught doing something of that nature. 'So the woman gets a thrashing and the man just watches her as if nothing...'

'Nonsense. They both get a hundred lashes. Both of them,' I said triumphantly. 'You see, in a way, the Prophet Muhammad was actually the first Arab feminist. He liked women. The way they'd been treated before him was really appalling.' I had recently shared this theory with Mad who was more familiar with the Quran than I was. He paused dramatically.

'You might be right,' he said after a while. 'The only problem is that hardly anyone in this country has read the Prophet's book and absolutely nobody knows what a feminist is.'

'And you know what it is?' I asked, suddenly surprised that Mad knew exactly what I was driving at.

'Of course. A feminist is someone who likes women and thinks they're better than men. Which means that, apart from Muhammad, our Grandpa is also a feminist. And so am I.'

'And Mad, who told you what the word feminism means?'

After a long pause he uttered the word I would never have expected him to say: 'Mother.'

Mad was now standing in front of the gynaecological examining table, unable to stop his little eyes darting from the foot rests to the bolster and to the clean white sheet placed under each patient's rear. He had never been to the clinic before. As a boy he had no business being here, after all. However, John used to spend a lot of time with our Muhammad and was very fond of him. He had often engaged him in learned debates on religion, polygamy, the origins of the world and the infinite nature of the universe. They created a peculiar mix of English, Dari and Russian only the two of them could understand. It seemed to me that Mad was telling John things he had never told anyone in our family, including me. I gathered they often discussed Russia, the things Soviet soldiers had done in Afghanistan and I thought it strange that he had never talked to me about it. Visibly thrilled by these discussions, Mad blushed and his ears were stiff with excitement. I felt a pang of jealousy and realised with sadness that Mad, just like every other child, would grow more and more distant from me and that, one day, I just wouldn't be enough for him. John had never raised the subject of Mad's condition either, which confirmed my suspicion that he knew much more than I did and was reluctant to involve me in his little friend's intimate problems.

'Girls, here you can take off your burkas,' Nafisa hollered and the three ladies timidly began to pull the rustling garb over their heads.

'John is a doctor, he can keep a secret,' Nafisa was very proud to have pulled off her secret expedition. I smiled, thinking it was all for the best. But then the smile froze on my lips. The tall figure, the one who took longest to take her burka off, the well-built woman standing next to Mad, turned out to be Freshta.

I cursed in Russian and everyone looked at me.

Freshta had had serious health problems for a long time. My husband informed me with a mysterious air that 'that moron' had probably given her some kind of a disease and if they had another child it might be born blind. He must have heard it from Nafisa. Freshta, in her turn, had hinted that her ability to perform her marital duties was rather limited since the periods between the times of impurity were getting increasingly shorter.

It took me a while to realise that John had stood stock still ever since Freshta had taken off her burka. His eyes were wide open and he couldn't take them off my sister-in-law. The way they looked at each other made my flesh creep. It was obvious that any healthy man was bound to fancy Freshta, that she was attractive as hell since her perfectly-formed features were capable of driving other women into a jealous frenzy while in men they inspired whatever it was that had prompted the Prophet Muhammad to command women to be chaste and abstemious.

'I've met this lady before,' smiled Heidi, interrupting the silence that began to feel oppressive. Fortunately, she didn't remember her from that first encounter at our house when we fell through the glass, only from my consultation room for the wretched souls where Freshta had turned up after she discovered Roshangol had abandoned us.

'So you have sorted out all your family problems,' Heidi pestered her.

'Yeah, yeah, everything is OK,' I answered for Freshta who didn't understand a word anyway.

'Herra, please, try to interpret and don't take it upon yourself to think for everyone.' Heidi had repeatedly pointed out to me that I was too authoritarian with my clients and never let them speak for themselves. Of course, Heidi didn't realise that this was different and that Freshta and I were related.

'Let's start,' Mad said, taking the initiative as usual, and I was grateful to him. We left John, Nafisa and the first patient in the clinic and went outside to wait in the garden. The patient was infertile and beyond help and the second patient's turn came very soon. Besides, poor John could hardly concentrate and he evidently had no idea how he should behave once the Madonna whose sight had taken his breath away mounted the trestle.

'I'm not going back in there, Herra,' Freshta whispered into my ear, on the verge of tears.

'Don't be silly,' Mad lost his temper. 'He's just a doctor. He's examined millions of women before.'

'Well, maybe not millions...' I said, tempering Mad's enthusiasm.

'OK, tens of thousands.' He insisted on the highest possible number to prove to Freshta that she was just one of many and that the tiny part of her that was of any interest to a gynaecologist was exactly the same as in every other female, so it didn't make the slightest bit of difference who the doctor had on the table.

'If it makes you feel better, put on the burka. He's not interested in your head at all, you know. It's the other parts of your body he'll be examining.' Mad went on the offensive and Freshta turned as red as a lobster.

'Hmm, that might not be a bad idea,' I joined in, thinking that wearing a burka would definitely make things easier for Freshta. 'Besides, Freshta, John is not actually going to examine you himself. He'll be only assisting. Although lots of women eventually let him help them and examine them directly, without an intermediary...' I lied a little. So far only one lady had showed that much courage, throwing John into such an apoplexy of shyness he had no idea what he was doing and it was left to our Afghan nurse to diagnose the patient.

'I bet you'll carry on examining patients through a mirror once you're back at home... it will be quite spectacular, you'll have more patients than you can handle,' Heidi teased him and John lowered his eyes so chastely he would have made the most die-hard Muslim happy.

Oddly enough, neither Freshta nor I thought it strange to discuss such fundamentally intimate matters in Mad's presence. He listened with his ears pricked up, beside himself with suspense. I think his ability to predict events came to the fore again at this point. And that is why, unlike us, he knew that it was absolutely crucial for Freshta to meet John.

'C'mon,' a rollicking Nafisa peered out of the surgery and waved to us. Freshta covered herself with the burka and went in. I felt sorry for her. She must have found it quite an ordeal.

'Tell the believers to lower their eyes chastely and guard their sex,' Mad mumbled a quote from the Quran which was hardly appropriate for this situation – quite the contrary.

'I'll do my best to guard it,' Freshta tried to joke.

'You've misunderstood me, my dear Freshta. You have to guard yourself so that you are healthy, serviceable and capable of performing your main functions...'

Luckily he didn't have time to go into more detail. John looked at the veiled Freshta in surprise, and all he managed was a quiet 'Why?'

'She's my sister-in-law, John,' I came clean. Mad nodded to indicate he understood our English conversation. 'We would like you to take special care of her.'

'And she's OK with that?' wondered John, blushing gently.

Meanwhile Freshta started to climb on to the table. The Afghan assistant adjusted the angle of the mirror and helped to hold on to Freshta's burka to stop it from getting entangled in the metal foot rests. Mad started chasing everyone out of the room.

'If Qais knew about this,' he giggled once we were outside in the courtyard.

'Keep your mouth shut, please,' I shuddered in horror.

'How come you've managed to get away from him today?'

'He sent Freshta and me to Nafisa's hospital and we're supposed to stay there till the evening. She's in no danger at the gynaecological ward, especially when I'm with her,' Mad laughed.

John came out together with Nafisa and Freshta. She had thrown the burka casually over her arm as if it were a coat she had just brought along in case the weather might change. All three were blushing, as pink as babies.

'She'll require longer treatment. We've arranged everything,' said John and squeezed Freshta's shoulder, shocking both me and Mad with his gesture.

'She knows no English words,' Mad croaked almost without a mistake.

'We've arranged everything,' John retorted handing Freshta a bag full of medicine.

Nafisa took over the supervision of Freshta's visits to our surgery. They made Qais and Mad believe she needed long-term treatment, that Freshta had to come for a check-up once a week and that the various procedures would take a full day at a time. Qais seemed to regard the hospital environment as beyond reproach and wasn't particularly worried. Besides, he wasn't allowed to enter the ward and the staff at Nafisa's hospital had been instructed what to do in case he turned up suddenly. After all, Nafisa sometimes had to perform surgery, which could last several hours, and Freshta wasn't allowed to leave the hospital without her. As a matter of fact, since Roshangol had disappeared Qais' hatred of Freshta, whom he blamed for the whole tragedy, seemed to have given way to a growing indifference. He was spending more and more time away from home, claiming he was earning money for Grandpa's, Mother's and Mad's pilgrimage to Mecca and Freshta once boasted that he had almost stopped demanding physical contact.

Heidi would sometimes ask me about my sister-in-law and I knew it was John who was behind her questions. I told her the truth and Heidi was shocked. She even forgave me for keeping our family ties secret for such a long time.

'But you see, Heidi, what happened to Freshta is not typical. I mean, it does happen but it's not typical. It's just that Qais is a particularly stupid bully.'

'Can't she get a divorce?' Heidi once asked me and I went numb. Clearly, John had asked her to take care of the practical side of things. Freshta had by now visited the surgery at least ten times and was referring to John as 'John'. This was quite scandalous, as it was rare for us to utter the names of males who didn't belong to our family.

'If Roshangol were here I would love her to find a man like this,' Freshta quivered in excitement, clearly speaking of herself. 'If I were Roshangol's age, everything might be different,' was what she really wanted to say.

'Well, she could get a divorce but there's a small snag,' I gently explained to Heidi.

'You mean you'll slaughter her, won't you...' she fumed.

'Nobody will slaughter her. I mean, provided she has serious grounds for divorce.'

'Such as?'

'Oh, all sorts of things. But the problem is that her husband will get custody of all their children, you see.' Heidi raised her eyebrows and exclaimed: 'But that's inhuman, that's vile. How can you be so stupid?'

'What do you mean by "we"?' I objected. 'That's how things work in this country... after a divorce young babies stay with the mother but the older children belong to their dad. And once the baby is able to get dressed on its own, off it goes to the father's family. But sometimes even that isn't taken into consideration and babies are taken away while they're still being breastfed and the family hires a wet-nurse. Such things are usually not handled by the courts, the families come to an agreement, that's how it works. This is one of the reasons why so few women get divorced because if they do, well, they have to give up their children.'

Heidi came back the following day, having apparently passed my primitive interpretation of Islamic family law, or rather its local version, to John. I was in the middle of advising Leila. She was quite a tragic case. The Russians had killed her husband, her son had joined the Taliban and was now in hiding in the mountains and Leila was left with seven children and relatives in various refugee camps.

'There's something else I wanted to ask you, Herra...'

'Let me finish with the lady here and then we can have tea,' I suggested and Heidi agreed. I knew something serious was brewing. Mad was entering data on to index cards, and then transferring them into neat tables on the computer, an art that, unlike me, he had mastered so fast and to such a degree of perfection that Heidi was thinking of giving him a full-time job. The only thing stopping her was international conventions against child labour but Mad had almost persuaded her by arguing that in his case nobody could tell if he was a child or an old woman anyway. Now Mad showed an almost ostentatious lack of interest in matters he usually found extremely fascinating. He stared at the papers, muttering under his breath. Only his ears gave him away. They had turned translucent and quivered the way they only did at the most thrilling moments.

'Leila,' I said all of a sudden. 'If someone offered to send your children to Europe to school, would do you do that?' The woman, whose once beautiful face was now drawn, with her nose protruding from her wrinkled face in an almost shocking way, said without hesitation: 'Yes I would, right away.'

'Even if you couldn't go with them?'

'I wouldn't want to, anyway.'

'And wouldn't you miss them?'

'No.'

Leila stopped to think for a moment. 'My eldest daughter,' she said. 'The boys can make ends meet anywhere but a girl can meet a tragic fate... you know what I mean.'

I gathered she was alluding to a bad marriage. Afghan parents took credit for choosing the right partners for their children and blamed themselves for a failed marriage.

'And would you like her to marry a European?'

'No, I wouldn't want that,' Leila said firmly. 'But I'm sure she could find a Muslim there, couldn't she? After all, so many of our people have gone abroad. And now they own houses and cars and clean clothes. She could marry one of them and bring her siblings over later so I could die in peace.'

'Hmm, I don't think it would be so easy,' I sighed handing Leila a food stamp, which would get her a few kilos of rice, a couple of bars of soap, if available, and perhaps even a litre of rancid cooking oil, if she were willing to fight others in a queue.

I found John sitting at a table next to Heidi in the garden. He was lost in thought. Mad didn't even try to gatecrash our conspiratorial meeting, which I found rather suspicious. It upset me that John and Heidi stopped whispering when they saw me, as if I had just been the topic of their discussion. Besides, I didn't exactly feel like talking to them about family matters, although that was obviously what they wanted to discuss.

'I'd like to help Freshta,' John started bravely. Luckily, he hadn't yet acquired the Afghan habit of chatting about the health of assorted friends and family, the weather, the construction of a house, politics, earthquakes, and this year's harvest before broaching the true purpose of a meeting. John knew I was inured to these local rituals. He avoided looking me in the eye, as if he were ashamed of associating with my sister-in-law. I had guessed that Freshta was visiting the surgery more often than necessary, that Nafisa was doing her best to cover up for her, and that it no longer had anything to do with her health problems.

'Well, you've already helped Freshta a lot. She says she's feeling much better,' I said coolly.

'I meant helping her in a more fundamental way. Dragging her out of the gutter she's been living in.'

'She's not been living in a gutter. We have a nice house, a wonderful family, the place is clean and we have enough to eat. Her children are healthy and her parents are fortunately still quite young.'

'She's terribly unhappy,' Heidi whispered.

'C'mon, what do you know about that?' I fumed. 'She doesn't speak any English, what could she have told you...' I realised that Mad was often present during John's meetings with Freshta and that he would have made an ideal interpreter and organiser of a small family conspiracy.

'I understand her completely,' John whispered as if someone could hear us. Nobody said a word for a while and it was just a question of time before someone spelled things out. I couldn't take it any longer.

'If you fooled her into thinking you could take her away from here, you've done her a terrible injustice, John,' I said, tears welling up in my eyes.

'But I mean it, Herra. I want to marry her.' I was left speechless. John was an honest man. Handsome and masculine, perhaps a bit timid, which was at odds with his tall and muscular build.

'Herra, nobody needs to know anything, except for you, Mad and us. And once she's gone you can say it was all done behind your back...' Heidi was in her element. This is what she had dreamt of before coming to this country. Of rescuing oppressed Afghan women and smuggling them to Europe wrapped in Persian rugs if need be.

'You've lost your mind,' I said, raising my voice to stop myself from crying. 'You have no idea what might happen. The family will report you to the police and there will be an international row. Your organisation will be expelled from the country and you can count yourself lucky if you don't get your throat slit in a vendetta... Does Dominic know about this?' I blasted away, really scared now. But John seemed determined and wasn't really seeking my advice but my cooperation.

'None of that will happen if you help us, Herra.'

'And what about Freshta?' it suddenly struck me. 'Has she agreed to any of this? I bet she has no inkling of it! Perhaps she thought John recommended a different kind of ointment when in fact he was telling her he would take her to Europe...'

'Hardly,' John said unusually sharply. 'Hardly. I've discussed it with her many times. Yesterday, most recently. And we've also discussed her children.'

'That's exactly it, her children. Can you imagine us secretly driving Freshta to the airport with all her children, trying to look inconspicuous? That would be a laugh. We'll get busted before you board the plane. An Afghan woman is not allowed to travel anywhere without explicit approval from her husband, brother or father... Nobody will issue her a passport without one!'

'You see, that's what Freshta has been saying too. And she understands that she won't be able to take all her children with her and has agreed to take just two... the youngest ones, of course.' John surprised me with his expertise. 'And she also said you could sort it out.'

'What do you mean?'

'Well, you could get your husband to support her passport application. Before they realise at the airport that she's got a husband as well as a brother, we'll be long gone...' Heidi said triumphantly.

I shook my head in disbelief. 'Never. I shall never do that. They might kill my Nazir,' I said getting up and swiftly going back to where my women were waiting. I was confused. I felt John and Heidi staring daggers at my back and I knew they knew that they had already persuaded me only I didn't yet realise it. And I also felt great envy. How come it had never occurred to them that I might want to leave, too? And that Nazir might want to leave? And Mad? After a few steps I couldn't help it and turned around: 'Do you want me to lie to my whole family? What kind of people are you? I really don't know what kind of people you are!' I spat out the words really loudly, making Heidi get up and run to me.

'Herra, please, don't be mad. It's not against the family, it's for the family.'

'Except the family will never understand the good you've committed on its behalf. And I will never be forgiven for having even discussed it with you.' I was beginning to cry.

'Don't be silly, Herra, we worked it all out with Mad a long time ago,' said Heidi, stroking my head really gently for the first time since we met.

chapter 22

MAD AND I crouched in the courtyard outside our windows playing marbles.

Mad was winning, as always. Nobody else stood a chance as his little sausage-like fingers flicked the marbles with great precision every time. Not even my husband, who was past master at this Afghan game.

'The Ministry of Defence have started recruiting for the army,' Mad said out of the blue.

'Yes, the Germans and the Americans are training them. I've heard about it.'

'But they've just launched another huge recruitment drive because they've realised that the former Mujahideen don't pass muster, even though they have been fighting for twenty years,' said Mad and shot a marble into my face. It hurt and he laughed. 'Whoops, that was meant for your eye!'

'Are you thinking of signing up? They only take men over eighteen,' I said, disinclined to point out that in Mad's case age would hardly have been the greatest obstacle.

'No one knows anybody's age anyway. If you tell them I'm your son and that you remember giving birth to me eighteen and a half years ago, they'll buy it.'

'Usury and lies are forbidden,' I said, trying to lighten up the conversation.

'I see, you think they'll sneer at you if they hear I'm your son,' he continued pestering me.

'That's not fair, Mad. Nothing could be further from the truth. I'm just worried that...'

'I could sign up for an intelligence unit. Spooks don't have to be well-built, they just have to be inconspicuous.'

'Oh yeah, sure,' I replied, thinking that the only creature that might be more conspicuous than Mad was the two-headed calf recently shown on TV.

'OK, I do rather stick out but that wouldn't be a big problem. The main thing is, it would never occur to anyone that I, of all people, might be a spy. And besides, my voice sounds a bit like a woman's and that's quite unusual for intelligence men, too.'

I had to concede Mad had a point there. Mad sounded less like a fourteen-year-old child and more like an ageing woman who had made a conscious effort to lower her high-pitched voice by smoking thirty-five Pakistan-made cigarettes a day.

'And I can keep a secret,' he whispered suddenly and fixed me with his stare. I knew what he meant.

It amazed me how easily I had let myself be persuaded that the idea of Freshta eloping with John was realistic. Mad had the logistics worked out down to the last detail. All we had to do, he insisted, was wait for an opportunity. Which presented itself much earlier than we would ever have predicted. I couldn't help feeling I was reading a book by an author who – like the German Karl May writing about Indians without ever having visited an Apache village – set out to write this improbable story of an Afghan woman without having a clue where Afghanistan was on the map.

Mad was much better at persuading me than Heidi and John. He pursued his goal slowly but single-mindedly. Day after day I was inching closer to the idea of faking documents, helping Freshta pack, and deciding which of her children she should take along and which ones she would leave behind. I tried my best to convince myself that by helping Freshta to desert us all, to abandon the family that meant everything to her as well as the certainty that we would always be there for her, was indeed the best thing I could do for her. We kept passing each other as if nothing had happened, although she was bound to know that I knew. For all intents and purposes Qais had moved out by now. He lived with his parents, visiting his sons from time to time and showering them with presents. The boys loved him, for instead of bossing them about or telling them off he would just play with them for a while and bring them Japanese toy cars. My husband said Qais had been gambling and had a lucky streak at cards, and that Allah would punish him one day. He was not to know quite how soon that would happen.

Qais had changed and we all knew that he was grieving for Roshangol more than the rest of us put together. She was the only woman in the world for whom he was willing to make a sacrifice. He had fretted about her chastity from the day she was born, and ever since she turned about two, around the time I arrived in Kabul, he seemed to be on the lookout for slightly older boys who would make suitable bridegrooms. We'd always laughed at him and it had never occurred to us that he might really mean it. After all, he would never have been able to marry Freshta if her tears hadn't overcome her parents' resistance and for at least six months after the wedding he'd been on his best behaviour to show how much he appreciated their consent.

'But Mad, I thought you wanted to go to Mecca, and also to Europe. They won't let you go to either of those places if you become a spook,' I pointed out, hoping to distract Mad from the secret he was obviously dying to discuss with me.

'Europe will have to wait until after I've been to Mecca,' he said. He took his role as Grandpa's and Mother's escort very seriously. He realised the journey would place the greatest demands on him as the one responsible for his two fellow pilgrims. The only thing that worried him was what he would look like wrapped in the white robes, the customary outfit for those who visit the holy sites. He made a few attempts to wrap himself in old sheets and admitted he looked dreadful.

'It doesn't really matter in Mecca,' I assured him. There was no point in claiming the sheets suited him. He had to leave one shoulder bare and tie the ends of the robe on the other shoulder. That's what tradition dictates. The sheets mustn't have any buttons or zips, nothing that might distract from prayers.

'Getting a passport for the journey to Mecca won't be difficult, and then it will be easy to leave for Europe later,' he said and stopped playing with the marbles.

'You're quite wrong there, actually. Pilgrims get one-off passports, only for this purpose. It's a special kind of passport that can't be used for travel anywhere else. And when you come back you have to hand the passport in.' I was surprised that Mad, who was otherwise exceptionally well informed, wasn't aware of this hitch. The Ministry for Pilgrimages to Mecca charged every single Afghan pilgrim 1,500 dollars for this special travel document, the plane ticket, and board and lodging in Mecca. In the case of our family that would add up to a hefty 4,500 dollars.

The passport problem did nothing to discourage Mad.

'Never mind, you'll sort out something when we get back.' It made me laugh and I found it reassuring to learn that he had the same die-hard faith in me as in Allah. 'And don't you laugh – you'll have to arrange one for yourself too.'

'Oh yeah, and where will I be travelling?' I didn't take him too seriously at this moment.

'Well, of course with me, to visit Freshta and John, and later we'll go to Russia together,' he declared.

'Is that what they've promised you?'

'They would like me to come along right away but I can't because of the trip to Mecca. And because of you. You're not ready yet, you would refuse to go. Or wouldn't you?' he asked, to check he didn't get me wrong.

'I'm not going anywhere now or in a year's time. Except perhaps on a little trip with Nazir, and you'll be coming with us of course. But that'll be only for a few weeks or so. Surely we can't leave Grandpa, Mother and Father alone for too long?'

'We can't. But we will,' he said mysteriously, returning to the marbles.

The next day Mother wasn't feeling well. My husband, Mad and I drove her and Father to see a local doctor who was officially employed at the central hospital but spent most of his time in his private practice where he earned five times as much. There was a big crowd of people outside the little house with the sign for Dr Shafiq. We left the parents to their own devices and drove off to work. Mad was whistling, evidently in high spirits. One thing I couldn't get my head around was why all his plans, the short-term as well as the long-term ones, involved me but never my husband. I didn't dare ask him for fear that his reply might break my heart.

Mad rushed to the advice centre and I was immediately summoned to the clinic where John had a patient whose case involved complex social and medical issues. The woman, Navida, had breast cancer and her husband wouldn't give his consent to her treatment. They lived in the tiny village of Nau Nioz about an hour's drive from Kabul.

'Tell them it's still treatable. But they must go to the Russian field hospital. That's where they have all the facilities.'

I translated John's plea.

'We don't have the money,' the woman's emaciated husband told me. 'It took us two days to ride here and now you're turning us away.'

I was surprised to hear him use the word 'ride' as I assumed they had walked, which must have been extremely exhausting for his wife.

'We're not turning you away. I'll come with you. It won't cost you a penny.'

I still don't understand why I offered to accompany them, even though until then I had made a conscious effort to avoid meeting any Russians in Kabul and the mere idea made me break out in a cold sweat. But it was too late now and John was beside himself with joy. He had begged me to go and see the Russians with him several times as he was dying to see their place and knew I would make a perfect guide.

'I'll let Mad know,' he shouted happily and ran to the advice centre. Resigning myself to the situation, I helped the woman walk out of the clinic and started looking for a driver.

'We'll go on our own,' her husband announced firmly and I could tell from the tone of his voice there was no point arguing. 'Just drive slowly and we'll follow you,' he added.

Mad was euphoric. We got into the car, drove out of the gate and started looking for the couple. The emaciated little man stood on the roadside as if to attention, holding the handgrips of a primitive wheelbarrow, the kind market sellers use to transport melons. He was blocking the flow of road traffic. A woman in a burka lay on the dirty wooden platform. So this was how her husband had transported her for two days. Awestruck, we stared at this almost preternatural image. Mad was first to react: 'Hey, brother, leave the wheelbarrow here, we'll bring you back and you can collect it later.'

The man shook his head: 'A friend from Charasia lent it to me. If it gets stolen I'll never be able to repay him till the day I die.' And so we set out. Our shiny, huge white Toyota boasting a long aerial and diplomatic number plates, followed by the scraggy man pushing the wheelbarrow with his wife. We drove at walking pace without uttering a word. After around five hundred metres John suddenly signalled for the driver to stop. I thought he was going to make one more attempt to persuade the couple to join us but I was wrong. John got out of the car and said with a smile: 'Keep going real slow, I'm not too fit.' He went up to the stunned fellow with the wheelbarrow, and with a pat on his shoulder that nearly made the man fall over grabbed the handgrips from his hands. Then he started pushing the wheelbarrow along the bumpy road with such speed and tenacity our driver had to step on it. People turned their heads to look at our peculiar humanitarian convoy, some waving, others roaring with laughter. Only Mad and I stayed deadly serious.

The Russian field hospital was surrounded by a wall made of sandbags and topped with barbed wire. An endless queue stretched from the main entrance. Although we were not the only ones to turn up with a wheelbarrow, the queue parted at the sight of the red-faced, sweat-soaked John. I exchanged a few words in perfect Russian with a surprised young soldier sporting the insignia of the Russian Ministry for Disasters and a few minutes later a fat officer in fatigues arrived.

'Dr Vorobyov,' he introduced himself, shaking my hand.

'I'm Herra,' I replied trying to put on a heavy Tajik accent.

'How the hell did you get here, my lovely?' laughed the officer and I realised for the first time in years that what in this country might pass for intimate banter with a stranger did not necessarily amount to sin. It made me feel great and not even the sight of my husband appearing around the corner would have wiped the blissful grin off my face.

chapter 23

NOBODY NOTICED at first that Qais had really left, that he hadn't just gone off to his parents' place to sulk for a few days but that he had left for good. Only Mad knew. And he also knew that something was brewing.

'I think this might be a good time for Freshta to get her passport,' he said to me one day, looking around cautiously. We had never discussed Freshta's departure before but Mad knew I could barely think of anything else. Not that I cared about Freshta that much; it was more out of concern for myself, Mad, my husband and for our whole family, for it's one thing for a husband to leave his wife giving her a chance to mend her ways and perhaps come begging a few months later for him to take her back, and quite another for the wife to elope from Afghanistan with her white lover, and one who wasn't circumcised at that and – worst of all – to take along her children who belong to the father's family come what may, whatever scoundrel, drug addict or murderer he might be.

'But who will give the consent, Mad...'

'I've got it all figured out, don't worry' Mad said and I was sure he really had figured it all out. But even he wasn't ready for what happened a few days later.

Our first thought was that the reconciliation phase had arrived much earlier than expected. Qais' parents' car stopped outside our house after Friday prayers. A vast number of people emerged, some of whom I had never seen before. As soon as we saw them, Mother and I retreated into the closet where, not having learned my lesson, I installed myself next to the glass wall, which had since been fixed, and although it no longer had a spyhole, it still allowed us to hear quite a lot. Before launching into a self-important speech, Qais' father polished off a small bowl of almonds and three cups of tea. Freshta sat in the corner of the closet pretending to have no interest whatsoever in what went on next door. Baby Yunus, as if sensing it was preferable to keep as low a profile as possible right now, refrained from his usual howling. Freshta didn't come out to welcome her father-in-law, nor her mother-in-law who, contrary to tradition, was also part of the delegation. Father, with Grandpa by his side, assumed a courteous sitting position and asked my husband to keep quiet. Situations of this kind, quite common in Afghan families, which only resort to the courts to settle family affairs in extreme cases, required great composure and restraint, qualities my husband wasn't exactly blessed with.

Kamal was holding little Hamayun in his arms, Rustam served tea, and all three boys were extremely proud of being admitted into male company. They felt this was their rightful place, rather than being with us women. I shuddered at the thought that even two-year-old Hamayun, by virtue of being physically present in the more important room, now wielded more decision-making power than Freshta, myself or Mother.

Following a prolonged exchange of introductory pleasantries, with everyone asking about everybody's health at least six times and thanking Allah for sparing everyone's life for the past fourteen days, silence ensued. It was broken by Qais' father, a fat and rather unpleasant man who had fathered so many sons he didn't remember all their names. His wife didn't join us in the closet, to signal that this was no friendly visit, staying instead with the men, something she, as a woman of advanced age, was entitled to on exceptional occasions such as this.

'We'd like to take the boys away. No ill feelings but it'll be better this way,' Qais' father suddenly announced quite amicably.

Giving him the same kind of look my Dad used to give my Mum when he had had a drop too many, Father said: 'The boys are happy here and their school is nearby. It will be difficult for them to get here from where you live in the *Mikrorayon*.'

'We also have a school in our *Mikrorayon* and the teachers are just as good as the ones here,' Qais' father replied solemnly.

Whenever my Dad had come home giving us the look our Father now gave Qais' father, we knew he had drunk at least two badly-rinsed milk cartons of beer, washing them down with vodka that hadn't been chilled or distilled properly. He would babble some nonsense and call Mum names. She would take his clothes off, clean him up and put him to bed. Then she would wash the jumper he had been sick on while walking home and stay up all night wiping the sweat from his brow while he slept. But neither my husband, nor Father, nor his father had ever drunk beer from a milk carton or been drunk enough to be sick. They had never made Mother undress them while they were wasted, or made her clean up a messy bathroom after them. Nevertheless, following what seemed a rather cursory discussion, they gave their consent to Rustam and Kamal leaving our house and following their father to a musty block of flats with no running water where the toilet had to be regularly unblocked with a long piece of wire because it wouldn't flush properly and the accumulated excrement had very nearly driven the inhabitants out of their living quarters, and where everyone could hear every squeak due to the poor soundproofing. An hour later our family also agreed to sacrifice Hamayun. I felt like leaping up and storming into the men's room to say something but glancing at Freshta I saw she was sitting in the corner with a contented smile. And I realised this really was none of my business.

Mad kept pouring tea, stoically enduring the curious and disdainful looks of the visitors, which showed sympathy as well as a certain respect, albeit directed at us rather than at him. Not only did we tolerate a creature like this in our midst but also dared to present it in public. Had he lost a limb or been a hunchback he would, of course, have been deserving of more care than a newborn baby or a pregnant wife. But this sort of thing? Rather than sympathy, Mad aroused a degree of disgust few people were able to conceal.

The boys got up and gave Father a questioning look. He just nodded and said: 'Anything you take with you now is yours forever, whatever it may be.' I had never seen anyone actually raising these kids. They lived in the street, learned how to wait on guests and having been surrounded by males from an early age they acted the way they had seen others behave. That's probably why they stood up and went off to pack a spare Afghan suit each, their marbles, three chequered scarves, a catapult and two broken toy cars that had once been driven by a flywheel.

I looked at Freshta. 'Aren't you going to say good-bye to them?'

'No,' she snapped.

At that point I heard Qais' mother in the room next door and my heart sank. 'And where's baby Yunus?'

'He's asleep,' Father said curtly.

'Bring him,' Qais' father intervened, getting up to signal that the negotiations were over.

'Let Yunus stay with his mother. She is still breastfeeding him. That's what the laws say,' our Father said, standing up too, in a fighting mood.

'Unless you want us to tell the judge how you've brought up your daughter, that you allowed our granddaughter to leave the house, what sort of clothes you made her wear and how you made her go to a school where she wasn't being properly raised, as well as all the things you've taught our children, you'd better bring Yunus and we'll part in peace,' Qais' father said emphatically. Freshta looked at me from her corner and opened her mouth as if to say something. I put my finger across my mouth to silence her. Mother crossed her arms on her chest and started weeping soundlessly.

'Mad, bring Yunus,' I heard Qais order the boy in an unusually soft voice. 'It'll be better to sort everything out peacefully,' Qais added and I was grateful that he didn't make a fuss.

'Don't do it, it's not good for the child whom you love as much as we love him,' said Grandpa in what was a highly significant contribution to the discussion, since he was the oldest person in the room and it wasn't the done thing to oppose him. Qais' father was aware of this but he was ready.

'You know, brother,' he said gently, 'we're not happy with the way our children have been raised in this house. It's because of you that we have lost Roshangol whom we also love very much. We can't let anything more happen to other members of our esteemed tribe that might bring so much shame on us that we may be barred from the mosque. You've let the children watch films that are banned everywhere in the country, Yunus' mother has been visiting foreigners on her own and has made friends with a woman who spends all day unsupervised with Europeans wearing short trousers...'

Everything Qais' father said was true and it was impossible to object. Against all expectations my husband, instead of exploding, said quietly but very firmly: 'One more word about our women and there'll be trouble...' Nobody said another word. Mad returned to our closet, his chin crumpled like a headscarf. I knew this expression of his well. I don't think he was particularly attached to baby Yunus but he adored Freshta almost as much as he adored me.

He thought she was a goddess and claimed she resembled Miriam, who had given birth to Isa beneath a palm tree while remaining a virgin, which was a proven fact, as it said so in both holy books, the Bible and the Quran. He was right. It certainly did say so. For him Miriam, as well as Mary and Freshta, were symbols of beauty while Isa, or Jesus, was the epitome of meaningful suffering even though Mad wasn't quite clear who was right, the Christians who believed that Jesus was the son of God, which was why he had to die on the cross, or the Muslims, who claimed that the other religions only believed that he died on the cross. In any case, Mad was the only one among us who realised this was the moment of the Last Judgment and later described the scene in these terms. Freshta got up and said with hatred: 'Here, take him, he won't bring them any joy, only pain and unhappiness.' This was the only time in my life I've seen a loving, breastfeeding mother curse her own baby. The visitors had already gathered in the hallway and some started putting on their shoes waiting for Mad to bring baby Yunus. Freshta didn't pack anything for the baby. No clothes, not even the fancy glass bottle my husband and I had bought her two days after Yunus was born at the bazaar from a seller who imported amazing commodities like this from Germany, not even the little hat that said 'I ♥ NY' which Heidi had once given to me for Freshta.

We all went to bed very early that night. There were no children in the house apart from Mad, who behaved in an almost inappropriately grown-up way. This must have been the first time Freshta slept in her little room alone.

'Perhaps I should join her,' Mad said quietly.

'Perhaps you should,' my husband replied as both of them sat up on the mattress to assess the situation. My husband lit a cigarette. He put the packet back in his pocket, then looked at Mad and took it out again. Opening it he courteously stretched his arm out toward Mad. The boy pulled out a cigarette without batting an eyelid.

'I have one great advantage,' he said in that deep feminine voice of his that seemed to have got a whole octave lower today.

'You have lots of advantages, Mad,' my husband smiled but didn't dare to list them.

'But there's one fundamental one.'

'You're as clever as a monkey.'

'That I am, too, but that's not what's most important,' Mad grinned.

Suddenly I knew what he was going to say and I felt a pain in the pit of my stomach. I sat up on the bed, took my husband's hand and said, looking Mad in the eye: 'I know what you mean, Mad.' I really did. My husband put his arm around me and asked roguishly: 'C'mon, out with it, you two.'

Mad inhaled deeply, stared somewhere above our heads to signal that what he was going to say would be quite a revelation and then enunciated slowly: 'My greatest advantage is that nobody apart from the two of you wants me. Which means I'll never leave you.'

chapter 24

MOTHER'S HEALTH deteriorated after the children had left. In fact, we all felt there was something improper about a house devoid of chattering little beings. Mad tried to tempt some of his friends to come over to our house but they soon got bored with him as Afghan children love to run around and are not too keen on browsing through books. Freshta barely spoke and her visits to our clinic, in Nafisa's company, grew ever more frequent. Although Qais stopped coming to our house, officially he was still her husband. According to Afghan custom this was a kind of trial separation and there was still the danger that after a few months the husband might invite his wife to come back to him, once she had mended her ways and been punished. Women often accepted this generous offer for the sake of their children. Freshta, however, seemed to have become fixated on something quite different. One day I caught her in the little room with Mad, swotting up on basic English vocabulary. They both looked sheepish. By now we all realised that our secret plan boiled down to organising a passport for Freshta and coming to terms with the bitter truth that she would never see her parents again.

That Friday morning Mother wasn't feeling well and looked like a wizened apricot. After driving her and Father to see Dr Shafiq again, my husband took our car, which was perennially breaking down, to the garage. Freshta and I were preparing lunch in silence. It was broken by Freshta's quiet observation as we peeled some scalded tomatoes: 'You ought to get out of here.'

'Who do you mean?' I said, pretending I didn't understand.

'You and Nazir.'

'Oh yeah, and where do you suggest we should go?'

'To Russia. Via Europe. John could help you and you've got plenty of relatives in Russia, haven't you? Or you could ask the Russians who are stationed here to help you. They can fly you over by helicopter. They fly back and forth all the time.'

'But Freshta, I've got relatives here, too. Just like you. Do you want to leave Mad to look after Mother, Father and Grandpa? Besides, Mad said you want to take him with you.'

'But he doesn't want to leave until he's been to Mecca. Although Nafisa doesn't think that's a good idea. She thinks he ought to stay here.'

Lately Nafisa had been dropping increasingly forceful hints that Mad had only been loaned to us and that she wasn't quite sure how much longer he would stay with us. She would say this with an inscrutable face and I couldn't tell if she was referring to his illness and inability to live to an advanced age, or to some kind of obligation towards whoever had lent him to us.

'Nazir will never leave his parents behind,' I said reservedly and was relieved to hear someone knock on the door and put a stop to our conversation. Mad came in, panting and jabbering excitedly: 'Get a mattress ready, Grandma has to lie down.' Freshta and I peered out into the street and spotted a weird couple in the distance, swaying like young poplars in the wind. Something was towering above their heads but they were too far away for us to tell what it was. Only once they came closer did I recognise Mother in a burka with Father by her side carrying a wooden pole, to which a hospital bottle filled with a yellow liquid was attached with a piece of cloth. A tube from the vessel passed under the burka. Father was walking quite fast, reinforcing the impression that he was walking Mother on a leash and spurring her on with the pole from time to time. Mother pleaded with him from under the burka to slow down, crying that he was pulling the needle out of her vein. In his defence Father cited the doctor who had said she should go to bed immediately as her blood pressure was reaching critical levels, and that was why they had to walk faster. There was a risk that Mother might not live to lie down on her mattress. As soon as she reached the courtyard we pulled the burka off her, revealing a face that had turned completely green. With her left hand she was clutching her right arm, into which a needle was stuck. Apparently forgetting that he was connected to Mother by a tube Father dashed into the house, dragging the exhausted woman behind him. He didn't stop until they were inside their room. He placed the pole in a corner and Mother collapsed under it. Grandpa, who observed the whole scene from the far corner, said after a long pause: 'You've got to get better. I'm not going to Mecca without you.' Mother responded with a grateful smile.

Freshta, Mad and I held a stormy discussion outside in the courtyard. 'Let's take her to the Russian hospital,' Mad suggested.

'Would you be up to it, Mad?' I asked him.

'Herra, if you don't come she won't get proper treatment. That officer, you remember, he couldn't take his eyes off you.'

Our visit to the Russian field hospital had been among the most dangerous and horrendous experiences of my life and I had no intention of repeating it, not even for the sake of my family. It was a miracle that my husband hadn't found out about our breakneck expedition. Or at least I hoped that he hadn't. I was sure that, had he as much as suspected that I had crossed the threshold of a Russian military base, he would have reacted a hundred times more ruthlessly than Qais.

The Russians had been genuinely happy to discover I was their *zemliachka*, a fellow-countrywoman. And in spite of my valiant effort to mangle my native tongue they figured out that I had had the benefits of a higher education.

'You've got to come and work for us. We'll pay you as much as you want. You can use our *banya*, the steam sauna, we get our food flown in from Moscow regularly and we have enough vodka to swim in,' the officer boomed. He spent his days performing one reamputation after another, operating on rotting tumours, tinkering with wounds that had been potentially fatal weeks before he started treating them, constantly muttering under his breath: 'Tough as old boots, these Afghans. No wonder we lost the war against them. This fellow should have been dead long ago and still he makes it to our hospital on his bike and demands aspirin.'

We spent three hours at the Russian hospital. John inspected all the wards thoroughly, showing his appreciation for the excellent air conditioning of the tent and for the equipment the Russians had promised to bequeath to an Afghan hospital when it was time for them to go back, and enjoying the hospitality, particularly the red caviar. He scoffed it with great gusto, dropping a few globules into his lap with every bite. Picking them up carefully he lovingly stuffed them back into his mouth. He was offered a big shot of vodka in a plastic cup and before long his eyes had glazed over and his movements had become languid.

'We might have to load him on to the wheelbarrow on the way back,' Mad whispered into my ear but he didn't seem to be angry. Quite the opposite. He was in seventh heaven and seemed quite at home there. For a moment I reflected on how surprisingly well he fitted in and how much he resembled these nice and friendly smiling Russian faces around us. Once the doctors reached a sufficient state of inebriation after emptying a large number of plastic cups, it was impossible to tell them from Mad. That's what it was: of course, I finally had it – Mad resembled a drunken Russian. Strangely enough, the doctors weren't really struck by his bizarre physical make-up and only commented on how many Russian words the kid had picked up.

Two Russian nurses looked after our patient and her husband, and after separating the horrified man from his faint wife started to attend to her, loudly cursing, 'the Afghan conditions that have brought so much suffering to the people of this country'. After a while they asked me to explain to the little man that his wife's breast would have to be cut off but not to worry, it wasn't a big deal and would be done in a couple of days. It occurred to me that other field hospitals run by assorted peace corps would not even have looked at the woman, since Afghans were not allowed in. Besides, they would spend months examining her, to ensure she complied with the standards of hygiene, checking the family's medical history and God knows what else until the weary husband would end up driving his wife back home on his wheelbarrow half dead.

As we staggered out of the hospital all three of us felt quite strange. It was as if we had been to the cinema after a long time and watched something that was strictly forbidden and immoral, and that we actually found rather repulsive. But instead of leaving during the interval we stayed on and now John was totally drunk and we had to get him home somehow without attracting too much attention. Throughout our drive back our driver held a dirty rag in front of his face, probably something he used to clean the engine, so that he wouldn't have to inhale the smell of alcohol that John was exuding.

And now Mad was suggesting that we entrust Mother to the care of the Russian doctors. I remembered we had left the entire hospital team totally drunk and in the hands of the uncouth officer who had emptied a bottle of vodka in fifteen minutes, biting into pickled gherkins in between swigs. If he didn't have to perform more surgeries that day he would have stuffed himself with dried fish between the gulps of vodka. He reminded me so much of my Dad that I had trouble concentrating on a proper conversation with him. John ate everything that was proffered but wasn't capable of the simplest activity, let alone a breast amputation. For example, he had trouble getting out of the car in a dignified manner. Our Russian hosts who, unlike John, managed to stay upright, laughed and shouted at me: 'Hey, Russian beauty, we're expecting you tomorrow, we'll all go to the *banya* together, starkers!' A chortle of rather obscene laughter followed but for some reason I didn't really mind. I guess because it was free of malice. Fortunately, John was almost totally out of it and let us push him along. Mad pushed him from behind by his haunches, shouting at the Afghans who stood around gawping: 'Get out of the way, this man has a serious and highly contagious illness. If you get any closer you and your family are doomed.' It worked: the crowd let us through and followed us with embarrassed looks. Those among them who had been in the queue when we arrived still remembered that John had had no problem pushing the cart. He hadn't struck them as someone who could infect anyone with anything but good spirits and now they couldn't figure out what the hospital had done to this man who had presented a picture of health only a little earlier. Their willingness to seek medical attention in this place was waning rapidly. Seeing anyone else in this state, the Afghans would have treated him with the utmost contempt. But everyone loved John and people always forgave him before taking offence.

We laid him in his Dubai-made bed, in which he normally refused to sleep, preferring a mattress, and covered his head with a wet cloth.

'Is he going to sleep for a long time?' asked Mad, who lacked practical experience with alcohol.

'I hope so. And when he wakes up he'll have a terrible headache,' I said, giving my expert opinion.

'Is it true that drunken Russian soldiers used to rape our Afghan women?' Muhammad asked out of the blue. I was dumbfounded.

'Maybe…' I said, flushing with embarrassment. 'Maybe the odd rape did happen, you know what it's like in wartime… and they might not have been drunk. Afghan women are beautiful and perhaps it wasn't necessarily rape, not all Russian soldiers are that ugly after all. You see… we all sometimes do something we might later regret,' I stammered as something told me Muhammad wasn't asking out of mere curiosity.

'So why did he do it if it's going to make him unwell?' Mad asked, abruptly changing the subject and giving John a gentle prod. He had passed out and didn't respond. He had just started snoring horrendously.

'He hoped it would make him dream of something beautiful. Something that would let him forget his problems, that sort of thing.' I wasn't really sure what to say.

'Oh, so he's probably going to dream of Freshta. And of me. Of all of us walking down the streets of New York or Moscow,' Mad said dreamily, as if he had also downed a few shots of vodka.

The experience with the Russians shocked Mad profoundly. Up until then he had imagined them as dim, ugly soldiers who would take to their heels at the first war cry of *Allahu Akbar* and the only thing they were good at was bombing Afghan villages in the most cowardly way imaginable, from the relative safety of a fighter jet. Vodka had been part of Mad's idea of Russians so it surprised him that it was John who got drunk rather than the Russian officer or the nurses who had gulped down much more liquor than our unfortunate Polish–American friend.

'I thought they would be much worse,' he told me back at home that night, after we got ourselves thoroughly scrubbed and perfumed to make sure not even a trace of the alien smell, the mixture of Russian sweat with vodka and caviar, would cling to us.

'Much more stupid,' he said, lost in thought. 'But that officer was quite nice. And he was a wonderful singer. And he treats our people, too...' Mad mused aloud and I was surprised to realise I found his positive attitude towards my fellow countrymen rather heart-warming.

'And none of them has noticed how strange I am,' he suddenly said, surprised as if he had only now realised it. 'And they didn't ask any questions. Just like you, Herra, haven't been asking me any questions either.'

'And what on earth should I ask you about?'

'Well, for example, how I ended up in your family. And why Nafisa brought me here.'

'I don't care,' I lied. 'You've just fallen from heaven, He has sent you to us.'

'Hmm, except that you don't know if He's sent me as a reward for your good deeds or as a punishment for your sins. Do you have any great sins, Herra?'

I pondered his question. Not that I couldn't think of any sins, I just didn't know which one was the greatest.

'Well, I do have one rather big one,' I answered after a while. I knew I couldn't explain to Mad what trouble I had got my husband into on our wedding night.

'Perhaps it's because of this sin that God has deprived you of the chance to bear your own children. Because God is the only one who can punish our sins. Nobody else has the right to do that. "As for those who slander virtuous, believing women who are careless, cursed are they in the world and in the hereafter. Theirs will be an awful doom.".' Mad sang out in his croaky voice, rather out of tune. I found it quite terrifying that he was able to read my thoughts so accurately. Whenever my husband was really angry he would say he should have killed me that night but the torment caused by my infertility was a much greater punishment. He was right, but only to an extent. It was a greater punishment for him than for me. I couldn't help it, I just wasn't a true Afghan woman who would rather die than become the object of mockery, contempt and compassion just because she can't bear offspring. I would never exchange my own life for child bearing.

'And then God had mercy on me and gave me you,' I smiled at Mad.

'No. It wasn't like that, Herra. Nafisa just brought me along because she didn't know where to put me. Nobody wanted me. You were the only one who we knew wouldn't turn me away. And your family is very tolerant...'

Mad pronounced the word tolerant with a strange emphasis and in an almost English accent.

'I learned it from the dictionary yesterday,' he giggled. 'It's a good word.'

'You have some siblings, don't you, Mad?'

'I do.'

'And where are they?'

'With my mother.'

'And why aren't you with her, too?'

'Her husband was scared of me. Or rather, disgusted by me. He thought I was *shaitan*, the devil.'

'And where is your dad?'

'In paradise. Or in hell. It's hard to tell.'

'I see. So your dad died, your mum remarried and the new father didn't want you. But hang on, something is not quite right here, Mad. If a woman remarries she has to give her children to her late husband's family. That's almost a law, isn't it?'

'Only almost. There are exceptions to every law. The man who married my mother is quite old and he needed someone to look after him. So he married mother with her children. But he knew I would die soon, sooner than him, so I wouldn't be around to wipe his brow on his deathbed. It was he who would have had to do it for me. And besides...' Mad paused pointedly and gave me a look that was meant to emphasise the importance of the situation. 'Besides, my dad's family doesn't even know I exist. And they wouldn't want me. I don't think they really respect this law of ours, you see. I don't think my dad was a decent man. In fact, I think he was a bastard.'

'Are you angry with your mum for having abandoned you?' I asked, shocked by an urgency that was quite rare in Mad, and hoping to bring this awkward conversation to an end. In fact, I had no desire to find out who his father was. It struck me that a kind of loneliness and otherness compared with everyone around us wasn't the only thing we shared and that we might have more in common than I had guessed before. And the fact that I had friends in Russia wasn't the only reason Mad was so keen to go there but that he was attracted to the place in some profound way.

Frowning a little, Mad sang out again: '"And we have ordained that man be kind to his parents, for having borne him in great pain his mother had weaned him off after two years, and we said: Be grateful to Me and to your parents, as I am the ultimate goal." This is what Allah has said according to the Prophet. So I'm grateful to my parents, even though they produced me by accident. It really was a mischance.'

'So Mad, who was your real dad then, if it's not a secret?' I couldn't resist asking after all, even though I already knew the answer.

'That's a big secret,' he said softly.

chapter 25

I RAN OUT of the courtyard as soon as I heard the hysterical screaming. For the first time in twelve years I did not bother to cover myself with a burka or even a headscarf or throw any other piece of cloth over my head. My hair that was the colour of peed-on straw, as my husband used to say, was down, flapping behind me like a banner, and I ventured out among people dressed only in a light shirt down to my knees that would have showed off every kind of shape, let alone my rather voluptuous one, and a pair of trousers that had shrunk in the wash and shamelessly revealed my ankles. I don't know where my sudden fitness came from but I found myself flying in huge leaps and bounds, and although I was aware of not being too graceful my movements were quite purposeful and pragmatic and did achieve their goal. I advanced much faster than usual. I left the gate open, and stumbling on a piece of wood that was lying outside the door I flew several metres ahead, falling flat into the dust of the road like a frog. People were running past me, someone helped me get up and went on running without taking any notice. Behind me Freshta was puffing and Mother, for whom this was the second run in her life, was panting. The first time it happened was when the Panshir Valley was under Russian bombardment and she was convinced the shells would hit their hut of all possible huts. Grandpa laughs to this day when he describes how Mother's fat body quivered as she yelled: 'Nazir, Nazir, get the goat.' Then she remembered it wasn't just the goat but also Freshta who was still in the house. 'Forget the goat, get Freshta,' she screamed as she reached the outhouse. Nazir and Freshta apparently stood in the courtyard laughing so much they couldn't move, as this was the first time they had seen their mother run. I would have been about ten years old then. I hadn't seen my Mum run too many times either. Only once, when our dog chased after a cat did Mum start to run, screaming: 'Herra, Herra, move it, for goodness sake, make sure the dog doesn't end up under a car!' I also laughed so much I couldn't move as I watched my Mum bounce up and down in pursuit of the agile, disobedient animal.

There was blood on the palms of my hands and sharp little pebbles got stuck in my skin. I felt a searing pain. Without looking back, I kept racing ahead following everyone else to the place that resounded with the sort of screaming a crowd generates whenever something exciting happens. Freshta, who was much fitter and could run faster than I, caught up with me and stayed by my side instead of overtaking me. She was wearing a burka and looked like a ghost who had seen itself in the mirror and given itself a fright.

Mother lagged behind, for her legs still didn't serve her as well as they should have, even though her health had improved since she had been on the drip. I didn't have the slightest intention of waiting for her.

When I first arrived in Kabul and my husband allowed me to go to the bazaar for the first time with Mother, as the two of us strode among the market stalls, dignified in our burkas, Mother kept hissing at me: 'Don't run so fast, we walk slowly here.' Later at home she told me off for being too distracted and unfocused, for bouncing and undulating like some kind of ballet dancer, giving myself away as a foreigner, and said I shouldn't be surprised if boys tried to pinch my hips through the burka. Once when my husband and I went to collect material for my new dress, my prancing must have been too provocative making me look more bouncy in my burka than other Afghan women, I felt someone stroke my buttocks from behind. I turned around and thrust my fist right into the nose of the person standing nearest behind me. He was an elderly short man, who probably just happened to be passing by. He started waving his arms and muttered something I couldn't understand, angrily spluttering green and brown spittle all around. He must have been happily chewing on his snuff when he suddenly found himself in the line of fire. My husband pounced on him and grabbed him by the neck but the man hastily pointed to the side where a crestfallen one-legged man stood, looking lonely and humble. As my husband approached him, I cowered behind his back. All he said was: 'Aren't you ashamed of yourself, a hero like you?' I don't know if they were acquainted and the legless man just failed to realise I belonged to the famous warrior, or whether my husband just assumed that anyone missing a limb must have lost it in the righteous struggle against one of the country's many invaders. The invalid didn't say a word. My husband looked down on the ground, thought for a while and then, with a quick flick of his left leg tripped up the cripple's only leg, the one he had been standing on. The man collapsed in a helpless heap without even trying to hold out his hands to cushion his collision with the hard surface, or trying to close his eyes to avoid seeing his own humiliation. He just tumbled down staring at my husband all the while. My husband spat at the man, taking care not to hit him right in the face. He hit his sunken chest, and I guess it didn't hurt too much as the cripple didn't protest. I pulled my husband's sleeve to signal I wanted to leave but he broke free from me in fury and gave the hero a big kick in the stomach. Then we left. The circle of onlookers that had formed around us parted respectfully and as long as we were within sight, nobody approached the poor wretch to help him get back on the one leg that was all he now had to carry him around the world. We handled the situation with dignity. Later at home I had to listen to my husband's hour-long angry lecture on how I shouldn't prance and run around the bazaar and that I had to hold on to the front of my burka to make absolutely sure nobody could glimpse even a bit of my thighs covered in trousers loose enough to hide several nuclear warheads. Basically, the main thing was that nobody should get the idea that the being underneath the garb was endowed with anything remotely resembling a female shape.

'This is not Moscow,' he yelled at me, as if I hadn't noticed a long time ago. 'They are wild and famished and they're idiots, lechers, morons...' He shook me as if I were to blame for the fact that thirty-year-old unmarried men lacked opportunities to satisfy their lust without getting married, or that their permanently pregnant wives didn't provide sufficient opportunities for sexual gratification either.

It seemed as if I were running faster and faster but the place I was trying to reach seemed to be getting ever more distant even though originally it was a mere two hundred metres from our house. Once Roshangol had run out of the house like this and Qais followed her, yelling like a lunatic: 'You go one step further, you little bitch, and I'll shoot you dead!' She was running away from him and I think she couldn't care less that he wanted to shoot her. This was after he had discovered that in a box where she kept some rather worn-out face make-up, she had hidden the photo of a muscular blond man, some American actor wearing a pair of exceedingly tiny swimming trunks. His extremely well-endowed manhood was squeezed so tightly into the puny shorts that the picture elicited sympathy rather than lust. I have no idea where she cut it out from but judging by how well-thumbed it was she must have consulted it quite frequently. Freshta wanted to run after her but Qais stopped her by the gate and with a violent push sent her flying back into the courtyard, making her collapse on the path. We still had the wandering rabbits back then. Thinking that something highly interesting was happening they dragged their cage towards Freshta, who was lying on the ground shedding angry tears. Gargosh and Margosh pushed their snouts through the bars, hoping for something to eat. Freshta got up, lifted the cage a little bit and carried it back to a grassy patch. The rabbits, the ends of their claws barely touching the ground as they tried to keep up with her, looked like ballet dancers performing on a stormy sea. Pouncing on her bent body from behind, Qais gave her a mighty kick in the bum. She tumbled over the cage, her head sinking into the grass. The children laughed, Grandpa was asleep, Mother sobbed and my husband and Father were fortunately away from home. 'He looked at you in his rear window,' Qais shouted and I was the only one who knew what had upset him so much, apart from the blond hunk with his swimming trunks. He had taken Freshta and the baby to see the doctor in a taxi. Qais installed his wife and children in the back seat where they belonged, while he himself settled into the seat next to the driver, engaging him in small talk. I tagged along as well and was quite happy to have another chance to look at the faces of people who couldn't see me. I was increasingly fascinated by the view of the world from behind the grille. The burka seemed to endow me with a degree of freedom that allowed me to entertain mischievous thoughts about people without them being able to read any malice in my face. Admittedly, the taxi driver did glance into his rear window once or twice and Freshta, shrouded in a burka, was indeed in his field of vision. I'm not sure if he could have seen her huge eyes and her long eyelashes through the thick grille and noticed her attractive and sexy look and the infinite passion emanating from every blink of her eyes. It's rather unlikely. It's much more likely that he just checked he wasn't being tailgated by another car or about to be overtaken by some madman on a motorbike.

Qais controlled himself while we were at the clinic but back at home... 'He looked at you in his rear window,' he yelled. He then cited this story as evidence of his wife's depravity for a full week.

'Did he really look at her in his rear window?' my husband asked me that night in bed, as I was massaging his forehead to rid him of a headache.

'Bullshit, he was just looking back, like every driver.'

'Qais is an idiot but when I drove a taxi I also used to look at women in the rear mirror, you know.'

'So what could you see, if they wore a burka?' I laughed.

'Everything,' said my husband with a mysterious grin, closing his eyes with glee.

Just like he had done in Moscow a few weeks before our departure for Kabul, when he declared: 'We must wait until later and it will be wonderful. We won't forget the night until the day we die.'

'And we're going to have a beautiful bedroom, aren't we...?' I said.

'It'll be the most beautiful bedroom in the world,' he said dreamily and it wasn't really a lie because at that moment the dilapidated little house with all its holes and bomb cracks struck him as infinitely preferable to the room in his hall of residence in Moscow or my parents' flat on a housing estate.

I had never pointed out to him that not only did that wreck of a house not contain the most beautiful bedroom, it had no bedroom at all. I didn't mind. We arrived on a Thursday, I still remember that because the next day everyone went to the mosque and nobody had to work. On Saturday an Afghan wedding was held. It was my wedding. As early as Friday they started dressing me up in horrid folds of white nylon and veils, forcing me into shoes two sizes too small, jabbering something in a language I hardly understood and pinching my cheeks. There were only women, of course. I had barely glimpsed any men in the house. Apart from Grandpa, who slowly traversed the house until he sat down in a place where he was most in the way. He muttered something about how no sooner had one lot of Russkies gone than he had another Russian delivered straight to his home. But apart from that everyone was very nice to me.

On Saturday morning they made a real spectacle of me. I had henna rubbed into my hair, which made me look as if my fingernails had long been afflicted with scabies and a fungal infection and left untreated. The gold jewellery hanging from my neck and ears weighed so much I was certain my ears would either fall off any minute or distend to a stupendous length. The chain around my neck was as thick as my thumb and my wrists were adorned with gaudy shiny bangles. My eyes had been enhanced with suspicious-looking bits of coal they called *shorma*. It was supposed to provide best protection from conjunctivitis, which I promptly contracted. And I had so much make-up plastered on my eyelashes it took me a full second to see anything every time I blinked. The kohl that was supposed to have healing properties elicited a constant stream of stinging tears that smudged the paint around my face. Sometimes my upper eyelashes would get glued to the lower ones, blinding me completely and the only way I could tear them apart was by twisting my face until the sticky tangle got unstuck again. '*Khoob*, *khoob*, OK, OK,' was my answer to every utterance addressed to me. Hordes of relatives arrived and we all went to a restaurant. It was a large and ugly building. Women were seated in one room and men in another. Before the dinner we had been to see a mullah. I don't know what he said or what the old men standing around him wiggling their white beards said, perhaps something about the daughter of the Prophet Ibrahim, the one we apparently share with the Muslims and call Abraham. Finally they mumbled something and nodded their heads, thereby allegedly sealing our union. Forever.

'You mustn't smile, you have to frown and look desperate,' my future husband whispered in my distended ear. Later I was told this was customary, to make sure people did not get the idea that the bride might be looking forward to the wedding night and desire her husband much too much. Yuck. Just imagine the disgrace. I put on my fiercest expression and managed to keep it up till late at night. I had pins and needles in my face. Afghan music played all afternoon at the party, the traditional elements enhanced by an amplifier and an electric guitar; the singer wore a European suit and a tie as wide as two hands instead of traditional Afghan male attire. All the songs spoke of unhappy love and suffering caused by male–female relations. The women giggled, ogling me with unbridled curiosity, while the men never even glanced at me from the corner of their eye, except for old geezers with one foot in the grave, and Father. Back in Moscow it occurred to me that I ought to invite my parents to Kabul but Nazir rejected the idea and he was quite right. My Mum would have felt out of place without my Dad, the heavily made-up and dressed up women bedecked with gold would have frightened her, while the absence of alcohol and the monotonous clapping that accompanied the two drummers in the men's room would have driven Dad crazy. The drummers were remarkably persistent, drumming non-stop for about six hours.

Nazir, as the bridegroom, was allowed to enter the women's room and stand with me on a stage for an hour receiving felicitations. Nobody talked to me though everyone exchanged a friendly word with him, especially as many people hadn't seen him in years and now respectfully addressed him as Engineer Nazir. Everybody who had returned from a university in the Soviet Union was addressed as engineer, regardless of whether they had graduated or not, and regardless of the subject of their studies.

I had pins and needles everywhere, my legs were hurting and my neck was growing stiff under the weight of the chain. Nazir's parents had left the house for the wedding night; Freshta, Qais and their children went to spend the night with relatives. We were driven to our house and dropped off at the front gate around midnight, and as we were getting out everyone laughed and patted my freshly-minted husband on the back, cheering him as if he had been about to enter a high jump contest. We went into the house and this was the first time I felt it might have been a mistake for us not to have had sex before. We used to snog and cuddle in Nazir's halls of residence, while his roommate made out with a student from Ghana next door but Nazir would always sigh heavily and jump out of bed at the crucial moment. I didn't really mind at the time, although it had crossed my mind that he might have contracted something.

'He's probably got the clap and because he really loves you he doesn't want to give it to you,' my friend Nadia said. Much later, when we started talking about marriage, he was adamant that we should wait and savour a genuine wedding night. Except that I had no idea, no idea at all, and had actually been anticipating this moment with a gentle tingling in the groin. If he had told me back then, everything could have been different.

I reached a cluster of people. The men had formed a circle so tight I couldn't get through. Women were shuffling about behind the men, maintaining a respectful distance and wringing their hands, most of them in burkas that made them look like moths whose wings had got wet and who were now trying to take flight in vain. The noise they made sounded like lamentation, and seemed appropriate to the moment. I was standing behind them and couldn't understand why the crowd wouldn't part to let me get closer to the spot. But they didn't know who I was, as almost nobody had ever laid eyes on my face. They just guessed that Engineer Nazir's wife was white.

Freshta was standing next to me saying nothing. Mother soon joined us. We stared in the direction everyone was looking but couldn't see anything. And then Mad appeared in front of me. His fat cheeks hung so low on his face they looked as if they didn't belong there, as if he had just glued them on, the way we used to stick white cotton wool on to Father Christmas' chin. He wasn't crying, he just stood facing me, looking me in the eye and shaking his head gently. There was something weird about him. It took me a few seconds to realise it was the strange colour. He was covered in blood. As if he had just been born. And I knew it then. He had been born of mortal sin.

'Don't go there, Herra,' he said calmly, taking me by the hand. I turned around obediently and allowed him to guide me home slowly, very slowly. And that's why I've never seen what was left of my husband. All I knew, from people talking under their breath so I wouldn't hear, was that he had been torn to shreds, only his legs remained intact and his head, the way it happens in these cases, had been blasted off his body in time to remain unscathed. All other body parts are too soft to survive and the entrails end up all over the place without anyone even trying to collect them because they're quite liquid and eventually, mercifully, soak into the earth. Where they belong.

That same day there was an attempt on the life of the Minister of Defence, Kasim Fahim. He was on his way to Jalalabad in Nangarhar Province where he wanted to tell farmers to stop growing poppies and producing opium because it was forbidden. And to start growing wheat instead because that was a noble endeavour, which enjoyed the support of the UN and the US. After listening to his speech the farmers went happily back to their poppy fields. Fahim got into the car and as it started moving a roadside kiosk exploded, the bomb smashing it into pieces and killing four passers-by and wounding eighteen others. Fahim survived. He narrowly escaped soaking into the ground.

The eastern part of Afghanistan continued to be troubled, and so did the north and the south, only in Kabul did we enjoy relative safety, due to the Peace Corps and stones that had been painted red by soldiers to indicate land mines. I really don't know why the damned roadside near our house hadn't been marked by a red stone. Weeping later that night, Father said someone must have deliberately planted the mine there. He had stopped there so many times with dear Nazir to buy some snuff at the kiosk, and there had never been an explosion.

'Oyoyoyoyoy,' Uncle Amin lamented, arriving hot and sweaty, for he couldn't miss an important event, let alone one where collective lamentation was prescribed. 'There will have to be a proper investigation, I have a few cousins at the ministry, I'll go and see them first thing tomorrow,' he boomed, tossing handfuls of raisins and nuts into his mouth, sometimes missing in his excitement and flinging the dried fruit behind his back. Mad served us tea and flatbread, looking so calm I was getting angry with him. I almost suspected there had been nights when he had wished my husband dead. Or that he had known this was going to happen, and regarded it as something that just had to occur and that it wasn't advisable to resist.

'You've already had a kilo,' he told Amin with a smile, after being asked for more raisins. I was helped into black trousers and a dark brown top. Then Freshta, Mother and I locked ourselves in the women's closet where we had two well-rolled hashish cigarettes with the tacit approval of the men. Mad joined us after a while, sat down next to me and put his head in my lap.

'Tell me, Nazir didn't know about our visit to the Russian hospital, did he?' I asked him.

'No, he didn't,' said Mad. I had never felt so relieved.

Our wedding night also began with Nazir and me having a cigarette. We shared one. He licked the paper affectionately, kneading it in his mouth and sucking on it, placed the little roll between my lips and stroked my face. Mother had prepared our mattresses, covering them with snow-white sheets and placing stiff hand-embroidered pillows at the head. We rolled around our wedding bed touching each other and three times managed to spill the tea meant to wash down the hashish cigarette. It was a wonderful night and my husband enjoyed it so much I started feeling romantic. He smeared the make-up all over my face making me look like a smudgy image of a golden pheasant. Then we had sex for the first time and Nazir started crying. He wept bitterly for a very long time, his chin trembling. I kept taking his face into my hands but he kept moving away, then lying down in my lap again. I stared at him, rather put off by the sight of a strong man shedding tears and sobbing, with snot running from his nose, so I put on a stupid smile hoping to gain some distance from this festive moment.

'How could you do this to me... Why didn't you tell me in time?' he lamented about an hour later.

'You never asked,' I replied. He looked at me feeble-mindedly, then got up and took out of his pocket a flick knife we had bought together at the Tishino market near the Belarusian station in Moscow, and made a swift incision on the inside of his left thigh. Blood covered the snow-white, now slightly creased sheet, leaving a decent-sized stain, a virginal stain the size of a plate.

'Here we go,' he said with satisfaction. Then he remembered he was actually in despair. 'Do you know what you've done to me? Do you know who I am now?' I shook my head naively. 'I'm no longer an Afghan. I'm not a man.' He caressed me, then crumpled up the sheet and took it to out into the hall, leaving it in a basket that had clearly been left there for this purpose. The next day as the whole family returned home, Mother made a point of washing the sheet so that everyone would see. I was met with meaningful winks from everyone and Qais was the first to address me as Herra jan. It was a sign of respect, affection and closeness rolled into one and in later years I would recall this moment whenever I felt like killing Qais. One of the main reasons why I had never done it was that he was the first one to break a kind of distrust inspired by my foreign origin. I think Freshta was initially jealous of me and took much longer to accept me. It was Qais who showed me how to use the type of Afghan pressure cooker that had killed several housewives, he laughed when I made it explode, sending noodles flying all over the hallway till they got stuck to the ceiling while the pot cover with its steam piston lodged in a rotted wooden beam where we had left it as an eternal memento of Afghan-made pressure cookers. It was quite touching to hear Qais complain that no matter how hard he tried, he would be ridiculed by his father-in-law and brother-in-law and that Nazir patronised him, preventing him from developing his business skills, and labelling him a useless idiot on account of a few small mishaps.

What happened was that Qais had hired a lorry to import a truckload of chickens from Pakistan, and blew all the money the family had set aside for a rainy day. Alas, the animals didn't survive Qais' business acumen. On the way back he stopped for a chat with his relatives near Jalalabad, a few kilometres after the Pakistani border inside Afghanistan, and lost track of time. It was 40-degrees Celsius in the shade and the chickens slowly fried, squeezed as they were into poorly ventilated containers designed for sheep. Not a single chicken made it out alive. He arrived in Kabul with a pile of foul-smelling little corpses, which he tried to resurrect in our courtyard, desperately flapping the wings of select individuals and trying to get them back on their little claws. But the little corpses had given up the ghost. Even stray dogs turned up their noses at them and since this kind of merchandise wasn't even suitable for fertiliser, the men in our family had to dig a hole behind the house and bury the results of Qais' business skills in a moving ceremony. I was the only one to approach Qais, gently putting my hand on his shoulder. I was about to tell him not to worry when he squealed like a woman who had just been grabbed between the legs by a stranger and pushed me away, his eyes ablaze. Everyone noticed what happened and I was given a lesson later that night on the mattress.

'You mustn't touch anyone, ever, you understand,' my husband whispered, all worked up and the urgency in his voice made me worry that I'd done something truly awful.

'I felt sorry for him, because of the chickens. And I felt sorry for the chickens, too.'

'I mainly feel sorry for myself, for having a moron for a brother-in-law and an idiot for a wife.' My husband had never called me by such a name before, he had never insulted me and if he had ever said anything that might have been construed as an insult, he would say it so gently the coarsest words sounded almost affectionate.

'Surely everyone must understand that the odd nudge or touch of a hand or shoulder means nothing...' I said defending myself feebly.

'Don't be silly. Nobody in this country knows anything about you and doesn't want to know. Now you're here and our customs are different.' I turned my back on my husband, feeling offended. He cuddled up to me, wrapping his arm around me. It was the loveliest position we had ever found together.

We chanced upon it on that first, unfortunate night, when he realised he had been misled and hadn't married a Russian virgin, and that he would have to suffer the consequences for the rest of his life. When he left to take the bloodied sheet to the hall, for a split second I felt like packing the few bits and bobs I'd been allowed to bring, running to the airport, and catching the first plane to any destination, waving goodbye to this weird country from the plane window.

'You'll have to shave,' he told me when he returned. The wound on his thigh was still bleeding. I gestured to him, and when he approached, I licked the cut thoroughly, sucking the wound clean and gently pressing it together with my teeth to stop the blood running... 'Our women must never see you like this, hairy like an animal. Yuck.' It was only then that I saw my husband didn't have a single body hair on him. He was shaven clean in all the places where my body was covered in tangles of curly brown hairs, and he was perfumed like a ballet dancer. He shaved regularly, sometimes insisting that I assist him in this revolting operation. 'What if I get run over by a car and am taken to hospital in a helpless state,' he argued. 'If I am hairy in these places, I will bring our entire tribe into disrepute.' I'm quite sure that on the day our neighbours collected bits of him and put them into a bag he was also properly shaven and nobody could have reproached our family for its lack of cleanliness.

chapter 26

FIRST THERE WAS the diminutive man in a uniform who tried to stop us, waving his arms above his tousled head as he thought we were driving too fast. I slowed down and smiled.

'Try smiling, too, and wipe that awful strained expression off your face,' I hissed at Freshta who was sitting stiffly in the seat next to me, as pale as if she were about to faint any minute.

'I should have been in the front seat, she looks as if she were carrying half a kilo of explosives in her knickers,' Mad shouted from the back. Freshta and I ignored his insolence.

'And you too, you look as if you were to fly the plane yourself,' said Mad, directing his criticism at me and sticking his melon-sized head between us. We ignored him.

'A delegation, we're an official delegation,' he yelled out of the open window at the policeman, who stared into the car, mouth agape. A woman at the wheel was a rare sight to behold and a woman driver in Afghan dress was regarded as an almost mystical phenomenon. I heard that a driving school catering to the fair sex had recently opened in Kabul and the first twenty-five brave women had signed up, but so far the only kind of woman who dared to drive outside was the odd extravagant foreigner who enjoyed making the whole city stand to attention.

Mad pushed half of his body into Freshta to get as close to the window as possible, frowning fiercely.

'We have diplomatic immunity,' he shouted at the petrified little man whose eyes darted from me to Freshta, as if not sure whether he was dreaming or awake. A woman at the steering wheel, her hair covered by headscarves with only her eyes visible and next to her a startlingly beautiful, Afghan-looking lady with a scarf gracefully and rather casually thrown over her shiny black hair tied at the back into a plait as thick as five fingers. And between these two weird creatures a giant melon, pretending to be a talking head with a threatening expression on his face, screeching something in an unpleasant voice about a delegation and gesticulating with tiny arms that couldn't possibly form part of his body. The policeman must have forgotten every single regulation hammered into his head over the past few weeks by his German instructors, and decided to rely on his intuition. Even before the car came to a complete halt, instinct made the little man raise his right arm to his forehead and perform a salute with his mouth open. Clicking his heels together, he yelled with a mixture of awe and admiration: 'Have a good journey!'

Mad returned his salute and shouted: '*Allahu Akbar*, officer, we serve our country!'

We were attracting unwanted attention, and people trudging around the access road to the airport building started turning around to see what sort of people there were in the car that was allowed to drive up right to the strictly guarded building, which was out of bounds for most of them.

Three white Toyotas with blue UN signs were parked outside the entrance. There was one last empty space left for our unmarked car. I parked and Mad jumped out of the car to chase away any other strict security guards. I don't know what he told them but they certainly stopped at a respectful distance, watching us with reverence. I switched off the engine and shut the windows.

'Let's go,' I declared resolutely.

'Wait,' Freshta whispered.

'What should I wait for? We've got to go, you need time to check in and I can't leave the car here for very long.'

'I forgot my *taskara*,' Freshta whimpered and I realised she was looking for any pretext to slow things down and put off the painful decision.

'*Taskara*?' I asked in surprise. 'You won't need any documents there, let alone a *taskara*. You've got your passport, that's enough. You won't have much use for a birth certificate, especially a fake one. There's no way we're going back.' Freshta knew full well that she had all the paperwork she needed. All John had been doing for weeks now was arranging her visas and documents certifying that Freshta was going abroad for medical treatment. For a small bribe Afghan officials did not require a husband or brother to be personally present when passports were issued, and they accepted my husband's fake signature, which Mad and I had been studiously practising in the evenings, mine eventually reaching a greater degree of perfection.

'You'll have to find a way of getting rid of these people gaping at us. What if someone recognises me?' Freshta didn't stop pleading.

'C'mon, Freshta, how could anyone recognise you, nobody has ever laid eyes on you. The burka makes us all look the same so you can rest assured nobody will recognise you. Just act normal, don't talk too much and pretend you don't understand.'

'If Nazir were alive he'd kill you,' she said.

'Why me?' I asked, forgetting how painful I still found any mention of Nazir. 'What about you? Am I the one doing a runner?'

'But you're condoning it,' she stated not very logically and burst out laughing.

'No, Freshta, I don't condone it. But it's the least bad of all the very bad solutions.'

Just then Mad, who was taking the luggage out of the boot, started to complain there was too much stuff and it was too heavy. When we secretly loaded the car in the morning we were too excited to assess the monstrous amounts of luggage.

'You've got around 120 kilos here. I don't understand what it is you're dragging along, do you think you'll be walking around there dressed like this? Have you never watched TV? People hardly wear anything except for swimming costumes and sunglasses, and some restaurants don't even let them in wearing anything else. And what's this? I can't believe it! Herra, come here. Look, she's completely lost it! Just have a look at this,' Mad squealed in an irritating falsetto, rummaging through the luggage. I hadn't checked what Freshta had packed, I didn't really care, although in the morning I was quite stunned by the combined weight of everything. I got out of the car and found Mad pulling assorted clothes and headscarves out of a huge Chinese holdall, tossing several pairs of shoes to the ground and fishing out additional objects from the bottom of the bag. He dropped a photo album on the tarmac sending our family photos flying in all directions. 'And what's this, oh no, I can't believe it...' he said, fishing out a six-litre *kazan*, a special cast-iron pot for cooking rice, which alone would have made the luggage overweight. 'She's gone round the bend,' Mad rasped furiously, placing two three-kilo bags of rice next to the pot. 'And look at this! Herra, I think we should go back and have her committed to an institution for violent lunatics.' He had just discovered baby clothes Yunus and Hamayun had worn. Right at the bottom, carefully folded, he found Roshangol's baby dresses and her finest shoes. Freshta finally got out and watched us in silent reproach. 'Are you planning to open a restaurant there, or what?' Mad fumed, unzipping another piece of luggage. 'And do you think you're going to shrink to a smaller size there, or why else are you taking these children's clothes?'

I walked around Mad's back and picked up a smaller bag, making sure he didn't see me. I put it down on the ground next to the car, out of his sight.

'Say something, Herra. Tell her she can't take all this stuff along.'

'He's right, Freshta, you probably can't take this,' I said and as I put my arm around her I realised I must have looked really bizarre next to her. Freshta was wearing tight black bell-bottomed trousers Mad had secretly bought for her, and a long top, which wasn't long enough by Kabul standards. It ended just below her rear, exposing her firm thighs and sensuous knees to the hungry eyes of male bystanders. She obviously felt naked.

'Where's your underwear?' I asked.

She gave me a surprised look and silently pointed her finger at her left breast. Then she whispered: 'I'm wearing it.'

I rolled my eyes. 'Yes, obviously, but what about your spare underwear, which bag is it in?' She pointed to a white, slightly grubby wheelie bag with Mickey Mouse on it. I crouched down to the pictures strewn on the ground and hastily selected some that didn't show any of Freshta's children. Only Father, Grandpa... I hesitated over a family photo showing all of us. It showed Nazir smiling happily with his right arm over my shoulder and his left over Freshta's. Grandpa and Mad are sitting by his feet, and Mad is holding chubby baby Yunus in his scrawny arms. Next to me stands Roshangol cradling Hamayun. Rustam and Kamal proudly stare into the camera, their defiant, fierce and ruthless expressions reminiscent of their father. Qais is not in the picture. He must have been the one who took it. As usual, Mother has got out of having her picture taken. Everyone bares their teeth to demonstrate we're in an absolute state of bliss. I turned the picture around. There was a date on the reverse: 15th November 2001. In my handwriting. Baby Yunus had just turned one month old and it was the first day of Ramadan. I put the photo aside. Freshta watched me. After a while, she asked with resignation: 'Why are you taking them away?'

'A new life without old memories,' I replied but couldn't look her in the eye. 'Why were you taking the rice and the pot?'

'He said their rice isn't as good as ours. He likes it. And you can't get these special pots there either...'

'Freshta, there's so much food there, you'll see,' I said dropping the remaining photos into the bundle of children's clothing.

'But I'd like to take at least some of these,' Freshta said but didn't make a move, as if she knew that Mad and I would have our way anyway.

'Freshta, come to your senses.' Mad joined the conversation and helped me gather up the stuff from the ground.

'I'll have more children,' Freshta suddenly declared with great determination.

'So what?' Mad didn't stop working but nevertheless responded a bit more gently.

'And I want them to have nice clothes.'

Mad stood up, raised his head so he could see eye-to-eye with Freshta who was much taller than him, spread his arms akimbo, which made him look like a bottle opener, and announced sensibly: 'Do you realise there are thousands of shops there with millions of lovely children's clothes? And do you know you're not allowed to wear Muslim garb there? Do you know you might land in prison because of that and your children might end up in a children's home? There are loads of children's homes over there and if a mother doesn't look after her little tots properly or stuffs their heads with all sorts of nonsense and reads them the Quran instead of fairy tales at night, they come for her and lock her up in an asylum. So take my advice and leave all this stupid stuff at home...'

'Good grief, Freshta, you can't be serious!' Now it was my turn to scream. Both of them looked at me. I was getting really angry. We were pressed for time and having to repack Freshta's entire wardrobe outside the airport hadn't been part of our plan. Seeing what I was pulling out of the next bag, Mad gave himself a mighty slap on the forehead and said: 'Our Prophet Muhammad was right after all. Sometimes it does no harm to give a woman a lash of a whip.'

Mad and I had agreed we would avoid saying farewell. We didn't tell Freshta but we were determined to find the right moment to sneak away so we wouldn't have to wave goodbye.

'It'll be better for her that way,' Mad brooded as we laid our plans at home.

'And for us, too,' I added.

'I don't really care,' he said, trying to sound courageous. 'I just hope she'll send me an invitation soon. At least for a few weeks. As soon as I'm back from Mecca, we're done here, Herra.' Mad had recently bought a satellite dish with the money he earned and his understanding of the world had greatly expanded. His encyclopaedic knowledge was starting to get unbearable. And although John declared the boy a genius, spending twenty-four hours a day with him was quite an ordeal. 'It's quite cold now in Western Europe, a cold front is also affecting Eastern Europe so it would be better for us to leave our trip till nearer the summer,' he jabbered. Weather forecasts were among his favourite programmes and he often knew the temperature in Burma, whether they had rainy or dry weather in Moscow, or what weather fronts would cross Poland the following week.

'Of course she'll invite you in the summer,' I lied, for I was quite certain that the airport would be the last place Freshta would ever see Mad, although I didn't know whether it would be because Freshta would forget him or because Mad wouldn't live to receive her invitation. Both possibilities were rather likely. Either way, I was certain this was how it was going to end.

I locked the car, Mad threw a pile of luggage back into the boot, and started to push the wheelie bag.

'What's that you've got there?' he snarled at me, noticing I was holding a small bag that I had put next to Freshta's pile.

In the heat of the moment I couldn't come up with a convincing explanation. Mad pulled the bag in silence, having pushed his head through the grip that normal people hold in their hand somewhere around their thighs and fastened it above his visibly protruding chest. His eyes darted from the floor to the small bag in my hand. But he didn't say anything. We were able to enter the departure hall without passing any checkpoints. Freshta looked like a foreigner while Mad and I elicited sympathy rather than arousing suspicion that we might blow up a plane. An aircraft was just landing. The plane started taxiing along the runway, spitting out little balls of fire. As Mad had explained to me many times before, they were meant to confuse enemy bullets, which are attracted to heat and might be fooled into hitting the fake bait instead of the plane. We stopped at the end of a line consisting of a couple of Afghans and a few foreigners. It had been agreed that John and Heidi would meet Freshta on the other side, behind the check-in counter. Just in case. Two weeks ago, when we started planning the details of Freshta's disappearance, John amazed me with the number of conspiracy theories he came up with. At one stage he even suggested he wouldn't sit next to Freshta on the plane, to make sure they didn't get turned back. This in spite of the fact that his fierce struggle for Freshta's visa had made him enemies in every embassy that had by then opened in Kabul. But, of course, not in order to issue visas to Afghans.

'Her first guy was a brute and a sadist, and now she's got herself a sissy,' Mad assessed the situation. 'If the plane were to be shot down and there was only one parachute, John would be the first to grab it,' he fumed, although John was the person he loved most, apart from me.

'Give it a rest, Mad, he's just being careful, after everything that's happened.' Then I spotted Heidi waving cheerfully. She had already checked in and was standing behind the glass.

I pushed Freshta in front of me, keeping an eye on Mad, who was still wedged into the wheelie bag. There was only one more person ahead of us.

'It's lucky that you found her burka. I wouldn't put it past her to stroll around New York wearing it and giving those little Americans a fright,' Mad laughed. Heidi kept waving frantically from behind the glass. I noticed John standing a few steps behind her. He didn't wave, he just looked in our direction and even at a distance it was obvious that he was shit scared.

'Actually, I've put it back in her bag,' I admitted in a fit of truthfulness.

'A burka? You're letting her take a burka to America?'

I shifted from one foot to another in embarrassment. 'I'm taking mine, too,' I finally found the courage to say. He looked at me with toxic flames in his eyes.

'Don't say that, Herra. Please don't say that.'

'Here's 500 dollars, Mad. A hundred is in small change. Go and find a driver outside the airport and pay him enough to drive you home in our car. I'll be back in a few weeks.' I put the money into his shirt pocket. He didn't say a word. Then he pulled the money out of the pocket and threw it on the floor, without looking at me. He flung my bag on the scales. The pointer on the scales was broken and it was impossible to tell how much it weighed anyway. But it can't have been more than six kilograms. The attendant labelled it with a piece of paper that said Frankfurt and smiled at us.

'Anyone else?' he asked. Freshta stared at us. 'This way, madam,' the attendant said in English, motioning to Freshta. Freshta went ahead while I quickly picked up the money from the floor.

'Mad, please...' but he was no longer there. I found myself alone with the hastily collected dollars in my hand. Meanwhile my bag landed on a cart and I was told to follow Freshta. I felt faint. I caught up with the man with the cart and tugged at his sleeve: 'Mister, I've forgotten something important.' On the other side of the glass Heidi and Freshta were hugging and John stood next to them with a shy smile on his face. Freshta tried to turn around in the embrace because she realised we hadn't said goodbye. She started looking for Mad and saw me talking to the man with the cart. She opened her eyes and seemed to be saying something. Then she pointed to me, and Heidi and John stuck their faces to the glass. They had spent the last month trying to talk me into leaving and had nearly given up. However, their efforts hadn't been wasted: I had got myself a passport and visas and agreed to deceive Mad. This was a bigger sin than my tarnished wedding night.

'I can't give it back to you, it's already been checked in,' the attendant claimed. 'Go and get whatever it is you've forgotten while we load your bag on the plane. It won't get lost, don't worry. Just come back quickly.'

'No, I really need it, please...' but the man held firm. I took out the crumpled banknotes and found a hundred dollar one. It was slightly more than he earned in a month. Without further comment he pulled out my bag and handed it to me. I tried hard not to look to where Freshta, John and Heidi were standing. I turned around quickly and started running. Out. Someone shouted at me that they couldn't check me in again and that the plane was due to depart in a few minutes. I ran out of the building and stopped. The car wasn't where I had left it. The security guys remembered me and greeted me with a cheerful smile.

'Over there,' one of the men said, pointing to the car park. That's where our Toyota was, its door opened. The car was surrounded by a bunch of wildly gesticulating policemen. I ran so hard the lower part of my headscarf slipped down, revealing my mouth and chin.

'Mad,' I yelled, as the policemen were obviously looking at something much smaller than themselves that had just climbed out of the car. As they drew aside one of them inquired: 'Is this yours?' It wasn't clear whether he meant Mad or the car.

'Yes.'

'He wanted to drive away but couldn't reach the pedals,' laughed the youth in uniform, holding Mad's shoulder. The boy kept his head low and didn't say a word.

'Mad, my dear Mad,' I sobbed. 'Did you really think I was going to leave you here?'

The policemen let me pass and I got into the driver's seat. Someone picked Mad up and threw him into the seat next to me like a bag of rice. His head was still hanging down and he didn't resist at all. You could have kicked him like a football at that moment. I started the engine and we got going, past the old airport with the bombed-out Soviet jets with red stars on their wings, then past *Mikrorayon* No. 3 and the road that passes the centre of the Wazir Akbar Khan district, all the way to the road towards Taimani. Neither of us said a word. I stopped far away from our house to make sure nobody would hear the sound of the engine and wouldn't see us arrive. At that moment a plane took off from the airport. It circled above the northern slopes and headed south-west. I started laughing.

'We did it, Mad, we did it.'

His head was still low. I stroked him as gently as I could. At last he looked at me. The corners of his mouth were drooping, his chubby cheeks were lined with deep furrows and tears were streaming down them. They kept dropping into his lap at regular intervals, forming a huge moist patch around his crotch.

'I would die, Herra, I'd die here without you,' he said very softly.

'I'd die without you too, Mad.'

acknowledgements

THIS BOOK could have not been written without the help of my Afghan friends who cannot be named for obvious reasons. I am also grateful to Lenka Weberová, who not only read the manuscript many times and patiently discussed the book's contents with me, but who, together with my mother, provided me with a base in the Czech Republic without which it would have been impossible to work while I was posted in Afghanistan. Last but not least, credit goes to all those involved with my NGO Berkat to whom I am grateful not only for their financial support but also for their ability to overcome stereotypes that limit humanitarian aid to flour handouts and the export of 'Western' ideas of democracy and human rights.

about the author

PETRA PROCHÁZKOVÁ is an award-winning Czech journalist, humanitarian worker and writer. In 1994, with fellow journalist Jaromír Štětina, she founded the private news agency Epicentrum, dedicated to war reporting. They have covered events in Abkhazia, Afghanistan, Cechnya, East Timor, Georgia, Nagorno-Karabakh, Kashmir, Kurdistan, Ossetia, Russia and Tajikistan.

On her return to the Czech Republic, Petra founded the humanitarian organisation Berkat for the support of children and women in Chechnya and Afghanistan (where she has acted as a correspondent in recent years) and for refugees living in the Czech Republic. In 1997 she was awarded the Ferdinand Peroutka Prize, and in 2000 the President of the Czech Republic presented her with a Medal of Merit. In 2001, the Hanno R. Ellenbogen Citizenship Award was bestowed on her by Madeleine Albright.

Freshta *(Frišta*, 2004) is Petra's first novel to be translated into English.

about the translator

SLOVAK-BORN JULIA SHERWOOD was educated in Germany and England and settled in London, working for Amnesty International and Save the Children. Since 2008 she has been based in the US, translating essays and fiction from Czech, Slovak, Polish and Russian. Her published literary translations from the Slovak include Daniela Kapitáňová's *Samko Tále's Cemetery Book*, and the short stories *Birdsong* by Leopold Lahola and *Lace* by Uršula Kovalyk. *Before the Breakup* by Balla will appear in Best European Fiction 2013.

also available from stork press

Madame Mephisto **by A. M. Bakalar**
ISBN Paperback: 978-0-9571326-0-3
ISBN eBook: 978-0-9571326-1-0

Illegal Liaisons **by Grażyna Plebanek**
Translator: Danusia Stok
ISBN Paperback: 978-0-9571326-2-7
ISBN eBook: 978-0-9571326-3-4

The Finno-Ugrian Vampire **by Noémi Szécsi**
Translator: Peter Sherwood
ISBN Paperback: 978-0-9571326-6-5
ISBN eBook: 978-0-9571326-7-2